TROY CITIZENS GAS LIGHT CO. OFFICE
South line of Lot 10
HALL
Levi Smith
A
N 72°25 W in 1885 486
Levi Smith?
B
C
GH HOME
Site where Robert Ross fell
Mounds Weeds & Debris
PATH
cinders & ashes
THIRD DISTRICT POLLING PLACE
Orr's St
FITCHBURG RAIL ROAD
TROY AND BOSTON
20 inch
Levi Smith
J. H. Winslow
H. F. House
Hutchins
Patton
Giles
L. Bu
John Crall
Donahue
D. Corning
D. Corning
H. Ingalls
ST SEWER
N. FOURTH ST
STOVE FOUNDRY
Burdett Smith & Co.
NINTH ST
TENTH ST
WARD LINE
72 inch
AV

THE TRIAL OF BAT SHEA

THE TRIAL OF BAT SHEA

A NOVEL BY JACK CASEY

Warmest wishes

9/30/08

DIAMOND ROCK PUBLISHING COMPANY TROY, NY

Published by

Diamond Rock Publishing Co.

744 Broadway

Albany, New York 12207

ISBN 0-9639886-0-3 (hc)
ISBN 0-9639886-1-1 (ltd ed)

Design: Frances Johansson
Typsetting: Mike Klein
Photography: Larry Roberts
Expeditor: Robert T. Farley
Special Consultant: Charlotte Foster

Grateful acknowledgment is extended to
The Times Record
The Troy Public Library
The Rensselaer County Historical Society
Holmes & Watson
Clinton County Historical Society
New York State Department of Corrections
and the New York State Library
for their courtesy in opening their archives and in permitting the use of the illustrations appearing in this work.

An earlier version of this book appeared in excerpts in The Sunday Record, Troy, NY, May 29 - September 25, 1977.

Manufactured in the United States of America
at Hamilton Printing Co., Castleton, New York.

First Printing March 6, 1994
Second Printing May, 2002

For my children

MOLLY and **JOHN**

"May they chart their courses long and true
Knowing from whence they have come."

CONTENTS

BOOK ONE — THE KILLING

BOOK TWO — THE TRIAL

BOOK THREE – THE EXECUTION

THE TRIAL OF BAT SHEA

PREFACE

The nagging, unresolved theme of Jack Casey's moving tale about Gilded Age Troy is a question which has troubled moralists since the dawn of history: do the ends ever justify the means.

To Bartholomew Shea, as one of the least promising representatives of Troy's downtrodden working class, the stuffing of a ballot box seemed a small enough price to pay to even the scales of an oppressively hopeless system of economic injustice.

To the self-righteous avengers of the martyred young reformer Robert Ross, the opportunity to railroad the criminal justice system to restore order and civility seemed to be a public obligation all decent citizens should applaud. Each side justified its illegal acts by the noble end to be attained, and each, in turn, produced tragedy.

It is difficult for modern day Americans to comprehend the intensity of class struggle and ethnic rivalry so prevalent in nineteenth century America. The roles which were played out in the brief lives of "Bat" Shea and Robert Ross were cast for them and their contemporaries long before their births and had their roots in the bloody history of Ireland. England's systematic displacement and debasement of Gaelic stock Catholics with loyalist Protestants created an open sore which has not healed to this day.

But the world of the Rosses and Sheas was not the Old World. An insatiable need for stout hands and strong backs to run the engines, looms and machinery of industry transformed America into a nation of immigrants. In 1894, nowhere was this more true than in the neighborhoods of Troy.

To the laboring classes of Troy, the mill owner, the landlord and the factory manager all meant the same person, the man who could cut wages, raise rents, hire and fire, blacklist and evict. Long days, short wages and child labor were prevalent.

The gentry of Troy were only too aware of the deep suspicions, resentment and hatred felt for their class. The invisible but efficient walls of segregation by housing patterns, churches, schools, fraternal lodges and even secret societies perpetuated the power of "respectable" Trojans.

Two unstoppable forces intensified this class struggle. The first was economic. In 1894, Troy was declining. The great urban industrial giant which had introduced the Bessemer process to America, provided millions of horseshoes for the Union cavalry and had sent its elegant cast iron stoves around the globe was trapped in a losing war with emerging steel giants of industry closer to the Mesabi range out past the Great Lakes. The intense struggles between union labor and desperate management only aggravated and kept alive the old ethnic rivalries which should have never crossed the Atlantic.

The second force was political. The American system, despite all its faults, extended to these armies of new workers not only the protection of citizenship, but the privilege of the ballot. Just as unions were evening the scales of justice for the laboring classes, political parties and the all-pervasive machines provided strength to the powerless. The writing was on the wall. Government by the masses was inevitable.

The pressure of these forces and the violence of confrontation erupted finally in the murder of Robert Ross and the sensational trial of Bartholomew Shea. A hundred years ago, the trial of Bat Shea captured the attention of Victorian America. In the larger picture the principal players became almost pawns in the struggle between anarchy and civilization, oppression and justice. The results were tragic irony.

In his attempt to gain power through the improper use of ballot box stuffing and the bullying of voters at the polls, Bat Shea and his followers compromised the very institution which offered the only possible hope for their struggling class.

The reformers, in their zeal to preserve democracy, corrupted the very thing they were sworn to save. Packing the grand jury with prejudiced jurors and tampering with witnesses to insure a total triumph were no less despicable tactics than the very abuses they preached against.

Jack Casey tells this tale not just as a storyteller but as an attorney whose familiarity and respect for the law, coupled with a labor of love on behalf of his native city, have restored to us the memory of a time and place critical to the development of our democracy. He has also resurrected in Bat Shea a tragic character who emerged from the bottom of society's rankings to achieve in the nobility of his death a dignity denied him in life.

JOHN J. McENENY
Member of the New York State
Assembly and former Albany
County Historian

BOOK ONE

THE KILLING

1.
THE REVOLVER CAUCUS

Ballot Box

A cold wind's howling out of the north. The canals are frozen, the river icebound. Like battlements of a medieval city, brick mills and warehouses line the frozen river, taking the brunt of the wind. Within the city, snow rises like fine white sand and blows into drifts and dunes. Except for an occasional trolley or horsedrawn sleigh, the streets are deserted, the city like a ruin.

Winter is harsh here where the Mohawk meets the Hudson, here in this mill city, here in Troy, New York, on the first Saturday in February. The wild north wind spins weather vanes, bangs signs and shutters along rows of brick tenements; it rips through stone belfries where bells hang frosted and silent; it blows horizontal the black smoke from stacks of foundries and steel mills; it backs up chimney flues. Now and again the winter sun appears like a white communion host behind dark clouds passing. Shifts in the mills don't end till after dark, and then the wind will drive workers indoors to coal fires and parlor stoves to wait out the long, dark winter night.

In an abandoned storefront the caucus was called at noon. Four men in greatcoats and derbies stood outside in the snow, waiting, stamping with cold, passing the flask.

"Yeah, Bat, you'n Jack sure gone and done it this time," Jerry Cleary said. Jerry was a big, clumsy thug with thick features and a low-pitched laugh. "Jack in there. Chairman of the goddamn Republican caucus. George'll be on the goddamn ballot as a Republican. An Irish Catholic Republican! Now there's a freak'a goddamn nature for ya."

"Aye," the leader of them said, swigging from the flask, then passing it on, "but that's how we get George in."

"Sure, Bat," Owen Judge said in jest, "and when George is in, Jerry here'll be a-pestering him for an appointment. Inspector of the Line." The "Line" was a six-block string of bordellos by the railroad station and Central Police Station downtown. The madams paid protection and the police got their weekly take, a share to the party, and everyone was happy with the arrangement.

"Already am, Owney," Jeremiah Cleary spoke with pride. "Already goddamn am," he held up the flask, "official goddamn inspector of the goddamn Line."

"Ah, but there'll be good times, and we'll all be getting fat when George is in." Owen Judge smacked his lips.

"Now stop that there, Owney," Bat Shea cautioned. "I don't want nothing more said about that till George is in." Bat Shea was dressed in a black bowler and a greatcoat and boots. He was young, rawboned, lean, and he sneered when he smiled, as if the entire human race merited only his contempt. "Step at a time, boys. Today we win the caucus, then George is on the ballot. In March, the election, and in April he's sworn. Only when George is in do we worry who gets what. Now gimme that." And the north wind screamed in the telegraph wires overhead as Shea took the flask from Cleary.

Inside the dim store, Jack McGough was worried. Nervous by nature and trigger happy, and being an Irish Catholic Democrat in a room of Protestant Republicans, Jack sensed much could go wrong. The room was cold and dim and the hot iron stove did little more than raise a stink of wet wool when the wind blew fine snow through chinks. Jack McGough and Bat Shea had pulled a master stroke by packing the party with phony enrollees and electing Jack chairman of the Republican caucus. Republicans outnumbered Democrats in the thirteenth ward, and if they got George on the Republican line, victory was virtually certain. But the Republicans were grumbling now, the Ross brothers openly hostile.

"And last, for alderman, George Dunlop is nominated," McGough called, all business. "Show of hands? Thirty-one. The nominees for alderman are Isaac Lansing and George Dunlop." Loud protests rose.

"What about Eli Hancox?"

"There weren't thirty-one hands for Dunlop!"

"There weren't three hands for Dunlop!"

McGough stared down the general grumbling. "Like it or no, gentlemen, that's the slate." McGough rapped the gavel. "Let the voting begin. Lansing or Dunlop." Lansing was the weaker of the Republican candidates, a mean-spirited old miser who had entered politics at the age of fifty. Eli Hancox was the favored candidate, Dunlop's only competition, and McGough had just neatly set him aside.

"I protest the consideration of George Dunlop!" A man in the shadows slowly pulled himself to his full height. The dull glow from the whitewashed showcase window was helped little by the smudged kerosene lamps, and it was dark in the corner.

"You there, you're out of order!" McGough squinted. "The rest of you, let the voting begin."

"But there was no discussion about Dunlop," the man in the shadows continued, opening his arms frankly. He was a big man, well over six feet, with a strong jaw and high forehead. "You simply mentioned his name, counted some imaginary votes, and now he is being considered by this body as a legitimate Republican candidate for alderman? There were no thirty-one votes." He turned to his fellow Republicans. "This is an outrage! George Dunlop is a saloonkeeper, a policeman dismissed from the force, a union agitator . . ."

"Vote!" McGough commanded, hammering his gavel.

Noise of protest and grumbling rose again in the room, louder now, and as dissent, confusion and anger spread, McGough whispered aside to the clerk, "Who's that one there, the one what keeps talking, the big one?"

"Why that's Robert Ross, sir."

Jack hammered his gavel again. "Mr. Ross! Mr. Ross!" The room quieted some. "Like it or no, nominations are closed. We can neither strike names nor place new ones into consideration. Now if you'd allow us to continue our caucus in an orderly fashion, you can voice your opinion with your vote."

"Why, this is a travesty!" Ross insisted. He stepped from the shadows, and addressing his fellows, he pointed at McGough. "This man, this Irishman steals in here and takes control of our caucus! To advance a saloonkeeper as a legitimate Republican candidate . . ."

Another stood up next to him: "Robert, there are far more of us than there are of them. Let us proceed to an orderly vote, and beat this George Dunlop at his own game."

"But Lansing?" In the faint light, Robert Ross's eyes flashed with anger. "I don't like it, Bill. I don't take to this compromise. Eli Hancox is our candidate . . ."

While he was talking, other Republicans rose and threaded along the wall to the ballot box, a glass fishbowl in a steel frame. There were mild protests as they deposited paper ballots under McGough's watchful eye. Suddenly one of them stepped back and cried, "Why, here's a hand coming in!" He revealed a hand in a black glove sticking through a hole in the window sash, depositing paper ballots into the box.

"I demand to see those ballots!" Robert Ross cried out, turning upon McGough.

"Now, now, gentlemen," McGough stood up, hiking up his trousers, trying to look nonchalant, "these are secret ballots. Once they're in the box . . ."

"Move that box away from the window!"

"Terminate this whole proceeding!"

A great hubbub went up.

"You're certainly free to vote, Mr. Ross," McGough said.

"And look here!" another cried. "Here comes the hand again from outside, and more ballots!" As a dozen paper ballots were dropped into the box, one of the Republicans grabbed the hand and held it. Two others took hold. "Go outside and see who's there," someone ordered.

"This is a locked caucus," McGough called above the rising protest. "No one in, no one out."

Outside, Jerry Cleary was cursing and sputtering, his shoulder against the building, his arm inside. "Bat, Jesus Christ, they got my goddamn hand!" Owen Judge and Gene McClure laughed uproariously and grabbed for the flask in Cleary's free hand: "Jesus Christ, Jerry! Let the APAs have your arm, but don't spill the bottle!"

"Let go!" Jerry cried. "Let go, goddamnit!"

"They're playing a very dangerous game," Shea said ominously, folding his arms. And the wind roared down River Street, raising clouds of snow as Jerry put his foot against the wall and struggled for his freedom. Owen Judge and Gene McClure grabbed him by the waist and pulled.

"Let it go!" McGough commanded inside, rapping the gavel. The Republicans were shouting and pressing forward.

"Call the police!"

"That won't do no good. They belong to Murphy!"

"Go out and see whose hand it is!"

"Probably Dunlop!"

"It's Murphy's in any event!"

To take back the meeting, McGough stepped on a chair, pulled a pistol from his coat pocket, raised it above the crowd and fired a shot into the tin ceiling. The muzzle flash and loud report brought silence then in the unsettling stink of gunsmoke. Released, the hand in the black glove slipped like a snake out the window.

"Now, gentlemen," McGough grinned, "like it or no, I'm chairman of this here caucus. You get along and you vote nice and quiet and proper and nobody gets hurt. Otherwise . . . " He looked up at his pistol and smiled.

"Why, this is intolerable! A revolver?" cried Robert Ross, advancing.

"Vote, you son of a bitch!" McGough cried, leveling his gun at Ross. "I've had a bellyful of you today!"

"You'll go back into the hole you crawled from!" Robert Ross leapt at McGough. McGough cocked back the hammer.

"Don't shoot a man like that!" someone cried. Arms flailed to knock the pistol up. McGough brought it down upon the bridge of John Boland's nose, and Boland bent over, screaming in pain. From behind, someone kicked out the chair, and McGough fell into a swarm of fists and boots down to the floor, where they punched and kicked him. Robert Ross stamped on McGough's wrist and the pistol fell aside. John Ross bent down and hauled McGough up by the lapels. Boland hauled back and punched McGough full in the face.

"Bat! Bat!" McGough screamed. "Come now or they'll kill me! Bat! Help me! Help!!"

Suddenly the showcase window exploded. A rush of cold wind and wintry light caused all faces to turn upward. A large form filled the window casing in a halo of steam from the escaping heat. A revolver pointed down at them. "Leave Jack go," Bat Shea said in a low, raspy voice. These three words achieved their effect. McGough brushed himself off, retrieved his pistol and hat from the floor, and backed toward the window. Once in the room, the wind played havoc with blank ballots that fluttered about as all the men stood still, mouths open in fear and astonishment.

"Now, gentlemen, you've had your vote for today. And if there ain't enough in there for Dunlop, why, we'll just add us a few more. You there, hand me the box." He pointed his gun at George Cooley. Cooley resisted. "Hand me up that box, you son of a bitch, or I'll blow your head off." Jack elbowed past Cooley and handed up the box.

"Here, Bat."

"You can't take that box!"

"No worry, gentlemen," Shea said. "We'll bring it back and guard it till Sergeant Butcher arrives."

"Yeah, that we will." Glaring at his assailants, McGough stepped onto the ledge and jumped to the walkway outside. Cleary, Judge and McClure greeted him warmly. "Gimme a slug, Owney." Jack grabbed the flask. "Christ, that's thirsty work!"

Shea fired two shots at the ceiling, and as the men ducked and covered their ears, he disappeared.

John Ross was first to the window. The five were running down River Street, holding their hats, Shea with the ballot box under his arm. "They've stolen our ballot box!" John Ross cried impotently into the wind: "They've stolen the nomination!"

2.

THE BOSS

Senator Edward J. Murphy, Jr.

The malthouse of the Excelsior Brewery loomed above the railroad tracks across the street from the county jail downtown, seven stories of windowless brick streaked by coal soot and grime. Day and night its smokestacks belched black smoke from the cooking fires and white steam from the copper malt cookers. Whistles called two twelve hour shifts to work each day from nearby tenements, rough-looking men with lunchpails. Water was drawn from a spring gurgling at the base of high clay hills. Rails brought rice up from New York Harbor and hops in from the western counties to a siding in back.

Founded by William H. Kennedy and Edward J. Murphy, Jr., the Excelsior Brewery was among a dozen breweries in this factory town rolling out countless barrels of strong ale and porter to slake the thirst and dull the monotony and give a bit of cheer to legions of millworkers. The brewery also housed the offices of the Honorable Edward J. Murphy, Jr., United States Senator from New York, the New York State Democratic Chairman and former Troy Mayor. A big, intelligent Irishman, Murphy had a fine head of white hair, and kind, sentimental blue eyes that belied the ruthless politician filling out his capacious vest. For twenty years he'd ruled as absolute dictator of this mill city. While mayor, he built Troy City Hall, and showed great aptitude at keeping the Protestant manufacturers happy, the starched churchgoers filled with piety and patriotism, the Irish mollified, and the city sated with beer.

Murphy ran a "wide-open town." Whether you were a rough canaler from Buffalo or a cardsharp from the Rondout, you could find a game, a woman and a bottle in Troy anytime, day or night. "The party" took its cut of the bribes to the police, and it was rumored a healthy share found its way back to the boss. It was widely rumored, too, that the boss profited from the franchises of streetcar lines, the gas company, paving contracts and construction of the new municipal sewer system, any contract he could steer to his cronies. In the plans now was a commodious new county courthouse, and the "honest graft," as Boss Tweed termed it a generation before, would be most gratifying.

But more important than wealth, Murphy controlled people and events. Murphy decided who filled all municipal offices, from the police commissioner to the streetsweepers. Even young women wanting teaching positions in the public schools made a pilgrimage to the brewery where they "voluntarily" donated a portion of their meager salaries to get and keep appointments. Few spoke openly about this tyranny. Those on the inside winked, and those on the outside scowled and shook their heads. For two decades, Murphy walked a narrow line between the flaring tempers of the Catholic laboring masses and the greed of the small but wealthy enclave of Protestant merchants and industrialists.

The Irish admired Murphy for he vindicated their most cherished illusion that every Irishman is a king. Affectionately they called him "Boss." The Scots Presbyterians and the Anglicans despised but tolerated him. Murphy was useful: he could soothe the laborers when strikes were imminent, and he knew how to "invest" a trunkload of greenbacks in Washington to get tariff bills through. Yet it galled these teetotaling Protestants that Murphy controlled Troy's civic life from offices in a brewery. From the brewery, they believed, flowed a constant stream of political corruption and lawlessness, awash in Excelsior Pale Ale.

Nearly four weeks after the caucus, a thaw loosened the iron fist of winter, and yellow fog rose from the river. Up Ferry Street snorting teams waited by the curb while their drivers ducked into saloons for a quick nip. A lamplighter and his dog were ambling along Fifth Avenue past the jail, a string of green gas globes lit behind them in the mist.

"Well, Buster, 'lectric streetcars and 'lectric lights is here, and they say the gas lamps'll soon be gone altogether." He snorted. "Boss Murphy settin' over there in the brewery, and his Troy Gas Works, why, they're resistin' the 'lectric lights. And we should be obliged to 'im for keeping us in work. Heh, heh. 'Lectric lights don't vote, lamplighters do, heh, heh. That's what he says. Yet stopping progress is like stopping a freight train. Everything's going 'lectrified these days. There in the jail? Hah! The gallows fer murderers? No more, Buster, no siree. Now they set 'em in a chair up to state's prison and run 'lectricity through 'em with wires. Heh. Heh. Progress."

Hoofbeats interrupted these ruminations and suddenly a horse and rider galloped past the lamplighter and pulled up before the brewery. The horse reared, slipping on the cobbles, and the rider jumped down and hammered his fist on the heavy oak door.

An old maltster opened the door a notch. "Yeah?"

"Senator Murphy!"

"Sorry, sir. After hours."

"Aside!" the man commanded, brandishing his riding crop, and he pushed into the dark malthouse.

On the curb the lamplighter shook his head. "Hah, Buster, look at that. Triflin' with the boss. On'y one place that feller's hurrying, and that's a place I'm afeared we'll all be reaching sooner or later. C'mon, boy." The lamplighter took an old meerschaum from his pocket, lit it from his taper and ambled to the next lamppost in the fog.

Robert Ross strode through the sweet-sour darkness of the malthouse seeking Murphy's office. The maltster followed him, protesting. Ross threw open a door, and two clerks peered up from their ledgers.

"Where's Murphy?"

"You can't go in there!" one of the clerks glanced at the double door to the great man's office.

"Aside!" Ross raised his riding crop and threw open the door.

The enormous room, paneled in oak, a Persian rug on the floor, was bathed in soft gaslight. Behind a wide desk Boss Murphy was eating his dinner, sent in gratis from a nearby chophouse. A pretty young woman with a massive pile of red hair was seated nearby on a chaise lounge. The senator was pouring wine and, flushed with conviviality, he turned, bottle in hand: "Yes, what is it?"

Ross was startled by the opulence and by interrupting a man at his dinner. He swallowed and walked across the room.

"I am Robert Ross of Oakwood Avenue, Senator."

"Yes?"

"Ross Valve?"

"I know the firm. I know your father. George Ross." The senator cleared his throat, impatiently wiped his moustache on his napkin.

"Miss O'Leary, would you please excuse us? I should like to save you the offense of Mr. Ross's lack of manners."

The young woman covered her plate and left the room.

"Now, Mr. Ross," Murphy's expression darkened, "what brings you unannounced into my office at this hour?"

Ross advanced. "At a Republican caucus last month in the thirteenth ward, your thugs stole the ballot box, filled it with fraudulent nominating votes and got a saloonkeeper onto the Republican ticket."

"My thugs?"

When Murphy got angry, his complexion reddened, and the flush was now rising above his high starched collar.

"Yours. All the saloon brawlers in Troy are answerable to you, and I mean to put an end to this lawlessness. This group has polluted the Republican ticket by placing George Dunlop there. Dunlop, you may recall, was discharged from the police department and he's now a common saloonkeeper. Well, we held another caucus and we have our candidate, Eli Hancox, on a third line. I mean to see that the charter election next Tuesday is a square and honest vote. Your thugs and repeat voters are on notice that my men will be at the polls to ensure an honest vote." Ross pointed his riding crop across the desk. "I do not take threats against my life lightly."

Murphy's face was now crimson, and his blue eyes bored into Robert Ross. "Mr. Ross, I suggest you speak with Police Chief Markham. I have not been involved in local politics for years."

"You lie!" Ross slapped the whip on the desk with a loud crack. Two of Murphy's aides tumbled in the door from where they'd been eavesdropping, and the senator rose from his chair, planted his two fists on his desk and faced off.

"Now look here, Ross, I have done nothing but benefit you and your family. When I was mayor, your father came to the Manufacturers Bank, my bank, looking for a loan to start in business. I advanced him credit and he has seen success. I have nothing to do with these people you speak of. I would suggest that before you barge into a man's office, brandishing a whip in his face, accusing him of voting fraud, you get your facts straight and you weigh what such rash behavior will earn you. Now, I'll ask Mr. Fitzsimmons to see you out."

"My father has nothing to do with this, sir," Ross glared at him. "That was business, and it gives you no license to force an election. I am putting you on notice, that my life and the lives of my family were threatened today. I was warned to stay at home next Tuesday or I would be harmed. I am now returning the warning, Senator. I shall have a posse at the polls Tuesday armed with clubs, and any force on your side will be met with force on ours."

Ross slapped the riding crop upon his thigh, turned and strode past the two ledger clerks. Murphy adjusted his collar and cravat. "Fitzsimmons, would you tell Miss O'Leary I shall not need her . . . her assistance tonight. See her to her rooming house. I shall send a carriage for her tomorrow. Gavin, you call the chief and have him station Officer Ryan up here through election day. Then get Halloran to take this note up to Dunlop's Saloon." He scribbled on a paper, folded it and handed it to Gavin. Now Murphy was all charm, streetwise, exuding control.

"You see that fellow? That there Robert Ross, boys? He has one small misperception, and it could be his undoing." Murphy paused, looked up, his blue eyes twinkling. A brogue crept into his voice. "He thinks I run a goddamned democracy." Then Murphy's expression turned hard, and the clerks laughed politely.

"Anything else, sir?"

"Why, yes. Yes, there is." Murphy again flashed his winning smile, though he was clearly perturbed: "Don't let that fellow past you again. Street him. You must have more skills than accounting. If an Irishman can't lick a Scotsman in an alley fight, then he ain't worthy of the designation."

3.

DUNLOP'S SALOON

Troy Saloon

Dunlop's Saloon was a gilded emporium of whiskey, ale, laughter, music, gambling and, it was whispered through the parish, female "companionship," just off the electric streetcar route in the city's north end. George Dunlop, a plump publican with gray muttonchops, was a theatrical, bellowing sort of Irishman who abhorred silence, pined for the old country, though he'd left Ulster at the age of two, and sought, by serving drink and jokes to his countrymen, to advance his station in life.

Although he had an English surname, George Dunlop had been raised Catholic by his Irish mother, and he married a Catholic girl, Mary Gleason. Dunlop served on the police force until rumors spread he was looking the other way too often at the freight yard while the boys broke into the cars. After Dunlop left the force, he drove a team of horses for a year, but such work was too physical and too demeaning. When his wife inherited the saloon last winter, George had a headquarters to launch his first bid for public office. An English surname was a valuable asset in the thirteenth ward, particularly if you backed it up with Irish muscle. George now knew politics was his true calling: you could dress well and take what you wanted; you could even lie and cheat if need be, and people respected you for it.

Each night Dunlop waxed his moustache, pulled up his arm garters, adjusted the flare in the gas lamps, slipped Sergeant Butcher a pint of porter, a five dollar gold piece and a "tip o' the wink," then threw his saloon open to the neighborhood. And it was as if George Dunlop opened his expansive bosom as well. For the next six hours he joked and sang and argued with the regulars, kept a watchful eye on the kitchen girls, pretended the upstairs girls didn't exist, and maintained a healthy banter of jokes and doggerel and song swirling in the cigar smoke. Yes, George Dunlop was the neighborhood host, his saloon within earshot of hymns from St. Patrick's. And because this neighborhood host was about to be elected alderman, the conviviality had never been louder or more joyful, for there's no more fun-loving person on earth than a man running for office.

Bat Shea, a street tough, had come to George at fourteen asking how to become a cop. George knew his old man, Bartholomew Shea, Sr., over on River Street, a thin, sour, bent-backed molder nicknamed "Weary" who'd used his fists too often on the kid. George recognized talent in Bat Shea, his large fists and his thick skull, the brooding resentments and his love of brawling, and so George recommended Shea to Liam Gleason, his father-in-law, who gave Shea his meals, a room over the saloon and work as a handyman, bodyguard and bouncer.

Bat's accomplishments with the drunks and lechers and welshers around the bar were much celebrated. By eighteen he was a legend in the north end, and though the velveteen bordellos downtown offered him better pay, nicer girls and a bit of class, Shea preferred Gleason's where you could hear and talk about baseball, horses, prize fights and game cocks.

A punch-up two years before with an Albany politico out slumming who had roughed up the "wee blonde whore," as Jack called the consumptive Jenny, brought Shea an indictment for assault. Shea went on the lam, riding the rails westward to Chicago, St. Louis, Silver City, then San Francisco. He stayed away a year till tempers cooled, then he returned to Troy, more serious and thoughtful, matured from what he had seen in the hobo camps, the meatpacking yards, the mining towns, Chinatown and the 'Frisco docks. He understood now how men exploited each other, and he was determined to take his share.

This change in Shea worked to Dunlop's advantage in his first bid for office. The publican gave Shea a room and enlisted him as leader of the gang that would elect him alderman of the thirteenth ward. There'd be jobs for everyone in city hall, George promised, after he was in. Shea immediately called on a friend from childhood, Jack McGough, to serve as lieutenant in the enterprise.

Now Jack was something of a dandy. Where Bat wore simple wool trousers, coat and vest, scuffed boots, flannel shirts and plain neckties, McGough liked tweeds and plaids and flashy neckwear. Jack had a quick and devious mind that often got him into trouble. At thirteen he'd been "sent up" for stealing a pair of shoes, fancy shoes of yellow alligator hide. "Inside," Jack became adept at a variety of trades: pickpocketing, cardsharping, various forms of fraud, forgery and larceny. But Jack really craved power and prestige. When Bat Shea offered to bring him on board and Dunlop dangled visions of a sinecure in city hall, Jack signed on.

With Shea, Jack McGough was the perfect henchman, flattering, deferential, "nimble and quick" as Owen Judge put it. Jack considered himself smarter than Shea, but he envied the brawler his pride and air of command. Jack gained a measure of self-respect in planning for the gang, and he believed his cunning and craft would save him if things ran amok, for then he could cut and run. Bat welcomed Jack's agile mind. Jerry Cleary was a brute, Owen Judge a complainer, Gene McClure unreliable. Jack livened up the enterprise and gave it some balance and flair.

The boys were all at the bar rail "cutting the phlegm" from the raw March evening when Halloran shuffled in. Dunlop was regaling the saloon with an embellished version of last night's poker game: "So my boy Bat here says to him, he says, 'You got a watch, ain't you? You got fillings in your teeth? And what about that wedding band?'" The men laughed and lifted their pints of Kennedy & Murphy's Excelsior Pale Ale into the mellow gaslight. "'Twas a fleecing rare."

"Bat'd relieve a man of his trouser braces, then the trousers as well," Owen Judge said in admiration.

"Don't sit at the table if you ain't prepared to lose," Shea remarked.

The group at the bar noticed Halloran, but George had to complete the tale.

"So the man folds. Bat takes the pot. Seventeen dollars, boys, more'n a week's wage."

"Aye," Shea said, working his jaw around a mouthful of ale, "and naught but five mutts in my hand. Not so much as a single match."

"That little feller from Cohoes was holding queens and threes!" Dunlop cried.

Laughing and shaking their heads, they finished their pints, filed into the backroom, and took places around the circular card table topped with green felt. Katie came in and lit the lamp, and they waited for her to leave.

"So, Terry, what's the word at the brewery?"

Halloran handed George a note and cleared his throat: "Seems one of the Rosses came a-visiting the boss tonight." He licked his whiskered lips. "Powerful hot in here, George."

"Which Ross?" Shea demanded as George read.

"Robert. The youngest. Big son of a bitch he is. Said he'd bring a posse to the polls Tuesday armed with clubs."

"Clubs?" McGough scoffed. He pulled out his revolver and twirled it about his index finger. "I got something better'n that."

Halloran's eyes lurched about the room. "Sweet Jesus, me tongue feels like a feather duster."

"What else?" Shea demanded.

"Ah, well, the boss was mighty agitated when he heard about the caucus last month. He don't like the infiltratin' that went on with the Republicans. 'Leave 'em their side of the street,' says he, 'and they'll leave us our'n.'"

"So why the visit, Halloran?" George was visibly upset with the message. Getting on the Republican line was his idea. His father-in-law had crossed Murphy ten years before when he first opened the saloon. Liam Gleason, a big proud Irishman from County Limerick, thought he could sell whatever ale he chose. Barrels of Kennedy & Murphy porter and ale began piling up in his barn and customers boycotted the place. Gleason suddenly saw the light when he found his dog hanging in the hayloft. Since then the taps poured only Kennedy & Murphy brew.

The old drunk clacked his tongue. "I wouldn't mind enjoyin' a taste of your hospitality, George."

"Owney, get Katie there to bring in a pint of porter," George said impatiently.

"And a shot, too, George, just to cut the phlegm, mind you. It's cold and mighty damp out . . ."

"And a shot," Dunlop ordered.

"All right," Halloran said with satisfaction, "the boss sent me up here to warn you's. Said the thirteenth ward's been stepping out of line. Said there won't be no antics next Tuesday that could embarrass him nor the party. Said to get the votes in early with no guns nor knives nor knuckles."

The pint and the whiskey arrived, and Halloran took a long pull of the porter. He hooked the shot right down, then took another swallow of the porter and licked the foam from his whiskered lips. "Ahhhh. Now that's better, George, much better. Any-hoo, seems that the Ross feller there's been threatened of late and he's hotter'n a bitch in an August lather. The boss wishes you well, George. He was right sorrowful when they had to dump you from the force, and he'll be glad to see you on the board, if you make it, but it won't do to embarrass him nor the party in tryin' to get there."

"Now we weren't planning nothing extraordinary," Dunlop candidly opened his arms, "were we, boys?"

They shook their heads innocently.

"Just a few repeaters from down Kingston way to slide some extry votes into the box and assure us our deserved victory. Nothing unusual there, now, is there, Halloran?"

"Nah." He gulped the last of the pint. "You ax me, that Ross feller's in line for a fall. He appears far too high and mighty to last long in this here town. Someone got a chew?"

"Owney, give him a cut of your plug."

"This guy wants everything. Want me to chew it for him too?" Owen Judge grumbled. Halloran took the plug and cut off a chew. "Well, time to catch the last car downtown. I can report to the boss we're all of one mind?"

"Business as usual," Bat Shea said.

"And there'll be no weapons nor violence?"

"Business as usual."

"I knew we could count on you boys." Halloran winked, stood and shuffled out of the back room, and the men looked at each other for a long moment.

"I don't like this," George said at last. He kept folding and unfolding his plump hands. "Ross has been tipped off. You boys were too free with the guns and fists at the caucus."

"Nah, it weren't the caucus," Shea said. "Something's happened since. He said something about a threat." Shea looked around the circle of faces in the lamplight.

Jack McGough cleared his throat and looked sheepishly at a cigar burn on the green felt.

"You, Jack?" Shea asked.

"Not me."

"Why the long face?"

"No reason."

"Jack," Shea's eyes bored into his, "what did you do?"

"Aw, I ran into Hayner this afternoon. You know how it goes. We got to talking, and I said something about Ross, you know, Bat. It weren't nothing. This'n that, you know. Hayner must've told him."

There was silence as Shea scrutinized McGough. "What'd you

say?" His quiet voice suggested a deep breach of trust.

"Ah, you know, that he better watch his step, this'n that. And Hayner was taunting me real good, so I turned it around. You know."

When Bat Shea scowled, his brow clouded and he seemed capable of great cruelty. "That warn't smart, Jack."

"Aw, come on, Bat, for Christ sakes. Son of a bitch had me pinned at the caucus. Holier'n thou. I see Ross in the carriage with his little brunette, Josiah Patton's daughter. Temperance leagues and tea parties. Rotten bastards. Then they all pull on their black hoods for the APA meeting and plot how to keep us poor and miserable. You wanna hear what he said about you?"

"I fight my own fights, Jack."

"I don't like this," Dunlop said nervously. "I don't like it one bit. I seen people cross the boss and they don't last long. Now, boys, we all stand or fall together. Please, think of yourselves, think of me — "

"Aw, stop yer sweating, George," Shea snapped. "What does Murphy know of the thirteenth anyway? He ain't been up here in ten years."

"Goddamn right," Jerry Cleary agreed.

"We got things under control, George. Jack made a blunder, but it was a small one. Let Ross bitch. He's been belly-achin' around his mill all winter. Come election day he'll be one surprised son of a bitch, and you'll be sitting in city hall, alderman from the thirteenth."

"You worry me, Bat."

"Forget it, George," Shea said.

"Well, if you guys are through," Owen Judge said, "I think I'll be heading home. I've drunk my fill."

"What's with you there, Owney?" Shea's deep raspy voice now confronted Judge. The resolve of the group seemed to be unraveling.

"N-n-nothing, Bat."

"Why you so anxious to give your friends the slip?"

Judge laughed through his nose. "I got a new bride. Ain't that reason enough?"

"And she's drawing all the meanness outta you," Jerry Cleary laughed crudely.

"You leave her out of it," Judge protested.

Shea quieted them. He fixed Judge with his blue eyes. "I just want to make sure you're on board, Owney."

"I'm on board, Bat. Of course I'm on board. Have I ever been anything but on board. I'm on board . . . on board."

"On goddamn board," Cleary slapped him on the back.

"That's good." Shea peered closer, pointed with his finger. "Now you remember, Owney, we're going all the way to the end of the line. And you're either on board or you're overboard. There's no middle ground."

"Geez, Bat, what gives? I'm on board, on goddamn board, don't you understand? I'm with you guys. I just got to get home to see Peggy. She's waiting and I promised."

"Very well, then, you run along to your little wife. But we're counting on you Saturday for an overnight to Kingston, by boat if the river's open, so you better clear things with the little lady." The others laughed at having to seek a woman's permission.

"Sure, Bat. See you, guys. Right." And he exited out the back door, grinning and rubbing his hands together.

"Well," Dunlop slapped the table with his plump palms. "I'm real goddamn thirsty now. Let's go back inside, drinks on me."

"Yeah," Shea said. "I'm powerful dry too. We're all of one mind now, boys, that it's business as usual?"

"Business as goddamn usual," Cleary laughed.

"Business as usual. Ha, ha, ha," Jack McGough sang, and pocketed the gun he'd been spinning. "Business as usual. You got a way with the language, Bat, I swear to Jesus."

4.
THE VIRGIN

The next afternoon, knowing his father to be at the stove foundry, Bat Shea walked the four blocks from Dunlop's to his parents' home to fetch his revolver. With the assault charge still pending and such talk circulating about the caucus, he'd grown cautious, keeping the gun there until things cooled. There'd be a showdown at the polls, he could feel it. He had a good sense of such things.

The Shea family let the second floor of a small frame tenement on River Street, the back yard facing the river. Bat Shea paused to look up and down the frozen river. The Springs City Express was crossing the railroad bridge across a Mohawk tributary toward Saratoga, and its whistle was shrill and long. The clatter of the wheels came clear over the river. Shea spat in the yard and climbed the back stairs.

There were voices inside, and as he opened the door, young Mamie Halligan was sitting at the kitchen table with his mother, both women bundled in shawls. Coals glowed in the kitchen hearth.

"And look who's here, Mamie, would you now?" Mary Shea was a plump matron with graying reddish curls and protruding blue eyes. She talked in a loud voice due to her poor hearing. "Barry, my first born." Mrs. Shea loathed the nickname "Bat" and insisted on calling her son

"Barry" to differentiate him from his father, Bartholomew Sr., whom she called "Bart."

"Hiya, Ma."

Mamie turned, and a knowing look passed between them.

"I won't be long," he brushed past. Tim had taken over his room. Bat slid the dresser aside, pried up the floorboard and took out his Smith & Wesson, oiled and shined and wrapped in chamois. There was something comforting about the fragrance of a well-oiled revolver and he hefted it admiringly. He retrieved a box of cartridges and dumped out a pocketful, then put the chamois and the cartridge box back, replacing the floorboard and shoving the dresser back into place. There was a knock. He stuck the revolver in his belt, buttoned his coat and stood up as Mamie came in.

"How have you been, Bartholomew?"

"Good."

"You look fine."

"Yeah." He stared at the floor. "So what?"

Mamie seemed confused. "I have missed you is all." She went to him, took his large calloused hands in hers. Her hands were like small white birds, soft and delicate and chilled. Then he looked at her eyes. There was great sadness in her blue eyes, and her lips looked as though they expected a kiss.

"I told you, Mamie, I ain't for marrying just now."

"Can't you just relax?" Her voice dropped into a whisper.

"I got a lot on my mind today." He was whispering too. "What we said we said, and we can't unsay it. I can't get married now. Maybe when I get somewheres, but I ain't going to be working day in and day out like the old man here for you and six or seven squalling brats. You want to wait till the vows are said. I respect that. You can wait. But I ain't waiting and I ain't saying the vows'll ever be said neither. So there's no use putting each other through the aching and frustration of getting halfway there every time."

She dropped her eyes, and held his hands in hers. She had her long red hair pinned up. He smelled her perfume. Yes, he wanted to lie with her, talking as they had done so often before. She was a good gal, with much sense, and she had a big heart. The physical ache could be cured some other way. He wanted just to talk with her, to tell her of his fears and his ambition. But he knew she'd misunderstand, and be critical, and chide him for his friends and his way of life and his methods, and then things would get complicated and it would be worse than now.

"I've been giving a lot of thought to it, Bartholomew."

"Yeah?"

"And I think, I think I'm ready."

He shook his head. "Naw, Mamie, don't say that! Don't do that! Don't cave in like that. You ain't ready, and that's all right. I respect that. You won't be ready till the vows are said. Don't you give in. If you do, I won't be around later. Don't you see? Can't you see that?"

When she looked up, tears were streaming down her face. "I don't understand you, Bartholomew. You and your friends. You'll fight to the death over some silly little job in city hall, when you could make an honest living just as easy and be able to sleep nights. Like my brother Tom."

"Tom's had his problems."

"But they're getting the union underway now. Why can't you join with Tom instead of this here fraud George Dunlop."

"George ain't no fraud."

"He's no friend of yours, Bartholomew Shea. And no friend of mine, neither. Why, when he was bounced off the police force for that ring of robbers at the Delaware & Hudson car barn, I knew he was no good."

"I ain't going to argue with you, Mamie."

"Why don't you get in with the union? These politicians will sell you out soon as look at you."

"They're my sort, Mamie. You never understood. Let Tom work for the working slobs. That's his say. I'm working for myself and no one else."

"But what about me?" This was plaintive and insistent.

"I ain't getting married till I can afford to, Mamie. And I never told you otherwise. Now you can either wait or you can find someone else. That's your choice, and it's all the same to me." He was gentle but firm in saying this. She sobbed quietly and pressed her face to his breast. He placed his hands on her back in a clumsy embrace.

"I'm awake most nights, thinking about you, wondering where you are and who you're with."

"Now, I can't help that." He stepped to the side, toward the door, but she embraced him and kissed him, raising her body up to his. Abruptly she pulled away and opened his coat.

"What's this?"

"My revolver."

"Oh, I don't like this. Carrying a gun now, are you? And where will that get you?"

"Where I want to be. Listen, Mamie, it ain't your say-so. Let it rest. You don't control me. You watch your brother Tom work with the labor people, and you watch old Tom get locked out of the factories and get his skull busted as thanks for his efforts. Me? I'm taking what's mine. That's the only way you ever get what you want. You got to take it."

"You were never like this before . . ."

"You never saw me before. You were blinded by the thought of marrying, and children. I was only the groom."

Mamie began to sob audibly. "What is it you want? I don't understand this. What exactly is it you want?"

He took her by the arms. "I want to be somebody. I want to say 'Do this,' and it gets done. I want to say 'Go,' and they go. That's what I want. I want for people to look at me on the street and say, 'There goes Bat Shea,' instead of looking right through me like I were a tub of dish-water. Living low and out of sight may be all right for you and Tom, but I ain't built like that. George offered me this opportunity . . ."

"George ain't doing you no favors, I'm thinking."

"Well, that may be or it mayn't be, but it ain't for you to judge. Now, if you'll be kind enough to step aside . . ."

In desperation Mamie reached up and encircled his neck with her arms. He kissed her perfunctorily, then wiped his lips on his sleeve. "Tell old Tom I said hello. Now, I got to go. I'm sorry it ain't the way you planned, but it ain't exactly the way I planned neither."

He left her in the room, passed through the kitchen under the skeptical eye of his mother, "Bye, Ma," and was in the backyard again. He took three deep breaths of the wintry air. The afternoon had darkened and it would surely snow before evening. This was a perfect afternoon to lie with Mamie and talk as they had done the winter before he went West. Yeah, but there were other things to do now. He felt the revolver, and he needed a drink. He spat and wiped his mouth on his sleeve. Good thing George didn't mind if you took a nip while you tended bar.

* * *

Much later that night, Shea and McGough and Cleary were in Paddy Hannan's basement gambling "hell" behind Daisy LaFleur's two-bit house where the girls were fresh in from Pittsfield. A bigboned blonde in a fringed brocade dress cut up past the knee kept beckoning to Shea. She was wearing a hat with a veil, and her full red lips formed a kiss at him.

"Go jump her, will you, Bat?" McGough said in disgust. "She's poisoning my dice. I swear, Jerry, you ever see a five dollar hat on a two-bit whore?"

"Go on, Bat!" Jerry Cleary urged. "She's after you."

"I don't want her," Shea said, his arms folded. He had been moody all evening, snapping at George's regulars, then not wanting to come downtown, then coming downtown, the drink souring in him until there'd be a fight for certain unless something took the edge off him.

"Here, Dolly," McGough said. He had a flashy silk tie and a loud plaid suit and derby hat tipped back, a cigar in his mouth, and he flipped her a silver dollar with a flourish of his hand. "Take the big guy out for a while and give him whatever this'll buy."

"Gee, thanks, Big Spender." She took the dollar, and picked up Shea's hand. "Wanna go to heaven?"

"I'll go but only so's I won't have to look at these two," Shea explained.

"Such flattery!" she said with practiced irony.

"Put a smile on his kisser," Cleary called as she led him up the stairs to the alley outside. The wind was up, blowing the fresh snow off roofs.

"In here," she said, pulling open a stable door. The fragrant warmth of horses and the smell of oats and hay met them.

"What's the matter with Daisy's?"

"Don't ask. I ain't welcome in there no more."

"Oh, this is a good thing."

"Relax. I'll earn the dollar and more."

The girl led him up a ladder into a hay loft. On a blanket she plied her trade well. Afterward, Shea lay looking into the darkness where his breath steamed upward. "You like doing this?"

"It's all right. Better'n the mills. Besides, I get to meet such interesting guys like you."

He ignored the sarcasm and took a swig of the flask she offered.

"Ah, this is no good. What you do this for?"

"Money. What else?"

"Here." He tossed silver coins on the blanket. "Here's money. That make it better?"

"Sure. Makes it a whole sight better. Don't make it no worse'n it was, I'll tell you that."

"You go back in and tell them I went home. I had enough of it and I went home. Maybe you had enough too?"

"Me? No. I ain't had enough."

Shea adjusted his clothing, then climbed down the ladder. The horses had patiently endured the few minutes of human groaning, and they moved aside to let him pass.

Outside the Montreal Express was pulling into Union Station, clanging and gasping. A thin snow was falling, beading on the hot metal of the engine, coating the steaming backs of horses in the traces of cabs and wagons that waited for passengers by the station. Up the street, gas lamps gave the fronts of the whorehouses a greenish cast for few still had their red lamps lit. Shea's breath clung to his lower lip. The engine gasped again, and a great cloud of steam rose into the snow. The metallic heart of the engine throbbed as it waited by the platform like some impatient beast to be off again into the wilderness.

"This ain't good no more. I must be getting old, or soft, or something. Losing my touch." And then he thought of Tom Halligan, the labor union organizer, and Mamie, Tom's freckled kid sister, and he remembered the great fun they had in the innocent days, swimming in a pool up the gorge near the Frear place, and he remembered how she wept that afternoon, wept because she loved him. "She don't understand me," he muttered to himself, and then he thought of the girl in the hayloft. "None of 'em do."

5.
THE BETROTHED

J.C. Ross *Robert Ross* *William Ross*
Adam Ross, 2d

Next morning, Robert Ross stood at a window of the spacious family home, gazing down the steep hill to the worker tenements, the mills, the factories and the river far below. It was Saturday, and John, the eldest brother had summoned him from the foundry by telephone to discuss an urgent matter. A thin blanket of snow had fallen in the night, and it gave a stark purity to the maze of tenements and saloons below. Yet with the smokestacks it would not remain pure for long.

"Thank you for coming so quickly." It was John. Adam and Bill came in behind.

"Your message was rather cryptic."

"Sit down, please."

The four Ross brothers arrayed themselves about the starched linen of the dining room table in the places assigned long before by the patriarch. George Ross, an immigrant from Edinburgh, had not weathered this winter well. He was upstairs bundled in blankets.

"We met with Senator Murphy and the police chief this morning," John began.

"What?" Robert's eyes narrowed. "Why wasn't I informed?"

"Please hear me out, Rob. Senator Murphy asked us to come see him about Tuesday's election. He was alarmed about a call you made upon him which, he said, could lead to violence at the polls."

Robert's jaw clenched, and his face flushed. He was the youngest and most beloved of the brothers. He had fierce brown eyes and an unyielding will and was accustomed to getting his way. "And so I was excluded?"

"The senator said you'd already had words with him."

"I doubt they will be the last."

"Robert," Adam said in a conciliatory tone, "the senator assured us there would be no trouble at the polls Tuesday, that the police superintendent would detail a police officer to each of the three polling places in the ward, and that the prohibition against carrying weapons will be published in all the newspapers Monday. He had some concern about clubs?"

"Yes?"

"What clubs?"

"I had Townsend turn out some clubs on the lathe. Like this." Robert took a long club of purple and yellow wood from inside his coat. "This is what the Irish will meet if they try to force the vote at the third district."

The three older brothers exchanged glances.

"It is a felony to carry a weapon Tuesday," Adam said.

"You weren't at the caucus, Adam!" Robert became agitated. "Bill and John were there. They saw that character McGough pull a pistol when a hand was coming through the window with illegal votes, and then that other one, Shea, crashing through the window. These are desperate men, and they must be stopped."

"But the police will be watching for weapons among our poll watchers as well. You could be arrested."

Robert stood and walked to the window. "So this is all I have succeeded in doing, shackling us with our own morality. Thursday when I went down to see Murphy, I had received a taunt from the Irish through Ellis Hayner. They threatened my life, and your lives as well. I responded, and now I'm the villain?"

The older brothers nodded. "I'm afraid so," Adam said. "And Murphy has the police force on his side."

Robert turned from the window. "Well, I am not altering my plan. If I have to go to jail to ensure an honest vote, I shall. I will be a martyr to our cause. The problem we face exceeds the very narrow issue of this election, *friends*." Robert deliberately used the word "friends" to remind his brothers of the APA pledge. "Sure, Murphy can try to confine this to a simple charter election in our small city, but the problem is nationwide. This is a class war. In every city the Irish have propped up their corrupt bosses to steal our taxes and bleed the merchants and manufacturers dry, lining their pockets with our money. They put their hacks and layabouts on the public payroll, and frame corrupt contracts for public works to reward their cronies. They must be stopped! Government must be returned to Americans, friends, to its rightful heirs and guardians, us, gentlemen, the only race morally fit to rule."

"Caution, Rob, caution," said John.

Robert Ross flashed his dark eyes at his brothers, and slapped the club in his palm. "Caution does not win a class war, John."

"But this is America!" Adam protested. "We live in a democracy!"

"If we don't act now," Robert said, "it won't be a democracy for long. I am going to stop Dunlop and his Irish thugs if I must do so alone."

"We'll be with you, Rob," Adam promised, but there was little commitment in his voice.

Robert Ross did not return to the foundry. Slighted by his brothers, he rode his bay gelding out the snowy lane beyond the city line to the home of his fiancée. When the butler answered the door, Nellie was at the piano in the drawing room.

Nellie Mae Patton was a haughty young woman of striking beauty. She had high cheekbones, a high forehead and a strong chin and jaw. Her lips were thin and pale, accustomed to impatience. Her eyes were a dark violet, unusual bewitching eyes that narrowed often when expressing the authority of her intellect and will. Her luxuriant black hair fell in ringlets upon her shoulders and was fragrant and thick. She held her head high and looked down at the world and its creatures that did not often seem to interest her. Nellie had not yet discovered her mission in life, but she sensed that Robert Ross was worthy of her, and so she allowed herself to love him. They would be wed in June.

She came through the high foyer to greet him. "Why, Robert! Are things slow at the shop?"

"Nell," Robert disregarded the teasing. "I needed to see your smile."

"It wouldn't hurt to see yours as well."

Robert Ross shook his head. "I suppose I am rather distracted." When his expression brightened, Nellie's violet eyes flashed, and she smiled triumphantly seeing her power over him.

She escorted him into the drawing room and dispatched the butler for coffee and cocoa. Muted sunlight, reflecting off the snow, gave great clarity to objects in the room. Once seated, Robert seemed to awaken to the rich spacious home, the beautiful young woman, the station he aspired to reach from the soot and noise of the shop.

"What is it?" There was a hint of impatience in her voice.

"Oh, politics. What else? The Irish question again. They seem to be everywhere, their labor unions and their Catholic schools. Now the election Tuesday. There are so many rumors going about, threats of violence, murderous talk."

"Are you alarmed?"

"No, of course not. The Irish are cowards as well as liars, and they won't dare to face our organized resistance."

"So you will carry the day. I don't know why you spend so much time and energy on these trivial matters. What has local politics ever done for anyone?"

"You are right, my dear. But it galls me how these Irish oppose us, try to extort guaranteed wages from honest capitalists who must risk everything to keep the shops open, how they insist on cutting back on their hours."

Nellie stifled a yawn. "Oh, let us talk of something else, Rob. I find it so tiresome. Let me share plans for our wedding and honeymoon with you," and she reached for a great album beneath a table and they fell to reviewing it together.

The butler entered and set the coffee and cocoa on the table.

"And this is the silver service pattern I have chosen for us. It complements the crystal and the dinner service. Mother's Aunt Letty has ordered the most elaborate silver flatware. See the tea service?" She showed him a catalog. "Look at the sugar tongs. Have you ever seen such sugar tongs?"

He confessed he had not.

"And there's ever so much arranging to be done. I was out to the house yesterday. It seemed so large and empty. We'll need furniture and draperies and servants to hire. And we'll take the night boat to New York for Mr. Tiffany's lamps and perhaps a window and a bauble or two."

Robert regarded her, his concern for the election gone. Her father was giving them a home, furnishings and all. He found discussing the details somewhat embarrassing. Although the Rosses were well off, they had not a tenth of the great wealth of Josiah Patton. "Of course, Nellie, of course."

And then she was off again, imagining the grand tour through France and Switzerland and through the Alps to Italy. Italy! And while she spoke, he marvelled at his good fortune in having so handsome and intelligent a wife-to-be. At last she paused: "There, you seem less crestfallen now." She held his hand in hers.

"Is your father at home?"

Nellie dropped his hand. "Yes, he is." She regarded him suspiciously. "You did not come to see me at all, did you? You came to see him. Perhaps we should request that he move in with us this summer?"

"Nell, your father is a very influential man."

"More influential than his daughter, at least with you." She pointed toward the door. "He's upstairs in his den, probably plotting how to corner the market in milliner's ribbons."

"Nell. It will all be over Tuesday."

"No it won't, Rob. It won't ever be over. You thrive on it, plotting and scheming with him. I suppose I should feel lucky that you are looking higher than the shop and the valve trade. But I don't. Go to him. He's upstairs. Plot and scheme and Tuesday will come and go, and you'll either win or you will lose. And I won't care either way unless it discourages you from further involvement. If it does that, then I will applaud."

"Nell!"

"Go."

Robert left her in the drawing room, and ascended to the study of Josiah Patton, merchant prince.

"Enter!" the patriarch called to Ross's knock. He peered up from a great ledger, squinting through octagonal spectacles. "Yes?" he asked impatiently. Josiah was fond of Moorish architecture, and reds and ochres and rust colors dominated the room in exotic Arabesque patterns. He had travelled extensively in Spain, and he was something of an authority on the Inquisition. "Oh, Robert! It is you. Come in, dear boy." He put down his pen. Patton had piercing blue eyes and a long gray beard separated into halves by the cleft of his chin. He wore a fez in his study, and satin slippers.

Ross bowed to the butler, discharging him, and crossed the carpet and sat in a carved throne of a chair facing the enormous black walnut desk.

"So good of you to visit. I am just going over some figures from the shop before I venture down into the chaos that is our fair city." He looked through his spectacles. "Is everything all right?"

"Yes, sir. I saw Nellie downstairs and we visited. She is an extraordinary young woman."

"And my favorite. Five daughters, and she is my favorite." He wagged his finger at Ross. "You are a lucky young man."

"I know, sir." Robert Ross cleared his throat and adjusted himself in the chair. "I have some news, though, that may be unsettling. Murphy and the police commissioner are stepping up patrols for the election

Tuesday, and our plans have come under scrutiny."

The old man's face clouded. "But how were our plans made known?"

Ross grimaced. "I am afraid I confronted Murphy the other day. My brothers met with him this morning. He knows about the posse and the clubs. He has made guarded threats."

Josiah sighed. "Not wise, Robert. Plans are to be hidden until executed. Now we must adjust. The Irish will certainly be armed. We must be as well. Are the clubs distributed?"

"Yes, sir. We gave them out."

"Revolvers would not be a bad idea."

"But they say it's a felony."

"It's a felony for clubs too, is it not?"

"Yes."

"So what's the difference? You should indicate that none of our members will be discouraged from carrying revolvers. We might also float a promise to provide legal representation should anyone be arrested."

"That would be an incentive."

"Yes, and Frank Black is interested in helping. Do you know him?"

"The new Republican chairman? I have met him."

"Yes. A brilliant attorney, though he primarily handles commercial matters. He will provide legal representation to fellow Amoreans if any of them should fall afoul of the police. Pass the word. Meanwhile, are the poll inspectors prepared?"

"Yes, sir."

"Very well. And you are ready for tomorrow's meeting?"

Ross nodded.

"Good. Good. We shall prevail Tuesday, Robert. It is critical we keep the alderman in the thirteenth ward Republican. Not only would the balance on the council shift if the seat were to go to that saloonkeeper, but with our plans for mills up the creek, we need a champion in city hall. Our plans call for streets, sewers, lights. It looks like Whelan is finished in the city, and Molloy won't be so favorably disposed."

"But we shall prevail, sir."

"You have a very bright future, Robert, and I have many friends. Say goodbye to Nellie on your way out or she will be intolerable all afternoon." Josiah stood and shook Ross's hand in the secret handshake of the APA brotherhood. "Good to see you. Now let us both get back to work."

6.
THE CITY

Downtown Troy In The Horsedrawn Days

In the age of water power and water travel, this city had advantages. Troy was founded as a market town on a gravel floodplain at the head of Hudson River navigation, and farmers and horsebreeders traded here, their produce and stock boated downriver to Albany or New York City. Troy won the designation of county seat from the older village of Lansingburgh in 1792, and here the courthouse, jail and gallows were erected. Incorporated as a city in 1816, Troy awoke from its rural slumber in the 1820s. In 1825 the Erie Canal was complete and snubbed canal boats by the thousands streamed down the watery staircase cut in black shale across the Hudson to unload along Troy's four miles of waterfront.

The Atlantic tide reaches up the Hudson to Troy, a hundred fifty miles north of New York Harbor, and steamship lines plied the Hudson to and from the metropolis. With the Erie and Champlain canals ending here, Troy became the transfer port for Adirondack lumber and Indiana grain and barrels of salt from Syracuse and Caribbean molasses and salted meat from the Chicago slaughterhouses. Along Troy's waterfront walked browned "canawlers" from Oneida and Erie, Rochester and Champlain, Quebec and Niagara, and swarthy deckhands from Brooklyn and the Antilles, and occasionally sailors from Liverpool and Belfast.

In 1894, before Lansingburgh was annexed, Troy was a rectangle, four miles along the river and a mile and a half east from the riverbank. Although the city line ran through high clay hills that rise up suddenly from the gravel floodplain to form a high irregular ridge, the businesses, parish churches and clusters of worker tenements crowded together in the six blocks of level ground along the river. The rectangular grid of streets laid out in the 1790s generally ended at these hills, though in places developers had surveyed and were building along Eighth, Ninth and Tenth streets for worker families who'd saved enough to cross the railroad tracks. It was every worker's aspiration to "live on the hill." When "'Tis sure I'll have me home on the hill," was spoken with irony, it referred to one of the cemeteries in the hills above Troy.

Before the 1870s, the hilltops were farmed. Wealthy merchants and manufacturers built great brick and granite mansions downtown. Washington Park, an exclusive enclave of manufacturers built in the 1840s, boasted industrialists and abolitionists who helped Lincoln win the Civil War. Here lived an attorney who defended the notorious Veiled Murderess and saved a fugitive slave from an angry mob. Here lived matrons who secretly forwarded escaped slaves along the Underground Railroad. Bankers and merchants built their mansions on First and Second Streets, and over on Fifth Avenue to be near their docks, their commercial counting houses, their banks, and Union depot.

But in the waning decades of the Victorian era, the noise and the smoke and the grit and the grime of the city forced a new generation of Troy's elite up into the hills. The earlier mansions were neoclassical, but as the age turned darker and architecture gothic, peaks and towers and heavy wrought iron made these mansions appear like birds of prey, watching over the activity in the valley below. The Gurleys, the Pattons, the Frears, the Eddys, the Warrens, the Tibbits, the Vails, the Griswolds and the Burdens all escaped the soot and squalor, and from their lofty pastoral seats they peered down upon the masses sweating, toiling, occasionally rioting, like barons, safe and secure above the Darwinian struggle. They raised their children in an elite world of gardens and coaches, soirees and golf and tennis, saving for the young men, after a sojourn in the Ivy League, the nasty secrets of business and oppression of the laboring class. Yet in the center of the ridge rose the spires of St. Joseph's Roman Catholic seminary, as if a papist crown had been placed upon the city.

Three streams draining the Berkshire foothills spill over the ridge of clay hills to the floodplain and the river below, the Piscawenkill, the

Poestenkill and the Wynantskill. Men of industry and vision harnessed the latter two with millwheels and turbines to manufacture nails, horseshoes, textiles, wire, flour, paper, brushes. Indeed, Henry Burden built the largest waterwheel in the world on the Wynantskill. John Marshall enlisted Irish coal miners to bore a tunnel through a thousand feet of black shale for an underground millrace, powering turbines in the basements of mills down the Poestenkill gorge. Only the Piscawenkill remained to be harnessed, and Josiah Patton quietly purchased the incorporeal water rights so he and Robert Ross might exploit the waterpower there.

Troy's energetic ruling caste is quick to seize an opportunity, an invention, the corner of a market, and the city supplies the world with detachable collars and with iron stoves. By 1894 steam engines have replaced many creaking millwheels and the gasps and explosions of driving pistons reverberate in narrow brick alleys where the two twelve-hour shifts of workers trudge to and from their tenement homes. Before sunrise each day, legions of men tromp to work in hobnail boots, swarthy vulcans who labor and sweat all day in the showers of sparks. Thousands of single young women, too, board the streetcars to work the spindles and looms, hoping only to exchange the drudgery of the mill someday for the drudgery of motherhood. Many miss this mark when local madams come recruiting among the ranks for comely lasses to staff the bordellos, yet another form of industrial slavery.

Children work in these factories, too, ten- and eleven-year-old children earning pennies for twelve hour shifts in the foundries, in the forges, at the shuttles and spindles. These children cannot read or write. They are malnourished, filthy, ragged, vacant-eyed, turning out piecework for the wealthy industrialists who rule as respected and unquestioned as feudal tyrants. The children grow up with deep resentments for the wealthy folk on the hill, and the new generation is forming unions.

The overnight industrial revolution that propelled Troy from a market town of shops and cottage industries into a factory city was worldwide. Since Queen Victoria ascended the throne of the United Kingdom in 1837, the world has seen an unprecedented surge of city building. Inventions — the elevator, the locomotive, the suspension bridge, the telegraph, the flush toilet, the telephone, the electric streetcar, the electric streetlamp — have brought quicker and easier transportation and communication, have illuminated the night and allowed buildings to rise above three stories. But the expansions and prosperity have extracted a heavy price. From the clanging iron and steel mills of South Troy to the vast complexes making detachable collars and cuffs in North Troy, this city in 1894 throbs with manufacturing day and night. At night the sky is lit a rosy orange from the blast furnaces. Smokestacks blow tons of coal soot and sulphur toward the sky that coat and streak the buildings and monuments when a merciful rain clears the air. Heaps of black slag stain the riverbank. Sewers vomit metals and washwater and bleaches and dyes into the river, and the municipal sewage system, recently completed, dumps raw human waste into the river that then lies in a stinking clot for hours until the tide turns and it can flow south to the sea.

The congestion of people, as in the Old World from where they fled, breeds vermin and disease. Flies, fat on horse manure in the streets, mosquitoes and gnats fill the summer night. Bedbugs and headlice are common; rats large as cats prowl for food in the kitchens of the poor, and can be heard racing through the ceilings at night. Scarlet fever, malaria, rheumatic fever, typhoid, venereal diseases of syphilis and gonorrhea from the "cat houses" by the rail station, and a virulent strain of tuberculosis rage through the community. Homes are occasionally boarded up, families quarantined during outbreaks. Medical science is primitive in diagnosis, treatment and surgery as industrial accidents, boiler explosions, railroad crashes and runaway horses send victims to the hospital with burns and fractures, blindings and lamings.

Not so long before, this same Hudson River was the subject of a school of landscape painters. They idealized the Hudson in a rapture of man in harmony with nature. Now at Troy the river is an industrial sewer, and it breeds contamination in human form as well. Troy's waterfront in 1894 is a tenderloin of vice and thievery. The riverboat from New York brings the fancy folk, like trussed birds for the pickpockets and robbers that lurk along pierheads. Cardsharps and confidence men mingle in crowds that travel elegantly in the great floating wedding cakes of the Citizens Steamboat Line. Brawny canalers, browned and calloused by the waterway from Troy to Buffalo drink and gamble and whore with abandon at this, the eastern end of their long haul, before they must load their boats and return westward.

In the center of town by Union Station stands the crowning scarlet insult to the repressed Victorian, Catholic and Protestant alike, the Line, long city blocks of bordellos, whose lights in the night glow like a harlot's ruby necklace. Friday and Saturday nights are long and dark, filled with honky tonk piano and ragtime tunes pouring out of the saloons, women's screams and gunshots. Few are the Sundays, while the bells of Troy's many churches toll, where no murder investigation is underway by Superintendent Willard's bluecoats.

A generation before, the Civil War raised Troy industrialists into national prominence, Henry Burden, John Griswold, John Winslow, men whose eye for business and invention saw beyond city and state borders, envisioned national and international markets that the fledgling rail and steamship networks can now reach. While there is no Rockefeller or Carnegie here, survival of the fittest has raised up certain blood lines in local business.

Yet the second generation of millowners lacks vision and times have changed. New anti-trust laws and talk of an income tax strike at concentrations of wealth. The challenge of the frontier is gone. Markets are everywhere shrinking. Pittsburgh has emerged as the predominant iron and steel capital to rob Troy of the designation. English exports threaten Troy's collar and cuff industry. The technology, too, is changing. Waterpower and muscular energy of men and horses is being replaced by steam engines in ever-new applications. In Schenectady a dozen miles to the west, Thomas Edison works on new marvels to lead the steam and gaslight era into the electric age, and the age of internal combustion.

Seven decades of iron and steel making have coated Troy with a thick blanket of coal soot. The warehouses, factories and tenements, built of brick baked from the clay of the hills, and of the native oak and pine, cherry and maple and walnut, are packed tightly together along the cobbled streets. There is no planning, no zoning, no oversight. The city has grown haphazardly by leaps and bounds since it was half destroyed by fire from a locomotive's spark during the Civil War. Brickyards mine and bake the clay of the hills next to schools; saloons are adjacent to churches; factories are surrounded by worker tenements and factory stores; and through the streets electric and horsedrawn streetcars pass, connecting the neighborhood pockets of Poles, Italians, Jews, French, Danes, Germans, Irish and Scots.

The public buildings and concert halls are built of imported building stone from Vermont quarries, marble and granite, with wrought iron balconies and balustrades. Though it aspires to Victorian elegance, and by 1894 good Queen Victoria has been on the throne nearly sixty years, Troy can never cleanse the grime and grit of its furnaces and smokestacks, the sweat and vice of its people. Troy's citizens have built a gracious Music Hall in the center of the city boasting the finest acoustics in the world, yet Troy's daily symphony is one of locomotive and mill whistles, immigrant brawls, and the clang and throb of machinery.

Out of this welter of economic, ethnic and social forces, Edward Murphy, Jr., emerged. First elected alderman, Murphy rose quickly through municipal offices to become the city's first Irish mayor. "Boss"

Murphy is a born executive. His blarney deflects pointed questions and tough issues into the milder fields of humor while his organizational skills have built an invincible political machine and ingratiated him with the great Tammany Hall that runs New York State. Murphy masquerades as a gentleman, but when crossed has the will and tactics of a street fighter. He distances himself from the dirty work. His party's secret weapon is voting fraud. His minions fix elections by stuffing ballot boxes with false ballots, and relying upon elections the party faithful rigs, his candidates then pay Murphy homage while in office.

This year, 1894, Senator Edward Murphy serves as New York State Democratic Chairman as well, a handsome, dapper gent in a top hat with a strong and honorable statewide presence. While mayor, Murphy erected Troy's gothic city hall twenty years before and brought the project in under budget. As a decorative flair he had shamrocks carved above the gothic windows. He gave the downtown a new system of granite streets, gaslights and watering fountains for stock. He won the hearts of the people by saving a bank from closing, and by turning back his Irish from halting the Orange Day parade. He is entrenched. The brewery is his fortress. His excesses are legion. He has even taken to paraphrasing Louis XIV's "*L'état c'est moi*" into "What's Troy? Why, that's me!" This vanity and tyranny galls the industrial aristocracy.

In 1893, a recession closed many plants and mills across the nation, and Troy was hard hit. The elegance of the Victorian era was darkening, the styles rococo and gothic. While plump belles and beefy young men danced at cotillions and promenades, dirty-faced immigrant children starved and shivered in their tenements with no Charles Dickens to assay the purity of their hearts. The poor and disenfranchised are looking beyond the show and ornamentation that Mark Twain snidely dubbed "The Gilded Age," asking why in a free country they cannot earn a decent living. The underbelly of Victorian respectability is about to be exposed in hot blasts of William Randolph Hearst's yellow journalism, and the calliope and ragtime tempos of an age are drowning in a loud and steady throb of steam pistons.

Across the land, captains of industry have seized control of the economic heart and arteries of the republic, and in their iron fists vast profits are to be squeezed. Yet the overlords are worried, their absolute control is slipping. In February, an army of unemployed rose up in the Midwest under a populist hero, Jacob Coxey, to march upon the nation's capitol and demand jobs from Congress. In response to the dire financial times, a secret organization has formed in Iowa, the American Protective Association, the APA, an anti-immigrant, anti-Irish, anti-Catholic fraternity of white Protestant males who meet in secret, dress in black robes, observe odd rituals, and call each other "friend" and "Amorean" to signify friendship with the flag and love of native American values: temperance, public education, the free and honest ballot. The APA targets the Irish as scapegoats. Solve the Irish problem, abolish Catholic schools and, they believe, society will be saved. The APA has opened a chapter in Troy and membership is growing. Indeed, Robert Ross has just returned from Iowa, indoctrinated and zealous to purge city hall of Irish machine politics.

Thus, in the early months of 1894 Yankee English and Scots Protestants wield the economic power in Troy, and the boss's Irish Catholics hold political power. The manufacturing and mercantile families want to rule the city they own, and the Irish want economic parity and labor reform. The industrialists lack only a leader and a single purpose to shake them out of their political indolence and forge them into a unified force to depose Boss Murphy. On the other side, though, Murphy could care less about labor reform. He is in power, God's in His heaven and all's right with the world.

In 1894, this city of sixty thousand is comprised of thirteen wards, each electing two alderman to the board. The board passes local ordinances and its standing committees oversee city finances, assessments, the police, the streets, alleys, burial grounds, city clocks in the public squares, gaslamps, railroads, streetcars and the common schools. Troy holds its charter election on the first Tuesday in March of each year and the aldermen's terms are staggered so they run every two years.

The present mayor, Dennis Whelan, a bottler of soda water along the Poestenkill, has recently ignored Murphy's directives in appointing party members to city jobs. Dennis Whelan mistakenly thought that while Murphy was away in Washington, he could curry favor with wealthy Protestants whose temperance leagues endorse his "birch beer" and "root beer" and "ginger ale," alternatives for beer and whiskey. He believed the Protestants would protect him in a power struggle, and he would prevail. But word is on the street that Boss Murphy has ordered Whelan's independence punished, and has anointed Francis J. Molloy for mayor. Marching bands of repeat voters must be ready March 6 to assure a Molloy victory.

The Irish Democrats undertake their work with zest and zeal. Their resentment and bruised pride at being socially shunned enjoy vindication at the polls. The Protestant Republicans are sullen — they have been beaten so many times before, the conclusion is almost foregone: Whelan will be out. And with Murphyites in city hall, in the district attorney's office and even in judicial robes, there is no higher redress for the election fraud.

On the eve of its seventy-ninth charter election, Troy, New York, is a microcosm of the Gilded Age, containing between its breezy hills and brown riverbank all the vices and virtues, the hypocrisies and bigotry, all the pent up sexuality and aggression of the Victorian era. Spring will be here soon, and from the hills, after the flooding subsides and the land turns green, you may watch the steamboats and the railroad join Troy to the fertile West of infinite possibility, and to the vast metropolis downriver. You can hear its mill whistles blow, and its church bells ring the Angelus. And from a distance of time, the city may even appear picturesque. Yet the struggles are brutal and the winners few.

This spring the mayor's race is the battleground between the millowners and the boss, and the boss is predicting an easy victory. "What's Troy? Why, that's me." Yet no one sees what is about to erupt in this small manufacturing city where few secrets are kept and four daily newspapers ferret out the interesting and the curious, for very few are paying any attention to a small tinder box and the wild sparks flying in the race for alderman in the last voting district of the city's last ward.

7. PREMONITIONS

Troy City Hall

You could lie in bed in the dark and listen to the harnesses jingling and the horseshoes on the cobblestones outside. When one of the new electric streetcars pass, blue-white sparks lit up the dark of your windowpane. You could hear the laughter from George's saloon below, and when the piano player arrived, sweet tenors giving voice to sentimental Irish tragedies of lost love and lost rebellions. And you tried not to hear the laughter and the squeals of the girls next door and upstairs. If you enjoyed a cigar in the dark before going downstairs and you tried to keep your mind fixed on the single purpose ahead and how it was to be accomplished, and you tried to render an honest evaluation as to who was strong, who was weak, and how it would all play out, it was damned annoying when there was a knock at the door.

"Yeah?" Shea called. One of the paying customers was no doubt too drunk to read the room number a girl had scrawled and slipped him. "Who is it now?"

"Bartholomew?" A woman's voice. Mamie Halligan. He stabbed out the cigar, pulled his trouser braces over the shoulders of his union suit and opened the door.

"Hello?" Her voice trembled, her eyes glanced up at him, then were cast at the floor. "Can I come in?"

"Sure. Sure."

He struck a sulfur match and lit the gas lamp, and the light rose white then ebbed into a soft green.

"And what brings the likes of you by?"

"I thought you'd be happy to see me."

"I am. But it's unusual for you to come to a place like this."

Indeed, she had difficulty disguising her distaste as she peered about the barren room looking for a place to sit. He offered her the only chair and he sat on the bed.

"You have no curtains?"

"I got nothing to hide."

They stared at each other for an uneasy moment.

"Perhaps I shouldn't have come," she began haltingly, "but Tom heard some things, and I got to worrying, and I was upset about seeing you yesterday at your ma's and how you stormed out of there, and I wanted to set things straight between us."

"What things?"

"About, you know, us!"

"No. What things has Tom heard?"

She sighed in frustration. Politics was always more important than their courtship. "That the Ross boys was arming a posse of fifty so as to stop you Tuesday."

"Is that so?"

"They mean to beat George, Bat. They have that suffragette lady Susan B. Anthony speaking tomorrow night at Music Hall on the evils of the all-male vote, and they've picked three more races other than George's so's they can take control of the board. They're organized and determined, and I," she peered up at him, "I got premonitions that if you run up against them there'll be trouble."

"Premonitions?"

"Don't scoff! Remember when I had the premonition just before Christmas and they found little Maggie dead in her cradle? Or last fall when I woke up dreaming of the Kellys and lightning bolts and the next night their house burnt down."

He started to laugh. "That was a chimney fire!"

"It was a premonition still. Oh, Bat, I can feel there's to be evil doings here, and I come tonight," now her demeanor changed, and she pulled a small flask from her handbag, "I come to have a sip with you."

"Well, now you're talking." He rubbed his hands together.

The couple in the next room had just entered a certain phase of their transaction that caused the iron bed to bang against the wall. Shea pounded his fist on his side of the wall.

"Pipe down! There's a lady in here!"

"Yeah, ain't they all?" came a man's voice, and then the laughing. "Waist-down, anyhow."

"I oughta . . ."

"Never mind." Mamie took a sip of the whiskey and her eyes bulged as she swallowed carefully and then her eyes watered. "Want some?"

As he reached for the bottle, she held it to his lips and guided his hand to her waist. When he took a long swallow, she slid from the chair onto his lap and kissed him in a way she had never kissed him before.

"Where'd you learn that?"

"Never you mind. I have a secret or two."

She kissed him again. She took a swig from the flask, then gave him one. "Why don't you turn out the light? That bare window spooks me."

"For what? What you got in mind?"

Mamie laughed and held the flask again to his lips. He drank, regarding her suspiciously.

"Now what's all this about, Mamie?"

"What do you mean? It's what you want, ain't it?"

"Yeah, I suppose so. But why the sudden turnabout?"

"Look who's stalling now." She was coy.

"Wait, Mamie, get off my lap. Sit over there. Now, what's this all about?"

"I come to be with you."

From the next room a woman's laughter exploded, then a man's deeper laugh. "Goddamn them!" Shea stood up, clenched his fists. "I don't know, I don't know about this. It ain't, it ain't . . . right."

"And who's advising you now, Father Swift?" She giggled. "You been a-pestering me for so long to visit you here and we could . . . you know . . . so, here I am."

"But it ain't the right time, is all. I got a lot on my mind. I don't want to be distracted."

"Oh, so it's a distraction is it?" She lay her head back and laughed a throaty laugh. "A distraction he calls it where before he'd sooner get my petticoats up over my chin than have his liquor."

"I thought you wanted to wait. You always said you wanted to wait. Why don't you want to wait no more?"

"I'm tired of waiting. Waiting did me no good. The nights are just as long for me, and the mornings just as empty. So let's not wait. Put out the lamp."

"No, Mamie." Shea was agitated. "You don't just come barging into a man's room and start telling him what to do. You don't come in here with this new way of acting, a new way of kissing, for Christ's sake, and a bottle of the good bonded and start acting like a saloon tart. How do you think I'll treat you afterwards?"

"I don't care. I'm tired, tired of waiting."

"Well, I don't like this."

"You don't like it?" Mamie Halligan cried, and she rose suddenly in anger. "You don't like what you been a-troubling me for these last two years, and I screw up my courage to get the bottle at Flynn's who knows my da, and purchase new bloomers without my sisters getting wind of it," she raised her skirts.

"Don't, Mamie! For God's sake. What the hell's got into you? This world's turned upside down, I swear." He sat her down. "Now, I want you to put your shawl over your head and I'll get you down the back stairs, and you skittle off through the alley so's no one sees you. Understand?"

"But . . . !"

"No arguing, now. I don't want what you come here to give, least not tonight."

Now she began to sob. "I don't believe you, Bat Shea! I come to give you what you want, and you throw me out. Smuggled down the back stairs and out into the alley! Like some shameful trollop. What's the matter with you?"

He went to her, took her arms and she embraced him. "I got a lot on my mind, Mamie. Look, it's the election. There's lots of talk. Even your brother's hearing things. I ain't myself just now. I got to pay attention to my work. It'll be all right in a week. Then we can make plans. After George is in, we can make plans, big plans."

"The election!" she made a spitting sound. "Politics! You men and your games. As if the world dangled on a string. You think you can master it, and you'll wind up being its victim. I know, Bat Shea." She tapped her head. "I have premonitions. The Ross boys are arming, and there'll be trouble. Oh, Bat, please don't go through with this! I fear you'll get hurt!"

Shea went to the window and looked up the street. The night was damp and foggy and the cop on the beat, Officer Daley, was pacing along on the other side in the gaslight. Shea needed something to say, and he needed time to think.

"This is the only show they give me, Mamie. It's this election or nothing. George picked me up to do this for him. Otherwise I'd be breaking my back in the foundry. Who else'd have me? No, I thought it through, and this is my show, and I'm taking it."

"But there are other ways."

"There are?" He sneered and gave a laugh. "No, there ain't. There's only one way, Mamie, the strong eat the weak. That's all there is. You can pray and you can hope and you can wait for a better world, a better life, but if you clear away all the lies, that's what it comes down to. There's them that kicks and them that gets kicked, and I'm goddamned tired of getting kicked. I been kicked my whole life. I got kicked in school, kicked in the mill, kicked around in the neighborhood and kicked around out West. It's only when I kick back that others give me a show."

"It ain't like that, Bat. Not as bad as that."

"It is! The APA is sweeping the land with their chapters and secret meetings trying to crush us. Sweet Jesus! Ask your brother Tom. He's been kicked a few times. They meet in secret dressed in hoods, won't show theirselves together in the daylight. Like snakes. Now I don't want to be kicked no more, so there's only one choice, I gotta kick back. After the election, when I am in a position of being able to kick back at them, we can make plans. You and me. We'll see, and there'll be plenty of time for this here then."

"You always take everything so personal. It don't have to be that way. You ain't the only one who hurts."

"I may not be the only one, but that don't make it hurt any less. Now, let's get you collected and down the stairs and out the back."

He dried her tears with a handkerchief, then urged her up from the chair. Mamie pulled her shawl tight about her face, and Shea led her down the stairs while the laughing and squealing continued above, and the singing below. Out in the alley he gave her a kiss, holding her face in his hand. She looked like a child then, and it was cold and there was the smell of wet ashes.

"Good bye, Mamie. Thanks for stopping in."

"Sure." She turned away, then stopped. "You be careful."

"No need to worry 'bout me," he said jauntily. And as he turned into the saloon, he shook his head and muttered, "Premonitions."

But Bat Shea had trouble drinking away the jarring feeling Mamie's visit left in him. That slut the other night in the stable that Jack paid for, then Mamie wanting to raise her hem, that part of life confused him. He saw all manner of men undone by women, and he considered marriage and children nothing but obstacles to his ambition. Yet he loved Mamie, even if he had trouble admitting to the soft side of his nature. If he could just raise himself up to some decent level, she'd be the wife he'd choose. Her worrying upset him, her premonitions, for Shea was superstitious. He feared he was losing his edge of toughness and control and others could see. There had been so much reaction in the ward to the "revolver caucus," there'd be a battle Tuesday sure.

To keep occupied he helped George prepare for the parish "feed" tomorrow, boiling briskets of corned beef and baking bread. With a pail of beer on the stone table in the center of the kitchen, even Gene McClure lent a hand. It was hot work over the great kettles and ovens, and when Shea ventured outside the bar about ten for some air, he was surprised that the cop on the beat, Paddy Daley, called him over:

"So, what's the word, Shea?"

"How so, Officer?"

"For Tuesday. I hear you got plans."

"George is a good bet."

"I heard you got plans is all, Shea." Daley tipped back his tall hat and backed Shea into a brick wall. "Hah? You got plans, Shea?"

"I got plans, Paddy. So what?"

"And them plans is what?"

"They's just plans at this stage. What's eating you?"

Officer Paddy Daley snarled and pressed his billyclub against Shea's throat, thrusting him against the brick wall. Shea coughed. With his right hand the policeman patted Shea's pockets looking for the revolver that was under the mattress upstairs.

"There's a warrant out for you."

"It's two years old. Is it any good? Don't they get stale?"

Daley ignored the wisecrack. "I oughta run you in right now just on a hunch. But that might look bad for other boys in the organization. We been instructed to pick you up on that warrant if you so much as show your face election day. The chief himself give the order after Dunlop whined. So you just keep that ugly kisser behind closed doors all day Tuesday, 'cause we don't need your brand of trouble."

"Sure, Paddy, sure. Why's everyone so jumpy this year?"

"I never liked you, Shea. You're too stubborn and you don't take nobody's say. I'll come up here for you myself if I hear anything between then and now. Understand?"

"Clear as a bell, Paddy." Shea smiled despite the choke hold of the club and his sarcasm was ill-disguised. "And don't think I don't appreciate the advice."

"Get the hell out of my sight." And the cop released him and Shea swaggered up the street, adjusting his collar, and he circled the block and returned to Dunlop's. As he walked into the barroom, his name was called merrily by Jack McGough: "Bat Shea! Where in Christ's kingdom have you been?"

"Getting some air."

"Don't be so hangdog there, bucko. Wait'll you hear the news from Kingston — " and McGough briefed his leader on the trip south. Owen Judge, who'd gone home to be with his wife, had comported himself well, and they scoured the Rondout waterfront for eight of the roughest stevedores who, for a ten dollar gold piece, their trainfare, meals and lodging, would stuff the ballot box full of votes for Dunlop.

"What's got into you, Bat? It's all done. We're back the same day. All the preparations are made, and now we just sit tight and wait till Tuesday and George is in, and we'll be getting fat."

"I wish't it were over, Jack, is all, and we could get along to do something new. There's been a flurry of attention to this thing that I don't like."

"Ah, nothing worth doing don't have its unpleasant side, so let's enjoy!" Jack ordered another round of drinks. George Dunlop came over to the table in the midst of their sweet intoxication and he expressed his satisfaction with their work, yet he seemed apprehensive too. News of Protestant resistance came repeatedly from various sources.

About midnight, little Harelip McGee crossed Shea: "They're awaiting on ya, Shea. Ya think yer a big man, but they'll cut ya down to size. They're awaiting on ya."

Shea told him three times to keep still. "I don't want t'be picking on a cripple, McGee," he said, but when Harelip taunted the big thug again, Shea crammed his face into a spitoon. Harelip surfaced with a brown sludge running down his face, sputtering and cursing. George saw it and came rushing over in his apron.

"Boys, boys, enough of the horseplay. We got to be respectable, least till after Tuesday, ha, ha. Now, please, could I ask you to, uh, you know?"

"Sure, George, turn us out into the cold," Jack called.

"You're a real pal, Georgie," Shea said. "Is this the treatment we can expect come Wednesday? After you're resting your boots on a desk in city hall? The bum's rush to your loyal supporters?"

George looked this way and that, his plump fingers in the air. "Boys! It ain't nothing like that, you know, but would you, please?"

The last streetcar was passing when Shea and McGough tumbled into the street, and they caught it downtown. The city was empty and dark.

"Let's hit one of the houses, Bat, get the pipes cleaned. Ain't seen Gerty in weeks. Got to keep track of her time of the month, you know."

"What about Maggie Riley? She's a good gal."

"Ah, we had a fight. I broke it off with her. I'm better off, Bat. I don't need all that talk of marrying."

"Agreed." Shea took him by the arm and led him firmly along. They rounded the corner by the Episcopal church and city hall rose before them. City hall was a great gothic structure of brick and granite with a clock tower.

"Look at it, Jack! City hall. Ain't it grand?" He gave a drunken sigh. "We're going to be in there soon. First thing is, I'm going to buy me a dozen linen shirts and three dozen collars, half a dozen silk ties and a diamond stickpin. I'm going to buy three new winter suits and three new summer suits, and a new derby and a pair of gaiters. We'll turn some heads, eh?"

"We'll own this goddamned town, Bat!" McGough was stepping up and down from the curb.

"Aye." Shea stood for a moment, folded his arms with great satisfaction. The vision of city hall, empty in the darkness, illuminated only by his dreams of the future, was enough to erase all the premonitions of Mamie and the cop and the harelip, to soothe his ugly resentments, his disgust with the present and his dread of the future, for Bat Shea knew with certainty that political power, even in the small measure he sought it, would solve all his problems.

8.
THE MEETING

Robert Ross

The following night, while George Dunlop threw open his saloon to the parish, and voters came swarming in from the frigid March night for a free boiled meal, the renowned suffragette Susan B. Anthony addressed quite a different crowd at Music Hall about the evils of an all-male vote. After her speech, the men of substance escorted their wives home, and then re-entered their coaches and gave their drivers the Patton address.

It was nearly eleven o'clock when carriages passed through the gracious wrought iron gates and up the circular drive of the Patton estate. As he opened the door, Fitch the gatekeeper inspected each carriage to be sure there were no infiltrators. Up the steps and into the mansion men moved silently, talking in low voices of their solemn and grave purpose.

The ballroom of the home was resplendent with light, the crystal chandeliers and mirrors reflecting many-fold the gas and candlelight. From a side door issued a line of men, having slipped black robes over their suits for this solemn ritual. Then Josiah Patton emerged with Robert Ross and a tall lean man with circular spectacles, Frank Black. The three mounted the dais.

"Gentlemen," Patton began, holding his hands over the convocation, "we assemble this evening for the purpose of retrieving control of our beloved Troy. The men who join me, no strangers to you, Robert Ross on my right and Frank Black on my left, are deeply concerned Americans, and will shortly address you concerning the mayor's race in this Tuesday's election . . ."

In the upstairs hall, Nellie saw her sister Jane peeping through a hole in the panelling where the Thomas Cole landscape was pushed aside.

"What are you doing?"

Jane whipped about, a guilty, defiant look upon her face. "Nothing."

"Let me see." Nellie peered through the hole, and below in the ballroom she saw about a hundred men assembled, wearing black robes like judges, yet with hoods at the collar. On the dais, there were three men. Their demeanor was weighty and solemn. In a moment, Nellie was surprised to see Robert rise to speak.

"Let me see!" Jane hissed.

"No! It's Rob!"

"Gentlemen," Robert Ross stated nervously, "there is a great likelihood of violence at the polls in the thirteenth ward. Our sources indicate the Irish will be armed, and they are desperate to get George Dunlop into office. I have enlisted all the millhands from my shop to appear at the polls in shifts of six throughout the day. But six men, or a dozen or two dozen will be nothing to these Irish."

Ross shifted his stance and seemed to grow in confidence. "Therefore, I appeal to those of you, gentlemen, who live in the thirteenth to send whatever force you can muster." He leaned forward, his palms upon the table, his expression intent, and Nellie, despite her disdain for politics, was surprised that her Robert had such a commanding presence.

"Last week, gentlemen, I went to the devil's lair myself. I stood face to face with Boss Murphy, and I warned him that his tactics would work no longer. I told him in no uncertain terms that we would tolerate no voting fraud. Now is the time to fulfill my promise. Now is the time to assure an honest vote. Now is the time to wrest back the board of aldermen and the control of city hall from these corrupters. We must keep Dennis Whelan mayor!" A ripple of applause grew until the room resounded.

Nellie was delighted. Until now she had seen Robert as a rather ordinary young industrialist. This showed a side to him that held promise.

"Nellie!"

"Hush!"

"Nellie!" Jane tugged at her gown, and when she turned, she gasped: Mother watched from the other end of the hall, her arms folded.

"Young ladies! What are you doing?"

"Uh, uh, Mason showed it to me," Jane explained about the peephole.

"That meeting is for men only and it is secret."

"We won't be telling anyone," Jane said. Nellie replaced the plug.

"Get along with you to bed now. It's late."

The sisters ducked beneath the stern gaze of the matriarch and hurried in the direction of Nellie's room.

The tone in the meeting progressed from expectation to cold determination when Frank Black rose to speak. Black was a New Englander, a tall, lanky, caustic attorney who had little patience with sentiment, corruption or the boozy politics of Senator Edward Murphy. Recently elected Republican chairman in Rensselaer County, his involvement in politics was an outgrowth of his law practice where he specialized in commercial claims, litigating on behalf of the merchants and industrialists. He stood before them, as tall as Robert Ross, a commanding presence.

"There is a question that occurs to us, gentlemen, one simple question, when we think of Senator Edward Murphy: How? How did he rise to such a height, and how does he remain there? A United States senator and chairman of the State Democratic Party who boasts he never lost an election. How? It is simple. He cheats. He rigs the elections. And yet someone who poisons the very root of our freedom in this country, the free ballot, is respected and honored from Troy to Washington. This leads to a second question. Why? Why do we allow him to do it? Why?" Black let the question hang.

"I drafted legislation last year to make his form of voting fraud illegal by assuring adequate poll inspectors. I was laughed out of the state capitol. 'Go home,' they told me, 'tend to your law practice. You don't understand politics.'" Black paused for effect, and his voice dropped: "I understand politics, and I understand voting fraud."

Frank Black leaned back, glaring at the assembled. "It is a sad comment upon our system of government that this dictator, this demagogue, this corrupt boss can be tolerated, let alone heaped with honors and high office. Now, gentlemen, now is the time to topple him."

The men began to clap slowly, then more loudly, and their clapping found a slow and steady rhythm. It was a strange and moving scene to witness a hundred men in black robes clapping, their faces solemn, determined. Black raised his arms for silence: "This is what we shall do. We shall form a committee of one hundred, gentlemen, as they have in other communities. We will organize and we will meet to wrest from Murphy the control of our public institutions. No matter what crony of Murphy holds public office, the sanctity of our public institutions still rests in our hands, for, gentlemen," he paused once more, "we are the people. And we shall prevail! We shall restore our public institutions to their former glory, free of the corruption of the Irish and the Church of Rome."

The applause began again, but Black cut it short with his outstretched hands.

"On Tuesday, let us do our duty. Let us go to the polls as concerned citizens and assure ourselves that there will be an honest vote. These Irish do not outnumber us if we band together. They have only ignorance, violence and lawlessness on their side. It is time they are stopped. Let it stop here, and let it stop now. An honest vote will retain Dennis Whelan as mayor and will turn control of the board of aldermen out of the hands of the Irish, and into the hands of Americans."

Black's laconic style caught them unaware as he suddenly sat down. The applause was as short as his message was incisive. The meeting was an unqualified success, and there was an air of expectation as Josiah, with the forked beard of a patriarch, adjourned in prayer, assuring the assembled that God was on their side.

Afterward, Patton escorted Black and Ross through the foyer, discussing how they had forged a resolve in the "better citizens" of the city this night, and now that the issue had been raised, it must be kept alive through the charter election and beyond until Murphy's machine was exposed, discredited and dismantled.

"And you, gentlemen, shall be my lieutenants in the fight," he clasped their hands. "Thank you for your participation tonight, friends, and Godspeed at the polls."

Melody, the maid, cleared her throat, and as the triumvirate parted, she whispered to Robert Ross.

"Yes," Ross said, "I shall come." He looked at Patton. "Nellie is still up and would like me to see her."

Patton frowned. "She should have retired long ago. Go along, Robert. Love!" he said with distaste. "Young people must be indulged, I suppose, in their great delusion."

Robert entered the drawing room, dark except for a single candle. Nellie did not immediately look up, but when she did her violet eyes gleamed with excitement.

"Nell?"

"I saw your speech, Robert."

"But you weren't there!"

"I heard you."

"Yes?"

"I wanted to wish you good night." She stood and offered herself to him. Ross was hesitant. Nellie was usually so reserved, so imperious, he distrusted this intimacy in the candlelight. He looked into her eyes, trying to read some message there. Her lip curled and her eyes held a superior knowledge and approval he had never seen. Robert Ross sensed something had changed, but was unsure of the new boundaries.

"You may kiss me," she whispered. He did so. Her lips were soft and he could feel her breath. This new intimacy was unexpected and so doubly thrilling.

"Oh, Nell!"

"I saw you speak to them," she whispered.

He took her into his embrace and held her, the fragrance of her hair, the soft press of her breathing, the unspoken words of praise, all woven together into a delightful spell. He could feel her body tremble. She pulled back then and looked up at him with admiration, a strange tranquility in her violet eyes, "Oh, Robert, you shall be a leader of men!"

Ross then closed his eyes. His beloved at that moment had perceived his most sacred and, till now, hidden ambition. Not only did she approve, but she shared it!

"Albany, surely; perhaps even Washington! And I shall aid you in the quest." She pressed her face to his breast. "We shall have such a wonderful life together."

"Oh, Nellie, I love you."

"We shall be so happy, Rob."

9.
ELECTION DAY

"Boss" Murphy Slays the Tariff Dragon to Save the Damsel of Troy's Collar Industry

He awoke with a start, and he could not breathe. It was dark and he felt a great suffocating weight upon his chest. Had he missed it? He breathed slowly then, and deeply, to calm himself and he lay for a moment, watching his breath rise in the cold dark air. No, today was the day. There had been dreams, dark, torn dreams with suffering and weeping by unseen people. Yesterday, a bleak, dark, sleeting March morning followed by a gale, had been wasted in drink in saloons about the ward, talking big, swaggering about, sending out threats on networks of gossip that Protestant opposition would only draw trouble. And later, back to Dunlop's, a party.

The good booze George brought out for once was still singing in his veins, and Shea smiled remembering the antics of those "wild things" from Kingston, "brawlers, maulers and buggers" George called them, trying the lockstep like a chorus of them dancing tarts in Belle's Blue Revue downtown. Sweet Jesus, they were funny! Eight of the hardest creatures along the waterfront from Brooklyn to Black Rock, with iron vices for strangling and fists for smashing, low of brow, thick of jaw, experts who would show the Troy poll watchers a bit of the way it's done by Tammany pros. The quality of the thug this time was pleasing. Owen and Jack had done a good day's work in getting them, but the four that couldn't read nor write'd need help in making out the ballots.

He gave George a thought, too, for George was a politician and you never could trust him. He was no stand-up guy, always wheedling and whining out on you. Sure, he wanted to lay low when he heard that Paddy Daley had his little chat, made his little threat, got his little speech off his little chest, but George'd be the first to squawk if the votes weren't there and he only had his saloon to fall back on. Hard times indeed, and there'd be no more on the cuff. Sometimes it made you sick how gutless and weak people were. Today there was nothing to do but keep a dead even course to the goal, vote these eight dancing girls four or five times in each of the ward's three districts, and it'd be cigars and better booze and maybe a five dollar whore tonight.

It startled Shea to feel someone stir next to him in the bed. That broadarse Kate? Or the girl from upstairs, the quiet deep one with the opium pipe, what's her name? Or Mamie? He had no memory of the end of the evening. Then he smelled Jack.

"Don't you have a bed of your own to crawl off to, but you have to go and pollute mine?" Shea cried and hauled Jack up by his shirt. "Some cat crawl up your arse and die?"

McGough started up in bed and felt for his revolver. "Jesus Christ, where am I?"

"Died and gone to hell where you belong, you heartless bastard."

A mischievous smile spread across McGough's face. "Ah, today's the day, eh, bucko?"

They looked into each other's eyes, sizing each other up. "Yeah. Sure is." They both smiled.

"They gonna know we're here, eh, Bat?"

"Come on, Jack. We got work to do."

The eight repeaters were snoring under horseblankets in George's barn around the corner. Shea and McGough kicked them awake, and they cursed and stumbled to their feet and pushed past the horses and shuffled out covered with straw into the cold, dark morning. Two milk wagons were on the street, but the streetcars were not yet running. Into Dunlop's they went for an eye-opener. There was coffee on and hot rolls from Dugan's Bakery.

"Jerry'll be here at five-thirty," McGough observed, as he lifted a shot of Monongahela. Owen Judge had sample ballots on the bar and names of voters from the registry books. He was writing laboriously with a dull pencil. Jack pulled out his pistol and loaded the chambers. George came out of the kitchen at that moment, his face red from the steam.

"You ain't loading that thing?" he asked nervously.

"Naw, George, I'm just gonna shove it in their faces and let 'em club me to death like last time."

"I don't like that, Jack!"

"Aw, quit your belly-aching, George," McGough protested. "I got Shea with me. He keeps me in line. Ain't that right, Bat?" Shea grunted assent. Lil was down in her flannel nightshirt having a morning shot, and she was reading to Shea from yesterday's paper about Boss Murphy's tariff battle in Washington. There was a cartoon of Murphy as a knight in shining armor, saving the Troy collar industry kneeling in the form of a damsel in distress.

"Sometimes I think you two are dangerous 'round each other," George shook his head in disgust and wagged his finger. "You be careful. It's an election we're trying to win, not a noose."

"Noose, George?" McGough scoffed. "Get with the times! You want to be alderman, you got to keep up with progress. The chair, George, quick as goddamn lightning." He clapped his hands.

Just then, mill whistles blew five-thirty, and the door opened to admit Jerry Cleary, whose drunken glow had persisted through four hours of sleep: "Hey! What's the story? Goddamn! Who's goddamn drinkin', and who's goddamn votin'?"

"Buy him a drink and shut him up," McGough cried uproariously. Shea was quiet and grim. "Gene's waiting over to his old man's place. Whyn't we go on over, Bat, and help 'em open the first?"

"Sure," Shea said. The walk would do him good. He finished his drink, patted Lil on the head and ordered the repeaters out the door. It was dark and clear, the stars glittering and hard, and the ground was crusted with frost. The cobbles and streetcar tracks gleamed. The streets were deserted, but you could see lamps on in the tenements as men were readying for the mills and for the polls. McClure's Saloon was across River Street from the first district polls, and as the gang pushed inside, half a dozen men at the rail looked up. The place had a confused air, a hungover feeling to it as the boys were trying to pour enough in so they could get even with the shakes.

Gene had bacon and eggs and beans and soda bread dished out on tin plates, along with whiskey and coffee. Shea didn't eat, but stood near the window, arms folded, watching the polls across the street. St. Patrick's bells began chiming the Angelus when he turned. "All right, boys, it's time." There was much confused shuffling and coughing and spitting. Owen Judge gave some last minute instructions to the repeaters about the ballots, and then in the dark the gang marched over to the storefront with a boarded window where the caucus had been held a month before.

Already a line of voters threaded up the street. Seeing the gang, Officer Patrick Cahill twirled his moustache, winked and nodded.

Shea swaggered up to the door and roughly shoved three voters aside: "All right, out of the way. Stand back there. Come on, boys," he sidemouthed to the repeaters, "in with you and be quick." He rattled the door, and when it did not yield, he stepped back and with a swift kick of his jackboot sent it swinging open.

With the regular voters protesting, Shea counted his men in, then shoved Jack inside to help the illiterates remember the names they were to swear. Voters were grumbling:

"I demand to go in there!"

"This is an outrage!"

"In the name of God!"

"I'd be shutting my face, if I was you!" Shea said evenly.

"Officer! Officer!" a voter complained.

"Don't push!" Officer Cahill shoved the repeaters back. "Back up there or I'll crack your skull."

"But Officer!"

"You just mind your business," the policeman ordered.

"This is criminal!" cried a voter. "I demand this cease!"

"You ain't seen the worst," Shea patted the bulge in his coat pocket and winked. The voters quieted then. "Hustle up in there, Jack. We don't want to keep these good people from their breakfast."

Jerry Cleary stood on the curb with his arms folded, looking up and down the street. "Jack's too goddamn slow in the morning," he observed in a brash, hungover voice. "Spends too goddamn much time joking. Gonna be a nice goddamn morning, though, soon's the sun's up. Good goddamn day for an election."

"Done!" cried McGough emerging. Out from the door of the polls came the eight of them, one directly behind the other, lockstepping through the crowd. "Candy from a babe," McGough said in a stage whisper to Shea. "We'll be thanking you for your patience," McGough cavalierly tipped his hat to the line of voters who glared at them and muttered.

"On to the second," Shea said.

The sun rose as they walked, and they cast long shadows in the street. A few teams of horses and wagons passed, but the streets were quiet and empty. It was a clear, bright morning with a lingering chill of winter. Rags of snow lay in the northern shadows cast by tenements and steeples. There was a faint promise of spring, and the air was rich with the smell of manure and ashes.

Polls for the second district of the thirteenth ward were located in an abandoned livery stable near a large outcropping of black shale, Mt. Olympus. Emboldened by success at the first district, Shea shoved aside the first few men in line, making room for his repeaters to enter. Jack followed them in and they seized paper ballots from the table, went behind curtains of the booths, and substituted their fraudulent ballots. Then, with McGough whispering the names from a sheet in his hand, the repeaters deposited the votes and swore in those that were challenged. All the while McGough glared at the poll watchers, his gun in his pocket pointed at them.

"Swear!" a Republican poll watcher cried, irate at the voting fraud. One repeater mispronounced "Mulholland" and McGough corrected him. "Address?" As the repeater gave it, a curtain opened and a man emerged: "Why I am Dennis Mulholland and that's my address. I challenge that vote!"

Jack grinned and stepped across the floor, pulling out his gun: "You want to challenge this?"

"No, sir, no, not at all, but, but that's . . ."

"That ain't none of your goddamned business, see?" Jack seized the ballot from Dennis Mulholland and crumpled it and threw it on the floor as the repeater swore in the false one.

On the street the line of voters was growing surly and impatient. Many had to get to work, and the delay for such a purpose was an outrage. Shea sent Cleary in to speed things up, and Jerry hauled Mulholland up and threw him into the wall. "You're not yourself at all today, Mulholland!" Jerry screamed, and Mulholland flinched when he cocked back his foot.

The third district polling place was set back against the base of the steep hill just below the railroad tracks. It was a small frame house along a dirt lane, Orr Street, with a pit across the way filled with brush and trash where a foundation had been started but abandoned.

Flushed with pride from their two easy victories, Shea and his gang rounded the corner about a quarter past seven, prepared for an easy score. But across the mud and the snow a large crowd of men in derbies and caps guarded the entrance to the polls.

"Sweet Jesus Christ!" Shea spat his first wad of tobacco into the cinders.

"Goddamn vigilantes!" Jerry Cleary said.

"Must be sixty of 'em."

At the sight of the repeaters, Ross's vigilantes bristled up and clustered together. Many reached inside their pockets.

"Well, whadda we do now?" asked one of the repeaters.

Shea considered. He never favored retreat, yet to attack would be rash given the numbers.

"Let's get some breakfast, boys. I'm feeling sort of peckish, and I'm dry, too."

"Yeah, I could use a drink," Owen Judge observed. In a group the dozen of them trooped a block back to Dunlop's Saloon.

"Look at them, John!" Robert Ross said to his brother. "They come swaggering over till they see our strength, then they skulk away. It's good we arrived early."

"Like dogs in a pack," John observed. "They have no courage."

"They'll be back when they get some from the saloon."

"But they won't be forcing votes here today," William Ross added.

"No," said Robert, "not at the third district they won't."

"How goes the war?" George Dunlop asked cheerily as the gang entered his saloon. The free lunch board was already laden with sandwiches and soup and a great wheel of cheddar to entice the locals to return his favor with their vote.

"Like a breeze in the first and second," Jack said, his boot instinctively finding the rail. "Give us a shot, George."

"Problem in the third," Shea said.

"Now I don't want no trouble," Dunlop cautioned, his plump palms in the air. "Get the votes in good and proper, but no trouble. The boss put out the word and it'll never do to go against him."

Shea cleared his throat and spat at the spitoon. "Give us a cigar, George. You worry too goddamn much."

In past years, cautious ward leaders voted repeaters on names of men who were out of town or dead. They carefully changed the ties and hats and coats of the repeaters before sending them back to the same polling place. But Shea and McGough cared nothing for subtlety. The revolver caucus, as it was now generally known, had changed the rules. Repeaters were voted on names of men very much in town and very much alive, and let the Protestants protest all they wanted.

The gang made another round of the districts at nine. Resistance was building. Word of the gang was circulating through the neighborhoods, and lines of voters were hostile and loud with protest, vainly calling upon the police to intervene. Yet the police force was answerable only to Murphy, and the cops in long blue coats and tall hats simply nodded and looked the other way.

In the second district this time, an angered poll watcher charged at Shea with the lid from an iron stove. Shea seized a crutch from a lame man to fend him off. This gave McGough and Cleary much delight as they swaggered along.

"A goddamn crutch! A crutch against a stovelid!"

"I never seen the like, Bat," McGough cried. "Why didn't you pull your gun?"

The day was not shaping up well for Shea. "I never pull my gun till I intend to use it."

"Well, I repeat my question . . ." and they burst into laughter. Shea regarded them skeptically. The liquor was taking hold of Jack and Jerry, he concluded, and that could be good or bad. These boys could be useless by noon.

"Goddamn it!" Owen Judge cried as they rounded the corner by a pile of building stone. Across the dirt lane and the trash pit, a larger group than before stood guarding the polls, their derbies and moustaches and dark suits blurring into a vast impenetrable crowd.

"You need your crutch," McGough taunted.

"Come on," Shea said, "we're going in." He swallowed hard, and the dozen started across the street.

"Gentlemen," Robert Ross called calmly, "let us meet them square."

The vigilantes moved forward into the street, John, William and Robert Ross in the forefront. The two groups met in the road.

"What do you want here?" Robert Ross asked Shea.

"We're voting. Get out of the way."

"None of you lives in this district," Robert said evenly.

"You're not wanted here," William Ross added. One of the Ross group shoved Owen Judge, and with that, Shea reached past Robert Ross and punched William Ross in the face.

"In the name of God!" William cried, holding his eye, reeling from the blow. Robert Ross put his hand on Shea's chest.

"Get your goddamn hand off of me!" Shea stared into Ross's eyes, and Ross glared back. Shea cleared his throat, worked the phlegm around in his mouth, considering whether to spit in Ross's eye, but Ross's intense glare dissuaded him.

"Take it, William," Robert counseled, still staring at Shea.

"You'll take that," Shea screamed, suddenly enraged, his fists clenched, "and I'll give you more." He reached over Robert Ross to strike William again, but Ross held up his arm.

"You are not wanted here. Please. We are trying to assure an honest vote, and we'd appreciate it if you left."

Shea glanced at the posse of burly millhands packed tightly behind its leader. There were clubs out and pistols and grim looks on the faces. Shea had eleven with him. They were outmanned more than six to one. He spit at the ground, narrowed his eyes, and muttered, "Come on, boys."

The repeaters turned and walked along the dirt lane past the ditch of brush and trash, back to Dunlop's Saloon.

"They're gone!" John Ross said with relief, dabbing William's bleeding lip with his handkerchief.

"They'll be back," Robert said ominously.

Shea stormed into Dunlop's Saloon and flung his hat across the crowded room. Harelip McGee was laughing at the bar. "Give us a shot, Tommy," Shea growled and he pushed into the back room where George was dispatching boys with free growlers of Excelsior Pale Ale to lure their fathers to the polls. George turned, a worried look passed across his plump features, then his blue eyes twinkled and he said, "Things are going well here at least."

Shea ignored him. "We got big trouble at the third, George."

"Sit down, Bat, and have your drink."

Tommy, the kid who laid out the sandwichboard, entered with a "shandygaff," a jigger of whiskey and a lager chaser. Shea hooked down the whiskey, then chugged the beer. "One more."

Dunlop nodded assent and sat across the table folding and unfolding his hands. "Look, Bat, I've been going over the figures. We might take it without the third. We got the first and the second in our pocket."

"We calculated this before, George. We need at least a dozen votes in the third to pull it off. Now how are we going to get them with the Rosses and their gang there?"

"Things'll work out, Bat." Dunlop became conciliatory. "Listen, I don't want no trouble. More than anything, I don't want no trouble. You got to understand. I'm in a hell of a position here. I got bounced off the force, and the boss didn't want me as the candidate to begin with, and he's sent warnings up three times for us to lay low. He's spread it around that the thirteenth ward is the black sheep of the family. Now I don't want to win the battle just to lose the war. We got to keep a sense of perspective here. If the Rosses put up such opposition, then we got to respect that and deal with that in a, a *professional*, shall we say, manner."

"Don't you sell me out, George."

"I ain't selling you out," George whined. "I'm only advising discretion. You have to know where to push and how hard. Now, you've done a bang-up job for me so far, and I ain't faulting you nor Jack. I just don't want no trouble."

The second shot arrived with a chaser and Shea hooked it down and then chugged the lager. "Gimme a chew, will you, Tommy?"

The kid produced a plug of tobacco and Shea bit off a chew. He thought a moment while the whiskey settled and his jaw worked at the tobacco.

"I see your point, George. But I also know that we need at least a dozen votes in the third. We don't get them, you're out on your arse, and then how's the boss going to regard you? You'll see his brand of gratitude at work then."

"Lay low, get some food into you — "

"I ain't hungry."

"You have to eat. Wait till noon when the poll watchers go home to their dinner, then steal on back over there and see what you can do. Here's some new names. Change their coats and hats. We got Officer Murphy at the door and Maloney on the inside. He's a good boy, and a bosom chum of Jack's. So you only have to get through the crowd. See what you can do then."

The sun burned off the lingering fog and by mid-morning it was a resplendent spring day. After a long winter huddled around parlor stoves, struggling to and from the mills and church and the stores, people were emerging from their tenements, stretching in the sunshine and breathing the easy spring wind off the river. A sense of buoyancy, a sense of promise was in the air. Many hitched up their horses and by mid-morning the streets were crowded with carriages and carts.

After glimpsing Robert's speech, Nellie Mae Patton had taken a keen interest in the election. Robert's involvement in Troy's civic life seemed to bode well for their future, and she saw him as a champion, a leader who would go off to Albany and then to Washington as a delegate from local manufacturers to pass protective laws. And she would be at his side, riding only in private cars, guiding him, comforting him, basking in the adulation and glory, and at night in the hotels . . .

All through the engagement, Nellie had believed she controlled Robert Ross. He was so struck by her beauty and her fortune and her father that he'd do whatever she wanted. The view into the ballroom, though, with a hundred of Troy's best men in black robes listening to her Robert had changed her thinking. He had merely allowed her to control the romance, and that was the trivial side of things, wasn't it? He was directing his energies elsewhere. Nellie was now determined to participate actively in this dimension of his life.

She ordered Melody to pack box lunches, called for the carriage and had Fitch drive her down to the polls. Along the brink of the hill on Oakwood Avenue they drove. The Hudson and Mohawk Rivers bristled in the sun, blue water, white ice floes. Because of the steep grade of Ingalls and Middleburgh, Fitch drove to Tenth, then to Rensselaer Street and to Ninth. As they came upon the polling place, Nellie was surprised to see so many men.

Robert recognized the carriage and came over.

"You should not have come, my dear," he leaned in. "The repeaters have been by twice now, and one of them has assaulted Bill."

"Oh, dear." Nellie was flustered. "I brought sandwiches."

Robert smiled at her innocence. "That was kind of you, but I'm not hungry."

"You must eat something, Rob. Get in here beside me. Your men can spare you for half an hour." Just then the bells of St. Patrick's Church pealed twelve, and along the river the mill whistles began to blow for the noon break. "See? It is time for you to eat something."

"Robert!" called John Boland from the crowd at the polls, and he pointed with a long purple club. The blackeye Boland suffered at the caucus had only recently healed. Across the dump and between two small houses there appeared a dozen men in derbies and caps. They had shed their long coats and they were pulled up by a pile of paving stone.

"Fitch," Robert ordered, "drive Miss Patton home immediately! Do not turn around!" He leaned in again. "I shall call this evening, Nell, and tell you of our victory. We've stood their attacks twice, and we'll stand this one as well."

"Be careful, Rob," she pleaded. He nodded grimly, and kissed the hand she offered out the window. Fitch flicked the whip and the carriage lurched forward, down Douw Street, past the dozen men near the pile of stone. Nellie pulled her veil down over her face and sat back, conspicuously ignoring them.

"There's as many as before," Jack said dismally.

"Goddamn-aye right." Jerry Cleary spat into the dirt.

"Righteous sons a bitches! I say we do 'em," Jack looked for Shea's approval.

"Jesus," Owen Judge cried, "here's George from the polls!"

Dunlop came bustling up, his hand to his hat. "Well, boys, I had a little word with Officer Murphy. He won't make no fuss, but advises that you come back later."

"We're going in," Shea said, looking dead ahead.

"I don't know, Bat. It might not be the right time. That's what he said, and he's the boss's cousin."

"We're going in," Shea said. "Come on."

Shea led his group across the dirt lane. Not wanting to be identified with them, George remained behind. When he saw a woman watching out her window, he adjusted his derby and hurried away.

"Here they come, gentlemen," Robert Ross said. "Let us be ready, but not provoke them."

The gang came on with determination, shoulder to shoulder, twelve lowered brows and twelve set jaws, and as Shea reached the poll watchers, he commanded, "Aside!" They did not move. He picked the smallest in the line. McGough, Cleary and Judge formed a wedge behind him and they marched the repeaters tightly through a path that reluctantly opened. There were cries of protest and anger as the repeaters lockstepped to the door. Officer Murphy was standing before the door, a fat cop in a long blue coat. Shea gave him a "tip o' the wink" and Murphy nodded.

"Away with you," Shea seized a voter by the coat and hurled him aside. "All right, let's go," and with his boot he kicked open the door. "Get in!" he grabbed the first repeater and shoved him inside, pushing the other seven back by back in behind him.

"You have no right — " William Ross began.

"Quiet or you'll get more of the same," Shea snapped. Behind the repeaters he went into the small hall and stood shoulder to shoulder with Cleary and Owen Judge to keep the vigilantes out.

Outside, Ellis Hayner was enraged. Recently the burly Hayner had broken a strike at the McLeod foundry behind Ross Valve, and Cleary's uncle and Shea's father were his sworn enemies. Hayner wanted to impress the Rosses, and he protested mightily to Officer Murphy. "I'm going in! If they can go in, so can I."

"Stand down," Murphy said to him.

"By Christ, I'll go in there."

"Shut your face!" McGough said. He was jumpy, his hand was on the pistol in his pocket, and he just realized he was outside alone against the angry mob. Hayner ignored him.

"I'm going in, Murphy, and you ain't stopping me!"

"You get back!" Murphy said. "I'll go in and see what's what." Murphy pushed open the door and with difficulty squeezed past Shea and Cleary and Judge.

Hayner whined to John Ross, and there was a general denouncing of the police force. "How can we expect justice?" Hayner cried and then he stormed the door. "I have as much of a right to be in there as anyone!"

"Shaddap," McGough said, and he pushed at the door trying to get inside too.

"Get out!" Shea cried. "No one else, Jack."

"If you can go in there, so can I!" Hayner cried, and he charged the door, pried it open and squeezed inside. Shea and Cleary cried, "Get out! You goddamn scab! Get out!" Then Officer Murphy's voice sounded from within: "All right! All right! Everybody out!" Shea punched Hayner in the face. Hayner's hands went up for the door jamb, but he missed and he fell into Jack McGough on the stoop. Shea and Judge and Cleary came spilling out the door and they crowded into Hayner who yelled: "But the repeaters are still inside!"

"You're treading on my feet!" Cleary cried, heaving Hayner away from him.

"You took another man's job, Hayner," McGough taunted him. "You go sucking up to the Rosses, licking their boots —"

"I'll not take this!" Hayner cried.

"You got no balls," Cleary sneered, spitting his wad of tobacco at Hayner. "You're a goddamn scab, that's the long and the short of it. I'll not talk to any son of a bitch who'll take a poor man's job." Cleary spied a friend. "Give us a chew of your plug, Jim."

"I'll not take this!" Hayner cried again.

"You'll take it, and I'll give you more!" McGough laughed nervously. As Shea turned to share the laugh with Cleary, who was biting off a chew, Hayner pulled a wrench from his overalls, cried, "By Christ, I'm going in there!" and swung the wrench at Shea, cracking him on the ear. Shea reeled into Cleary then he turned, his derby off, his eyes on fire, blood on his fingertips from his ear.

"Why, you scab son of a bitch!" Shea lunged forward, threw a right and then a left into Hayner's face that raised him off the ground and sent him sprawling into the ashes and trash in a gully beside the building. Then Shea dove on him and they rolled to the side of the building. The crowd roared and shook itself awake. "Club him, boys!" they cried and they began to punish Shea.

"Goddamn scab!" Cleary lowered his pistol at Hayner's forehead, cocked back the hammer, then his arm was knocked upward by a club. The gun went off in the air. At the sound of the gun, the crowd closed in, pressing the gang against the small house.

McGough's elbow smashed a windowpane, and he struggled to get his pistol out of his pocket and into the air. "Stand back! Stand back! Out of my way!" he screamed. The crowd surged northward and carried Jack with it until he found his feet and started through. It was an ugly mob, men shouting with anger and fear, clubs and pistols flailing about.

"Stand back!" Shea rose up, throwing people aside. "Back! Get back!" He led three repeaters through the angry mob until he met Robert Ross.

"Halt!" Ross ordered.

"Get the hell out of my way!" Shea shouted, and he pulled out his revolver.

Ross grabbed him by the shoulders, snarling: "I should have had you arrested this morning!"

"Let go!"

McGough had nearly made it through the crowd when William Ross confronted him. "You have no business — " he brandished his club, but Jack lowered his pistol and as William Ross turned to flee, McGough shot him in the neck. Ross screamed and fell to the ground.

Nearby, Robert Ross saw his brother fall. He hurled Shea aside and lurched at McGough, but Jack darted away, then started across the lane on a run. Ross chased him, caught Jack by the collar and hit him over the head twice with the club. McGough turned and aimed his pistol at Robert Ross's forehead, but as he squeezed the trigger, Ross deflected the gun upward and the bullet knocked off Ross's hat. Now Jack was away and running down through the dumps, Ross at his heels.

"Stop! Stop!" Ross commanded. Gunshots rang out over near the polling place. As he ran into the ditch Jack was hit with a bullet in the hip. He skipped and spun, and Ross rose up and tackled him down into the cinders and brush at the bottom of the ditch. Ross then let loose a flurry of blows upon McGough's skull, screaming, "You shot my brother, you cur!"

Meanwhile, Shea cleared a path through the crowd and with his men out of the polls, he started to run. A bullet grazed his skull, and he fell, rolled over, dropping his pistol. He saw men's feet running past him, and guns were going off. He crawled over to his revolver, picked it up, then reached out for the palings of a fence nearby to pull himself up.

"Bat! Bat!" Jack was screaming. Shea shook his head to focus from the booze and the clubbing and the gunshot. There were men running and gunshots and screams all about. "Bat! He's killing me. Help!" As Shea stood, shook his head and turned to look back, John Boland was running toward him, his pistol blazing.

Shea shook his head and started back, shouting "Jack! Where are you?" Shea fired at Boland and Boland fired back. Robert Ross heard Shea coming and he jumped off McGough, clambered up the side of the ditch and just as he reached the top, Shea fired again at Boland. Ross fell into a sitting position, his head lolling into his lap. Shea squeezed off another shot at Boland and Boland, behind Ross who slumped slowly over onto the ground, fired again at Shea.

Freed of Ross, Jack was up and running out of the ditch empty-handed. Shea turned away and saw Mickey Delaney.

"You potted him, Bat!" Delaney cried with delight.

"I'm hit," Shea said.

John Boland came running up then, a club in one hand, a gun in the other. "Get him!" he cried, waving the pistol, and he swung his club at Shea then set out after McGough, firing at him.

"There he goes!" someone cried, and a group of the poll watchers chased after Jack McGough who hopped on his good leg over a fence, skipping away from them.

Shea staggered along. "I'm hit, Mickey!"

Stanley O'Keefe helped Shea, then George Dunlop came bustling up. "You all right, Bat?"

"I'm hit. I'm hit."

"I didn't want no trouble, Bat!"

"I'm hit, goddamnit!"

"Go get a doctor, Mickey!" George said, and he and O'Keefe put their shoulders under Shea's arms and helped him away.

John Ross was the first to reach his brother Robert who lay upon the edge of the ditch. "Rob? Rob?" He bent over and raised Robert's head off the ground. The eyes were glassy and vacant. There was no breath. He reached behind Robert's head, and his hand was warm and dark with blood. "Robbbbbb!" he screamed, and he shook his brother gently. "Robbb!" he cried up at the resplendent blue sky. Robert's head fell to the side.

"My God!" John screamed. "My brother! My brother's been killed!" He bent down, sick at heart, tears welling in his eyes. "Rob," he whispered, and he gently closed the eyelids, and he embraced his brother. "Oh, my God!"

The scene by the polls was as quiet and empty now as it had been noisy and active before. "My brother!" John Ross cried to the sky. "Robbbb!" In the lane, Adam Ross was helping William Ross from the ground. "The blood of my brother is upon my hand!" John screamed, holding his hand in the air. "If there's an American citizen here, don't let them escape!"

But his words went unanswered. All that was left in the still afternoon was a lingering smell of gunsmoke and a train whistle blowing north along the railroad track.

10. AFTERMATH

Scene of the Murder (cross indicates where Ross fell)

Slowly four men approached John Ross who held his dead brother. John Ross's sleeve and the leg of his trousers were covered with blood. A neighbor brought a large blanket from her home nearby. When they could coax John to relinquish the corpse, they lifted it onto the blanket by its arms and legs, lifted the blanket by the corners and carried it across the cinders and the dirt of the deserted roadway, through a picket fence and into the front room of the Dugan home on Orr Street. Soon the doctor's buggy rolled up.

Two blocks away Bat Shea sat in the kitchen of Dunlop's Saloon with a doctor attending to the bullet wound on his scalp. A dozen men in caps and derbies looked on.

"Does it hurt much?" George asked. His usual florid complexion was white.

"Get me a bottle, will you?"

Mickey Delaney was loudly bragging how Shea plugged Ross.

"Shut up, goddamnit, Mickey!" Shea ordered.

"I told ya, Shea," Harelip McGee whined. "I told ya they was going t'get ya."

"Get that kid outta here!"

"Whiskey, Tommy, get Bat a bottle of my finest Irish!"

Officer Daley was elbowing his way through the ring about Shea. "So what happened there, Shea?" he bellowed. Shea looked up, worked his tongue around in his mouth and spat into the sawdust on the floor.

"Nothing."

"I shoulda run you in the other night. You're no good, Shea. Your old man was no good, your uncle's no good and you're no good. What you got to say?"

Shea looked up, their eyes locked, and Shea snarled defiantly: "I can't stomach your flattery, Daley."

The cop seized him by the collar and pulled him up, spilling a bottle of iodine and surprising the doctor. "That Ross boy is dead, shot through the back of the head, and you're going to swing for it, you son of a bitch. And that's as it ought to be, to my way of thinking. You went against the boss and now you're on your own."

The news of Ross's death brought quiet to the room, talk dropping into subdued whispers.

"Tommy! Goddamnit, bring Bat a bottle!" George's complexion had gone shades whiter. "All of you, get out of here. Get out! Leave Bat and me have some air."

The kid fumbled in with the bottle, and Shea removed the cork with his teeth and took five strong swallows. He nodded then, and looked stoically about as the people filed from the room, glancing back for a last look at him.

"What gives?" Dunlop asked when the cop was gone. Shea had relaxed, his head bandaged now. "Who shot him?"

"How the hell do I know? He was coming at me, I thought he stumbled on the edge of the ditch. He just fell down. That's all I know."

"You didn't fire?"

"I fired at Boland. I might have hit Ross when he rose up there, but it was in the front."

"But who did shoot him then?"

"How the hell do I know? Guns were going off all over. He must have caught a stray from over near the polls." Shea spat into the sawdust again. "Them APA bastards! Now there'll sure be hell to pay."

"If they hadn't come to the polls! If they'd stayed up on their hill!" George whined, wringing his hands. "You're right as rain, Bat! There'll be hell to pay now. The boss'll be taking this one out of my hide."

"Yeah, George," Shea took a long pull of the whiskey, then he looked at George with his head tilted back. "Looks like you really got a lot to worry about now, don't it?"

George ignored the sarcasm. "C'mon. Let's get you up to your room."

In waves through the city, news of the murder spread. Along the new-fangled telephone wires word flew that a young hero, Robert Ross, had fallen to the cause of an honest vote. Newspaper offices sang with the news as the presses were stopped with bells and whistles to print this story on the front page of evening editions. The electric streetcar up Congress Street was filled with whisperings of the murder, whisperings that Jack McGough, seated with a searing pain in his hip, tried to ignore.

Jack had dashed from the scene, chased by a dozen vigilantes. He'd dropped his gun in the ditch so he could not exchange fire. Despite his hip wound, he jumped the back fence, darted up a gangway, then ducked down the basement entrance under the front stairs of his father's place on North Fourth Street.

"Pa," he cried, limping into the kitchen, "I'm hit. There was trouble at the polls and one of them Protestants got me."

Owen McGough was sitting at the kitchen table eating a bowl of soup. A decorated veteran of Gettysburg, he knew how to dress a wound. "In with you, Jack, into the washroom." He peered out through the curtains and saw men prowling in the backyard with their pistols drawn. As Jack kept talking, Owen McGough grabbed his son by the shirt. "Don't do no more talking about it, boy. I don't want you to say one more word about it! Not one more word! Get up to your Uncle Bill's till we think this through."

On the streetcar Jack felt blood begin to flow from under the gauze of the dressing. The car jolted to a stop and a plump woman in an enormous flowered hat boarded.

"Here, ma'am," he said. "Would you care for a seat?"

He stood up, then saw blood on the upholstery.

"What a kind young man," the woman said.

He considered warning her, but instead he just smiled. "Enjoy the day, ma'am."

Now he could feel the warm blood ooze and run down his right leg and into his sock. His uncle Bill Doyle lived up on Christie Street. Where Congress Street became steep, it was clogged with horses and wagons and pedestrians, and the car moved slowly among them up the hill.

News of Ross's death reached Boss Murphy through a pale, stammering Police Superintendent Willard, who made a special humbling trip to the brewery. Murphy took the news with a serious nod, his cheek twitching, his face flushing and his blue eyes narrowing.

"Who did it?"

"No one knows. Ross could have been shot by one of his own men."

"They'll never admit to that."

"No."

"Who are they blaming?"

"Well, Bartholomew Shea was leading the gang. He told someone he potted Ross."

Murphy's brow knit. His executive powers rested in large part upon his attention to detail, his flawless memory and his ability to deflect blame. "Wasn't Shea to be picked up and held till after election day?"

Willard coughed and stammered: "Y-Y-Yes, sir. But one of our men, an Officer Daley, talked with him and extracted a promise that he would stay at home. In any event, there is every indication he did not do the shooting. He was at the scene, sir, but no one's accused him yet. In fact, he himself was shot trying to escape."

"Well, who are they accusing?"

"As I say, sir, it was most likely one of the Republicans who shot Ross. There's a good chance it was a man named John Boland who was behind Ross firing. They think it was Boland who hit Shea, too, as Shea was fleeing."

Murphy shook his head and beneath his white moustache his lips were set. "I hope you're not deluding yourself into thinking they'll allow one of their own to be prosecuted."

"Well, that's why we have Kelly, isn't it?"

John Kelly was district attorney.

"That's why I have Kelly," the boss corrected Willard.

"Quite so." Willard looked about in bewilderment. "So, what is the next step?"

"Goddamnit! Must I tell you how to do your job?"

Willard was exasperated. Certainly he was answerable for not picking Shea up before the election. That was a favor George Dunlop had extracted. Surely his future was on the line. But he highly resented the implication he was incompetent.

"No, sir, I am only asking if I can accommodate you and the organization in any, uh, official way."

"Pick them up for questioning. Every suspect. I must return to

Washington. I am getting the four-fifteen train for Grand Central, and preparations for my departure will occupy me the rest of the afternoon. Do not disturb me with this matter further."

"Very well, sir."

Murphy nodded, and the humiliated police superintendent, hat in hand, bowed and left the office. Murphy then called his head clerk: "Fitz, my boy, there's been some sort of trouble at the polls up to the thirteenth. Inform any callers that I have departed for Washington. If they press the issue, tell them I am going by the four-fifteen train for New York. In the meantime, get me a closed cab to take me over to Green Island. I want to catch the two-thirty Saratoga train down to Albany. Let all the reporters cool their heels at Union Station waiting for me there."

Fitzsimmons grinned. "Very well, sir."

Willard called the precinct house and instructed Officer Daley: "Pick up Shea."

"Everyone's saying now, sir, that Boland is the one. Shea weren't never behind the man."

"Well, pick them both up."

"Yes, sir."

"And Daley . . . the boss weren't too pleased that Shea was loose after he gave the order to pick him up on that assault warrant."

Daley nodded gravely on his end of the phone, certain blame would now be laid upon him.

Willard added: "I took full responsibility."

This brought Daley relief. "I'll pick up Shea immediately, sir. And Boland too. And thank you, sir, thank you." Willard slammed down the phone at the other end.

Daley reappeared at Dunlop's Saloon as Shea, a bandage showing beneath one of George's derbies, was stepping into McClure's carriage. "Where do you think you're going?"

"Who's asking?" Dunlop said. His face was flushed normally now, and anger had replaced the initial fear as word spread that Boland had accidentally shot Ross.

"I got to take you in, Shea." Daley ignored Dunlop.

"What for?"

"Can't it wait?" Dunlop asked.

"Now!" Daley said with impatience.

Shea turned to him, looked him up and down. "I got to vote, Daley. I ain't voted yet."

Daley shook his head. "Where?"

"I live in the first district, over to River Street."

"Be quick with you, then."

"I'll bring Bat down to Central Station when we're through," George promised.

As they drove through the ward, George Dunlop, ever the politician, waved and smiled to all the voters who still had a chance to get to the polls. Shea looked straight ahead.

"Here, Bat, have a smoke." George handed him a cigar from his inside pocket.

"This ain't the weed you been handing 'round all day to the voters."

"No, this is Cuban. My special stock. Nothing's too good for my boy Bat."

"Save the gas, George. You already got my vote."

The sarcasm hurt George, but he continued to smile and continued to wave to his loyal subjects.

As John Ross walked out Oakwood Avenue, he had a heavy heart. His father, George Ross, had taken the news very badly. "I am going to see my boy," old George Ross announced, and he threw the Ross tartan blanket over his shoulder and started to leave the house on foot. John had to get Penelope to restrain him and Cobb to bring the gig around to take him down Ingalls Avenue. Now John had the unenviable duty of telling Nellie Mae Patton her fiancé was dead.

Fitch was preparing ground in the flowerbeds: "Afternoon, Mr. Ross. How're things at the polls?"

"All right."

"That looked like a rough crew."

"It was. Is Miss Nellie at home?"

"She is."

John was shown to Nellie in the sun room on the south side of the house. The room was bathed in sunlight and so warm that Nellie had bared her shoulders. She was eating a fruit cocktail.

"Would you join me?"

"No, I'm not hungry."

"You look dreadful, John. I must say when Fitch and I happened by the polls that group seemed rather hard. You are to be admired. All of you. Of course, some romanticize the working people, but I find them repulsive."

John marvelled how beautiful, how innocent Nellie Mae Patton seemed at that moment, how oblivious to harsh reality, the mourning, the long years of sorrow and grief that lay ahead. He regretted having to change so much with so few words.

She went on: "That group was particularly unsavory. I do not wonder why you must protect the polls against them. You should hear Rob go on about their horrid unions! But, I talk too much. What brings you here at this time of day?"

She looked into his eyes and read their message: "Rob! It's Rob! It's Rob, isn't it, John? Tell me! Something has happened. What, John?" He stared at her. She clutched his hand. "What, John? Tell me! I'm not a child. Tell me, John! Is he all right?"

"No, Nellie. I am sorry. Rob is dead."

She stared at him, stupefied. "Dead?" That word alone. She shook her head, her lip quivered. "Dead?" She dropped her spoon with a clatter. "No! That's impossible. This is a cruel hoax. John, tell me, this is some sick practical joke . . ."

"No, Nellie," he shook his head, "it's true. I was there. I am sorry. He was shot while chasing those thugs from the polls. He's dead. I'm sorry."

Only now, after telling his parents, only now, looking into Nellie's eyes did he feel the tears come. "I held him in my arms, Nellie, as his life ebbed away." John cradled his arms to show her. "I used to hold him like that when he was a baby. Rob, dying in my arms. Oh, my God!" He bit his lip to stop it from trembling and he turned toward the wall. When he turned back, she was facing him with red eyes, struggling to control herself.

"I am sorry, John," she fumbled up her sleeve for her handkerchief, her voice suddenly husky, "I must leave you now," and she rose and swept from the room.

"So," John murmured to himself, "this is it. The end."

Aboard the rattling, clattering Springs City Local, Frank Black folded his arms and scowled. Black had been in Saratoga Supreme Court foreclosing on a farm, and he was in a hurry to return to Troy for news of the election. As the new Republican chairman, he hoped to pick up a seat or two on the board of alderman. When the train pulled into Green Island, Black was surprised to see Senator Edward Murphy stepping from a cab. Odd that Murphy was in Green Island on election day. Black detrained to catch a streetcar across the bridge to Troy. When he peered toward Murphy, Murphy turned abruptly away and boarded the train.

The whistle blew, the wheels grabbed and the train pulled out toward Albany. Black seized his briefcase and walked along the platform toward the corner to catch the streetcar. Along Railroad Avenue he heard the newsboys crying: "Extra! Extra! Read all about it! Murder at the polls! Robert Ross gunned down at Troy polling place."

Black pressed his lips together. He had been with young Ross just Sunday night at Patton's home. He purchased a copy of the paper, and read with curiosity and outrage how a gang of Irish toughs had gunned Robert Ross down at the polls only hours before. Black turned toward the train tracks where the Saratoga local was receding toward Albany. The whistle blew from Watervliet.

"So that is how the captain looks deserting a sinking ship." And Frank Black boarded the streetcar and crossed the Green Island Bridge into Troy with many plans forming.

BOOK TWO

THE TRIAL

11.

PULPITS AND BELL TOWERS

The Esek Bussey Firehouse

Innocent blood had been spilled, and so a cry for vengeance went out across the city. Grief, sorrow, outrage passed in waves through the populace, yet it was no mere eye for an eye retribution they sought. There would be no angry mob with a noose. This cry for vengeance was tempered with reason. The price to be paid for Robert Ross's death must be extracted slowly, methodically, according to law. Not only must the miscreant pay, but Murphy's political machine must be dismantled so there would be no reoccurrence.

The day after the murder the unpredictable March weather turned foul, overcast and warm. Along the docks, merchants, chandlers, river captains and stevedores tarred and caulked boats for the first downriver voyage. Spring was their most profitable season. With goods stored in warehouses and markets empty downriver, Troy's mills and factories were backordered. The spring thaw would bring an infusion of cash. The merchants and millowners had been praying silently that the Panic of '93 was behind them. Now avenging the Ross murder gave Troy's elite something other than business to think about.

Wednesday afternoon's papers carried an announcement that all good citizens, men and women, regardless of sect or political persuasion, were invited to a mass gathering at the Fifth Avenue Presbyterian Church Thursday night. And so, after the mills and offices disgorged their workers the following day, as the opera houses and saloons were filling, carriages lined up for blocks along the curb of Fifth Avenue. Church bells of Fifth Avenue Presbyterian ponderously tolled. The night was dark and blustery, barren limbs sprinkling rain from an afternoon shower. Men held their bowlers and top hats, women held their bonnets against the wind as they hurried inside.

In the long line of fashionable liveries, a small, closed black coach appeared at the curbstone, its horse with a black plume. "Beggin' your pardon," the driver said politely, and he urged people away from the coach as he opened the door. The coach seemed empty at first, and some craned to see who would emerge. Then murmurs of sympathy arose as Fitch helped down Nellie Mae Patton in a long black dress and black veil. The crowd stepped back respectfully, whispers in the gaslight spreading the news that the martyr's betrothed had arrived. "Widowed before she was wed," the phrase was whispered in deepest respect and sympathy. Nellie was ushered in a side door.

Within the great church, pews quickly filled, and an overflow crowd climbed into the choir loft. The leading citizens of Troy were arrayed in the chancel, somber, grave men in black broadcloth, ministers in black cassocks. Behind them a large American flag hung. Florist shops throughout the city had sent wreaths and baskets of flowers.

When the church was filled to capacity, the doors had to be closed against another thousand people pressing to get in. Suddenly the bell ceased its tolling and silence fell. Then an organ blast startled the congregation, and in a communal exhalation of sorrow, everyone stood and sang from the hymnal "He is Gone."

After the first hymn, the organ immediately intoned "The Star-Spangled Banner," and pious faces of the congregation gazed up at the red, white and blue, placing hands over their hearts and singing with passion and with pain. Upon the dying notes of the "land of the free and the home of the brave," the pastor, Reverend Lemuel Haynes, ascended the pulpit.

"Citizens of Troy!" he called in a clear authoritative voice. "Men and women who love righteousness and hate iniquity: we have assembled in this, a sacred house of God, to express our indignation against a dastardly crime, to locate in some measure the responsibility for that act and to punish the men who were directly or indirectly responsible.

"Standing this morning with the father by the body of his handsome boy," Haynes spoke with pathos, "I tenderly uncovered the silent face, and took oath in my heart of hearts that if there was anything I could say or do to overturn the infernal power that made such a scene possible in this bloodstained land I would do it."

Applause rippled through the congregation, and shouts of "Here! Here!" The reverend then described how a young boy had been shot at his side thirty-two years before on a Virginia hillside during the Civil War. "Without a moment's warning in the height of battle, a shell from the enemy's guns struck that boy on the side of the head, tearing it nearly off, and he fell at my feet, a martyr for the cause of human liberty." Haynes paused for dramatic effect. The Civil War had been the last great sacrifice that had winnowed through a generation of Troy's young men while the millowners grew rich with war contracts. "I declare to you tonight that Robert Ross was as much a martyr as he.

"Ladies and gentlemen, Robert Ross died because he dared to protest against the shameful infamy which has made our city a blot upon the land. He died while in the act of defending his brother from the assaults of an armed gang of remorseless ruffians. He died while on his knees crying for mercy. He had a weak ankle and he had already fallen when he was shot down in cold blood by one of the foul miscreants seeking by force to elect a mayor whom they feared could not be chosen by peaceable means.

"Who is responsible?" the minister called rhetorically, his arms outstretched, his intense blue eyes boring into the congregation. "Is the bullet that finally found its way to the dead man's brain, or the weapon that held the lead, or the miserable man who aimed the pistol, whoever he may be? No! No! A thousand times no! These, these *things*, including the man, were only incidental to the fray. The responsibility finally rests with the system of forcing elections which has prevailed in this city for so many years. When you ask who must answer for this system, I reply the man or men whoever they be, high or low, who have educated their too-willing slaves up to such treasonable methods."

Haynes then read a resolution that he and Frank Black had prepared. He asked that it be adopted, calling for a special term of the criminal court to be convened in Rensselaer County and that the attorney general be sent up from Albany to prosecute: "What say you, citizens of Troy, to these resolutions? Aye or Nay?" A resounding "Aye!" echoed in the vaults of the ceiling.

The Rev. Dr. Halley was next to the pulpit: "I will adhere closely tonight to the text of these resolutions." He bowed his head in respect. "An air of painful and unwanted solemnity fills our city. Paeans of victory are not chanted. The din of strife is hushed. What is the reason?

"Edmund Burke said in the British House of Commons that you can't draw an indictment against a whole people. We haven't drawn an indictment against the City of Troy, we have drawn it against one man. When Louis XIV was in the extreme arrogance of his power, someone asked him 'What is the state?' He answered, 'The state? That is I.' If you were to ask Edward Murphy, Jr., tonight, 'What is Troy?' he would reply familiarly, 'Why, that's me.' It is this arrogance, ladies and gentlemen, that has cut down in his prime a young man of peerless virtue. One shot has startled this whole community out of its indifference, abjectness and servility . . ."

Unnoticed in the sacristy sat Nellie Mae Patton in her black veil. She wore the veil to hide the redness of her eyes from two days of weeping, and to hide her complexion, pale from two nights without sleep. She had insisted on attending to see that her beloved had not died in vain, and she wrung her black gloves in her hands as the speakers talked of a martyr. The word was strange to her. Her grief was not assuaged hearing these words, seeing these speakers. And the speeches blurred together.

"Tuesday morning, fellow citizens, a young man was by a cruel shot murdered," this was a bald man with a blond moustache. "As I think of this noble young life summoned out of existence, I feel that the glory of Troy is not in its wealth, nor in its industry. No. The finest fruit which this earth offers to its Maker is a man. Robert Ross was such a man." Loud cheers sounded from the crowd, and people rose up, applauding. In the sacristy, out of sight, Nellie Mae Patton buried her face in her hands and sobbed.

Next speaking was a corpulent man with white muttonchops:

"There is one name that appears on the roster of the senate in Washington that disgraces that body, and which would never have appeared there if you had done your duty as citizens."

Nellie Mae Patton did not know that this plump, pompous old whitehead was Mayor Greene of Binghamton, and she did not care that Ex-Lieutenant Governor Woodford of Brooklyn too attended this evening:

"It is sad we never see our duty until we stumble over a grave." Nellie took her handkerchief down from her eyes. "It is sad that we never knew what slavery was until war took away our firstborn. Ladies and gentlemen, you never knew what evil power controlled your city until that brave boy lay dead before you. This is no time for passion. If this meeting spends its force as the wave breaks upon the shore, it is better you never gathered. Do you know what the ballot box is?" He paused, and his ringing voice hung, poised in midair like a musical note. "The air, the sunlight, these are common things. We prize them not until we lose them. But the ballot box! The ballot box is the sanction of authority. It decrees our rulers, it directs our laws. It is the symbol of all that is American.

"Men of Troy, if you attempt to wrest advantage to a party out of this uprising of the people, you do wrong to the people. What we want of the Democratic Party are loyalty and patriotism. What we want of the Republicans are men who will not make corrupt bargains with the other side. I know not whether I should mourn or congratulate that young man who lies dead in Troy. If it shall be proven that by his death liberty has gained, then his free spirit will come back here tonight and thank God because he has accomplished more for freedom and honest elections by dying than he could have by living.

"It is easy to live and hard to die, hard when the sky is blue and life is opening . . ." at this, tears streamed from Nellie's eyes, ". . . hard to pass away from this world unto the strange unknown. But never a soldier more truly died on the field of battle than did young Ross, shot to death on the field of politics. Never could a young man ask for a higher guerdon; never could a young hope seek a larger Elysium. I speak tonight what all Troy knows. I speak what the senator knows who fled from the avenging countenances of his neighbors, that no apparent honor or political preferment can bring that senator to a place of honor such as young Ross took when in one leap he passed from life into glory."

The congregation was on its feet, and it burst into the familiar strains of "America," the organist swelling the pipes with bass notes.

When the fervor had subsided, Frank Black was introduced. He quickly ascended the pulpit, drew up his lanky frame like a coiled spring. His rimless spectacles reflected in the light:

"I have been asked to speak for ten minutes, but I shall not take five. I could not express my sorrow, my indignation or my shame if I stood before you until my hair turned gray. There has never been imposed upon me a duty to which I have felt so unequal as I do to this." He paused to gaze at the assemblage. Frank Black was not given to bombast. He cut to the issue, and made no attempt to disguise where he rested blame.

"Words are of no avail unless they stir to action and action is worthless unless it shall produce results. If those results are not now to be accomplished, then this city is indeed lost. A call to action, even to the extent of revolution, now is heard. There has just been committed here a crime so shocking and gigantic as to put another scar on the face of a city long renowned for its crimes. To denounce it is only half our duty. The other half is to place the responsibility. The responsibility is already placed in the public mind, so it is your duty to give it public utterance.

"The fear that has so long rested upon this city must be flung off and the truth spoken. The responsibility is not upon the outlaw who fired the shot. He was as much a tool as was his revolver. He was the product of corruption as much as his revolver was the product of invention. Against him you must make the charge of murder. But you must reach above him before you place the responsibility for it. If he had not believed he would be protected, he would not have committed this murder.

"The load upon Bat Shea's shoulders is not half so great as that upon the shoulders of those who fostered him." There was a stir in the crowd. There'd been much speculation, but this was the first time anyone publicly named Shea as the murderer. Perhaps Black knew more than others?

"If they had been honest, Bat Shea would have been an impossibility. You may hang Bat Shea and all his friends, but their successors will continue to rise up and will finally destroy you unless you cleanse the ditch out of which they spring. You may as well hang a pirate sailor and heap honors upon the pirate captain to ensure the safety of your commerce. You can never stop the terrible evil that has cursed this city until you stop praising the authors of it and covering them with honors. As long as you denounce them in public and in private receive their favors, you will be their slaves and victims, for your actions will be neither sincere nor effective until your public utterances and your private acts are consistent."

Frank Black scanned the crowd. He spread his arms and shook his head.

"I do not understand how the leader of a disreputable gang of repeaters and criminals can be the personal friend of deacons and elders and straitlaced creed worshippers, and at the same time the pronounced enemy of every decency which those worshippers profess. You are locking arms too much and locking horns too little. If laws are to exist, you must guard their enforcement. You must resist the powers that defile them, whether weak or strong, whether repeaters, those cheap and detestable worms, or the protecting class above them in the disgraced garb of policemen's dress, or in the still higher form of corrupt and unscrupulous leadership."

Again he paused for effect. His eyes scanned the congregation. "This murder must be avenged. Its repetition must be prevented. The evil which now confronts you is a coward as well as a criminal. If you have the courage to confront it, it will crouch and slink away under the steady gaze of an aroused public conscience. Then there is nothing left to do but put grit in your determination, and there will not be the least doubt of your redemption. There is honesty and intelligence in this city, but it is cast down and nailed in. You must insist upon the laws being enforced."

Without waiting for applause, Black descended the pulpit and sat impatiently with the others while additional speakers addressed the assembly. Tonight was his forty-first birthday and his wife had planned a large party. Black loathed parties. He relished the task ahead. There was another such meeting to be held at the Baptist Church for the overflow crowd, and then work tonight in organizing the Committee of Public Safety. This public furor must be channeled properly so it did not rage out of control, so it did not dissipate before toppling Murphy. Frank Black folded his arms and gazed at the changeable mob, wondering how long this murder could keep their attention.

In the sacristy, Nellie Mae had heard enough. The public call to arms lay beyond the compass of her grief. Tomorrow was the funeral and she needed strength. Perhaps tonight she would sleep. She summoned Fitch, and they left by the side door.

The mood was glum in Dunlop's Saloon. George Dunlop had been elected by eighteen votes. The efforts of Shea and McGough had prevailed. Yet while they won the battle, they saw they'd lost the war. Shea and McGough were both in jail, Shea as a murder suspect and Jack McGough for assaulting William Ross. The murder had focused the attention of Troy's four daily newspapers, and the attention of newspapers in Kingston, Syracuse, Poughkeepsie, Rochester, Brooklyn, Buffalo and New York upon the boss, the thirteenth ward and George Dunlop. And the ripples were widening to other states.

George Dunlop had been drunk and depressed since the election. While he had great affection for his boys, he had even greater affection for his political career. The worst had happened. Now a hot wind of retribution, like some Old Testament plague, was blowing up out of furnaces of spite and hate and indignation, like some abolitionist passion returning with all the "Glory, glory, hallelujah," righteousness that vanquished the South. Soon it would scorch and blacken the meager holdings and lives of the Irish. Even though his barman was pleased with the depletion in liquor stock since the murder, George had been one of his own best customers and had given away as much as he sold.

When the piano entertainer arrived in Dunlop's that night, few took notice. At the bar they were discussing the public meeting. Timothy

Edwin O'Malley knew all the ragtime favorites and had a stock of risqué limericks and songs he bawled out after the boys got soused and the belles from upstairs were swaying about. He was from Waterford, across the river in Saratoga County, and paid little attention to Troy or Rensselaer County politics.

"What's the word, boys?" O'Malley called cheerily, throwing out the tails of his checkered jacket, pushing back his tweed cap as he sat at the piano. He launched into a ragtime medley and called out, "Why's everyone so glum?"

Dunlop glared at him.

"A few of the boys are in jail," Owen Judge informed him.

"I'd hardly call that unusual," the piano player stated with an ironic roll to his eyes.

Jerry Cleary went over. "We don't need no music tonight."

"Why, my good man, everyone needs music!" Timothy Edwin O'Malley gave a toothy smile that made Jerry scowl and nod. And Timothy Edwin O'Malley lay his head back until his adam's apple protruded, his fingers danced on the keys, and he began a lively intro.

"Yeah, now I s'pose you're right. Let's see how well you can sing!" and Jerry brought the keyboard lid down upon his fingers, and the piano man cried out, pulled his hands free and ran to the bar in shock and in pain. "He broke my fingers! He broke my fingers!" the man whimpered, shaking his hands in George's face. "My God! I'm ruined! My fingers!"

"Get the hell outta here!" George growled through his teeth. The piano player cried out he would have his revenge, and exited into the night. "So tell me again, Owney," Dunlop said wearily, his eyes heavy with drink, "they let poor Bat walk in the hall, huh? And smoke? He can smoke?"

"Yeah, George, they're takin' good care of him. They let him have special privileges. He told me to tell you to keep the hot meals and growlers of ale coming."

"Twice a day, Owney, twice a day till he's free, because he's gonna be, boys. I know that Murphy fled town, and I know they're trying to remove Kelly as the DA. But Bat's a good boy, and he didn't shoot no one, and he'll be set free just as sure as I'm now the alderman of this ward. Now, I'll be going down myself tomorrow. We'll stand by him. Tell Agnes it's to be mutton stew and dumplings. Got to keep his spirits up. Let's have another round, boys. On the house, Tommy. Set 'em up."

On Hoosick Street the next afternoon, the facade of Esek Bussey firehouse was draped in black and emblazoned:

IN MEMORIAM ROBERT ROSS
1868-1894

Across the street at Oakwood Presbyterian Church the coffin had lain open since late morning, Robert Ross in a morning suit, eyes closed and hands gently folded, viewed by hundreds of well-wishers. To the rear of the church sat Nellie Mae Patton in her black gown, apart from the crowd, observing with a dull and vacant eye through her black veil the comings and goings of the crowd. What did it matter to her, any of it? This was the first time in her life where she was not able to control her own destiny, and she felt adrift, disoriented. She had fastened so much hope upon her wedding day. The gulf of sorrow and desolation remained unfilled by any of this political talk. She knew not this stranger they talked of, this martyr. Her heart felt the uselessness of punishing anyone, the utter futility of doing anything at all.

At two-thirty, Rob's brothers and cousins closed the coffin and carried it out to the hearse pulled by two jet black mares with plumes of crows' feathers. The bell began to ring in a slow, ponderous tolling. The dreary sky added to the solemnity.

"Come, Nellie," it was John Ross, "we must go."

"The cemetery?" Her voice trembled.

"No. Downtown."

"Downtown?"

"Yes, there is to be a viewing at Fifth Avenue Presbyterian Church."

"But why?"

"It is important, Nell. If Robert's death is to matter, to change anything, to mean anything, people must see him."

"It was these vile politics that killed him!" Her voice grew stronger. "Can't they let him rest in peace?"

Adam Ross came over. "Would you prefer to be driven home?"

Her eyes flashed with anger beneath the veil. "No, Adam. I prefer to be with Rob. I shall be with him until the cemetery, until the end. It is these interminable speeches and this breast beating that I cannot tolerate."

"If Rob's death is to do any good . . ."

"Rob's death, Adam, has put out the sun for me. It cannot bring anything good."

"We understand, Nellie, we understand."

They escorted her to her private coach that fell in behind the hearse, and with the bell ringing, down the incline of Hoosick Street toward the center of the city the procession wended. Businesses throughout the city had closed for the day, and the long procession, to the beat of a single drum, included the volunteer firemen of Esek Bussey, the non-union workers of the Bussey-McLeod foundries, the non-union workers of Ross Valve, the Sunday school children that Robert taught, and a great crowd of the Temperance Union.

The bells of Catholic churches were silent: St. Patrick's, St. Peter's, St. Paul's on the hill, St. Anthony's downtown. Noticeably absent from the funeral procession were policemen. Though Superintendent Willard offered to detail a platoon of officers to the funeral, his invitation was seen as a concession to Murphy and was flatly declined.

In front of Fifth Avenue Presbyterian Church the crowds filled the street for four blocks. The casket was carried into the church and opened. A gasp swept through the church at the repose of the martyr upon his satin pillow.

Now came the floral tributes, unloaded from long drays by the curb, many bearing the word "MARTYR". There was a four foot cross of red roses and white lilies, a cross from John Boland, who was in jail suspected of firing a stray bullet that killed Ross, a pillow of flowers with "Gates Ajar" inscribed across it, and a floral sarcophagus from the Bussey Steamer carried in the procession on the hose wagon. Nearly lost in the mountain of flowers was a small ring of white immortelles with a ribbon across the front: "ROB." This from Nellie.

The gates of the church had to be locked against the pressing throng, and at three the bells stopped ringing, the congregation bristled with attention and the Reverend Haynes again took the pulpit to address the bereaved. Nellie sat alone. Her father was in the chancel, Jane and her sisters sat with the Ross family. She has wanted it this way, and they have honored her wish.

"What was that?" Jack McGough bolted upright on the top bunk.

"What was what?" Bat Shea was gazing through the window grate at the dingy brick malthouse and warehouse and office complex of the Kennedy & Murphy brewery across Ferry Street.

"Why'd them bells stop ringing?"

"Don't know, Jack." Shea rested his arms on the windowsill. "Maybe they got him planted. There's an awful row being made over this here shooting."

"It'll die down."

"No, Jack, it won't neither." Shea sighed, looking over the brick smokestacks, the mansard roofs, the tenements, the theaters, the merchant blocks, the heavy cornices thickly coated with rust and coal dust above the tangles of telegraph wires. Over the cold mud, teams and wagons loaded with barrels, empty and full, were passing to and from the brewery.

A train rattled up the pit behind the brewery, its black smoke billowing, then hidden under the Ferry Street overpass, and the foundation of the jail shook, then the smoke erupted as the train passed to the rear of the jail and slowed into Union Station. They said nothing for quarter of an hour, each man alone with his thoughts. Then up at Union Station the whistle blew for loading the three-twenty belt line to Albany.

"Reminds me, Jack, on my way West, I got sidetracked in Olean. Had a hobo camp there in the railyard. One of the old bums got set upon by a dog. Happened at night when he stumbled away from the fire to take a leak. Dogs ripped a hole in him so the blood started to pour. Then once they smelled the blood, in a pack like wolves they come for him. The other dogs." Shea turned from the window.

"You could hear them barking at first, when they got the scent of blood. But you know what's worse? When you hear them not barking. When it's all quiet, 'cause then you know they're feasting. That's what this is going to be. Don't matter they're waving flags or speaking from pulpits, or wearing robes or spouting legal hocus pocus whilst the church bells ring. It's the bloodthirst of them dogs you're gonna be seeing, Jack." He shook his head. "You should'a seen how they stripped the bones of that old bum. One taste of blood, I tell you, it's all it took and there weren't a spinster's gleam of hope for him."

"Ah, it won't be like that neither, Bat. Murphy'll fix things. He'll get us sprung. Anyways, you didn't shoot the son of a bitch. Boland did. You was in front of him. Boland was the only one behind with a gun."

Bat Shea shook his head and turned back to look out the window. "Yet it worries me, Jack. This here city's gotta have a scapegoat. Ross got gunned down so they gotta have someone to kill in return." He paused. "The boss? That's who they want, and by all rights, that's who it should be. But it won't be him, will it, Jack? Won't be him at all. That's the way of the world, ain't it, Jack? Won't be the man in the top hat and spats and silver-headed cane, eh? Never is, is it?"

McGough snorted. Since being in jail he had grown nervous and odd. "Yeah, but maybe it will too be the boss what falls, Bat. Look at Boss McKane down in Gravesend. Six years hard time at Sing-Sing where the smallpox just broke out. That's who they're after, Bat, the boss, not you, not me."

"But I heard many of 'em are saying I shot Ross."

"I heard that too. How can they say that? We was both hit, and now they're saying that we were the only ones with guns. You didn't shoot him, did you?"

"No. Not in the head. I was firing at Boland when suddenly he came up from the ditch. Might have hit the front of him. Might have squeezed one off at his heart as he came toward me. But I was dazed then. I, I can't be sure. I turned and walked on with Mickey Delaney. He called out that I potted him, but I ain't sure. You see anything?"

McGough shook his head. "Nah. The son of a bitch pummeled me so good down in the ditch, I dropped my gun. Never got it back. Next I knew he's clumb off of me and up on top of the ditch." Jack lit a cigarette and blew out the match. He was lying on the bunk with his right ankle on his left knee, his hands folded behind his head. "He was hit by a stray, Bat, and Boland was the one I saw firing. Now you'n I both know they can't convict someone of murder during a riot. Don't stand to reason. Everyone was looking out after his own skin, everyone was running and shouting, I'll tell you that."

"Aye, but you watch and see. Mark my words, Jack. Men're animals that travel in packs, like wolves. They say they're so principled and civilized, Jack, but they ain't quenched the bloodthirst yet, and they ain't never going to, neither. One scent of blood, that's all it takes."

Suddenly the bell at Fifth Avenue Presbyterian Church commenced tolling again, and Shea turned back to the window. A flock of pigeons rose up and flew above the tenements and steeples, circling from the green copper of the bell tower above the rail depot and the whorehouses and the docks and the white steamboats and channel markers out on the river. "There it goes again," Shea said. "That goddamned bell. Give us a smoke, will you?"

"Sure."

Shea lit a cigarette and folded his arms on the windowsill and gazed out the window toward the coal-streaked brewery as each ring of the bell reverberated in the stone heart of the jail. They smoked in silence.

Slowly the funeral procession moved up Fifth Avenue to Hoosick Street, then up the hill to Tenth and out to Oakwood. A silent tide of humanity followed, six thousand strong. The wet wind held a promise of spring but the skies were foreboding. In her private coach Nellie Mae

Patton closed out the world and lay back.

At the cemetery, volunteer firemen, Rob's friends and school chums, lowered the coffin into the earth. The cemetery and the prayers were a blur to her, and soon she was delivered home. Straight to her room she went and she drew the curtains. "Oh, Rob!!" she sobbed and threw herself upon the bed and she let the flood of emotions pour forth. "I took you for granted! I never knew it could hurt like this." In her hand she clutched a locket, and she opened it to feel the lock of his hair. "Oh, Rob, oh, my love!" She knew then that she would never marry, and she wept into her pillow, murmuring, "Oh, Rob! Oh, Rob! Why does it have to be this way?"

12.
A CONCERNED CITIZEN

Frank S. Black

Frank Black leased office space in the Hall Building in the city's commercial district. He was a successful bank and commercial lawyer with an expertise in negotiable instruments — bills of lading, bank drafts, chattel mortgages — and contract law. From the triangular plot where First Street branched off River Street, the elegant Hall Building rose above the storefronts and banks and warehouses and cranes at the docks, above the gaslamps and thick skeins of telegraph lines and the wires for electric cars. The Hall Building was orange-red brick with cream-colored gothic arches, exotic patterns of red and gray and black.

Amidst the hustle and bustle of trade, Frank Black avoided the criminal court. He detested the immigrant swarms who arrived in Troy by the shipload with their old world clannishness, accents, superstition and disease. His practice was clean, with moneyed clients. He mastered each case and fought each one with all the force of his stern, imposing will and his unyielding moral superiority.

Frank Black stood a lanky six foot three. He was sprung from the flinty soil of Limington, Maine, a younger son of a family too large to live on the farm. He had worked his way through Dartmouth College teaching school, married a girl from Freedom, New Hampshire, and after college migrated to New York State to serve as editor of *The Journal* up the Mohawk Valley in Johnstown. When the publisher sought to temper an editorial he'd written at the insistence of an advertiser, Black refused, quit the newspaper and relocated in Troy.

After the farm and Hanover and Johnstown, the pace of this river city appealed to him, yet he was ambivalent toward Troy. It was too large and busy to be pleasant, yet too small to forge a statewide political base. It was near the state capital, but irretrievably provincial. Worst of all, it was peopled with illiterate immigrants who, he believed, were unworthy of democracy because they lacked the moral fibre to lead useful lives and the judgment to make informed choices in their leaders. Black studied law, was admitted to the bar, went into partnership for a year, but found partnership distasteful. He was ever a solitary figure, a New England Yankee who kept his own counsel, trusted few and relied on no one. He opened his own office and practiced alone. He bought a large, breezy cottage on Pinewoods Avenue on the "east side" to keep his wife and only child away from the noise, smoke and corruption of the city.

If Frank Black had a choice, all things being equal, he would have been a farmer. The haggling of lawsuits, the vanity of attorneys, the unbridled arrogance of judges wore on his patience. Yet he kept criticism behind his thin New England lips and endured the law for it provided a better living then he'd ever realize by farming. Whenever he could, though, Frank Black packed up his wife and son and escaped to the farm in Freedom.

Black scowled through rimless spectacles at the tide of corruption and sensuality: the corrupt police force that openly took bribes from the madams along the "Line"; the Italian and Irish and Polish gamblers who ran gaming "hells" and horserooms under the noses of authorities; the drunks and the gluttons who filled smoky chop houses and saloons; even the wealthy and fashionable folk who paraded at the elegant Mansion House. Troy indeed was an "open" town for all sorts of vice, and Black considered that all its vice had one fountainhead: Boss Murphy, the jolly brewer who daily poured hundreds of barrels of beer into the city to fog and addle the brains of the citizenry, and seduce them from the steep, thorny path of righteousness.

Having grown up poor, books as his only companions, Frank Black secretly envied the warmth and capacious charm, the wealth and executive skills of Boss Ed Murphy. Murphy had nine children, and it was rumored a couple of mistresses. Black had an only son. Murphy was not shamed by his humanity, by his feelings, by his animal magnetism and his sensuality. He loved, he hated, he promoted, he demoted, he spread favors about like Kris Kringle among local charities, and ascended to high office on the helping hands of his adoring subjects. He also punished quickly and effectively.

Six years before, Black spoke at the statewide Republican convention. This past fall, he actively entered politics, assuming a post no one wanted, helmsman of the leaky, foundering boat that was the Rensselaer County Republican Committee. He had been elected chairman because no one wanted the task of laboring in the shadows and drawing down the wrath of Murphy's monolithic machine. Black had perceived opportunity. He would be around people and he could lead. Now the Ross murder gave him the issue he needed. Yet he was cautious, for he knew that stepping into the limelight exposed one to scrutiny and criticism from all sides. He preferred to remain in the shadows, shielded from public view by committees and citizens' groups.

Black had a fondness for Machiavelli's small book. In his analytical way he pictured Boss Murphy as a medieval prince, ruling absolutely over the city-state of Troy, his regime bloated with vice and greed and arrogance. Murphy had subverted the power of the merchants and industrialists by buying them off individually with promises. His own power came from the working classes, particularly the Irish, who kept the machine in power with their votes and voting fraud. The small enclave of wealthy people, like aristocrats in Renaissance Florence, resented Murphy's absolute sway. Black saw that their resentment could be exploited during a coup, provided they were assured a share in the power. Yet none of these men of wealth, preoccupied with mills and markets and stocks and tariffs, had the capacity to lead. He did.

Power was all leverage, Black believed, like prying up a stump in the potato patch. To seize power, Black saw he must elevate Robert Ross to the point of knight errantry, swell the wrath, the moral force and indignation of the aristocracy, then press that force upon the fulcrum of Ross's heroic death so that it uprooted Murphy. Then and only then might he plant what he would in the hole. Ever cautious, Black realized he must not be seen as an opportunist. The aristocracy could crush him if it saw he was using them for personal gain. The effort must always be a collective one, and he must guide events with an unseen hand.

In the past year, Black had been indoctrinated with the methods of the American Protective Association, the black robes, the secret meetings, the odd rituals and initiations. He viewed the trappings of the APA with the same disdain that he viewed Roman Catholic vestments, rites and ceremonies. Yet he saw the political utility of membership. He believed its anti-immigrant, anti-Catholic credo and he approved of its vigilante methods. He felt the heart throb of superiority over other men at the meetings, and with the APA's resources, both of men and money, he knew he could rise. Most appealing to Black were the APA's surgical methods that had been successfully employed elsewhere.

After exposing the grave threat posed by immigrant political machines, the APA first appointed a committee of one hundred of the "best" citizens dubbed the "Committee of Public Safety". That title suggested existing law enforcement institutions were unreliable, and that it was a populist group dedicated to maintaining order. All religious and ethnic groups were to be included in this committee to give an illusion of its broad base of support, but policy was set and steered by Anglo-Saxons.

On Friday evening that first week, Black convened a group of merchants and manufacturers at his office, and in the glow of the gaslamps, he listened closely, talked little, analyzed, weighed and schemed how best to orchestrate the backlash.

After appointing a hundred of Troy's best to the committee and giving them a variety of tasks to build community support and to keep them busy, Black then focused on the legalities of the prosecution. The current prosecutor, John Kelly, must be sidestepped. He was Murphy's lackey and, Black suspected, too fond of the bottle. Kelly had the ability, either by a faulty presentation to the grand jury or by prosecutorial discretion, to dump the whole matter. Even if there were indictments, the trial could become a circus. The first order of business, then, was to petition Governor Roswell Flower for a special prosecutor.

Next, Black saw that the panel of grand jurors must be instructed by the committee as to their civic duty. Since the grand jury was a body convened in secret, the committee must use the mail. Black delegated to Charles Baker the task of drafting a circular to send prospective grand jurors, apprising them of their duty and subtly alerting them that the committee was watching. Communicating with grand jurors was highly unusual, highly prejudicial and could result in a guilty verdict being vacated, so Black did not want his name on the circular.

Yet as thorough and far-reaching as Black's plans were, there was one major flaw. The enemy had slipped out of town and was even now ensconced in Washington deliberating a tariff bill upon the senate floor. If Boss Murphy succeeded in passing this bill, which imposed a high tariff on English-made collars and cuffs, half the industrialists in Troy would be grateful and sympathetic to him and the push to dethrone him could stall. As long as Murphy remained in Washington, he was beyond the range of Black's artillery, and so was able from a higher emplacement to enfilade Black's line. You could extradite common criminals, but not a United States senator while in Washington debating.

As he pondered in the gaslight late into the night, his long bony fingers to his chin, his blue eyes keen and incisive through rimless spectacles, Frank Black knew his plan would fail if all he accomplished was Shea's execution. Shea was merely an instrumentality, as he had indicated from the pulpit. Shea had been Murphy's instrumentality, and now Shea would become Black's instrumentality, the fulcrum. But Black perceived that Shea must not become the sole scapegoat, drawing all the blame away from Murphy. If he succeeded in executing Shea, he would have indeed only hung a pirate sailor, the pirate captain sailing freely away. Yet recently, two other urban machines had been dismantled: Boss John McHale in Gravesend, and Boss Divver in the banner Tammany district in New York.

And so Frank Black leased a large conference room adjoining his suite of offices in the Hall Building, and set about preparing the case as he would any civil matter — he called witnesses to his office. In each other's presence, he asked about the murder:

"Did you see the shooting?"

"Yes, sir."

"And what happened?"

"Robert Ross was a-chasing a young feller 'cross the dumps, which is what we call the broken ground over there, and they fell down together. Ross was hitting the young man with a club, then he got up, climbed up the side of the ditch, and here comes the leader of the group."

"Bat Shea?"

"I guess. And Ross slumps down and pitches over to the side."

"Did you see Shea pull the trigger?"

"Well, not exactly, sir. I saw his gun."

"And you?" Black turned to another potential witness.

"I saw Shea shoot."

"He was facing Ross?"

"Why, yes."

"But the fatal wound was in the back of his head."

"Well, Shea kind of circled, yeah, that's what he did, he kind of circled around back of Ross, and he put the gun to Ross's neck and he fired."

"Point blank?"

"Yes, sir. Point blank. Not three feet, not two feet, not eighteen inches away. I would judge Ross was dead by then."

In four days following the murder, Black interviewed a dozen eye witnesses, nine of whom said they could swear they saw Shea shoot Ross in the back of the head. Those who did not know Shea by sight identified him by his necktie. The work of the committee was proceeding well. Now an APA judge must be called in to hear the case. Even though a regular term of the Court of Oyer and Terminer was to be convened in April, Black and the committee sought to have an extraordinary term of the same court called and a judge from outside Rensselaer County, beyond the influence of Boss Murphy, appointed to hear the case. The committee drafted such a proposal to present personally to the governor.

Finally, Black conferred with criminal attorneys. As a civil litigator, Black was unaccustomed to the different concepts of the criminal law, the prosecutor's duty to accomplish justice not just put people behind bars, the higher burden of proof, the presumption of innocence that demanded nothing of the defendant and everything of the People. Black sought to educate himself quickly. The secrecy of the grand jury concerned him, for if this matter was heard out of public earshot, there would be no scrutiny and Murphy's influence might prevail.

"We must keep this case ever foremost in the public mind," Black insisted Saturday evening to Seymour Van Santvoord, a prominent criminal attorney. "Each proceeding must be reported in the newspaper if possible."

"But the accusatory stage is clothed in secrecy, Frank. That is to protect the innocent."

"How about the coroner's inquest, then? That is a public proceeding."

"Yes," Van Santvoord agreed, "but it is very limited in scope. The coroner's inquest must determine only that Ross came to his death through criminal means. That should be open and shut. He didn't shoot himself."

"But what if we treat the inquest like a deposition, a publicized deposition? What if we have the coroner inquire into all manner of factual allegations concerning Boland and Shea? What if we parade some of our witnesses, companions of the Ross boys, out at the inquest? That would fix Shea's guilt in the public mind."

Van Santvoord shook his head. "Highly irregular, Frank. Accusing specific individuals of crime is the function of the grand jury, not the coroner."

"But the coroner is Republican! He'll do it if I ask. Shea may not have an attorney at the inquest to make objections. Why not do it that way?"

Van Santvoord frowned. "This is all highly irregular, Frank: selecting grand jurors, sending a circular to them, interviewing witnesses here in your office. You were not elected by the people to prosecute this crime."

"Neither was Kelly. Repeaters stole his election too."

"But he is nominally in office. You are not."

"So I should do nothing?" Black was incensed.

"No. But you must keep efforts of the committee within the confines of the constitution. This is not a civil case, and you are not plaintiff's counsel. This prosecution cannot become a witch hunt or the conviction will be reversed on appeal."

"Listen, Sy, a peerless young gentleman of our city has been gunned down by a saloon thug. Bat Shea will not get away with murder if I can do anything about it."

"You mentioned this Bat Shea in your remarks the other night at Fifth Avenue Presbyterian. What convinces you it was he?"

Black sat up straight, light reflecting in his spectacles. "Everyone says so."

"No, that is not true. There was a general riot. Ross may have been shot by a stray bullet. Might even have been shot by John Boland as the Irish maintain. Boland's story about having only blank cartridges in his revolver is incredible as a matter of law. So far we have only heard from a dozen of the Ross people. A couple of them know Shea, but are uncertain he fired the shot. Only those who don't know Shea and identify him by a green tie are sure it was he."

"John Ross told me the day after the murder it was Shea."

"But John Ross had been tending to his brother Bill when the shot was fired. Don't you see my point, Frank? Some witnesses can say only that Ross was shot by a man in a green tie. Those who use the green tie to identify the murderer cannot identify Shea. Those who identify Shea do not refer to the green tie, and they only say they saw Shea turn and run toward Ross. Furthermore we have yet to hear from any of the Irish."

"Of what use would that be?" Black was indignant.

"A jury is entitled to evaluate all the evidence."

"But the Irish will lie."

"So, the jury will evaluate their credibility and find accordingly. Surely I needn't school you in the function of a jury, Frank?"

"Are you telling me you wish to dissociate yourself from our effort?"

"No, Frank. I am merely stating it is dangerous to jump to conclusions before hearing any sworn testimony. What these men say to you in this conference room may not be what they swear to on the witness stand. You don't want to get too far out on a limb."

"Surely you don't doubt that Shea is the murderer?"

"I was not there, Frank. I don't know. I am not the judge and I am not the jury. It is not my function to accuse and it is not my function to judge."

Black scowled. "So you would do nothing?"

"I think your naming Shea the other night was premature. I think the Ross people are biased, motivated by understandable outrage, and therefore unreliable. I don't believe in the midst of a riot that a dozen people happened to turn at the precise moment Ross was shot and observe who pulled the trigger. The worst thing you could do at this point is commit all these people to one theory of the case, and then have another one surface later. Everyone would look foolish, and Murphy would be more in control then than he was before the murder. I say, let the criminal process operate with its checks and balances. It works."

Frank Black stacked his papers, closing up for the night, his thin lips pressed together. He was unpersuaded.

13.

OTHER SIDE OF THE TRACKS

The Fitchburg Train

And what of the Irish? Huddled on the river side of the tracks, long rows of worker tenements amidst factories, brickyards, coalyards, warehouses, and in the center, in an upsweep of all their desperate immigrant hope, church steeples, how were they reacting? They talked of nothing but the murder, and their reaction ranged from violent outrage to shame.

In Irish neighborhoods of South Troy and North Troy the killing was outwardly condemned, but many workers and union agitators who'd been locked out and blacklisted by the APA were secretly pleased a gun had spoken for them. There was great confusion, too, as to who had pulled the trigger. Few admitted that no one really knew. Everyone had an opinion.

As he held court in McClure's Saloon, Tag Foley was certain in his heart of hearts that it was John Boland, an APA sympathizer, who was shooting at Shea as he ran. "That lardass's as useless as his old man," Foley ventured. "Couldn't hit the broad side of widder McClean with a loaded pecker," and he spat a line of tobacco juice at the spitoon.

"Naw, it warn't him, Tag," dour old Droop Halloran shook his head. "But I don't think it were Weary Shea's boy, neither. Some are now saying it was Jerry Cleary who come up from behind."

"No, no, no. He was to the south with Judge."

"I hear Jack McGough's name rumored too."

"Nah. Ross had knocked the gun out of his hand long before that. Anyways, the APA couldn't pin it on him, 'cause they'd never get murder first. Ross was clubbin' him just before he was shot."

"Aye," said Tag Foley, "and they sure need an electrocution with this one. Them APAs won't sit still for no life at hard labor."

"Horrible thing," Horace Bayly sighed.

"You know these boys was good boys, too, that's the pity," Lightning Kilcullen offered. They called him Lightning because it took him so very long to catch an idea. "Shea had some rough edges, surly when you cross him, mean son of a bitch, but Jack McGough was a good lad. Come to think of it, he could get on your nerves too. But George Dunlop, he'll do a lot for this ward now that he's in."

"Yeah, like what?" Droop challenged him with his sad watery blue eyes. "Weren't he the cop behind the railyard robberies?"

"I suppose you're right, Droop. But the boss, well, he'll stand back of 'em, just wait and see."

"The boss couldn't get out of town fast enough," Foley corrected. "He don't cotton to a whole gaggle of lily-white Protestants screaming from pulpits that he's to blame for a murder. How's that to look in Washington? How's that to look in Albany? Might have a slight impact on how he's got this state all tied up and hornswaggled."

"Yeah," Lightning agreed, nodded, then scowled. Independent thought was very difficult for him and so many considered him an able barometer of the community's mind. "So who are we t'be sorry for?" He ordered another round of drinks so they could mull over the matter a bit more sociably.

"For ourselves," Foley said. "We ain't heard the last of this, and they won't be satisfied with just a trial and a hanging neither. They're going to lock us out, bust the unions, temperance leagues closing the saloons — ."

"Wait up there a bit, Tag," Lightning said. "They'd never do that! Close the saloons."

"Oh, no?"

"Nah. You heard the one what was going around? Why did the Good Lord invent whiskey?"

"Why?"

Lightning held his amber shot glass into the air. "T'keep the Irish from conquering the human race." He drank it down, and smacked his lips. "My that's good!"

"Ain't that the truth?"

"And Murphy is the Lord's right-hand distributor."

"Aye, he makes a dry pale ale, he does there. And he's an able politician, he is, and he'll ease himself out of this one, he will, you just wait and see." And Tag Foley winked and tapped his temple with his finger.

Railroad tracks cut the city of Troy in half. Entering the city from the South and West and North, train tracks ran along the base of the hill, separating the worker tenements and neighborhoods by the river from residential sections of the well-to-do. These rail lines connected Troy with points south, Albany, Poughkeepsie, New York, and points west, Utica, Syracuse, Rochester, and with Montreal, Rutland and Boston and points north and east.

The eleven-twenty train from Albany chugged up the New York Central tracks from Greenbush, blowing black smoke and cinders, then the shrill white steam as the whistle blew and the train clattered into South Troy. Engineer Timothy Corcoran eased up on the throttle.

"You can feel the change in climate," he spoke to his fireman, Sparky Malone, who paused from shoveling coal and looked ahead, white eyes staring out of a blackened face. Sparky Malone's second cousin was married to Bat Shea's uncle. "There's a cloud over this city, Sparky."

"Always has been, Cork; place is accurst; wouldn't live here; moved to Albany." Sparky married Colleen O'Brien and moved into a flat her father, a Democrat ward leader in Albany, had to let them cheap and quick. Her father took the news in stride, though, "First one can come anytime, Sparky; rest'll take ya nine months. S'long as ya marry her, what difference?" Colleen being disgraced with a "big front at the altar," still stayed inside all day doting on the baby. So Sparky was no stranger to disgrace, but this murder gave him mixed feelings. His cousin by marriage was being framed.

The train moved slowly past sidings to the Burden Iron Works and the Rensselaer Iron and Steel Co., vast grimy complexes of coke plants, blast furnaces, foundries, puddling forges, warehouses, docks and smokestacks belching coal soot. "There's always kids on these tracks," Tim Corcoran remarked with a shake of his head. The boozers were open all night in Troy to accommodate the graveyard shift, and the children grew up hard from the cradle, clouted or ignored by their parents. They formed gangs in the clay hills and stole from the railyards, and they ambushed the trains, raining down a dark hail of mudclods and rocks and then it's only the whistle that you could blow to try to scare them off. But it still haunted Tim Corcoran how he deprived a young boy of his right leg last winter when the kid slipped underneath the wheels on some foolish stunt. "They'll never learn down here," he told Sparky.

In the shadow of St. Joseph's steeple the train passed and at the Clinton foundry siding it veered away from the river, then across the Poestenkill into Little Italy, "Guinea-town," where mustachioed patriarchs and round mamas in print dresses raised their dozen children on pasta and sausage whose spices hid the taste of the occasional horse or dog meat that made it into the mix. Each family had its plum tomato patch and its grape arbor in the little plot behind the tenements and each September they stomped the fruit of the vine into strong *grappa* stored in green bottles in damp cellars. The bakeries in Little Italy turned out the flakiest pastry and the lightest bread that was peddled on horsedrawn wagons to the Jews along First Street and the millowners in Washington Park.

With a blast of the whistle the train cut eastward across paved streets and dirt lanes, and a gang of children unleashed a shower of mudclods by St. Theresa's, the French Canadian church. Beneath the brow of the Warren property, behind Senator Murphy's Excelsior Brewery, the train dipped into the Ferry Street tunnel, then out into the light. Tim Corcoran laid on the whistle in the shadow of the county jail. Then it was under the bridge at Congress and a deceleration and smooth glide under the trestles, a wave to a gang of gandymen laying track, past blocks of whorehouses with girls in the upstairs windows, and into Union Station.

The great clanging steam engine halted at the depot. From the middle car emerged an older man with white muttonchop whiskers, a velvet waistcoat and spats. He adjusted his tall top hat and scanned the platform. Seeing no one, he proceeded through the vault of Union Station. On the street outside a coach was waiting with a spirited bay colt snorting in the traces. He walked to the carriage and peered in. Back in the shadows sat a form, the light catching only his spectacles.

"Mr. Black?"

"Thank you for coming. Please."

The elderly man stepped into the coach.

Black tapped the cab ceiling with his cane. "Drive on!"

"Who was that?" asked Officer Butcher of Officer Meagher. The two corpulent police officers were warm today, perspiring in their long woolen blue coats and high hats.

"'Twas Black's coach, t'be sure."

"Aye. And it seems to me that was a feller from the Attorney General's office that was pointed out to me once."

"Coroner's inquest begins next week," Meagher offered.

"Aye. And they're to get rid of Kelly, the DA."

"Black can't decide whether to spit or swaller on becoming a prosecutor here. See that nonsense in the papers? Wants to appear before the grand jury?"

"C'mon. We better report up t'the brewery."

"After I stop by Sadie's house. My envelope's there, and I need some bar-money for tonight."

"You ain't getting the pipes cleaned out today, are you?"

"Never can tell. Sweet new girls in from Bennington. Let's go."

Also on the platform, watching the two officers of the law move off toward "the Line," Alderman George Dunlop turned and boarded the train for Albany. He used to drink with them when he was on the force. Because of the circumstances of the election, he does not know whether to talk with people or remain aloof. Dunlop has an appointment with the state party boys to discuss the prosecution and his role in the episode, and he has looked with trepidation upon this trip.

It was difficult to shake the binge this time. While George Dunlop aspired to higher office, he hated to leave Troy, and insisted on sleeping in his own bed every night. The summons from the state boys was, no doubt, initiated by Murphy. George always carried in the back of his mind the image of his father-in-law's mutt strung up in the stable rafters. He feared this meeting was to discuss who will be offered up as a sacrificial lamb. The whistle screamed, the bells clanged, George boarded the train.

In the engine, Cork turned to Sparky. "Get the fire up now." He pulled the chain for the whistle, the conductor cried, "'Boarrrrrrrrd!" The steam engine gasped and slowly the wheels chugged to life, the couplings jerked, hauling the five parlor cars to Federal Street, then over the Green Island Bridge to veer south onto the Delaware & Hudson tracks back to Albany. Dunlop peered out the window. The river was filled with ice floes, and boats and ships in the river risked disaster. The river usually flooded the last week in March when the mountains loosened their hold on the ice, and then the streets were passable only by boat. A flood of a whole different sort is coming, Dunlop fears. "If only . . . if only. And I warned them, I told them, 'No trouble! I don't want no trouble!'" Yet the fact was squarely in front of him and he could not see around it. Murphy had released a version of the murder through a railroad commissioner, and the press howled at his suggestion that the Ross brothers were the aggressors. At Dunlop's first common council meeting a large crowd pressed into the room calling for Dunlop's ouster and for Francis Molloy to resign as mayor because of the election fraud.

The editors were daily drawing and quartering Murphy:

"The Trojan gentlemen who by virtue of past incidents of this character now occupies a Senatorial seat once the prerogative of statesmanship and manhood, is entitled to congratulations upon the logical fruition of his dirty work. He is privileged now to view the methods that he plotted and perfected from his soft retreat in the cushioned easy chair that once held a Seward, a Marcy, a Conkling. This smooth manipulator of thugs, cutthroats and hired assassins is permitted to run his eye over a spectacle of peculiar triumph. We wish him joy of it. We likewise wish joy to the pliant tool of Murphyism, Governor Flower, the saintly man of Watertown, the jelly-boned state executive who dares not say his soul is his own."

The state committee wanted answers from Dunlop, and State Democratic Chairman Murphy could mete out whatever punishment necessary to keep his skirts clean. Murphy was scared, and desperate men did desperate things.

As she looked westward over the Hudson from the Shea's back yard, Mamie Halligan watched the massive ice floes drifting south. Her premonitions had proved correct and now her beloved was in jail facing a charge of murder. Her recent premonitions were worse. Given to pulp romances, she was familiar with the dignity and grandeur of suicide, and the river seemed as cold and unyielding as the life she led. A yellow bar of light glowed in the western clouds and the ice floes drifted by, a faint blue. Life was so unpredictable!

Eddie Flynn had just offered to take her to Griswold Opera House where Ezra Kendall's latest comedy success was playing, "The Substitute," featuring the "famous little comedian Arthur Dunne and the charming little soubrette Miss Jennie Dunne." Going to a play in the midst of all this! And when she had softly declined, he persisted: "What about Miss Belle Archer in 'An Arabian Night at the Rand'?" Mamie sighed, shook her head, climbed the stairs with a tear in her eye, a sob in her breast. She needed to speak with Mrs. Shea, the doughty little spitfire, who refused to believe her son had anything to do with the murder.

"Electioneering? That there's my Bartholomew. But not murder. That's more Cleary or Owen Judge or even Jack McGough. Not my Barry." And in the parlor, huddled in front of his stove, sat old belligerent Weary Shea. They named him for his posture, gained through decades of bending over stove molds, sifting the damp sand and smoothing the pattern to perfection. Bartholomew Shea, Sr., has great skill in making molds for parlor stoves. Unfortunately, life is not wet sand and is not so easily molded.

"Mary! Mary!" he called. He was always testy these days. "Has that boy brought the damned newspaper yet?"

"No, Bart. I'll let you know when it comes." She leaned toward Mamie and whispered, "Since all this business began, he tortures himself with reading 'bout it. As if it weren't hard enough otherwise! He reads the papers not to find out anything, just to figure out what the neighbors are thinking. A change has come over him. Won't go to church even. And betwixt us, lass, I consider that would do him the most good of all."

14.

THE CAPITOL

New York State Capitol, as Designed

After three days of fiery sermons and secret meetings, the Committee of Public Safety issued a letter to the governor Sunday afternoon demanding Black and Van Santvoord be appointed to oversee the murder prosecution. Newspapers had the letter first. Monday's *Troy Times* demanded action, dubbed Roswell Flower "the gubernatorial numbskull in Albany," and accused him of conspiring with his political mentor Boss Murphy to deprive the people of Troy an honest trial.

Governor Flower acted swiftly to dispel suspicion. He telegraphed Black, District Attorney Kelly and Mayor-elect Molloy Monday morning, summoning them individually to Albany. He promised to appoint Frank Black as special counsel to assist Assistant District Attorney Thomas Fagan. Kelly and Molloy acquiesced. Flower then called Fagan down to the capitol later in the day.

Fagan was a young and able assistant in John Kelly's office, with few ties to the Murphy machine and perhaps enough independence to try the case credibly. He was a shy, retiring young man. He folded his arms, crossed his leg and bit his lip in the ostentatious red room of the executive suite on the capitol's second floor.

"This is the chance of a lifetime, young fellow," Flower said gruffly. Flower was a large, thick-fisted, bull-necked, blunt-talking north country yeoman who ignored those who criticized him as a blockhead. "Now you work with Black, that's what I'm telling you to do. He's a sharp lawyer, and he'll put you in touch with the right folks. Your future could not be rosier."

"With all due respect, sir, I think Frank Black will do nothing but inject politics into this prosecution as he already has done."

Flower chuckled and puffed on his cigar. "Son, I've been politicking around this state for longer than you've been alive. I never saw another place like Troy. Nothing in Troy is ever free from politics, and you got Ed Murphy to prove that. Now Black says Kelly and Murphy are up to some shenanigans. You say Black is. You're probably both a little right and both a little wrong."

"But Black has no authority to act. He has not been elected."

"Take him on, my boy. I'll give him the authority. He'll show you things."

"I'm sure he will."

Fagan left the capitol displeased that a citizens' group would be peering over his shoulder. Yet short of resigning and losing the chance to try the case of a lifetime, he had no choice.

That evening a letter arrived at his office and Fagan's eyes narrowed as he read. Then he took the letter to Kelly. "Black does not just want to participate, he wants equal power. He refuses to participate at all unless he gets it! No one in this committee has been elected to office, and they ignore the law as being an inconvenient little formality, demanding equal power with you and me, constitutional officers, to present this case to the grand jury."

"So what?"

"I thought their involvement would be passive. What's to happen when there's a disagreement between me and Black? Who decides the matter? And since the law's being ignored by appointing him in the first place, what rules apply? For openers, is an indictment jurisdictionally sound when another party is present in the grand jury?"

"To hell with 'em," Kelly growled. His eyes were a boozy red and his posture slumped. The past week had aged him a decade. Never under any illusion that he was his own man, the public outcry against him as Murphy's hack had stripped him of all dignity, and a bottle had never been far from his hand. "I'm tired of this whole goddamned mess!"

"Yes," said Fagan, "but it won't go away, sir." As he left the office he heard the drawer open where Kelly kept his comfort.

The coroner's inquest began the next day. The steps of the courthouse were thronged with people on that damp, blustery Tuesday morning, and the narrow corridors were wet and impassable. The press shouted questions as each party entered the courtroom and all was bustle and confusion. The scope of the inquest was narrow. The coroner was simply to inquire into the cause of death, and rule whether there was probable cause to bind over any of the men, McGough, Shea or Boland, for action by the grand jury.

Fagan squeezed into the courtroom by a side door. The gallery was packed and the reporters' table full. A murmur outside rose into a roar as the shackled prisoners came up the steps into the courthouse. The courtroom door opened and first there was Boland, then McGough and then, the crowd aflame with anticipation, Bartholomew Shea. Boland and McGough looked ahead at the bench. Shea looked at Fagan, sizing him up. Shea's eyes were hard and a sneer curled at his lip, as if he were daring Fagan to step out of line with the boss. Contrary to Black's prediction, attorneys had been appointed for Shea and McGough. Boland had hired his own. The attorneys filed in behind their clients and Fagan turned toward the bench as Coroner John Collins emerged.

The clerk announced the commencement of the inquest, John Norton put his appearance on the record for Bartholomew Shea. Fagan appeared for the People, then Collins nodded to Frank Black. "The court recognizes Mr. Black."

"Thank you, sir," Black rose and paused for silence. "We of the Committee of Public Safety have sought authority from the governor to participate in this prosecution. Our participation in this matter must be clarified before the inquest proceeds."

Fagan stood: "I object, Coroner Collins. At six-thirty last night I received a letter from Mr. Black wherein he declined to act unless he receives equal power as a prosecutor," Fagan held up the letter, glanced at Black, and Black scowled darkly. "To express it more fairly, sir, Mr. Black declined to accept the governor's appointment unless and until he was clothed with the same authority I possess. Of course I cannot deputize Mr. Black, and he has not been duly elected or appointed. Therefore I appear alone in this case."

The chant of "Fraud, fraud, fraud," was accompanied by the stamping of feet. Coroner Collins banged his gavel. Black turned to the crowd and raised his arms to quiet them. "Mr. Collins," Black spoke when there was silence, "I request an adjournment of this inquest so we may go to the governor and clarify the committee's status in this case."

"I oppose any adjournment," Fagan said. Catcalls erupted from the gallery. "This committee had its opportunity to participate, and declined." There were boos and cries of "Fraud!" Collins banged his gavel hard and repeatedly.

"This is a very serious matter," Collins said, leveling his eyes at the crowd, "I will not have this inquest turned into a sideshow. One more outburst and the courtroom will be cleared."

"Mr. Black has no standing here, sir," Fagan protested, "and no authority to seek an adjournment."

Now Shea's attorney, John Norton, rose. "I agree completely with Mr. Fagan, sir, and I will so stipulate."

"And yet, gentlemen," Collins leaned back, "Mr. Black represents a very legitimate committee of our citizens . . ."

"But he has no authority to act here!" Fagan insisted. "He has been neither elected nor appointed, and he has declined our offer to participate as an *amicus*. I have made Mr. Black a fair proposition, and now he is haggling about it. I shall proceed in the case and pay no more attention to him."

Black leaned forward, his fists on the desk. "Mr. Collins, I ask only a one day adjournment so I may see the governor and be clothed with such authority as I require."

"I am inclined to grant Mr. Black's request, gentlemen," Collins said, and he banged the gavel. "Matter adjourned until two o'clock Thursday. Sheriff Ford, escort the prisoners back to jail."

Collins was through the curtains, the prisoners on their feet and the attorneys dispersed before the crowd could react. Black would not look at Thomas Fagan, but collected his papers and exited immediately.

After a day of phone calls and dispatching telegraph boys on bicycles, Black contacted the entire committee. Early Thursday morning eighty-one members of the Committee of Public Safety took the belt line to Albany to meet with Governor Flower. Because Flower had refused to sign into law the so-called Troy Inspectors' Bill before election day, and because the newspapers speculated that the law would have saved Ross's life, the committee felt the governor would be shamed into granting three requests: the attorney general to prosecute, a special term of the court to hear the case, and permission for Black to present the case to the grand jury alone.

The belt line ran down the west bank of the river along the canal. Canal boats and small sloops in dry-dock were being tarred and caulked for the opening of shipping. Already the more courageous captains had small steamboats out among the ice floes. Some Albany boats had been running, and navigation south to New York would officially open the following Monday when the first boat of the Citizens Line reached Troy from Manhattan. The train made its quick local stops, Green Island, Watervliet, Menands, and reached Albany's Union Station at eleven.

"We shall march to the capitol, a city united!" Black called as they collected on the platform beneath the cast iron clock. "Let the governor look from his window and see a whole city marching upon him." With murmurs of assent, these four score industrialists, merchants, bankers, clergyman, capitalists, philanthropists and educators marched two by two up Steuben Street to the crest of the hill.

High upon the hill cranes swung blocks of granite into place atop a massive structure, large as an Egyptian pyramid. The New York State Capitol had been under construction since the end of the Civil War, nearly thirty years, and was not even close to completion. Padding of contracts and collusion in the bidding spread a dark cloud over this vast public project, its corruption surpassed only by Boss Tweed's courthouse behind New York City Hall.

"Cast your eyes upon corruption!" Black cried as they paused for a streetcar to pass. "The state capitol. A monument to boss rule!" Black's words were met with a righteous rebuke from eighty throats: "No more!" Black led the men in bowlers and top hats across the cobblestones and streetcar tracks, across the brown grass of the capitol lawn and up the great staircase to the executive chamber. Flower had been warned and was waiting.

After the obligatory pleasantries, Dr. Ferguson cleared his throat and spoke: "We are here, your Excellency, to request that you authorize the attorney general to prosecute the election fraud and murder cases in Rensselaer County. Like you, I myself am a Democrat, and I had the unhappy task of performing the autopsy upon the unfortunate boy."

The governor nodded.

"Not only does our District Attorney John Kelly daily render himself incapable of this task by imbibing alcohol, he is a mere puppet for Senator Murphy. As you know, if this matter is presented to the grand jury such that there is a no bill, a murder will go unavenged, election frauds will persist and the integrity of our whole system of government will be laid open to the most cynical of criticisms. Just yesterday, an upstart assistant of Kelly's office flagrantly insulted Mr. Black by ignoring his request to appear before the grand jury."

"I have talked with Mr. Fagan and with Mr. Black," the governor said. He seemed impatient.

"Here in this room, sir," Ferguson continued, with a wave of his hand, "are virtually all the persons of substance in the city of Troy. There are Republicans and Democrats alike, Protestants, Catholics and Jews. We have personally come here this morning in a body to ask your Excellency for the intervention of the attorney general both at the coroner's inquest and at trial so that the process of justice is not subverted."

Flower scowled. "And yet you have constitutionally elected officials charged with these duties. If they do not discharge their duties, is it not the ballot box that allows you to throw them out of office?"

A loud murmur arose. "That is precisely our point, your Excellency," Ferguson said. "Boss Murphy and his machine have corrupted the ballot box. Mr. Kelly is simply his lackey, and these criminals could very well go free if the case is not properly presented."

Professor D.M. Green then stepped forward: "We utterly and absolutely distrust the district attorney's office and any officer connected therewith. And we feel we have ample reason for this distrust."

George Warren, a former mayor, spoke up: "Governor Flower, thugs and assassins now run our city. They are more in evidence today than during those perilous times when I was mayor and I include the draft riots of '63. One man is responsible. Edward J. Murphy."

The governor drew in a deep breath, then he shook his head and spoke firmly: "Gentlemen, the city of Troy is itself responsible for the deplorable state of affairs you indicate prevails. I will not say I will not in the future direct the attorney general to take up this prosecution, but I will not take such action today."

Flower's refusal was met with murmurs of disapproval, but Black held up his hand to quiet the men. One by one the industrialists took issue with the governor's position. And yet Black did not himself speak. He was conductor of the orchestra, and he nodded for the doctor to proceed.

"We have other requests, sir," Ferguson stated. "We seek a special term of the criminal court to hear these cases, and we ask that Mr. Black be authorized by your Excellency to appear before the grand jury in this matter."

Flower glanced at his counsel who grimaced. "I will grant that one request. You can have a new court of Oyer and Terminer. As for the other, I spoke with Mr. Kelly and with Mr. Fagan. Kelly agreed in concept to have Mr. Black deputized as an assistant district attorney, and to make available the full resources of his office. The district attorney is a constitutional officer. A bill could be passed in the legislature giving Kelly the power to appoint two additional assistants authorized to appear before the grand jury. Do this and your proceeding would not look so much like a persecution, but a prosecution. It could be done in twenty-four hours. Go on with the coroner's inquest. Mr. Fagan is an honest man. He appeared too manly before me to justify taking any step against him. Conduct the inquest now, and if there is a finding of probable cause, we will take up the other matters."

Flower rose, signalling the meeting was over, then he walked among the men, speaking to them individually and unofficially. "Deplorable, this whole business," he shook his head, "but we must be careful and we must be prudent, gentlemen. We must not overreact." Black watched him with disdain. His calculating eye measured the room, the stature of the man, the vicious little counsel with his slim moustache.

As they left the red room, Troy's committee picked its way down an inside stairwell under construction, and paused on the ground floor. Workers covered in plaster dust walked to and fro on scaffolding and catwalks; outside, workers dressed blocks of stone with chisels and whining machinery, and cranes lifted high the massive stones for mortaring and placement. Frank Black considered the trip wasted, a miscalculation, yet he needed to save face before these disgruntled men.

The committee had formed small groups grumbling over the outcome of the mission. While in Troy their combined economic and political might was formidable, here in Albany where swirled currents and eddies of statewide and national concern, where the cities of New York and Brooklyn and Buffalo sent their problems and their voting blocs, Troy's local problem seemed minuscule, their political clout paltry. Black mounted a large granite slab and called the men to order.

"Have you seen enough, gentlemen?" Black waved his hand. "This is government by collusion and corruption. Thirty years to build a state capitol. Have you seen enough, or do you wish to see more? Plaster and masonry contractors pocketing millions. This capitol is a symbol of political impasse, a cathedral to corruption, to the raw thievery of one-party rule. Too long has our state been subjected to these grafters. Too long have we turned the other cheek and averted our eyes. Have you seen enough, gentlemen?"

They cried out, "Yes!"

"Do you wish to see more?"

"No!"

"Our battleground is small, gentlemen, it is only Troy, but our cause is as great and as noble as free government itself. And we shall prevail!"

There was a momentary spark of excitement and outrage, but despite Black's attempt to rally them, and to put a good face on their visit, the industrialists grumbled as he led them to the train.

"Gentlemen, I have a legal matter to attend to," he announced as they were boarding. "I shall be back to Troy this afternoon." The grumbling was renewed.

As he walked up Columbia Street, Black measured what had been and had not been achieved. The insensitivity of the governor was a setback, yet he saw three positive results: they would attain a special term of the criminal court for Shea's trial; the governor could be blamed if things ran amok; and he personally had ducked being deputized as an assistant district attorney. This was important, for not only was the prosecution of a criminal beneath Frank Black's stature now that he was a protector of the commonweal, but success in a murder trial is never guaranteed, particularly here where Ross had fallen during a riot. Black was comfortable stirring the cauldron of emotions for a time.

15.
THE INQUEST

John T. Norton

As the inquest resumed Thursday afternoon, Black was not yet back from Albany. He had telegraphed Dr. Owens, a member of the committee, to appear for him at the inquest and to obtain another adjournment. On the train he cursed his luck in missing the one-thirty belt line. He knew he must not stumble again. He had arrived in Troy with nothing and his credibility as a leader was now being evaluated by Troy's first citizens.

Legally, the focus of the inquest was narrow: had Robert Ross died by criminal means and if so, was there probable cause to bind anyone over for the grand jury. The inquest was not to accuse or even investigate beyond that limited issue. Usually prosecutors kept their evidentiary showings minimal to give defense counsel as narrow a view of their case as possible. Accustomed only to civil litigation, Black took the opposite view. Airing much of the evidence now in the newspaper, he believed, would compel both an indictment and a conviction.

Despite a spring shower, lines of people extended for a block from the entrance of the courthouse, and the stairs were packed with a solid wall of humanity as Shea, McGough, O'Keefe and Cleary were escorted in by Sheriff Ford and his deputies. Again they took seats and McGough greeted those about him while Shea stared straight ahead. The coroner emerged and Dr. Owens stood:

"Mr. Collins, sir, I have received a telegraph from Mr. Frank Black, who is out of the city today on his private business. He is leaving Albany as we speak and he asked if the inquest could be delayed until he can be here on the two o'clock belt line."

John Norton, Shea's appointed attorney, rose: "I object, Mr. Collins. We are ready to proceed and Mr. Black has no standing to appear in this proceeding."

"I join in the objection," said Thomas Fagan, the prosecutor. "Black has no standing, and his committee is not a party to this proceeding. We cannot hold this inquest open for anyone." The impatient crowd, too, began to object. Coroner Collins hammered his gavel and glared at Fagan. "It is not for you to decide whether we will hold the inquest open," Collins admonished him.

"Of course, I am your servant," Fagan said. "This hearing is under your control and you must exercise your discretion."

"Adjourned until a quarter past three," Collins called, rapped down the gavel and vanished.

The press, the crowd, the sheriff and the prisoners registered surprise, and Shea and the others stood and passed out of the room to the holding cell.

The proceedings reconvened at three-thirty, with Frank Black present, and the first witness, Dr. Ferguson, was called. He had performed the autopsy, and he testified that the fatal bullet weighing seventy-eight and one-half grains entered Robert Ross's head behind the right ear, that it split into four fragments upon meeting the skull, and then lodged in the brain causing instant death. The doctor observed that in attending William Ross, still laid up, the neck wound of William was quite similar to the wound that killed Robert.

John Ross was then called. He was hesitant and tentative in taking the stand, but once Fagan established a rhythm to the questions, he held the courtroom spellbound, the only noise was the scratching of reporters' pencils.

"Could you tell us about the so-called 'revolver caucus,' Mr. Ross?"

"Objection," Norton called, rising. "The scope of this hearing is to determine whether Robert Ross met his death by criminal means. What relevance can any encounter a month before have to such issue?"

"Overruled. Proceed."

"Exception." Norton sat down slowly.

"I was present at the Republican caucus early in February, a Saturday afternoon," John Ross said. "McGough was chairman of the caucus . . ."

"The Republican caucus?" Fagan asked.

"Yeah, he enrolled as a Republican and then got some committeemen to appoint him chairman. We objected strongly. Anyways, a fight broke out when we noticed a hand coming through the window from outside with illegal votes. McGough drew his revolver, struck John Boland on the bridge of the nose, and pointed it full into my brother Robert's face and threatened to shoot him."

"And what, if anything, did you do?"

"I grabbed McGough's hand and forced him back, and as we were subduing him I heard the breaking of glass. Looking around I saw a man, who they told me was Bat Shea, entering the room through the broken window. I couldn't see his face. He drew his revolver, held it at George Cooley's head and demanded the ballot box be handed over or he would shoot the son of a bitch." Ross was becoming agitated. Seeing this, Black stood:

"Would you care to take a moment to compose yourself Mr. Ross?" Black asked sympathetically. All eyes were upon him since he had no authority to speak, then all turned to the coroner who instructed the bailiff to get Ross a glass of water.

"No, sir. I wish to get this out and have this matter resolved."

Ross continued testifying to Fagan's questions: "Well, as you could expect, tempers ran high for a month all through the ward, the Dunlop people threatening to steal the election . . ."

"Objection!" Norton called.

"Overruled."

"Then at the polls March 6, a crowd of them came over. When Hayner challenged them, McGough drew his gun and shot my brother William."

"Objection!"

"Overruled."

"Robert caught McGough in the middle of Orr Street, wrestled with him; McGough shot at Robert's face and Robert's hat spun into the air; McGough then broke free; Robert chased McGough down into the dump, tackled him and beat him with a club."

"And what, if anything, happened then?"

John's voice fell into a whisper. The assembled leaned forward on their pew benches. "Robert arose and climbed out of the ditch. Robert had his hand up in the air and a man behind him was firing into the air. Then Robert fell." There was an intake of breath. John Ross paused for effect.

"And was his falling like a man who has been wounded?"

"Objection!" Norton was on his feet. "That calls for a conclusion."

"Overruled. You may answer."

"No, sir."

"Please explain."

"Robert had suffered a badly sprained ankle. When he fell, it was as though the ankle had given way, and he pitched forward. As soon as he had done so, this Shea," Ross pointed at Shea across the room, "ran up behind him and shot him in the back of the neck, then continuing to run, shot again at the front of Robert. I rushed to my brother, and held his head in my arms, and I called to the others, 'If there is an American citizen here, catch that man.'"

"Now where was John Boland at this time?"

"Boland was the first to reach me, and I cried out that he should catch the murderer if possible. I heard a woman shout, 'There he goes, through that gangway.'"

Seated close to the railing that separated the gallery from the suspects, Bat Shea was dressed in a black suit with a white silk scarf. As he heard Ross, he slowly shook his head. He kept his left hand to his chin, listening to the testimony, and his eyes glittered with cold disdain. McGough seemed agitated and kept turning to his aunt and his sisters to agree or disagree with each assertion.

Back through the dark streets they paraded at six. The lamplighter was making his rounds, and he paused with his mutt on the curbstone. Boland, Shea and McGough, the suspects, were handcuffed. Cleary and O'Keefe, material witnesses, were allowed to walk freely.

Up through the dank jail the prisoners climbed to a cell on the top floor. The deputy then unlocked the handcuffs.

"Been quite a day, eh, boys? Your supper'll be here straightaway." And he shuffled out of the cell.

"I can't believe the lying of that Ross," Shea said through clenched teeth. At last he might talk freely with Boland in a cell on the floor below. "They're trying to nail me, Jack, and they're using perjury. Way I remember was, you called for help and as I started over, Boland was firing across the yard and Ross suddenly come up from the ditch. I fired at Boland as Ross grabbed for me and then Ross went down. When

I saw Ross off of you, I lit out of there. And all that nonsense about them running after me. They all chased you, Jack, not me. I went on unmolested till them sons of bitches came by Dunlop's as my wound was being dressed. Jack, you see anything different? You got to think. You got to remember."

McGough's eyes held a faraway look: "I seen Boland running up, I seen the fire leap out of his pistol, and then Ross crumpled down. I ran for my life with them all on my tail."

"Don't you see, Jack? They're lying. It's all lies! I might be many things, but I ain't a liar. I got some honor left. Don't they? Who are these men? Why are they trying to bring me down? What am I to them? What have I ever been to them?" Shea was working himself into a state, and he wheeled on McGough. "Jack, you gotta remember, you didn't shoot Robert Ross, did you?"

"No, Bat, I didn't. I swear on my poor ma's grave. Not that I didn't want to, but when he was clubbing me, I dropped my gun, and I couldn't find it getting up amongst the briars and ashes. I just lit out of there. I know you didn't kill him too, 'cause you was in front of him, not behind. I'm telling you, it was John Boland. He was running up behind and he was firing at you. When Ross poked up from the gully, he caught a stray bullet."

"But John Ross said he saw me reach down and fire into his brother's neck! And if there's others that says the same thing, I'm a dead man."

"There'll be contradictions plenty, Bat."

"I can't believe these holier-than-thou-blackhearted Protestant bastards are lying under oath, Jack." His voice rose and he was pounding on the bedstead. "They can't succeed. And all that stuff and nonsense about the caucus." There was a sound in the hallway outside.

"Relax, Bat, here's our supper. The boss has been pretty quiet so far, but I'll bet he has a surprise or two awaiting."

"Yeah, his surprise is throwing me to the wolves so he can live to fight another day. No one in politics has clean hands, Jack. And the ones that get to the top are the worst of all." McGough took a lid off the steaming plate. "Boiled beef and spuds, Bat."

"Naw, I ain't hungry. Give us a smoke, will you?"

The coroner's jury contained William Armstrong, a man who had been in the polling booth when Shea's repeaters tried to use his name, and also Augustus Paul who told the police he'd seen the gang threatening to "do them." An editorial observed of the prosecution and Black's committee, "These brandishing tomahawks will go for but little if they fail to show any scalps."

Day after day the inquest ground on, witness after witness telling an identical story: Ross chased McGough after McGough shot William; Ross fell upon McGough, then rose off of him to confront Shea; Ross fell, slumped forward, then Shea circled behind him and shot him in the back of the head. The stories were so identical, Norton argued to the jury, they were contrived. As it came out on cross examination, most of the witnesses had been to Frank Black's office to discuss their testimony.

"Your honor, it is highly irregular to have a private party interviewing prosecution witnesses. I object to their testimony."

"Oh, come now, Mr. Norton. This is just an inquest. Your client has not even been indicted."

"Well, then, why can't he post a bond and be released?"

"Take that up with the Assistant District Attorney."

Norton rolled his eyes at Shea.

But for minor imperfections, the stories harmonized perfectly. Not only had most of the witnesses been schooled by Black, but when Osborne Lansing took the stand Friday afternoon, he was the eighth witness to admit membership in the APA.

"Have you ever heard of the American Protective Association?" Norton advanced upon him.

"I might have."

"You must answer yes or no," the coroner instructed.

"I don't remember."

"Are you in fact a member of the APA?"

"Uh, . . . no." Lansing shot an imploring look toward Frank Black. Black was instantly on his feet.

"I object to Mr. Norton's question. He is dogging these witnesses about their membership in a secret fraternity and it has no bearing on this case. Mr. John Ross is a Mason, is that relevant? Thomas Lee who just testified is in both the APA and the Odd Fellows. Mr. Fagan here is a member of the Knights of Columbus . . ."

"Your honor," Norton turned, "I object to Mr. Black's presence at this inquest. He is not with the defense and he has not joined the prosecution. He purports to represent a self-declared Committee of Public Safety that cannot be recognized under our law, and he is hampering our investigation. I am trying to show that stemming from their membership in the society, these witnesses have all been coached by Mr. Black to give the same version of the facts."

Thomas Fagan sprang up. "You accuse Mr. Black of coaching

these witnesses? There has been no coaching. Where a man's life is at stake there can be no coaching."

"Well, what in blazes is Black doing here? He is here to see his pupils remember their lines." Norton was dramatically pointing at Black who placed his palms upon the table and leaned forward.

"You have made an accusation against me, Mr. Norton, of tampering with evidence," Black said softly. "I must now remain to answer your outlandish accusations."

"Your honor," Norton implored, "Frank Black is not on trial here. His committee is not on trial here. The only issue before this inquest is whether Robert Ross was killed by criminal means."

Coroner Collins nodded. "That is true, counsellor, but I have allowed Mr. Black to sit here pending the announcement of who will prosecute the case when it comes to trial." Shea looked on impassively as Norton raised his hands in exasperation. "As far as your questions about the APA," Collins conceded, "you may continue so long as you don't require a witness to divulge secret rites or oaths."

Norton turned once more to the witness: "So, Mr. Lansing, you are not a member of the APA?"

"No, sir, not in this city."

"Are you a member elsewhere?"

"In Lansingburgh."

"I see. And when you became a member, did you ride on a goat and recite an oath?"

"I might have. I don't remember."

"And did that oath pledge you to keep Catholics out of jobs and persecute them wherever and whenever you could?"

"It might have. I don't remember."

"Isn't it true that the APA is bitterly opposed to the Roman Catholic Church?"

"It might be, sir, I really don't know that."

"Your honor," Fagan rose, "I can't see this line of questioning bearing any fruit. Mr. Norton is trying to shield his client behind the robes of the Catholic Church, of which I am a member, and he is deliberatey slurring this investigation with innuendo that Bat Shea is the victim of a political and religious conspiracy."

"Objection sustained."

"Am I to understand that no questions about the APA will be allowed?" asked Norton.

"That's correct," Collins said. "They are immaterial."

"No further questions."

16.

WEARING O' THE GREEN

Troy Stove Foundry Workers

The following Saturday was St. Patrick's Day. Legend held that good St. Patrick drove Ireland's snakes into the sea. Yet in their adopted land the Irish found America still had its snake: "Don't Tread on Me!" and occasionally it was roused from slumber and slithered forth with forked tongue and deadly fangs, and no chant or prayer could exorcise its serpent's hunger. Only an offering, a beast that it could slowly digest, appeased the American snake so it would crawl back into its lair to sleep for another generation.

The St. Patrick's celebration in Troy was dampened this year, and the weather did not cooperate. A parade was planned, but then cancelled when the grand marshall, Hon. Edward J. Murphy, Jr., was compelled to march with the Tammany boys in New York. In the precinct houses Friday night, in the Irish fire companies, in the rectories and church halls and the union temples, hundreds of men huddled this year, men who customarily saw this beginning of spring as an opportunity to get drunk, overeat, play music, then crawl home with a hangover to thank the little woman for nursing them back to normalcy. St. Patrick's Day plans were subdued this year in the backlash rising. Why rouse the snake?

Leaflets found their way into Troy and were posted on the shops at night, left in mailboxes and in tenement foyers, leaflets of the APA:

The Romish population furnishes the kind of material with which the ward politician delights to reckon. The Old World has unloaded upon us its paupers, criminals, illiteracy and Romanism, including its Jesuits.

Can a Roman Catholic be a good citizen of America?

How much longer will this flagrant violation of citizenship be permitted in America? Romanism is a political system, and as a political power it must be met. No ballot for the man who takes his politics from the Vatican!

In America today we have ten thousand American women shut up in convents and nunneries of the Roman Catholic church. They are white female slaves in this land of freedom. They are victims of a lecherous priesthood, a carnal class of so-called celibates who retreat under the garb of sanctity to conceal their debasing work.

How long will the six or seven thousand stall-fed priests of Rome in this country be allowed to travel up and down the United States of America recruiting American daughters for these retreats of priestly lust and religious mockery? Shall the great mother of harlots multiply her harlotry?

As if to reinforce this papering of the city with APA leaflets, the swollen gray clouds sent a soft blanket of snow to obscure the green grass and the shamrocks.

In her shawl, Mamie Halligan moved quietly through the snowy streets, a basket under her arm. Her brother Tom had a union meeting tonight. A contentious power struggle for control of union funds was brewing in the wake of the murder, and her da had fallen asleep with the newspaper in his lap, the checkerboard at his side. To perform a corporal work of mercy, yes, but more importantly to learn any news about her Bartholomew, she bought two bottles of porter at Shanahan's Grocery and stole over to River Street to visit the Sheas.

"Come in with you, come in, Mamie, darlin'. Ah, 'tis a sad night for the wearin' o' the green, ain't it now?" Mary Shea helped her out of her coat and shawl, shook off the snow and hung the garments near the kitchen stove.

"I brung the squire a couple of bottles of porter to drink the good saint's health."

"'Twas kind o' you, girl," Mary took the bottles, uncorked them and poured out three tumblers of the dark porter. She removed a loaf of soda bread from the bread basket, cut slices and dished up cold ham and butter. "Come in with you, and see the gent himself, Mamie."

The light was low in the living room and a slender man under a plaid blanket in a chair was gazing out the window.

"Pa? You awake, Pa?"

"Aye, Mary, unfortunately so."

Mamie set down the tray. "I've come with a drink for the holiday." She clasped his hand. "How're you feeling, sir?"

"Ach, horrible, horrible. But no use to grumble and scowl. It won't set my boy free." Bartholomew Shea, Sr., was forty-eight but looked sixty. "It was kind of you to come, girl. Sit ya down." He took a pull of the warm porter. "'Tis good, Mamie, and I thank you. Mary, this here leaflet come and I've had Timmy reading it to me. Not to alarm ya, but this is quite a pack o' bigots poor Bat's up against. Shootin's too good fer the likes of them that'd circulate such trash."

"Now that talk's dangerous, Bartholomew!" Mary said.

"Tom dashed out of the house to a union meeting," Mamie said. "Appears the circular's got union men all lathered up and there's a bickering between the hardliners and the softliners, Tom being one of the latter."

"There's an awful heap o' hate circulating, t' be sure. I'm alarmed that my boy will bear the brunt of it all."

In the past ten days the elder Shea had changed his thinking toward his son. During Bat's adolescence, battles royal waged between the two, expulsion from home was frequent, Bat's friends condemned as "low companions." But now that Bat was in the forefront of a class struggle, there was a certain respect tendered from father to son.

Looking out at the snow in the glow of the coal fire, the three reminisced of past St. Patrick's days, the carefree, drunken celebrations, the brawls when Orangemen opposed the Irish coming north of Canal Street toward city hall, then the mellow evenings with a quartet at the church hall, harp, violin, elbow pipes and *bodhran*, with a scent of spring in the air, flowergirls on the street corner with early daffodils, and young men walking with young ladies.

"Ah, it ain't the same this year, is it? And p'rhaps will never be again," and Weary Shea sighed a long and weary sigh. "But here's to old Saint Patrick," he raised his glass, "may he cast out the vipers from men's hearts."

The saloons were filled with disappointed Irishmen. Strangers in this land, first and second and third generation Irish have clung to their traditions, their faith and the wearing o' the green on St. Patrick's Day. Earning the lowest wages, they've dug deeply into their pockets to build churches: St. Joseph's in South Troy; St. Peter's and St. Patrick's north of the city; and up on the hill St. Francis de Sales and the new St. Paul the Apostle. They celebrate their heritage with songs, jigs, reels and drinking this day. And now to be deprived! The bottled resentments are pressing up and out. In the streets there are ragged shouts, occasionally a trash can rolls on the cobbles, the sound of glass breaking as APA pamphlets are answered with bricks through Protestant windows.

Father John Swift sipped a dram of whiskey for the holiday in St. Patrick's rectory, but he did not feel festive. As pastor to the flock that includes the Dunlop, Cleary, Shea, McGough and McClure families, much talk has reached his ears about the murder. The case cuts deeply into the fabric, the muscle and bone of his community. Yet until today it was a general feeling of unrest. Today he is in a spiritual quandary, for today a penitent has whispered in the confessional that lies were told to hide the murderer, and to place the blame on Bat Shea. The insidious whisper is still in his ear.

"They are lying, Father."

"Were you present at the riot?"

"No."

"Did you see the shooting?"

"No."

"Then how do you know they are lying?"

"Because I learned the truth immediately afterward."

"How did you learn the truth?"

"From the man who pulled the trigger."

"You have a duty to come forward."

"I cannot, Father. And, and it should be obvious why."

"But you must. Withholding this information is a grave sin, made even worse if it results in a false accusation or a false conviction."

"The man was boasting. Perhaps he did not do it."

"Then the accusations against Shea would be true?"

"No. I know that Bartholomew Shea did not kill Ross."

"How do you know?"

"I know." A long silence.

"Then you must come forward with this as well."

"I cannot, Father, and you know why." There was a long sigh. "Please, please forgive me."

"I am sorry, but I must withhold absolution until . . ."

There was a scraping sound, and the penitent was gone. Father Swift was left alone in the dark to ponder, as he listened through the remainder of the afternoon to the whispered litanies of gluttony, sloth, gossipmongering, petty theft, drunkenness, calumny, fornication, disrespect to parents, missed Mass, adultery, the two forms of coveting, masturbation, lies of all degrees.

Today, St. Patrick's Day, an APA leaflet was deposited in the rectory mail slot, and he read it in dismay. Minds twisted with hate and fear could invent lies surpassing the imagination of the darkest poets and heretics. And so he sat, alone, sipping his whiskey, gazing at the crucifix, marvelling at the sacrifice of God in sending His only begotten Son to die on the cross. Innocent death on the cross seemed different after today's aborted confession. Father Swift knows the penitent's voice and believes he knows who he is shielding.

Downtown, Frank Black took no holiday. Even though a Saturday, he had been interviewing witnesses since the inquest adjourned at two. One matter kept surfacing: the murderer wore a green tie.

"And did you perceive that the man you saw fire at Robert Ross wore anything extraordinary, Mr. Dodds?"

"No, sir. Cap, I think."

"A derby, perhaps?"

"Naw, a cap I'm pretty sure."

"Well, there has been testimony that Shea was wearing a derby, sir."

"Hmmm! Let me think. Now that I have time to consider it, could have been a derby. Yes, I believe it was."

"Anything else?"

"No overcoat. A short coat, a sack coat."

"How about a tie?"

"Green tie, I think. Yes. A large green tie. The tie was rather prominent."

"Loosely tied or four-in-hand?"

"Four-in-hand with the ends tucked into his vest."

"Now, you're quite certain of that?"

"Absolutely. The man who pulled the trigger wore a wide green tie."

"Good, Mr. Dodds. Now, let's discuss where you were when you observed the shooting. I have marked on this map the position of other witnesses when they saw the shots. Can you with accuracy point to where you were?"

"Well, I was here when the riot broke out, and I run back inside so's not to get shot."

"We are asking from what vantage point you observed Robert Ross being shot."

"Hmmmm! Must'a been hereabouts. Yep, right around here."

"So you did not go inside?"

"Yes, I did. But I ran along here, and I just happened to look over and I witnessed the murder, then I ducked inside."

"Very good, Mr. Dodds. Yes. It won't be much longer. We're nearly done." Black was jotting notes upon a legal pad. A copy of the APA flyer lay open on the table.

17.
MEN OF THE WORLD

Governor Roswell P. Flower

Early on the sabbath, Senator Edward Murphy slipped into Albany by train for a conference with Governor Flower. They met in a private sitting room at the elegant Delahanty Hotel, and they came alone. After a breakfast of coffee, melon, kippers, fried potatoes, eggs, biscuits and great helpings of small talk about Tammany's showing in yesterday's New York parade, they fired up cigars and settled back.

"You've had your problems of late, Murph."

"Ah, this business up in Troy," Murphy shook his head with a bewildered sense of humor, "them damned reformers howling for my blood. I hear they've come down badgering you no end. You're playing it right, a very good play so far."

From long experience Murphy knew it was best to lead with flattery to see from whence the wind blew. Flower had called this conference, and it could be major or it could be trivial, there was no telling with him.

"Keeping Frank Black and his committee off your tail is like trying to keep a stallion off a ripe mare. We been through a lot, Murph, ain't we? Together? Ups and downs, aiming high as the presidency. I wouldn't be straight with you if I told you there ain't been some talk."

"Talk. Talk. Talk. Everyone shooting their mouths off. Talk is cheap. No one gets rich but the newspapers. No one does anything anymore, Roz, it's just talk." Murphy was back-paddling and beginning to feel warm around the collar. The cigar tasted like a burning rope. The preliminaries were ominous and he wanted time to anticipate where Flower was heading.

"It's not loose talk, neither, Murph. Some of our money people, our biggest money people are concerned."

"I'm concerned, too. Who more than me? What do they propose? I'm always willing to listen to reason."

Governor Roswell Flower laughed a deep belly laugh. He was like a North Country bull, thick neck, broad shoulders and barrel chest, and just as fierce and just as stubborn. "Yeah, sure, you listen to reason, then do as you damned well please." They had a good laugh on that, and Murphy basked for a moment in his tough-boss reputation, the absolute despot who ran the small manufacturing city upriver.

Flower, a farm boy from Watertown, near the banks of Lake Ontario, prided himself on his horse sense, his rural metaphors and his identity as a self-made man. He never mentioned that his brother-in-law died suddenly leaving him a vast fortune to manage to which his own prosperity was engrafted. Flower was also a Presbyterian, and although a Democrat, he sympathized with white Anglo-Saxon Protestants squeezed from power in the last two decades by swarms of the unwashed Catholic poor. Republicans had no monopoly on bigotry.

"Well, some of the Tammany people, too, they want to take the heat off of you. Let's face it, Murph, you're a target now, and they came to me, asked me to have a talk with you."

"A talk? So talk." Murphy cleared his throat and stabbed out his cigar.

"There's great concern that this election fraud business is going to hurt us immeasurably statewide, Murph. The top brass thought it might be better if we go into the November elections with a new state chairman."

From decades of tough negotiating Murphy had developed a poker face, and no matter how bad or shocking things got, he was able to keep his poise, an even voice and a steady eye. This came as close as anything to staggering him. "What?" His eyes narrowed and a red flush stole up from his collar.

"It's just talk at this time," Flower tossed off Murphy's concern.

"Talk."

"Another cigar?" Flower offered his leather case.

"No. No, thank you."

"These folks are really looking out for your own good, Murph. This APA business, this trial up in Troy. It's bad. I can't ever recall seeing it this bad. Now, you're a man of the world, Ed. You know how quickly power whipsaws. This thing threatens to destroy you and the state ticket along with you. If we could just cut down the size of the target painted on your back . . ."

"The target's painted a bit lower, I'd say."

". . . we might lessen the damage considerably. You could certainly keep your senate seat, just give up the bother, all the details of running the state party."

"Well, I see a major flaw here, Roz, right off the top of my head. You're asking me to admit defeat, to relinquish the chairmanship with no judge nor jury, no hearing nor determination, only the say-so of a gaggle of rabble-rousing, blackhearted Protestant sons of bitches."

"Blackhearted Protestants," Flower repeated.

Murphy stared at Flower, the state's top Presbyterian. His neck and face were a brilliant red now. He had botched that one, even though it was bigotry for bigotry. It was hard arguing with an old friend, not because of loyalty or delicacy, but because you both knew better how to wound.

"I can't do it, Roz. I can't resign. Everything in my nature runs counter to that. I'm fighting Irish. I did nothing wrong, and I shan't pay for the mistakes of others."

"That's not the way they see it at Tammany."

"Well, we have a time-honored saying in the sacred halls of the United States Senate, Governor Flower: *Pogue Mahone*."

Flower saw it was the time to back away and approach from another angle. "Yes. Well, I just mention this, Murph, and I hope you'll consider. There's no malice, or ill will. But the Tammany people did indicate that there could very well be a floor fight when the delegation meets in July. The consensus is just informal at this time."

Murphy scowled and his cheeks trembled. "The consensus? You mean they've polled each other on this?" Flower could feel the full heat of his wrath. "They sent you to threaten me, Roz?"

"Murph. Murph. Murph. You have to get the statewide perspective here. This, uh, this situation is very bad. It could cost us the statehouse and our comfortable majorities in the senate and assembly."

"Oh, come on! Don't you think a few people are overreacting to what is clear vigilantism? This is absurd. To think that a ward election up in Troy could be perceived as having statewide implications."

"It reaches far higher than Troy, Ed, and we both know it. Now, we're both old pros at this game, and we've both done rather well by it. Let someone else run the state party. You don't need the headaches. Keep Troy to yourself, but give back the rest of the state. Cut your losses now. Throw whoever you must to the barking wolves and let's get cracking on November's election."

Murphy had regained his composure, but the purple hue to his neck had not drained. "Well, I will certainly consider what you've said. Tammany does not speak idly."

"Trust me, Ed. It'll be for the best."

"I was wondering, Roswell, how you were planning to take care of Black."

"Hmmm?"

"Frank Black. You must neutralize him. He is turning this situation to immense political advantage. Have you hit upon anything to neutralize him?"

Flower rubbed his chin in deep thought. "I've maintained my distance. A very delicate situation. Black has painted me with the same brush, and the newspapers in Troy are howling. I don't need that sentiment to spread. Crossing him would not be wise at this moment. Like the man said when they fetched the rail after the tarring and feathering, 'If it weren't for the honor of the thing, I think I'd rather walk.'"

Murphy smiled, but in truth he found Flower's North Country humor irksome. "I'm down in Washington, Roz, slugging it out with Georgia, Louisiana, the Carolinas over the collar and cuff tariff. It's their cotton going off to Britain to make the collars and cuffs, and they'll be goddamned if they'll support a tariff on the goods coming back. The labor unions are jacking the prices higher here at home, and it's a monumental mess. Consequently, I have no time to crush this upstart Black just now. We must cover each other's backs, right?"

"You know I'd do anything in my power for you, Ed. This fellow Fagan, is he all right?"

"I think he's spirited, wants his own head. Not a loyal party man, if that's what you mean."

"Well, let him dance independently. Either way you win. I granted them a special term of Oyer and Terminer. Half a loaf. Let them chew on that till the crust hardens. I'm thinking about the judge now. I have a friend in Watertown, Pardon Williams. Hell of a nice guy. I think he's in the APA, too. All the right credentials. Black and his people will love old Pardon." Flower chuckled. "And don't let the first name fool you. He's a blackhearted Protestant, too." Flower shook his head. "I have another recommendation, Ed."

"Another one?" This taxed the facial control of the great negotiator. "Always willing to listen."

"Cut your losses. Give them Barabbas, or whoever else they're clamoring for. Have they indicted yet?"

"No. Coroner's inquest is still underway."

"Whoever they accuse, cut him loose. Once the mob in Troy tastes a little blood, it will ease up and your people will learn not to bungle things. A doubly useful lesson."

"Make 'em feel the sting of the lash, eh?"

"Exactly."

These men of the world looked at each other, then Flower reached over and touched Murphy on the hand. "Step down from state committee. Then ram the tariff through to buy off your locals, those collar and cuff people. You can get back into state committee in a year or two before you need to run again."

"And you? What are you doing for me, Roz?"

"Besides showing you the wise way out of the swamp? I'm keeping the attorney general out of it. He wants to jump in and make a name for himself. He sees it as the way to get my job. Let the locals take care of their own problems, is my philosophy. Pardon Williams is a good judge, a tough judge. If they get a conviction and an execution, so be it. If not, well, they're inept. Either way, if we stay out of it and let it run its course, there won't be any fingers pointing at us."

"So we leave things where they are?"

"I know it's difficult for an old Troy alley fighter like you, Ed. But it must be done. This battle won't be fought in the alley, it'll be fought in the courthouse, in full view of everyone. And you can only lose if you get involved."

Murphy was nodding. The suggestion he give up the state Democratic Party directorship hit him hard, quieted him, sobered him. He could fight Tammany. He could fight Black. He could fight one of them or both of them or neither of them. He saw that he could not fight them both at once, and that he lost something anyway it went. It was better to choose what he was to lose and voluntarily give it up rather than allow a victorious enemy to strip him of an office or preferment.

That afternoon Senator Edward J. Murphy, Jr., met with his minions at Albany's state party headquarters, visited a supreme court justice who was seeking a federal appointment for his son, and dined with the majority leader of the state senate. All through the day he was haunted by the thought that his own power was slipping away, and these others were on their way up. Governor was to be his next bid, after Flower retired to Watertown, and from there, with a base built and expanded like Grover Cleveland, the presidency. This "whipsaw" as Flower called it infuriated him. He returned to his hotel in a foul mood.

He ordered a bottle of bonded whiskey then, and Senator Edward J. Murphy, Jr., formerly the most powerful Democrat in New York State, sat in his window gazing up at the unfinished capitol on the hill, drinking straight from the bottle as his father used to. It seemed to taste better this way tonight. It felt good to tie one on the old fashioned way, alone, anonymous in Albany. Yet in the long dark hours, the liquor took hold and Murphy descended down a long staircase toward oblivion, and when the whistle of the steamboat Cornelius Vanderbilt bellowed at midnight out upon the gleaming river, it sounded much like the grieving of his heart. The utter loss hit him hard in the stomach, sobs welled up, and this man of the world wept as he had not done for many years.

18.
A VERDICT

John H. Boland

Gavin and Fitzsimmons, ledger clerks at the Excelsior Brewery, watched with a sense of doom as a closed cab pulled up at the brewery office door Monday morning and Boss Murphy alighted. He was dressed in a greatcoat, top hat and spats with his silver headed walking stick, the very picture of elegance. As he entered, though, the gruff "Morning!" and his barked orders to get him the mayor and the district attorney in person in his office within half an hour, indicated something was very wrong.

Francis Molloy was not difficult to find. He luxuriated all day in his city hall office newly decorated at taxpayer expense. Molloy was enjoying his first cup of coffee and the morning paper, the bells tolling ten o'clock, when the two boys swept past his secretary like a strong wind and swirled him away. It was clear to the whisperers at city hall that someone was to pay for something.

Nor was Kelly difficult to find. He took his morning coffee with a shot of brandy at Doolan's Chophouse across from Keenan's horse room on Third Street. The clerks and Molloy swept him up as well, and were soon together in a gig trotting up Ferry Street to the massive fortress of blackened brick.

Gavin and Fitz went back to their ledgers, but they could hear the Boss ranting and raving within. "If they don't hang 'em, I will!" rose on the still air. "Throw them over, cut 'em loose! They'll pay dearly for crossing me! Dunlop too!" Gavin and Fitz occasionally rolled their eyes at each other. After a stormy hour, the mayor and district attorney emerged. The mayor was ashen white and the district attorney a florid red. Both walked dejectedly.

"Now, you talk to Dunlop, Frank!" the boss hurled after them, "And, John, you talk to Fagan! I want you back in this office by four." The two high officials looked at each other like scolded schoolboys. Again the door slammed, and the ledger clerks returned to entering figures, awaiting the next flurry of blame and retribution.

In his office, Murphy scanned the papers. Reporters from many places were attending the coroner's inquest: Brooklyn; Hartford; St. Albans, Vt.; Utica; Syracuse; Philadelphia; Chicago; Plattsburgh. From the *New York Tribune* there came a conjecture:

"The ease and apparent coolness with which Shea and McGough have taken their arrest and the indifference with which they have listened to the testimony have caused everyone to fear there is some plot afoot through which justice will be defeated. The case now seems to be as plain as ever a case was. There is no fear as to what the verdict of the coroner's jury will be, nor is there fear as to what the verdict of a trial jury will be. Between the two stands a grand jury, and in Rensselaer County grand juries are drawn in a manner which is a disgrace to the county and to the state."

"We'll correct that today," Murphy muttered, then Saturday's editorial in the *Troy Times* caught his eye:

"Yes, God's truth is marching on and the spirit of the martyred Robert Ross is abroad among us. Steadily the facts are coming out and the atmosphere is clearing with the remorselessness and majestic certainty of fate. The punishment of the guilty is approaching and the downfall of the machine drawing nigh. For the excesses and infamies of that machine one man is politically responsible for he made it, upheld it, and in all things it was his obedient, obsequious, fawning creature. The machine was made by Edward Murphy, Jr., and no one having intelligence to form an opinion will question that it was owned and controlled by him body and soul, if a thing so monstrous can be said to have a soul."

"Goddamned whore's rag!" Murphy balled up the paper and hurled it in the wastebasket. He walked to the window that looked down Ferry Street toward the river. Whiskey could cure only so much. The hangover had been steamed away by a barber's hot towels, and he was clipped and shaved and starched and pressed to perfection. Yet the inner man was in despair, for he felt his power slipping under a billowing, ink-black cloud of disgrace. He was infamous! Infamous! The builder of city hall! The paver of Troy's streets! Banker to industrialists! Director of corporations! These ingrates! Resign his directorship of the state Democratic Committee! Never!

"I made Flower," he murmured. "That hayseed knew nothing of conventions or caucuses or ward politics. I introduced him to Tilden and Van Buren! I masterminded his run against Astor! And this is his gratitude! Oh!" Murphy gripped the back of a chair and growled. "These ingrates! They came to me, all of them, on their knees, kissing my hand, imploring me for help and guidance. How they despised me even then! Now they desert me in my time of need. And I cannot make them feel the sting of my wrath!" He held his hands out, and he looked down at his fingers. "How hard it is to seize, how long it takes to build, yet how easily it slips away! Even now I feel it slipping through my fingers! And I am powerless to hold on." The senator gently clenched and pounded his fists on the back of the chair. "And yet I will punish those who have disgraced me. I will cut them from me like a diseased limb. I will whip my kingdom into order and I will live to fight again! That is all I can do. That is all I can do."

Later that morning, all the suspects were escorted to the inquest in shackles and leg irons. Rumors of escape plans circulated as testimony accumulated. Yet others winked. This was the beginning of Murphy's "payback" to humiliate the boys publicly.

John Boland, darling of the APA, sported a yellow jonquil bouquet at his lapel to freshen the air, and he seemed cheery. Boland smiled and nodded affably to the reporters. He did not look like a man suspected of manslaughter.

To dispel all suspicion, Boland took the stand Monday and testified he carried a thirty-two calibre Smith & Wesson self-acting revolver loaded with blank cartridges. None of the cartridges in the revolver he surrendered had been exploded. Yet even John Ross testified that Boland fired his gun. A revolver had been recovered from the ditch, a thirty-two calibre American Bulldog loaded with five cartridges, two unexploded. The bullets in the American Bulldog weighed eighty grains. The bullet fragments recovered from inside Robert Ross's skull weighed nearly that, and were undoubtedly a thirty-two calibre. Speculation ran high which was the murder weapon.

Meanwhile, Molloy and Kelly returned to the brewery at four to meet with Murphy.

"You got the word out?" he asked from behind his large desk.

"Yes, sir, Senator," the mayor stated, and he gave details how the organization was backing away from Shea and McGough. "Dunlop weren't too pleased. Said he wouldn't be where he is without them boys."

"Dunlop can kiss my royal Irish arse in Franklin Square. Neither would we. And you, John?"

Kelly was obviously drunk. "Tom Fagan's a good lad. Needs little direction 's all. I tol' him. He'll be all right . . . all right. I tol' him."

Murphy grew impatient. "Now can I return to Washington with the assurance that things won't further deteriorate?"

"Yes, sir."

"Yes, sir."

"I want it understood by you and by all the others, that I am more loyal to mine than any man I know. I will back my people all the way down the line. But when there's one that crosses me, well, he's turned his back on me. Whomever this coroner's jury names, and it looks like Shea, will be delivered up like a trussed pig. Give the APAs back Boland, and throw Shea to the dogs."

"Yes, sir."

"Yes, sir."

Coroner Collins gave the case to the jury at four-thirty the next afternoon with this instruction: "The only question you must determine is how, when and where Robert Ross came to his death."

The jury was back within an hour: "The jury finds that Robert Ross came to his death on the sixth day of March in the third district of the thirteenth ward from the effects of a gunshot wound from a revolver held in the hands of Bartholomew Shea."

"Objection!" Norton cried, leaping up. "That is not a proper verdict. This is not an accusatory proceeding. Accusing a person far exceeds the scope of this hearing."

"Overruled. Verdict accepted."

The gallery exploded, and the hand clapping was long and sustained while Collins hammered the gavel calling for order. Shea sat impassively, his arms folded. John Boland was standing, shaking hands with well-wishers from the audience.

"Thank you, gentlemen, for your attention to this matter," Coroner Collins addressed the jury. "I think your verdict will meet public approval." He rapped his gavel. "This inquest is concluded."

Being nearly the equinox, the lamplighter did not make his rounds until half-five. Fog mingling with the coal exhalations of a thousand chimneys hung in a filthy cloud over Troy. The wet cobbles gleamed, and the breath of horses was steaming as they waited after a long day to be taken to the stable, when suddenly the damp quiet was pierced with the shrill cries of boys running through the streets from the courthouse:

"Shea's accused of murder!"

"Shea's the one!"

The lamplighter paused upon the street corner with his quizzical dog to watch Sheriff Ford and his men hustle Shea and McGough and Boland back to the jail, and then behind them a roaring crowd emerged from the courthouse, spilling noisily up Ferry Street into the Italian section. Someone brought torches and lit them in the murk, and the crowd paraded north into the commercial district.

"What you think'a that, Buster?" he asked the dog. "Can't wait fer our old bones t'get the lamps on." The ruddy glow of the torches lit the mansions of Second Street, and receded up toward the square where a statue of Lady Victory held her trumpet high above the telegraph wires and streetcar tracks. After the crowd was gone, a tall lean figure emerged alone, Frank Black, with his aquiline nose held high and his top hat pulled down, briefcase in hand. He walked alone down Congress Street, avoiding the crowd.

Shea had been glum and moody, pacing like a caged beast in the cell. When he heard the newsboys below, he exploded: "I didn't shoot the bastard! I didn't. They're lying through their teeth! The rotten black-hearted Protestant bastards! They're waving the flag and crying out for justice! Where is the justice for me?"

"Calm down, Bat!"

He turned furiously on McGough. "You were there, Jack!" He seized McGough by the coat and lifted him up. "You had as good an opportunity as any to see!" He shook him hard. "Who shot the son of a bitch, Jack? Who? Who? Did you, Jack? Tell me! Did you?"

"Boland shot him, Bat! Put me down for Chrissakes!"

"Boland's walking out a free man tomorrow, Jack! The jurors agree that he had blank cartridges. I weren't hit with no blank."

"Me neither, Bat. Please! Put me down!"

"Who shot Ross, Jack? Who?"

"Boland!"

Shea released McGough and sat on the lower bunk, going over it again in his mind: "I was across the yard. I was shot in the head, bleeding. I heard you screaming and I come running, Boland was running toward me firing, and just as Ross stepped up out of the ditch, I fired once or twice, I can't recall and he pitched over forward, and as I run toward the ditch, Boland hit me on the head with his club, and I turned away. Then I met O'Keefe and Delaney and George and they helped me over to the saloon. That's all I remember."

"That's how it happened, Bat." McGough was brushing off his new suit.

"Now, I know I got myself into this mess, and I don't mind paying for what I done, thrown a few punches, maybe roughed Hayner up some, forced the vote." He stood. "But I didn't kill Ross, and I ain't going to swing for it."

"This is only the coroner's inquest, Bat. Look on the bright side. They haven't even indicted you yet. Nor me, neither. Hell, they accused me of assault first. That carries a twenty-year sentence, and I ain't worried." McGough attempted a laugh. "Let 'em prove their case."

Shea was gripping the bars of the grill. Below he could hear the newsboys' refrain in the foggy street: "Shea accused of murder! Read all about it!"

"Now the boss is selling me out, Jack. If he gives me up, he'll look honest. If he resists, they'll get me anyway, and they'll get him too for opposing them. That's how he figures." Shea shook his head. "I can't believe how simple it is . . ." he slumped down on the bunk, ". . . nor how stupid I was to think it were otherwise."

The next day was warm and blue and breezy. Navigation was open and the river was full of boats — canal boats, steamboats, sailboats — carrying all manner of goods and people. Trains clattered through the tunnels, over bridges, into and out of Union Station, and green and yellow and blue streetcars trundled up and down the steep hills of Troy among the horsedrawn wagons, carrying city folk to work and shopping.

In police court that morning Bartholomew Shea stood, hands cuffed together, looking worn and anxious, his eyes glancing about at the hungry inquisitive crowd. An artist sat nearby sketching his features.

Boland was escorted into the courtroom personally by Police Superintendent Willard, and he wore in his lapel a yellow nosegay. He bowed slightly to the applause and took his seat to await release.

Fagan stood: "Your honor, this matter has been before the coroner's inquest and it has been sifted to the bottom. The coroner's jury has placed the crime on Bartholomew Shea and has therefore exonerated Mr.

Boland. I know of no further charge against Mr. Boland, and therefore there is nothing left for your honor to do except set the prisoner at liberty."

"Let it be done," the magistrate called, and a resounding cheer went up among the assembled. Boland raised his fist in the air in a gesture of triumph.

"Is Shea here?" called Magistrate Donohue. Shea stood in the prisoner's box. "Mr. Shea," Donohue spoke, and Shea looked up at the bench, "you will be held for action of the grand jury on the charge of murder in the first degree." Shea stared at the floor as all eyes turned upon him.

Down the staircase John Boland passed, and out on the street crowds of men were opening packages of miniature American flags and distributing them to the assembled. A great crowd greeted Boland's release and brawny men hoisted him onto their shoulders, carrying him to the steps of a church where he stood to address them:

"Fellow citizens, today you have seen a miracle. Could my release have occurred in the Troy of old?"

"No!" the crowd answered as one.

"Under the very noses of the party boss and his machine district attorney I have had a fair hearing, and I have been exonerated and released."

Applause.

"But are we going to stop at this?"

"No!"

"As you know, Robert Ross was a bosom friend of mine. Not in this whole city, from Lansingburgh to the Burden wheel was there a more perfect example of Christian manhood. And today, freed from unjust imprisonment, I swear to you that so long as I breathe, I will see justice done. Are we going to allow Bartholomew Shea to get away with murder?"

"No!" And the cheer was loud and sustained.

"Well, come along with me, and let's march to the thirteenth ward!" The citizens accompanying Boland on his triumphal march into the thirteenth ward took the bags of small flags, waved the small flags high into the bright spring air and passed them out along the route.

A large American flag appeared, then a drum and two horns, and half a dozen police officers as an escort, until quite a retinue was moving up Third Street, through the commercial part of town, merging with River Street and into the collar and cuff district. The drum and the horns and the bright summery weather drew people from their offices and mills. Hundreds of spindle girls in white frocks poured out of the collar and cuff factories and lined River Street cheering for the freed hero.

Crossing Middleburgh Street into the thirteenth ward, citizens came flocking from every tenement, saloon, butcher shop, stove foundry, brickyard, green grocery, barber stall, lumber bin, and even up from the docks of the riverbank to cheer that champion of freedom, John Boland. Glen Avenue, where Boland lived, was decked with red, white and blue bunting, and neighbors were on their porches to greet the man who had been marked as a victim by Murphy's machine.

Boland was free! Now, as he kissed his wife and addressed them, was the time for all good men to come to the aid of their country!

19.

WOMEN'S TEARS

Troy Music Hall

Mamie Halligan, in the white frock of a spindle girl, stood on the curbside cheering and waving a small flag someone had given her. The day was warm and sunny and it was ever so nice to be out. She knew this man who just passed had something to do with that evil election day business, and it seemed to her a good thing he was released. Perhaps Bartholomew would be out soon too, and the evenings were lengthening and soon the fair grounds at Rensselaer Park would be opening and . . .

Rosie Cullen and Mae McBride were strolling arm-in-arm back to the collar factory, and Mamie picked up Rosie's hand.

"No," Rosie said curtly, "I don't know you no more, Mamie."

Mamie laughed as at a joke. Mae didn't join her. "Nor do I," Mae said.

"What's gotten into you two? No one's played this game on me since school! Now stop it."

"Leave off, Mamie," Mae scolded. "There's word around that you're still in love with Bat Shea."

"Well, of course I am. And didn't Mr. Boland just get himself freed? It shan't be long till this whole misunderstanding is put right, and Bat'll be out . . ."

"Mae, would you tell Mamie that my ma and my da were talking last night, and they informed me that Bat Shea was the one what fired the bullet. Said so right in the paper, tell her. And now that he's been accused of the murder, he'll be convicted for sure, tell her, and it'll either be the gallows or the electric chair, which in either case I find repulsive, and he'll die in disgrace. Also tell her that I've been instructed not to discuss nothing with her no more, just to be as civil as I need to be to her and no more than that. Tell her."

"Mamie . . ." Mae began, and then she saw Mamie's face, "I'm sorry."

Mamie ran into the factory, through the banks of looms and spindles, and she sought out the Ladies Retiring Room on the third floor. The progressive partnership of millowners, Lyon, English & Blake, had installed modern porcelain flush toilets in whitewashed stalls for the girls, not the tin two-seaters as in other mills, and also a lounge with a sofa where they might come with menstrual cramps. Mamie burst into the retiring room, and with two women talking in the lounge she sought the privacy of a stall. She sat there, alone, her face burning and her ears ringing with Rosie's words.

It was a long while before her pride rallied. If loving Bartholomew as she did meant losing friends, then so be it. If those two, and others like them, refused to talk with her, why, they weren't worth the effort. And then her anger gave way to the utter humiliation and disgrace, and the sobs and the tears came uncontrollably.

Sunlight flooded this room. The window was open and a fresh spring breeze blew from the river. The breeze smelled clean and new and carried the songs of birds and the far-off whistles and bells of the riverboats and channel markers. She wept, feeling sorry for herself, wishing this had never happened, feeling sorry for the family, and wishing she were away, down the river, far away from Troy. She felt sorry for Bat, yet less sorry for him than she felt for everyone else. Hadn't she warned him? Hadn't she gone to his room three nights before election and warned him of her premonitions? And hadn't he ignored her intuition?

And yet, this line of thinking led her to the inescapable question that lurked under all lines of thinking each day. Mamie preferred not to think this one dark, evil thought, but it was there, like a snake in an orchard, and she could not rid herself of it. She struggled with clenched fists against its coming forward, but as if in a recurring dream she saw Bat lower his revolver to the scalp of Robert Ross, just as they described vividly each day in the newspaper, and there was a loud explosion and orange flame and billows of black smoke as he summarily executed the Protestant.

"Oh, no! I must believe," she murmured, the tears streaming down her face, "I must believe in him! I must!"

And with determination she dried her eyes, pulled the chain of the flush box and left the stall to go back to her spindle under the watchful eyes of the floor supervisor and all the other girls who knew and who whispered.

Mary Shea had baked her Barry's favorite apple pie, and she entered the jail with trepidation. She heard laughter down the dim brick hallway, and the cobwebs and the grime of the walls and ceiling, the smell of the place, as of men in stalls, offended her.

"There you go, mum," the turnkey spoke and the iron door squealed on its hinges as it opened and within George Dunlop, Jack McGough and Owen Judge were playing cards while her son gazed out the window grill over the city. The sash was up and despite the rusted grill, the air was fresh, blowing from the west, full of spring sunlight.

The three men sprang up and offered their condolences. "So sorry, Mary," Dunlop said, his face immediately grave and sad. Jack shrugged and Owen Judge gave her a kiss.

"Well, after police court they thrung me in a cell down the hall," Jack said. "Whyn't we head down there, boys, and let Bat here talk with his ma."

The men shuffled respectfully out, and mother and son were alone.

"I baked you a pie, Barry, an apple pie." She placed it on the barrel head.

"Thanks, Ma."

He turned and shook his head. "I'm sorry, Ma. I didn't want you coming here, seeing me like this. I wanted better. I did."

"I know."

"I wanted a job where I could put on a collar and a silk tie in the morning, and have people say, 'Mornin', Mr. Shea,' when I passed 'em." He shook his head in disgust. "Not this. Not this here."

"It'll be all right, Barry."

"Naw, I don't think so, Ma. I think it's going to get much, much worse. I hear the boss has backed everyone off'n the case, and that Mr. Black has got a whole stream of witnesses to take the stand against me."

She hung her head. "You didn't shoot that boy, did you, Bartholomew?"

He stepped to her, took up her hands in his. "No, Ma, I didn't. Now, you know I never lied to you nor Pa, and it was the cause of much friction 'tween Pa and me that I was so truthful, 'cause if he asked me where I was and what I'd been doing, I'd sure as hell tell him. So, I ain't lying now, Ma. I had a gun, that's true, and I was there, and at the time I had a murderous heart to gun them down like dogs 'cause they was opposin' us, and him, 'cause he was hurting Jack. But I got no show. I circled back, hearing Jack calling for help, Boland was firing across the yard at me and Ross clumb up outta the ditch at me, and then he just collapsed, folded right up in front of me, and John Boland ran up and clubbed me and I'd been hit in the scalp, so I just spun away till I felt faint and there was Mickey Delaney and Stan O'Keefe and then George to bear me over to the saloon."

Mary Shea nodded as he gave his account. "That's the truth, you never lied to me, Bartholomew. I often told your father that there were questions I'd never ask because I knew you'd only give me the true answers."

They embraced, and Shea looked around the room, feeling oddly comforted with his mother there. "How's Pa?"

"Miserable as ever. He won't tell you to your face, but he knows you ain't guilty, and he's mighty proud of how you stand up to them all, both their side and our'n. You keep standing up to them, for him and for me, Barry, 'cause if you ever show weakness, then you're finished."

"That's right, Ma. That's good advice."

She stepped away and turned her back. "A mother, you know, a mother always, you know," she wrung her hands, "a mother always thinks there was something she might have done different, and if she did, you know . . ."

"Look, Ma, I'm twenty-three years old. I'm a grown man. I been working these past twelve years, and I been West to the mining country and the Coast and back. There's a lot more than this here hometown in my head. It weren't nothin' you did nor didn't do. It's just a bad season is all, and we got to get through it the best we can."

They talked awhile about the neighborhood, and Mary Shea urged him to have Jack write a letter to Mamie who was worried sick and did not know if she could visit. When she left, Mary Shea promised to return soon and she turned, her handkerchief to her face, her form bent over, and shuffled down the hall.

Now Shea felt a great sob well up and lodge in his throat. He turned to the window and looked out over the tarred roofs of the city. An Italian kid across from the jail had rigged up a pigeon coop, and when the bells rang each quarter hour the pigeons flew up, whole flocks of them, circling the steeples and towers of the city, then returning to roost. The kid was on the roof now with the birds, and he was tender and skillful with them.

Then Shea heard the boys returning from down the hall, and he knew his eyes were red, and then out the window he saw his mother making her way up Fifth Avenue. "Ah, Ma," he growled, and he saw her back shaking with sobs and her bonnet down and her fist to her eyes, "I'm sorry, Ma."

Indignation fired the Protestant women. To give form to their sorrow they organized a committee and issued shares of stock for a monument fund. Each night stock sales appeared in the newspapers. Local suffragettes saw this as a platform to advance the twin causes of temperance and the woman's vote.

A great convocation was called at Music Hall. George Doring's famous Civil War military band opened the program to a capacity crowd of ladies in bonnets and bright spring frocks. Plump Mrs. Tillinghast folded her hands in the gentle limelight and gazed approvingly over the crowd.

"Sisters and daughters, a man is gone from our midst. Shall we weep? Shall we don the black weeds as did the Trojan women of yore after their citadel had toppled? Shall we raise our wailing till it echoes from the welkin that our son, our brother is gone?" She paused for effect, her eyebrows rising in the light. "No. I say, no. The time for mourning is passed. Tears, though they soothe the heart, fall sterile on the ground salting the soil with bitterness wherein flowers should grow. No, ladies, now is the time for action." She clenched her fist. Then she read a poem she had composed and announced she would have this poem embroidered upon a pillow for the Ross family. She then introduced the ancient Reverend Fairlee.

"The old idea that the state is a divine institution is obsolete," Fairlee exclaimed, his veined fist clenched. "Troy belongs to its best citizens and they shall rule!" The reverend urged that one of the busy downtown squares, Franklin Square, be renamed "Ross Square" and the monument be erected there. Wild applause met his suggestion.

Martin I. Townsend, Troy's renowned attorney, now crippled in a wheelchair, urged that sectarian and religious principles not obscure the trial of "this miserable assassin."

Mrs. Lewis Gurley, wife of a local industrialist, then took the rostrum, adjusted her lorgnette and read her composition:

"What art's for a woman? To hold on her knee
Her darlings! To feel their arms 'round her throat
Cling, strangle a little! To sew by degrees
And 'broider the long clothes and neat little coat
To dream and to dote.

"To teach them, it stings there! I made them indeed
Speak plain the word 'country.' I taught them, no doubt,
That country's a thing men should die for at need;
I prated of liberty, rights and about, the tyrants turned out.

"And when their eyes flashed! O, my beautiful eyes!
I exulted; nay, let them go forth at the wheels
Of guns, and denied not. But then the surprise
When one sits quite alone! Then one weeps, then one kneels!
O, God! How the house feels!"

Mrs. Gurley looked up in poignant silence as her words registered.

"In such desolation as this sits one woman in our city today. We are here to mingle our tears with hers. We are here because it might have been ours who fell instead of hers — if we could have had the honor to be the mothers of such sons. We are here to make our woman's protest against the infamy which made that crime possible.

"It is not yet our role, sisters and daughters, to fight the battle of righteousness in public places. But it is our privilege to make knights to know that above all things else in God's world we prize a white soul!"

Applause, honest, impassioned, cleansing applause then resounded in the Music Hall, muted only by kid gloves, and the bonnets rose as they stood in unison and a great cheer rumbled deep in the breast of the crowd and flew out upon the air.

"It is ours, women of Troy, as those Trojan women of yore, to cry out for sorrow and for shame at our fallen city. It is ours to tune the public conscience to a truer key. It is ours to love truth and worship at her shrine that those who love us will not dare look into our eyes with a stain upon their honor." Loud applause sounded as the ladies settled back into their seats.

"We would raise up a monument to Robert Ross. What form shall it take? The Ross brothers when asked what sort of monument Robert would favor answered simply, 'A pure ballot.' And this is true. But we mothers and sisters and daughters would have something tangible to remember our hero.

"The monument should be beautiful. It should be inscribed with his name and his deed. It should stand upon a thoroughfare in this city where it may forever tell his story to the passing throngs. It should somehow catch up the spirit of the fallen man and pass it on to the youths who come after him — to multiply among young men the type of Robert Ross. It shall become a rallying place for young men who, like him, fear God, love righteousness and serve their country."

Loud and sustained applause greeted her suggestion, and Doring's Band struck up a rousing version of "My Country 'Tis of Thee." Other speakers followed in the limelight, and while the speeches were filled with sorrow, they were remarkably free of blame.

Margaret Ross was indeed weeping that day, as she had every day since the murder. Of the seven children she had borne, Robert was her baby, the youngest, the most handsome, the strongest and manliest of her sons. Because he was the youngest, she had spent more time with him than with the others. He had been her favorite.

Margaret Ross had no desire to attend the rally. Knowing what must be eventually done, she retrieved all of Robert's baby things that afternoon, short pants and jackets and caps that she had been saving to give Nellie, and sorting through the mementos on the parlor floor, she wept, reliving the joy and hope she had felt, the great prospects she envisioned for this son. There had been an unmistakable nobility to Robert Ross. He possessed an air of command, a stern, unyielding will even as a child. Robert had been marked by nature for great things, for high office, for leadership, where his firm ethics and purpose would radiate high principles upon those he led. Accomplishment would mark his tenure. And this paragon of a son had been gunned down by saloon thugs. True Calvinist that she was, there was predetermination in her thinking, yet she disagreed with those who considered Robert's murder an apotheosis. He had been predestined for greater things than martyrdom.

Margaret Ross did not follow the legal haggling and the pious moralizing downtown. She had no heart for it. Hers was a private grief. She was pleased, then, when her maid announced Nellie Mae Patton. She called for a pitcher of cold water, dipped a washcloth into it and applied the compress to her red eyes. Satisfying herself in the looking glass, she went to meet the betrothed.

"Nellie, my dear, thank you for coming!" The women embraced, and Nellie lifted the black veil that she wore. "I have been going through some of Robert's things, and I have set aside some items, some treasures for you."

The matriarch slid open the closed pocket doors and ushered the younger woman into the back parlor that looked down over the river valley and the factories and tenements on the other side of the tracks. Nellie went to the window.

"I had no heart to go to Music Hall today," she spoke haltingly. "I had Fitch inquire, and when I heard you were home too, I thought I'd pay you a visit."

"Why, I am so pleased, my dear." The mother was seated on the carpet in the middle of a semicircle of items.

"I sometimes think, Mrs. Ross," Nellie bowed her head, "I sometimes think that I didn't know the man they are deifying. Surely Robert was all the things they say. Yet above all he was a man. He was to be my husband, the father of my children, my lover and partner through life. He was tender and quiet and deep thinking, and I loved him," she began to sob, "I still love him, more than I love life itself."

"So do I, my dear. So do I."

There was silence in the room as Nellie struggled for control.

"I have been trying, Mrs. Ross, to understand. I have been trying to listen and to learn and to see what all of this means. And I keep coming up empty-handed. I, I just don't know where Rob is! I look but I can't see him. I speak but I don't know if he hears. I sense he is near and that he is saved and that his example can benefit us, but I cannot be sure." She turned imploringly for comfort. "Is death a veil, Mrs. Ross, as they say it is? Tell me if you know. The ministers do not."

"Perhaps."

"You have seen others die, the babies you lost, your parents. Is death just a curtain through which we cannot see or hear or understand? Or is it simply and utterly the end, and all this talk of morality and high-thinking just the prattling of fools?"

"I don't know. No one knows. No one can know."

"I call out in the night for God Almighty to send me a sign, an answer to this, but it is dark and still and, and so very, very empty." Nellie turned from the window and adjusted her veil. "I don't follow all this downtown, Mrs. Ross. I can't. It does not matter to me. Let them erect statues and name parks after him, and execute a dozen men, none of that will bring Rob back to me." She reached out, picked up a small coat and held it up. "This was his? Rob's?"

"Yes." Mrs. Ross searched Nellie's eyes.

"My God, what you must be going through!" Nellie started to weep, then. "And yet," she clenched the little coat in her fist near her womb, "I shall never know the joy of a life growing within, Rob's son. I shall never school and train a little boy in short pants and watch as he grows to manhood. Nothing, nothing can fill the emptiness I feel, and, which I will feel for the rest of my days." She swallowed hard and her tears were flowing, and sobs shook her petite frame. "I can't imagine what you are suffering, Mrs. Ross, for you have lost what I," she faltered, "what I shall never have!"

"And who can say which is worse?" Margaret Ross rose and crossed the room and embraced the younger woman. "You have a noble heart, Nellie. You were worthy of my Rob. And he of you. This poor human race has lost much in not seeing your children rise to assume their place in the world."

The elder woman called for tea, and they talked for an hour. Then Nellie departed, refreshed that someone shared her grief. And yet she knew she would not call upon Mrs. Ross again for a very long time. Her sorrow was private, and airing it only made it more painful.

20.

THE CELL AT DAWN

Rensselaer County Jail

In the dim hour between night and morning, the light is soft and the air clean. Listen to the birds. Don't mind the bars. If you try, you can remember the world outside these bars on a sweet morning like this, along the river how the canalers and stevedores would be up by now, cursing, dousing their hangovers with river water, and the slow trains moving up the Fitchburg track, across the Green Island Bridge. Remember being sixteen, hopping over back fences after a night in Katie O'Malley's bed because her ma was dead and her da was on the river, and how the birds singing at that hour in early spring with the great river coming alive and the green buds on the trees and the balmy weather made you happy.

And remember the teeming streets, the baker's cart and the green grocer's wagon and the ice man and the milkman working their way through the neighborhood, their horses familiar with every stop; the little kids jumping rope in the dirt of the roadway and the cop on the beat who'd clout you with his big fist if he caught you running from the pharmacy with a handful of peppermint candy. And remember Lent, the bells of St. Patrick's ringing for early mass, and the widows along with old men who'd taken the pledge drifting through the streets to church, always mumbling about how things used to be, and how you scoffed at their age and feebleness and humility for you were young and everything was possible and there were girls and saloons and money to be made by gambling.

And then after working up to it sideways, you might carefully unfold the memory of election day. The third district. St. Patrick's bells ringing quarter past noon. The press of the men as you went through the crowd, shoved your way into the polls, the fear and outrage in their eyes, and the repeaters inside voting when that sniveling pest Hayner kept pushing at the door, whining: "If you go in there, I'll go in too, I have as much right as you," and when the cop shoved you out you caught Hayner underneath the chin with a clean uppercut, and his hands went up to the doorjamb and he fell out the doorway, then Jerry Cleary was on him, the big fist down over Hayner's nose. And there was an uproar of protest from the vigilantes and you turned to talk to Jack, who was nervous, his eyes jerking about, hand fidgeting in his coat pocket for the gun, and you talked slow and deliberate to calm Jack when you felt the blow, and it was Hayner again screaming with the wrench, "By God! I will go in there!" and there was a lancing pain in your left ear, and your derby was on the ground; so you gave him a left jab and a good right hook in the face, and the burly son of a bitch flew off his feet and landed in the pit in a cloud of ashes.

Then the crowd closed up, screaming for blood, clubbing and kicking you, Jack with the gun out, screaming for them all to "Stand aside, damn ya's! Get back!!" And the Protestants were shouting in a deep-throated rage, the crowd like a frightened beast shaking itself to life, to action, and when someone fired, off it went like a runaway horse. It was tough to keep your bearings as the crowd pulled you south, but George's saloon was the other way, so you went against the flow until Robert Ross, one big son of a bitch, grabbed your hand to shake the gun loose. Jack was nearby, wrangling with someone, then he shot and spun away and was off, and Robert Ross threw you aside and lit out after Jack.

Then there was John Boland firing behind, and you felt a pain on the head and the ground came up fast, and blood was flowing, and the day grew strangely quiet and the spring sun was like hot liquid gold, and the screams and the gunshots were very far away, and as you got up, your feet seemed stuck to the ground and walking was tough, as if through thick mud; and Jack was screaming, "Help! Bat! Help me!" So you turned and started back, into the guns and the screaming of the riot to save Jack. Boland was lumbering at you thirty feet back, his gun blazing. Robert Ross was on top of Jack down in the gully, clubbing him, the fist and club raising up again and again. You returned Boland's fire. Robert Ross bellowed and rose up off of Jack, climbed up the bank and was reaching for you, and this is where it always fell apart. Nor did the pint of whiskey election day morning help the recollecting, but you recall squeezing the trigger, once or twice or three times, aiming at Boland, or was it Ross? And Ross buckled and slumped, and Boland was past him then, and he whacked you with a stick and you felt dizzy, and there was Delaney and O'Keefe and then George to buoy you up and help you over to the saloon.

And so now in the cell with the spring sun rising there are only simple questions, like the withered nun poised with her blasted catechism:

Were you willing to kill Robert Ross that day? Yes.

Did you shoot at John Boland that day? Yes.

Did you hit Robert Ross that day? No telling. Perhaps.

Did you think you killed Robert Ross that day? No. They announced he was shot in the back of the head.

Did you kill Robert Ross that day? Absolutely not. He was shot in the back of the head. If you hit him, it was in the chest. That didn't do the job. You were never behind him. You didn't kill him.

But life weren't no catechism lesson, and you always hated catechism anyway.

And so with Jack down the hall there was time and there was more here in this thing to consider now. Leave aside the remorse that stole upon you in the night because a man'd been killed over a ward election. Leave aside the sorrow you feel for his family and his girl. There will be plenty of time for remorse and sorrow. Murphy was off to one side now, and Black off to the other. They were pulling different directions, and George Dunlop and even Police Superintendent Willard and Mayor Molloy, they weren't even near to the deal. Your lawyers, what the hell did they know? Norton and that new fellow, the fat one, Galen Hitt, they were good men and maybe good lawyers, but they didn't understand this game. It was Black and Murphy waging this war, like dogs pulling apart a hare that one of them snagged. And you were the prize, and one of them, Black, was still pulling, and the other, Murphy, was all too willing to let go.

And for a long moment, too long a moment, the despair gripped you in the stomach and in the testicles. The dread and the despair made you feel light-headed and feverish. They would parade you out as the murderer, and the crowds would rage all about, cursing you as they did all through the coroner's inquest, only worse, spitting their scorn and hate, and the papers would print such lies, and you could only sit there and take it, while your head felt light and your bowels grumbled.

So that's how the matter stood just now, no denying. And it weren't too pleasant to think of, so you turned your thoughts to Mamie. That night she came by the saloon, willing to hike the petticoats to dissuade you from your mission. Her premonitions. She was a warm, loving girl and you treated her rotten by pushing her away. She'd wanted to encircle you during the past few months, fix up a warm nest of a place, a home for you with furniture and plates and candlesticks and wee ones, someplace to come home to after the foundry or, admit it, after the saloon, more'n likely. And what prospects did she have for a life now? Hell, even with the freckles and red hair she was damned fine-looking. She had a strong full figure and a nice way to her, pleasant and accepting. The only argument you had with Mamie was her brother Tom, and your falling out over George and Jack.

So you sat up, stood, went to the window. Thoughts of Mamie were pleasant as the birds banked and cried over the roofs of the city, over the boats passing on the river. There was a fragrant vapor of spring in the air that rose above the coal soot and burnt garbage. The buds on the trees of Mt. Ida were the faintest green. The grill of the window was cold. If you ever got out of here, you'd make it up to Mamie, marry her, get a job, have some kids. Listen to this, would you? Tow the line like a canaler's mule. But it'd be far pleasanter to be a lifer in the foundry than to be sweating out a trial like this. This was bad and more'n likely it would get a whole sight worse.

Send Mamie a letter, that's what you should do. Perhaps she could come and visit, snuck in by that new deputy, and you could urge her to get on with her life, find someone else. A letter, a plain letter with none of that nonsense that courting couples trade. Jack had some paper and pencils. Yeah, Jack'd do it for you, 'cause Jack knew how to read and write.

21.
THE GRAND JURY

The Hall Building

English nobles created the "grand jury" to interpose a body of their peers between the king and his arbitrary criminal prosecutions. It was called "grand" because of its size, as many as twenty-three members in New York, to differentiate it from the "small jury," the petit jury of twelve that heard cases and determined guilt.

The grand jury is both an investigatory and an accusatory body. It hears facts surrounding criminal charges, and then votes whether or not to issue a formal accusation, an indictment. Both the federal and the New York State constitutions require that a grand jury indict a defendant before he may be tried for murder. A grand jury had been seated in Rensselaer County during the week of the Ross murder, but District Attorney John Kelly adjourned it to give Murphy and his machine breathing time. Black and his committee howled that this was simply another tactic to delay and subvert justice. If no indictment was handed up, there could be no murder trial. With the coroner's verdict in hand, seventy-two members of the Committee of Public Safety took the steamboat "City of Troy" to Albany March 27th to demand another meeting with the governor.

Construction of the capitol was in full swing under the warm spring sun, blocks of stone rising on the booms of cranes, the fourth story complete over the legislative chambers, the fifth story nearly complete. Into the governor's anteroom Black led his committee. They were met by a Civil War hero, Colonel Buck Williams, who served as Flower's bodyguard, and who had been deployed after their last visit.

"I should like to accommodate you," Williams said officiously, "but you gentlemen have no appointment." He had a martial air about him, and long white whiskers that he shook in regret.

"Tell his excellency this is Troy's Committee of Public Safety," the imperious Black said with confidence. "He will see us." Williams went through the high doorway. Flower shook his head behind the enormous desk.

"I ain't going to see them, Buck. They're trying to break Ed Murphy's back, and I ain't going to be a party to that, despite what he's been saying about me. Now you just go along and invent something to get rid of them."

"Yes, sir."

Williams went back to the anteroom. "Gentlemen, Governor Flower is sorry that affairs of state occupy him to such a degree today he is unable to see you. If you would submit your proposals in writing . . ."

"Now just a minute," Black said sternly. "This is not some Sunday school class from Potsdam. This is Troy's Committee of Public Safety and we demand to see the governor." He collected business cards among the throng. "Present these six cards to him. Ask him for an audience with these six alone. He will see us then." Black nodded and there were grunts of assent in the crowd behind him.

Williams went through the door, waited a few moments on the other side, then returned.

"The governor regrets terribly that he cannot see you just now. He will be happy to review anything you care to submit in writing." A furor arose in the anteroom with cries of "open government." Williams then was shouting:

"Gentlemen, you'll have to leave! You're interrupting state business!" There was a loud cry and the cards were flung down. A spitoon sailed through the air, hit the door and fell, oozing its dark contents on the thick carpeting. "Let us have order! Some of you," Buck glared at Black, "are lawyers. It is a misdemeanor to interfere with state business. Now I will call the sergeant at arms if you persist."

The crowd grumbled into the hallway where Black called them to order. The high vaults of the capitol echoed with their impromptu demands and parliamentary proceedings.

"An elected official must be responsible to his constituents. This arrogant governor refuses to open his public office to us, a Committee of Public Safety, an office he holds only by our good graces!" Black summarized their position. The men of substance were disgusted they had given up a day's business for another fruitless trip. "We shall not file our papers with him!" Black cried. "We shall publish them in the newspaper along with the story of our rebuff! A closed door is the enemy of a free republic!" There was loud clapping at these words.

Then Reverend Haynes put pencil to paper: " . . . till now decency has submitted rather than be shot . . . the district attorney's office is corrupt . . . Kelly discharged a sitting grand jury the day after Shea and McGough were arrested . . . indictments against Shea, McGough and Cleary had been outstanding on election day . . . a successful prosecution depends upon the entire displacement of the DA's office and the police department . . . the conviction of Shea should be a foregone conclusion, but if the conviction of this miserable outlaw is all that is accomplished, justice will be completely balked."

After reading the submission aloud, Haynes handed it to Buck Williams, and the group left the capitol, filed back down State Street to the docks, and took the next boat north around the great arc in the river. Flower answered with a letter next day. He declined to dismiss Fagan upon the committee's "vague suspicion and innuendo. This committee is a self-declared body with no power under the laws of the state. They tried to bulldoze their way into my chambers and acted in an unseemly and unmanly way when denied an audience. I refuse to be bulldozed for the sake of their personal pride."

Reading the response in his office, Frank Black murmured to himself, "We shall see. We shall see."

The next step in the prosecution was obtaining a new and favorable grand jury. With its courthouse and jail in Troy, the county seat, Rensselaer County was governed by a board of supervisors, one supervisor from each of sixteen townships, and one from each of Troy's thirteen wards. The old courthouse was too small to accommodate the twenty-nine member body, and so the supervisors met monthly in the Troy city council chamber. Among their tasks each spring was drawing by lot names of men to sit on the grand jury. The procedure was simple. From a revolving drum names were chosen, and if any member of the board objected, that juror was excluded. If no objections were registered, the name went down upon the list of three hundred from which grand juries would be selected for the next twelve months.

At this year's meeting, though, there were more than the twenty-nine supervisors and staff. At the front table sat Rev. Haynes, lawyer David Greene, the Gurley brothers, and Frank Black. Though not elected as supervisors and having no authority to act, still they were busy interposing objections to names read under the auspices of the Committee of Public Safety. The board of supervisors had chosen nearly two hundred names when a string of Irish names came up. Haynes, Greene, the Gurleys and Black took turns objecting.

"Mr. Chairman! Mr. Chairman!" It was Supervisor John Winn from Greenbush. "I resent these men being here!"

Daniel Hull, a thick woodcutter from Berlin, was chairman. "Why's that, eh?"

"They have no authority in law for being here."

George Coutie from Troy's fourth ward was secretary of the meeting: "We will hear a committee of one hundred from Grafton or Greenbush when they are good, concerned citizens. We will hear a committee of one or of anyone else."

"You say that very well," Winn said sarcastically.

"Yes, and I can whistle it too."

"Go ahead, and I'll give you a penny."

"Gentlemen," Hull raised his calloused hand, "we represent the people here. We respect the right of petition, something Governor Flower did not do."

"Governor Flower did just right," Winn said. "He would not be bulldozed by vigilantes!"

"I resent that!" Frank Black stood slowly.

"I object to your talking anymore," Winn snapped back. "You have been talking all afternoon and we have said nothing. You don't belong here. You weren't elected to office, and we were. You have no mandate from the people, as we do, and so you are acting illegally. We have something else to do besides listen to your oratory."

"Please, Mr. Black," Hull said, "confine your words to objections." Black resumed his seat. "Gentlemen, let us proceed."

Over Winn's objections, and the grumbling of others, members of the Committee of Public Safety were allowed to stay until the list was completed, and then they were given a copy of it. Back at Black's office, they sat about his conference table and completed the final draft of a circular letter to send each proposed grand juror:

April, 1894

Committee of Public Safety
Office No. 20 Hall Building
Troy, New York

Dear Sir:

Your name is on the list of Grand Jurors. That is an important fact. It involves the punishment or protection of criminals. It means better local government or the removal of business from this county. The necessity for intelligent and determined action against lawlessness was never so great as at the present time. Either law-abiding citizens must unite and fight for their rights, or repeaters, thugs and murderous villains will rule in Rensselaer County.

The most encouraging fact in this county today is that the Grand Jury list contains an unusually large number of good names. It is in the power of the juries, which will be drawn from that list within the year, to make our county seat a desirable place of residence. For the next forward movement we suggest the following plan: Let those nominated as Grand Jurors meet at once in their wards and towns and organize a Local Committee of Public Safety.

Carefully enquire regarding violations of law in your localities. Let your neighbors know that your committee will listen to their complaints and aid in every meritorious case. Consult with the Committee of Public Safety on all offenses affecting this county.

Permit us to urge you to become familiar with the rights and duties of Grand Jurors. Such knowledge, if applied, will make your efforts effective. There is no more independent legal organization than a Grand Jury. It is a law unto itself. Its principal servant is the District Attorney. Unlike a trial juror who decides upon evidence presented by others, the Grand Juror seeks and presents evidence himself.

Here Black appended a list of the proposed grand jurors' names and addresses and a list of the county supervisors who had chosen them.

We would be pleased to see you at our headquarters. Our representatives will, if requested, visit any town or ward and explain more fully to the Local Committee the methods by which each Grand Juror can do effective work.

These efforts are not for political or sectarian effect. Our committee has two Roman Catholic priests, several Protestant clergymen and a number of prominent Republicans and Democrats. Above all, we are American citizens.

In behalf of our common cause whose importance merits united and earnest support, we ask your hearty co-operation.

Very truly yours,
DAVID M. GREENE,
Chairman.

"Shall we vote, gentlemen?" Frank Black asked. He understood the value of consensus — not only was there agreement and solidarity, there was also someone to blame if things went awry. They voted, the circular was accepted and directions given for its mailing.

Meanwhile in Washington, Senator Murphy, through secret and diplomatic machinations, amended and passed the Wilson Tariff Bill to protect Troy's collar and cuff industry from English imports. On the floor of the senate he took his bows when that body applauded. Its passage in the isolationist lower house of Congress was assured. Back home, one group of industrialists was very pleased indeed and Murphy's name was mentioned less in their talk about the murder.

At a Tammany Hall dinner in New York City's lavish Manhattan House, with twelve full courses, six different wines, Cuban cigars, French brandy, and a ballroom of doxies waiting to kiss and cuddle the men when their power mongering was sated, Senator Murphy, the honored speaker, sought to quell a rumor that he would step down as state chairman.

"Now, gentlemen, as my kind old ma used to say to me," he paused and let his eyes twinkle in the gaslight with his Irish blarney, "'Don't ye start preparing me wake'n windin' sheet, Eddie, till yer sure I'm cold.' Of course I've heard the rumors, and they shock me as much as they do you. But let me ask you, while I was chairman have we lost a statewide election?"

"No!"

"Don't we have majorities in both houses of the state legislature?"

"Yes!"

"Don't we have a Democrat in the governor's seat?"

"Yes!"

"Hold it there! Not so fast!" His eyes gleamed mischievously again. "Roswell Flower might say he's a Democrat, but he does not fight Republicans, he cow-tows to them. I say, gentlemen, it's a new gubernatorial candidate, and not a new party chairman that we need!"

"Here! Here!" And there was a resounding round of applause. Appealing directly to the members was Murphy's desperate ploy, for no one in Tammany's smoky backroom agreed with him.

The grand jurors received their circulars, and many did form committees of public safety in their townships, and many did visit the Hall Building and many did speak with Frank Black. The grand jury was finally convened May 14 in its room in a secluded corner of the courthouse.

A crowd packed the hallway to hear the judge address the new panel, and lawyers and reporters sat at tables in front of the bar. Frank Black sat there as well with three members of his committee. He was conspicuous and haughty, his arms folded and head held high, waiting to hear Court of Sessions Judge James Griffith, who brusquely entered the small room and sat:

"Gentlemen, you were chosen by lot and sworn to inquire into crimes in this county. Never in the history of this county has a grand jury been confronted with a more important duty than yours. You will inquire into crimes that have done more harm to Troy than if it was scourged with pestilence or afflicted with famine, crimes which strike a death blow to the vital principles of free government.

"That same voice which thundered at Sinai, 'Thou shalt not kill,' has again spoken. In view of mistaken zeal by some gentlemen in addressing a letter to you," he nodded at Black, "I charge that you not confer with any person in reference to the discharge of your duty, for the law distinctly says that a person who influences a juror is guilty of a crime, and a juror who willfully receives a communication, book, paper or instrument relating to a matter pending before him is also guilty of a crime."

Many of the jury panel looked toward Frank Black with rebuke, but he sat impassively. His strategy had worked.

The judge continued: "I believe there is a righteous sentiment abroad which will sustain every effort made by you in an honest discharge of your duty. Summon your inborn love of country which fills the heart of every true American citizen, and say to yourself, 'God help me, I will keep my oath. I will assist in preserving universal suffrage from corruption!'" He rapped his notes into a stack. "Be faithful to your country and to yourselves." He nodded, stood to leave, "All rise!" and the sheriff clapped his hands to clear the room of spectators.

When no one but the grand jurors remained in the room, the sheriff summoned Thomas Fagan, who slipped in through a side door, ignoring the clamoring reporters. Then the sheriff stationed two deputies at the closed oak doors of the grand jury room to assure the secrecy of the deliberations.

22.

VOX POPULI

Franklin Square

A week after the inquest verdict, bail was set for Jack McGough. Jack returned to the neighborhood, to George's saloon, to the railyard and the docks and the mills and the tenements, to life with his "old man" in the echo of St. Patrick's church bells. But it was nothing like before. A dark resentment hung like a pall over the neighborhood, and despite the airy spring weather, people were surly. No one acted the same to him. Few tried to hide their curiosity. "Going to George's is like having a tooth pulled," he observed to his father. One sentiment predominated, Shea was innocent, he was being railroaded and opposition was futile.

Day after day the newspapers battered Murphy. Outrage at the machine and its methods welled up in Troy and spilled in an iridescent tide of journalistic rage across the state, across the land. A new sheriff's deputy, a skinny kid of twenty with a pronounced adam's apple and undisguised awe of Shea, read to him in the dusty cell:

"Hey, listen here, Mr. Shea! They got clips from all over the bloody country in the *Troy Times* about the, the incident. Your name's a household word. Wanna hear?"

Shea, reclining on the lower bunk, boots crossed, arms behind his

head, blew cigar smoke at the upper bunk. "Yeah, sure, Jem, go ahead."
And Jem read excerpts:

AUBURN ADVERTISER

"Bat Shea has been found responsible by the coroner's jury. Put the screws to Bat and let us see if there is any justice in New York State."

HUDSON REPUBLICAN

"The thug Shea will now be tried, and if an intelligent impartial jury is obtained, he will be convicted of murder and executed. But what is to be done with the men who stood behind Shea, and whose tool he was? Is Edward Murphy, Jr., to sit unharmed in the United States Senate, and is Governor Flower to serve out his term of office as executive of this great state and suffer nothing for their responsibility? If Shea had not felt that he was carrying out the wishes, if not the instructions of these two Democratic leaders, a coarse bully like Bat Shea would never dare to commit the crime he did. The profound awakening of public sentiment in Troy has been a surprise to these men. It is to be hoped that it will not be satisfied until Shea is executed, and Murphy and Flower are held up to the contempt and execration of all decent citizens."

PHILADELPHIA INQUIRER

"Governor Flower of New York is committing political suicide."

MILWAUKEE WISCONSIN

"The Trojans as a class are active and aggressive citizens, and when they take hold of a thing, they do it with a will. They are determined that Bat Shea, one of the Murphy gang who murdered Robert Ross at the polls, shall be punished by death because he committed murder in the first degree."

CHICAGO INTER OCEAN

"Robert Ross was killed by a tough name Shea. He was killed in an election row promoted by his murderers."

NEW HAVEN SUN

"The city gallows is being sold. One fellow suggests chopping it up into souvenirs the size of clothespins and selling them to raise money to execute people on the most approved scientific principles, that is, the electric chair."

SYRACUSE STANDARD

"All good men have an interest in the punishment of those criminals and in the destruction of the political power of Edward Murphy, Jr."

NEW YORK TRIBUNE

"Francis J. Molloy, the Murphy Mayor of Troy, whose certificate of election is stained with the blood of Robert Ross, the young Scotchman who was brutally murdered by 'Bat' Shea, may not enjoy the fruits of his victory. Anyone injured through a fraudulent election can bring a *quo warranto* proceeding in the supreme court to compel the beneficiary of such wrong to show he is entitled to the results of the election. Mayor Whelan, who was challenging the rule of 'Boss' Murphy, has brought such a proceeding."

TROY TIMES

"It is true Governor Flower was only a puppet in the hands of Senator Edward Murphy, but his act has shown the Democratic thugs of Troy that the Governor of the State and a United States Senator were behind them, and that they would be protected in committing crimes for the sake of the Democratic Party. It was this belief that steadied the hand of Bat Shea when he aimed and fired the pistol that shot the life out of Robert Ross.

"Lately the City of Troy is moved as it has never been before. It will take nothing but justice in this matter. The people are rising in their might, and they will crush to atoms the men who may oppose them. The action of Governor Flower will only result in keeping this public indignation at white heat."

"I heard enough there, Jem." Shea rose on one elbow. "Them papers got it all figured out, just as if they were there. But it weren't like that, Jem." Jem's eyes lit up. Shea wanted to talk. He'd been so silent for so long. "Well, Mr. Shea, what was it like?" He kicked back in his spindle chair and pulled out a tobacco pouch and cigarette papers.

"It were like a thunderstorm when the wind's blowing and the sky rumbles dark and the ground trembles. Happened so goddamned quick, Jem, the shots. The shots. But as I think back, I should'a seen it coming."

"Yeah?" Jem licked his cigarette, then lit it. "So how'd it come about?"

Shea lowered an eyebrow. "You'd like to know, Jem?"

"Well, yeah, sure, sure, I would, Mr. Shea. Don't everyone?"

"It weren't nothing like in the newspapers, 'cause they weren't there." Shea fell silent.

"Yeah?"

"Yeah, what?"

"That's it?"

"That's it."

"You ain't going to tell me what happened?"

"Listen, Jem, I can't tell you how it happened. I can only tell you how it didn't happen. It didn't happen like all these liars and perjurers state. I ain't saying no more. Mr. Hitt and Mr. Norton instructed me not to, and I ain't. Only don't believe all the nonsense you're reading there in the papers, 'cause they weren't there, and they don't know. Read other news, lad."

So Jem read how Troy's women had raised three thousand dollars for a suitable monument to Robert Ross, martyr to the cause of pure elections, and how they argue that women's suffrage would eliminate such crimes on election day. The *Troy Times* editor picked up their cause:

"If women had the ballot as they should have, Troy would not have needed a martyr. No boss would ever control a woman's vote. If any bossing were to be done, they would do it themselves."

Jem read further that women were voting this year in Colorado and the April 4 election in Colorado Springs ran smoothly. Women were not voting in Missouri, and in Kansas City, Missouri, Catholics and the APA fought a pitched battle. A hundred shots were fired, one Catholic killed and five persons wounded.

Across the land the laboring class was rising. Jacob Coxey, a Populist hero, had marched on Washington with an army of six thousand unemployed to beg the federal government for jobs. He set up a shanty town on the banks of the Potomac, and was immediately arrested and hauled into court for disturbing the peace.

Hungarian workers struck in Pittsburgh, murdering the chief engineer of the H.C. Frick Coal Company. The detestable laborers are choosing arms instead of words in their frustration at the monopolies and lockouts.

Congress was considering an income tax. Its effect upon New York's Robber Barons is weighed:

"It would be rather an amusing site to see the long face of Russell

Sage frizzle up when he is asked to give Uncle Sam fifty thousand dollars a year out of his income. It is likely he would have the money brought out in barrels of silver dollars and paid out one at a time in order to hold on to it as long as possible."

Bids are being let for the new Rensselaer County courthouse. A modern commodious structure is planned to replace the small, cramped Greek temple. Contractors are anxiously bidding to supply the cut stone, hardwood, carpentry, plumbing, glazing, steamfitting and flooring that will reflect the wealth and grandeur of this mill city at the end of the canals. "And Murphy'll take his cut, murder trial or no," Shea observed. "They say it's a dime on the dollar."

"No matter how much things change, they kind of stay the same," Jem observed.

A scraping sound interrupted them: "Mind you, boys," called the sheriff and the metal door swung open into the small chamber and Jack McGough stood on the threshold.

"Thought you was bailed the hell out of here," Shea observed, peering up and down at him. "Look at the cuts of you!" Jack's wool suit was covered in cinders and burdocks.

"Yeah, so did I. But some son of a bitch squealed on the operation and so I'm in for grand larceny now."

"Who squealed?"

"Don't know, Bat, but they found all them cigars and hunnerdweights of tobacco we had stored in McClure's stables."

"The clay pipes and the chaw too?"

"Yeah. The Bobalink wads, the Jollytar plug, the clay pipes, the Sweet Lotus Tobacco, the pails of Gold Chew, all of it. Every last leaf."

"It's a good job then we fenced the ale and the whiskey. That's already sailing down the river having passed first through a variety of kidneys." Shea laughed with self-satisfaction.

"I don't see how that helps us now. We're the named scapegoats and everything amiss in North Troy is tagged on us."

Shea winked at the kid. "Now there, Jem, did we have an enterprise! Weren't nothing like trying to get George into city hall. No. Nothing so complex nor dangerous. Jacker here and me, we borryed a wagon. Y'see he won a swaybacked old mare in a card game. So, being winter, we crossed the ice to Green Island, and as the trains'd get moving, I'd climb up and bust open a car and toss and kick freight out on the railbed. Then along'd come Jack here with the wagon and pick it up, back over the ice we'd go, and a tidy little profit was thereby earned, with no bridge tolltaker the wiser."

"Yeah, and we'll swing now for it."

"Na, what's that there, Jem? New Haven? What? Gallows is old fashioned, Jack. It's 'lectricity now."

McGough shoved his hands deep into his pockets. "Just an expression. Wish I had some of that Gold Chew, though."

"Here," Shea tossed him a wad.

"Don't see how you can be so chipper, Bat."

"I'm just pleased to see your ugly kisser is all. When you're facing the worst, Jack, anything less ain't any cause for worry."

"Say, Mr. Shea," Jem snapped his newspaper. "Here's a letter from Lewis Gurley."

"Blackhearted APA bastard," Jack spat at the tin spitoon.

Jem read: "This city has been ruled by a despot more despotic than Russia's Czar. His control is complete. Every appointment in city government has been made not through advice of good citizens, but from the brewery on Ferry Street. The election day riots have borne their fruit, the death of one of Troy's best men. The murder has aroused the good citizens of Troy and a committee of one hundred reputable citizens embodying the intellect, wealth, power and respectability of Troy to rectify this evil if we can."

"Let me see." Jack grabbed the paper from him. "I got one for you, Bat, though I don't often read this Republican rag, I caught it this morning. Here it is."

"'Is Bat Shea, whom the coroner's jury has found guilty of the murder of Robert Ross and whom the grand jury is about to take up, so dear to Governor Flower and to Boss Murphy? No, they are not fond of Shea. They would like to have him snugly underground if he could be put there quietly,'" Jack looked up and paused, then returned. "'It is the trial they dread.'"

"Ain't that so, Jack? Ain't it, though?"

23.
SECRECY

Father John Swift

Like a great awakening beast, Troy's clay hills and gravel valleys shook out the frost. Deep gorges of black shale roared with meltwater from the Berkshires. Tenderly the warm sun decked the hills with buds of faint green like a soft breath, a sigh of fecundity, with yellow forsythia and pink magnolia, and spring warmth sweetened the rain that the gray clouds poured.

In a loud hubbub, reporters, spectators, attorneys and members of Black's committee filled the courthouse each morning. A thin, meticulous bailiff escorted the grand jurors to the grand jury room, and glancing nervously at the crowd down the hall, he closed and locked the heavy oak doors. Two sheriff's deputies, arms folded, necks bulging over uniform collars, guarded the entrance to the secret proceedings, scowling at reporters and any other curious people who ventured down the low dim hall.

Behind locked doors all was still, still with the stillness of the eye of a hurricane in the midst of the crowds and the press. Thomas Fagan made his presentation to the semicircle of twenty-three jurors:

"The grand jury as an institution evolved in England as a fair method of bringing criminal charges against a person believed to have committed a crime. You grand jurors have been chosen randomly from the population of this county, and your work is not to be hampered by rigid rules of evidence or procedure."

Thomas Fagan was a scholar, a small slender man with wire spectacles and a moustache. Peering through his lenses, he seemed cross-eyed, yet a sincerity, a reverence for the law weighed in his weak nasal voice.

"You have broad powers," he scanned their faces. "You can act on your own knowledge and you are free to make presentments or indictments of your own. You have two separate functions: you can investigate and you can accuse. I am your servant in these functions, and I shall discharge my duty to you as well as I am able, informing you about rules of law, and obtaining the witnesses you require.

"You may range far and wide in your investigation so long as these proceedings remain secret, and you will pledge to indict no one because of prejudice nor to free any man because of special favor." Again he scanned the semicircle. "I shall now administer the oath." Solemnly, with hands raised, the jurors swore not to divulge anything heard in the room.

Fagan then explained how witnesses would be presented, that the jurors could interrupt the proceedings at any time to ask questions of a witness, or to call other witnesses, and when they had heard sufficient testimony, he would retire from the room so they might deliberate and vote in secret. If at least sixteen voted to indict, they could hand the indictments up to the superior court and accused individuals would be arraigned and a trial would follow. If they returned a "no bill," the secrecy of the proceedings would ostensibly protect the target of their investigation. The jurors could lodge in Troy at county expense, or return home each night. The term would be one month long.

Yet as he packed his papers and left the grand jury chamber that first day, Fagan had misgivings. After the coroner's inquest and the verdict of the coroner's jury, this urging of secrecy was a sham. The coroner's jury had accused Bartholomew Shea. All the witnesses he would call had already testified in a public forum, their testimony reported at length in four daily newspapers. Although there was a side door through which the witnesses entered and exited, reporters lurked in the halls and could see them coming and going.

Black and his committee had so completely ventilated the matter, anything less than an indictment against Shea for murder in the first degree would be viewed as a rigged result. The circular Black sent to all grand jurors assured these jurors that the community was watching. While Black's maneuvers made Fagan's official task, getting an indictment, far easier, Fagan was an honorable man and he resented the meddling.

Not that he harbored any fondness for Shea or McGough. They were bullies, of the ilk that had terrorized him in the school yard, bloodied his nose, scattered his papers, forced him down to kiss squirming girls pinned on the clay, made fun of his spectacles and his studious habits. They were drinking beer and betting on sports and packing brass knuckles and riding the freights while he was reading Ovid.

Fagan was lace curtain Irish, a second generation "narrow back" who'd been encouraged by his mother to study and to advance out of the working class after his father was killed in the mill by an exploding steam boiler. Fagan grew up seeing only the feminine side of the rough mill city — the concerts, art, architecture, drama, poetry readings, temperance league meetings — the darling of his mother and two maiden aunts. Fagan attended Williams College, two dozen miles from Troy, and afterward he read for the law in Troy and was admitted to practice.

Although a Democrat, he despised machine rule. At Williams he had studied Athens in the fifth century B.C., and he believed in his heart that the principles of pure democracy could work, even in this gritty mill city. He resented the tyrannical control of Boss Murphy who ruled by perpetuating ignorance, drunkenness and cynicism. Like the black smoke pouring from the smokestacks night and day, Murphy cast a dark cloud over Troy.

Not that Tom Fagan was any revolutionary. He was contemplative and he respected due process and had little stomach for rabble-rousing and anarchy. He harbored a healthy suspicion of demagogues like Frank Black was becoming, who rose up decrying that the system was corrupt, promising that they and they alone could purify it. The system was not corrupt, only individuals were. Turn them out and the system would be cleansed. There were checks and balances, and they should be allowed to work without vigilantes demanding preferences. Adhere to due process, let Murphy and Kelly retire and the people choose their leaders. Honor the classical beauty of *The Federalist*, like the balanced lines of a Greek temple, and eventually the logic of Madison-Hamilton-Jay would prevail.

So Thomas Fagan advocated the rule of law that week in May as the blossoms opened and the river sparkled and the earth came alive. In the midst of nature's gaiety, his was a somber task. He called all the witnesses who had testified before the coroner's inquest. Interviewing them prior to their testimony, the harmony of their stories surprised him. He began to ask them an additional question:

"Have you ever been to see Mr. Black?"

Some nodded and set their lip purposefully. Some smiled assuring him they knew their script. Some sought to preserve the veil of secrecy Black had cast over his machinations, and they lied. Yet Fagan had no choice. He must present the case to the grand jury as the case existed, and let the grand jurors find as they would. Hour after hour, day after day the testimony flowed. Due to the secrecy there was a noticeable lag in news coverage.

Night after night as he pored over his next day's witnesses, Fagan ruminated. This most celebrated case in Rensselaer County history had fallen into his lap. He felt as though poised upon a high precipice. The Protestants, Frank Black in particular, were aiding him considerably. Yet why did he have such misgivings? If Black stretched the rules to assure an indictment and a conviction, did that diminish Shea's guilt? For surely he was guilty? Wasn't he?

After the hard winter, spring was intoxicating. There had been little flooding this year. Windows were thrown open to welcome the clean west wind into the rooms of coal soot from a winter of the parlor stoves. Children's laughter and songs were heard well past the lamplighters' rounds. In Rensselaer Park, baseball teams were practicing. Lovers walked arm in arm along the river. Father John Swift saw it all, the cycles, and the renewal was invigorating. Yet something tugged at him this year that was strong and dark.

The world had become a harsher place in the past two decades — the throb of steam engines, the rallying cry of labor organizers, the squeezing greed of millowners and merchants. The tyranny of the millowners who subjugated children for profits astonished him. The bigotry, the social ills, the poverty, the illiteracy, the drunkenness and sexual dysfunctions he saw daily among his parishioners caused him great sorrow, and but for his faith it would have bowed his shoulders. This murder wrapped a dark shroud about all his misgivings. The mystery of who shot Ross tantalized the public. His private knowledge was a heavy burden.

It was now breezy May, the Pentecostal season. School children had borne Mary Ever-Virgin through the neighborhood and crowned her with flowers to the strains of organ music in St. Patrick's Church. On a Saturday night, through his open window, a clean wind off the river lifted the page of his journal. He put the pen to his lip and pondered. Then he wrote:

"Tonight X again came to confession with his doubt. This is the third time. My dilemma is a moral one, for the spiritual question is solved. I can never reveal a penitential communication. And yet, possessing such knowledge, might I anonymously communicate such facts to the authorities? 'Shea did not shoot Ross.' That and only that need be said, anonymously. Would that breach the confessional's seal of secrecy? I have identified no party, no penitent, no agent. I have not identified the source of the information. I have not even identified myself.

"I wrestle with this decision, or more properly this indecision, each night. My only solace in not communicating henceforth has been the belief that no one would take my missive seriously. Another anonymous crank. Yet am I not obliged as an agent of God's justice to intervene in the administration of human justice? I hear that whisper each day: 'Father, I cannot come forward. I cannot. Please forgive me.' The despair in that voice! And I must withhold absolution until he does. And yet I shall correspond anonymously with the authorities, and tell them the conclusion I have reached."

The last four words he scratched in the soft lamplight while the spring wind toyed with the page and the jingle of harnesses and piano from Mullin's Saloon wafted through the window. Father John Swift sighed, opened a drawer and removed a plain sheet of paper, and he wrote. When he was finished, he left the communique on his desk for half an hour, his hands folded. He smoked a cigar. He read and reread the letter. Now that it was written, should he send it? Deliver it? He folded the letter finally, slid it into an envelope and put on his coat. He caught a late streetcar downtown to the Keenan Building, went upstairs to Fagan's private law office, slid the letter into the mail slot. No one was about when he reached the street, so he pulled down his hat, pulled up the lapels of his coat and hurried away.

Next morning, after mass at St. Paul's, Thomas Fagan ambled down the steep grade of Eagle Street toward the commercial district. Even on Sunday smokestacks poured rich black smoke into the air, and the river, swollen brown from upland mudslides, flowed beneath the bridges, with trees, branches and debris carried swiftly along.

In the bright spring weather, Fagan considered the case. His grand jury presentation was complete. Deliberations were over, the indictments were being typed today. The grand jury proceedings had been predictable. Fagan found no lack of proof. In fact there was too much. The jurors took their oath of secrecy seriously, and Fagan keenly watched their faces as they listened to witness after witness swear that his eyes were fixed upon Ross and Shea at the fatal moment. As the evidence mounted, Fagan's suspicion of Black's meddling grew.

It struck Thomas Fagan as unusual that in a free-for-all where guns were blazing, where a dozen and a half shots were fired in less than a minute, men screaming and fleeing, that so many eyes could be trained upon an obscure corner of the riot, and see the same exact same thing. Unusual, implausible, but not impossible. The weathered faces of the jurors, creased by the sun, sagging with the years, with the cares and frustrations of twenty-three separate lifetimes, never betrayed a doubt. Fagan overdid it, producing far more witnesses than he needed to. Place all the proof before them, and let them decide. It was their task. Black and his committee were major annoyances, and they would howl for his blood if the grand jury did not indict. He had successfully kept Black out of the grand jury room; but he saw how Black's genius had subverted the secrecy of the proceedings by using the coroner's inquest. Black and the APA understood secrecy and used it well. The witnesses were obviously coached. If the case were so clear cut, why was it necessary to coach witnesses?

As he unlocked his office that Sunday afternoon, he saw an envelope on the floor. He opened it and read it. Fagan immediately disregarded the note as the product of some Murphy sympathizer to undermine his confidence in the operation of the grand jury. Yet on that blithe sabbath afternoon, as he began to prepare for trial, reorganizing the testimony of the grand jury witnesses, and as he considered how best to announce the indictments tomorrow to the ever-hungry press, a doubt stole over his thinking. He retrieved the crumpled note and read:

May 19, 1894

Hon. Thomas Fagan
8 Keenan Building

Sir:

I am a Catholic priest who must remain anonymous. While administering the sacrament of Penance, I have learned that another individual, not Bartholomew Shea, shot Robert Ross. Please take this into consideration in performing your official functions. I am aware your task is not an easy one.

Yours in Christ,
CONCERNED

Fagan reread the letter. What if it were legitimate? Surely no priest he knew would trifle with the secrecy of the confessional. But what if? This note named no names, betrayed no confidences. It simply stated a negative proposition. He could picture the whispering through the grate, a slight brogue to the voice, generations of resentment and bitterness held back in the simple words, "They got the wrong man." The omniscient and omnipotent "they," Fagan thought. And now he was one of "them" even to his own race. "I know who shot Ross, and it weren't Bat Shea."

What ethical duty did this letter impose? None. The letter was unsigned. He could not subpoena a priest to divulge the contents of a penitential communication. While this note may pose a moral dilemma, there was nothing further to be done legally. This, this anonymous scribble, this hypothecation, this, this, this fantasy was not new evidence warranting new grand jury deliberations. Yet as he peered out the window with the afternoon warming despite dark clouds massing, as he looked out upon the brisk spring streets where horses passed and people called to each other in their Easter finery, Thomas Fagan believed there was now at least one other pair of eyes piercing into the dark murk that surrounded the murder, one other mind and heart that knew and felt the doubts that he dared not utter.

What was Mother's old adage? "Secrecy's the refuge of liars." Folding up the letter, he discovered a quote printed on the envelope flap:

"For God shall bring every work into judgment,
with every secret thing, whether it be good,
or whether it be evil."

Ecclesiastes 12:14

24.

THE INDICTMENT

Thomas Fagan, Assistant District Attorney

On Wednesday the heavy oak doors swung open at last and Thomas Fagan issued through them, lips tight, briefcase in hand. He was immediately accosted by a pack of newsmen who had been loafing and napping.

"What is it, Mr. Fagan?"

"D'ja indict him?"

"Murder first?"

"I cannot comment, gentlemen."

The heavy doors shut, and Fagan hurried from the courthouse to his law office three blocks away.

"Message from Mr. Black," Dory, his secretary, announced. "I think he wants to know the outcome."

"How does he know there is an outcome?"

"Mr. Black is resourceful."

"He certainly is that."

"Shall I ring him?" She smiled triumphantly. At Dory's bidding Fagan had finally installed a telephone in his office. He despised the thing for the bell interrupted his concentration.

"No, I'll go to see him personally."

Frank Black's offices in the Hall Building were spare and frugal.

Two scriveners at high desks copied the commercial notes and drafts, the deeds and wills and contracts and chattel mortgages, and a thin old man greeted clients and callers. Although three clients sat waiting to see the attorney, Fagan was ushered directly in.

"Has the grand jury returned its indictment?" Black asked in lieu of a greeting. He was at the large table in the adjoining conference room rented by the Committee of Public Safety.

"Isn't that rather presumptuous?"

Slowly Black let the map he was reviewing roll up. He fixed Fagan with a piercing stare and Fagan stared directly back at him.

"Are the deliberations complete?"

"You would have me breach the secrecy of the grand jury?"

"Oh, come now, Fagan! Don't be sanctimonious with me."

"Not sanctimonious, sir. I shall be brutally candid and straightforward with you. You have placed yourself in the vanguard of this citizens' group, and you can say what you like to congregations and even to the governor. But I will not have you inserting yourself into this prosecution. While this matter is proceeding in a court of law, I represent the people of this state, I represent them, not you, Mr. Black. I will not tolerate your high-handed meddling for political ends."

"Meddling, sir? I am not meddling. I am assuring that justice is done and that the people have a proper advocate in one of John Kelly's assistants."

The imputation that he was a machine appointee reddened Fagan's face, but he kept a rein on his anger.

"From where do you derive this self-proclaimed authority, Mr. Black? You have not been elected."

"No. I have not been fraudulently elected, that is true." Black stood up, head and shoulders above Fagan, and peered down at the smaller man. "Therefore I derive my authority directly from the people."

"You represent only a faction . . ."

"That is not so, sir. You and the district attorney are creatures of Boss Murphy, and you are the representatives of the faction. My mandate comes from a community outraged by Shea's cold-blooded murder."

"The state still must prove him guilty beyond a reasonable doubt," Fagan cautioned.

"Not the state, sir." Black's thin lips curled and he pointed with his finger. "You."

"That is right, Mr. Black. I. And I'll thank you to let me perform my duty untrammeled by your flag-waving and rabble-rousing."

"You should welcome our support. It can only help your case."

"You stand clear of this matter, Mr. Black, or so help me God, I'll bring obstruction of justice charges against you."

Black smiled broadly. "You do that, Fagan. Charge me with obstruction. See what that would do for your promising career."

The accusation of personal ambition infuriated Fagan.

"I am warning you, Black. Stage your rallies and your meetings, give whatever speeches you wish. I cannot restrain your speech. But stay out of this prosecution."

Black rudely looked over Fagan's shoulder and called out to a scrivener: "Have Fawkes send in my next client, would you please?"

Fagan turned and stalked from the room. When he reached the street, he drank in the sweet spring air to calm himself. Black had touched his one sensitive nerve: ambition. Although he professed to seek justice, Fagan suspected a good deal of ambition lurked beneath his desire for a conviction and this troubled him. Black knew it because Black's own ambition fueled his interest in the case.

"Ambition is corrupting him," Fagan muttered, yet passing along the crowded walkway in the sunny afternoon he thought about the priest's letter and he wondered darkly if maybe it were not corrupting him too.

The following morning the grand jury handed up an indictment to the superior court and the news ran instantly through the press corps.

"Now back up there, gents, there'll be time, there'll be time, all the time in the world, back up, please," Marty, the enormous deputy court clerk, waved them back and spread the indictment page by page upon the defense table in front of the jury box. Reporters climbed each other's backs to copy the contents of fourteen typewritten pages in which Shea was indicted on five counts of murder in the first degree.

News reached the jail a bit more slowly, and when Jem heard it, he shook his head and agreed to take the news up to Shea's cell. Bat and Jack were playing cards on the head of a barrel and the room was dense with cigar smoke.

"Cough up your greenbacks, Jem. Jacker here's just about bust." Jem did not reply and Shea turned at his silence. "What is it, lad?"

"Yer indictment's in."

"Any surprises?"

"'Pends on what you expect."

Shea looked from Jack to Jem and his mouth curved in a sneer of contempt. "Hope for the best, expect the worst, ain't that it, boys?" Yet the devil-may-care tone was belied by a twitch in his cheek. "Give it over."

"Five counts of murder in the first degree."

"Five, huh?"

"Yeah." Jem took a paper from his pocket. "One count of common law malicious killing, one count deliberate and premeditated killing under the code, then three counts of killing to effect the escape of Jack, here, after he committed three separate assaults — two on William Ross, one on Robert."

Shea dropped his cards, pulled his cigar out of his face and flicked his ashes on the cell floor. "Now ain't that there dandy? Just goddamn dandy." He stood and began to pace in the narrow cell. "Tell me, Jack, tell me what's what." Jem backed against the cell door. "With this here? What's goddamned what? These APA sons of bitches! I didn't do it and they know I didn't. Five counts! Five goddamn counts!" He hurled his cigar into the corner. "Five goddamn counts! This is a royal screwing, ain't it? A railroad job? Ain't it? Outta my way! Let me walk in the hall, Jem. Open that door. I got to walk in the hall!"

"Oh, I don't know about that, Mr. Shea."

"Let me into the hall, goddamnit, I need some air."

Shea pushed Jem aside and hauled open the door. In the dim and dusty hallway he walked up and down breathing deeply, clenching and unclenching his fists, his brow thick and troubled.

Jack kicked back in his chair and whistled: "Five counts. Whew. And three with me in 'em? Whew."

"Will he . . . should I call someone . . . what will he do?" Jem was worried.

"Ah, he's got a healthy temper. You'd need ten or a dozen guards if he were to get up steam, but he don't seem near to blowing just yet."

Shea reentered the cell, pointing his finger accusingly. "It's Murphy, Jack. Murphy what's selling me out. He's cutting me off and throwing me to the dogs so's they'll feed on me and leave him be. He don't believe in my innocence. He don't care about no loyalty, nothing at all. George is small potatoes. Molloy is a handpuppet. It's Murphy behind all this, trying to save his own goddamned skin and I can't do nothing about it. Nothing."

"That could be, Bat." Jack's face was twisted up into an odd angle. "Five counts. Whew! I can't believe there's five counts."

"What's the difference, Jack? One's enough when it's the death penalty. Give me a smoke. C'mon. I gotta think this through 'cause it looks awful . . . goddamn . . ." he turned and began to kick the door, "goddamn rotten right now." Violently, he lashed out with his boot, his eyes flashing, and Jem backed into the corner in fear.

The news flew through Troy like an electric spark. On the streetcars, in the restaurants and saloons, in the barbershops and the dry goods stores, the warehouses, the factories, the department stores, along the river bank where the great sidewheelers and the snubbed canal boats rode the incoming tide, in the lumberyards and mills, the foundries and factories, the body politic was galvanized, half pleased that retribution seemed possible for once, the machine could be defeated, and the other half angered at the oppression, at the strident flag-waving and at Bat Shea, the culprit who had brought it down upon them all.

News reached Albany by telegraph, telephone networks being small citybound systems, and Governor Flower, as his barber massaged his neck and ears and jowls with lemon soap, nodded with satisfaction.

"Those blackhearted Republicans come to me, they did, and said they can't get a fair show. I tell them Fagan's all right. He's a young Irish kid who wants to succeed, so he'll work double hard. And he did. Yes, by God, and he will."

Flower summoned Benson to the barbershop. Benson was his lieutenant dispatched to Tammany Hall each week on Friday's Night Line with orders and news. Upheaval had just erupted in the ranks. The sachems of Tammany had thrown out Jack Dugan when they discovered how much he was stealing. Although Dugan helped elect Flower by getting out the troops in Manhattan, Brooklyn and Queens for the upstater, Dugan became a political liability when his corruption was disclosed. Now Ed Murphy was following down the same primrose path.

"So, you were right, sir." Benson was congratulatory. "Their local officials rose to the occasion."

"That's fine!" Flower pulled the sheet from around his neck and slid a silver dollar into the barber's hand. "Smooth and clean. They did do that, Benson. But I think I'll grant them one wish now."

"And what's that, sir?"

"A new judge."

"But the election's not till '96."

"Hah! We can't wait for that, now, can we? No. I'll assign my old friend Pardon Williams to the case."

"From Watertown?"

"Yes. Now that this young district attorney has distinguished himself, Williams will preside over the trial. We'll call an extraordinary term of the Court of Oyer and Terminer up in Rensselaer County and assign Williams to it. He won't put up with any nonsense from the defense nor from Black neither."

"No, sir?"

"No. But Ed Murphy had better watch out."

"And why is that, sir?"

"Because they say Williams is a charter member of the Watertown Lodge of the American Protective Association," and Flower winked, eminently pleased with his own political skill.

25.
THE JUDGE

Judge Pardon C. Williams

Judge Pardon C. Williams presided over terms of the state Court of Oyer and Terminer, the superior court which "heard and determined" cases. Although he was Republican, he was an intimate friend of Governor Roswell Flower, and he was a tough, clear-thinking, Populist-minded sort who viewed an assignment to hear the Shea case as an honor, not a chore. Judge Williams emulated Abraham Lincoln in applying back-woods common sense to complex problems of a burgeoning industrial society. Having educated himself after he left the one room schoolhouse, Williams had little patience for the unwashed masses who were unable or unwilling to cultivate their minds. He loathed urban political machines that had arisen among the immigrants after the Civil War, and he detest-ed the violence and voting fraud they used to attain and hold power. A lifelong nativist advocating a return to simple rural values, Williams, if not a card-carrying member, was sympathetic to goals of the American Protective Association. He wished to turn back the clock to the time when good men sought public office not as a career, or as a path to wealth and power, but out of a sense of duty and sacrifice.

Williams boarded the train in Watertown on a bright summer

morning, and watched out the window as the train passed through the mountains, the rolling hills, apple orchards and pastures of dairy farms, over sparkling rivers, through the hardwood forests and the lofty shade cast by virgin pine. At Utica he boarded the New York Central for Albany. Alongside the tracks, the canal was glutted with boats shipping grain and salt, lumber and livestock eastward, manufactured goods westward. Occasionally there were passenger boats filled to the gunwales with immigrants too poor to buy a train ticket, German, Italian, Polish, Irish, whole large families seeking their fortune in the West.

As the train pulled into Schenectady, Williams scrutinized the brick factories of Thomas Edison's General Electric plant. The miracles Edison invented were changing the world in irrevocable ways, the incandescent bulb replacing whale oil, kerosene and gas lamps. There was talk of municipal lighting systems where giant turbines would generate electricity to light a whole city, and municipal gaslights would be obsolete. There were electric streetcars now, and these streetcar systems were interlocking to transport passengers through and between cities. The telephone, too, was linking homes and offices in many cities. Electric networks like great nervous systems were joining people to each other, and as these networks grew, the world became even more complicated. While every new step brought convenience and a benefit, Williams was old fashioned and skeptical — the inventions were godless for they minimized the value of labor, and encouraged children to leave farm and family for the ruby lights and clamor of the city.

The train swung overland to Albany, through sandy pine barrens, down a rocky defile to the broad Hudson at the north end of Albany where lumber from the Adirondacks was stacked high along the wharves. Williams detrained at Union Station, seized his portmanteau and climbed Maiden Lane to the unfinished capitol where he was announced to the governor. Flower waited until the door closed, then he stepped around the large desk and warmly clasped Williams' hand.

"Been too long, Judge." His eyes gleamed and there was irony in his use of the title since he had helped his old friend get on the bench. They asked about each other's families and talked of hometown matters, crops and the weather before easing into the topic at hand:

"We've got this bit of a mess upriver," Flower said.

Williams nodded. "Your old chum Murphy's got his hand stuck in the ballot box, eh?" Williams was a lean handsome man who bore himself gravely and rarely smiled.

"My old chum Murphy ain't been making the wisest moves of late. He has asked the Tammany sachems to look elsewhere for their gubernatorial candidate this year. He's trying to dump me. I hear Morton's coming back from Europe and he wants to run on the Republican line."

"Tough race. Morton's well-financed."

"Sure is. And so the party cannot afford a schism this year between its chairman, Murphy, and its highest elected officer, me. Only one course open. Get rid of Murphy. His voting record, hell, his attendance record for that matter, is no source of pride. And then there's this festering sore upriver in Troy . . ."

Williams folded and unfolded his hands. "It's been all over the press. You'd have to be a hermit not to have read about the case. Seems they have a dozen eyewitnesses who saw this boy Shea fire the fatal bullet. The trial should be short."

"But there is more, much more to the case."

"The voting fraud?"

Flower nodded. "Murphy's boys crossed the line. It wouldn't concern me a bit if all the techniques of his boys in stuffing the box are aired in the press."

"I'm not sure how relevant that would be." Williams considered.

"Shea's voting fraud, though, could show intent," Flower surmised. "The threat of murder and murder itself were tools of his trade."

Williams shook his head. "But that would be a general intent to shoot anyone who got in his way, manslaughter, perhaps. How would that be relevant on intent to kill Robert Ross?"

Flower lit a cigar. "Well, first of all, you get the right jury you don't need to prove anything. They'll take the cue. Second, this weren't a Sunday school outing these boys were on. They were there to force the election, and they did, and they killed Ross doing it. Bringing the gun to the polls shows premeditation, don't it?"

"Then every barroom shooting is premeditated because someone put a gun in his pocket before he left home?"

Flower glanced at him. "Which side are you on?"

"I don't take sides, Roz, you know that."

"Not much!" Flower broke into a belly laugh. "How about them boys that strung up the stablehand for raping Frank Witherspoon's girl? How about that young horsethief, Chuck Randall? How about the Canuck boatman that put a meathook in the paymaster?"

"You've been following my career."

"I get the paper, Judge." He sat back in his large chair. "Now, I'm mighty obliged to you for catching a-hold of this here hot potato. And there may be a spot opening on the Court of Appeals next year, and assuming I'm still here, we'll see about your candidacy. I ain't trying to tell you how to run your courtroom or how to hear a case. I'm only saying that I don't care if Murphy and his boys pay a good toll for travelling the road."

"Well," Williams stood, "I think I'll catch the boat upriver and get settled in tonight and see what's what."

"Train's much faster."

"That's why I'll take the boat."

North of Albany, the Hudson swung in a wide arc eastward toward the Green Mountains. A spur of the Erie Canal ran along the west bank, through the United States Arsenal at West Troy. On the east bank the belt line train chugged north, passing the sidewheeler steamboat where Judge Williams stood at the rail. As the boat followed the channel in its wide crescent away from the setting sun, the lush hills of Greenbush gave way to a hazy yellow cloud over South Troy.

Hundreds of smokestacks from the forges, foundries and mills smoked and steamed, and the warm muggy air had stalled in a cloud below the eastern hills. As the boat drew closer, sooty silhouettes of buildings and rusted equipment, and then, still closer, views through the sweatshop doors where men and boys stripped to the waist labored like sweating demons in the roiling infernos of flame and sparks and explosions, squeezing, coaxing, hammering iron and steel into shape.

Along the bank, wharves and warehouses bustled with stevedores and cranes loading crates into waiting canal boats and river steamships, and a rusted freight train blew white steam in a mournful blast and with a clang of couplings, began its trek toward Rutland. There was a sudden stench of sewage from the river that sent most of the curious below, but Williams stayed on deck. He had never been to Troy and he wanted a good look.

As the boat passed South Troy, Williams peered up the cross streets at block upon block of tenements, metal chimney pots and cornices rusted, unpainted porches, clapboards streaked with soot, the teeming streets, colorful advertising signs, teams pulling wagons, hawkers with their wares, children in filthy frocks, clusters of young boys on the corners, the open doors of saloons with dogs asleep on the cool stone of the steps. Steeples rose above the tarred and slate roofs where pigeons and swallows circled, St. Joseph's, St. Mary's and St. Anthony's, and high on the hill the four towers of St. Joseph's Theological Seminary presided like a papist crown over the city. Angelus bells were somewhere tolling. The tide was going out, the brown water lowering on wharf pilings revealing moss and algae.

To his North Country eye, the cloud of soot was an exhalation of the combined evils of industry, labor, slums, alcohol, Catholicism, promiscuity and, lording over the whole corrupt discordant labyrinth of noise and vice, Irish machine politics. It was time for a fresh outlook, time for a cold wind from the north to dispel that dark stinking cloud and bring fair skies.

Judge Williams took rooms at the Mansion House, a short city block from the offices of Frank Black, and two blocks north of the courthouse. He instructed the bellhop to get a message to the court clerk to visit him that evening, and after supper a meek balding man, Francis Riley, presented himself. Williams gave instructions that counsel for both sides were to be in court in the morning with any pretrial motions, and that jury selection would begin Monday, June 4. He gave instructions as to pens and inkpots and stenographers, how he wanted temporary chambers arranged, how he would modify local rules, and he gave so many detailed instructions that the clerk left the room shaking his head, yet secretly pleased with a sense of self-importance — the more orders this commanding judge from out of town gave him, the more Riley could relay to his three assistants. After setting things into motion, Williams took his top hat and cane and set off on a brisk stroll to have a look about the city.

Across the square, the enormous bulk of Frears Bazaar was ablaze with electric lights welcoming shoppers to its many departments. The square was thronged with pedestrians, but wagon and buggy traffic had eased since the afternoon. Williams proceeded down Second Street toward the courthouse. The young women of Mrs. Willard's Troy Female Seminary were conducting a candlelight ceremony on the campus, and across the street the courthouse was still lit. Farther south he reached Washington Park, the enclave of industrialists and the stately homes of attorneys Martin I. Townsend and young Seymour Van Santvoord.

Williams took a turn about the park in the gaslight, then passed LaSalle Institute eastward into the Italian neighborhood and the open air market where the men were haggling in Italian. Williams was used to hearing French Canadians and the Italian sounded spicy and exotic. He started north. Playbills for opera houses announced variety shows and dramas. The shops were open, and from saloons came curses and shouts and bits of ragtime piano. Farther north was Murphy's brewery, crusted with soot, coughing black smoke, then across Ferry Street, the jail. That brick fortress would keep them until Dannemora.

He heard a train whistle blow, and he quickly crossed the tracks.

A group of young men swaggered drunkenly past him. A block from the police station stretched a row of tenement houses, some of which had red lamps in the entrances, and women peering from the windows into the darkening street.

"Little companionship, Mister?" It was a female voice, and it startled him. Judge Williams peered into a mask of powder and rouge under a mop of blond hair. The realization of what she was unnerved him. "Why, you look like a real swell sort. Come on along with me." She hooked her arm in his and led him toward a staircase.

"Unhand me, madam!" He pulled free and raised his cane as if to strike. She backed away, whining, "Whatsa matter with you, anyway? You queer? Being on this street here and queer as a dance master!"

After this encounter, the street seemed to seethe with vice and evil. Every gangway held a pair of eyes. Laughter and harsh music echoed from the bordellos and saloons. Williams crossed to Union Station, got directions from a conductor back to the Mansion House, and immediately sought the refuge of his suite. For a very long time he could not sleep. The noise and the seething forces of this mill city excited him strangely, troubled his staunch rural propriety. He leaned upon the windowsill, peering down upon the tangles of telegraph wires, the gaslit square, the commercial signs, the warehouses at the bottom of the cobbled hill, and below where the river ran dark and gleaming.

Morning brought much activity. Overnight his presence in the city had become known and newspaper reporters from Troy and elsewhere accosted him as he passed through the lobby to the dining room for breakfast. No, he told them, the matter was pending before him and it would be inappropriate to comment. Although he maintained a stern demeanor, Pardon C. Williams was pleased with the notoriety. Frank Black and four members of the Committee of Public Safety were waiting in the dining room to welcome him. Remaining noncommittal, he listened to their arguments and their accounts of decades of voting fraud at the hands of the Murphy machine.

"This is not a homicide in the usual sense," Black stated pressing his fingers together. "The proof extends beyond who actually pulled the trigger, and who saw him do it. We believe, Judge, it is essential for the public good that the facts and circumstances of the voting fraud be brought out."

"For what purpose?" Williams was impatient. The food was excellent, the waiters professional, and he wanted only to eat a meal in peace before the trial began.

"Why, to show motive."

"But the People need not prove motive. They must prove intent."

"Well, then, to show premeditation."

"But surely, Mr. Black, the intent to meet and overcome opposition cannot suffice to prove murder in the first degree. Felony murder, perhaps, but not first degree. Therefore, of what probative value are the details of the fraudulent voting? The jury cannot convict someone of murder simply because he may have been leading a gang of repeaters, now, can it?"

Williams was testing them, and he saw disappointment in their faces. Surely if he was to be effective at all, he must establish his independence, and it would not do to suggest partiality. Black raised his thumb and forefinger to his chin and studied Judge Williams, who pushed away his oyster tray and began cutting his salmon with a fork. Williams was not as compliant as he had hoped.

"Gentlemen," Williams said, "I have been assigned to try this case, and I shall do so independently and impartially. The jury, of course, will determine guilt or innocence, and I will give this man and this community the fairest trial possible under the law. I appreciate your concerns, and they will either be satisfied by the outcome or they won't. I can promise you no more. Now I see the court clerk with the maitre d' and I must talk with him. Good-day."

Outside, Black reported to other committee members.

"It was a mistake," Joseph Warren said. He scowled at Black as if the rebuff were Black's fault.

"He's far too independent for my blood," Lewis Gurley stated. "Flower sent us a jack o' lantern!"

"You can never get a judge to make a commitment, Lew," Black explained, but he was impatient too, for he sensed his effectiveness with the committee was slipping. Everywhere he led them they were rebuffed with the same argument, you are not going through channels, you are not authorized, your actions are above the law. But wasn't law just the will of the people? Two misfires in Albany and now one in Troy. But there was an indictment at least, and there would be a trial.

The morning was resplendent and the streets shady, as Judge Williams walked slowly down Second Street. The courthouse was a small granite Greek temple with pediment and columns. Today its steps were crowded with the curious. Williams went up the alley and in the back door. An excited clamor reverberated in the halls and the courtroom was already filled to capacity. Clerk Riley was a petty tyrant to his people, and all was in order in Williams' new office, pads, pens, blotting paper, his robes ironed, ice water and a dish of rock candy.

The courtroom was filled far beyond its capacity and the balcony sagged, people craning to see the prisoner as he was escorted in. Sunlight streamed through the leaded windows and color from stained glass medallions dappled the crowd. The long mahogany bar separated the trial area from the gallery, and with the defense table on the left, the prosecution on the right, the room was dominated by the judge's mahogany bench. Behind and above the high leather chair was a pediment of wood upon which the goddess of justice, blindfolded, held aloft her scales. Down from this pediment hung maroon draperies, and as the clerk cried "All rise!" silence fell in the room. Williams swept through the curtains in his black robes. "Be seated."

"Read the indictment," the clerk called, and Thomas Fagan turned towards Shea, who looked pale and grim. Fagan read each of the five counts of murder:

" . . . Bat Shea, with force and arms, in and upon said Robert Ross, in the peace of the people of the state of New York then and there being, feloniously did make an assault, and a certain pistol, then and there loaded and charged with gunpowder and a leaden bullet in his hand had and held to, at and against said Robert Ross . . ."

Shea stared at the judge, sizing him up. Williams glared sternly down from the bench. Sentence after sentence, paragraph after paragraph were read, but Shea's and Williams' stares were locked until Williams looked away.

"Shea, do you have any preference as to counsel?" Williams asked when the reading was finished.

"Mr. Norton here has been with me from the first."

"The court then appoints Mr. John T. Norton, counsel for the defendant."

Mr. Norton rose and introduced Galen Hitt, his co-counsel. "We would move at this time, Judge, that this trial be adjourned until the next term of this court. I have only been just now assigned. With the inquest and the grand jury the People have had great opportunity to prepare their case. To go forward at this time would prejudice the defendant."

"Judge," Fagan stood, "this motion must be in writing. The defense must present affidavits to the court on any motion it brings. Otherwise relief must be denied."

"Gentlemen!" Williams declaimed, hammering the gavel. "Since the defendant has not pleaded to the pending charges, the question is not properly before me. There must be some reason for my appointment here, a judge from outside your judicial district, at the same time that there is sitting a regular term of the court. I can only presume it is to try and dispose of this class of case. Now counsel for the defense has had full and ample notice of this extraordinary term. These election cases are why this term was created.

"I will do all in my power to see this defendant has a fair and impartial trial and is not unduly forced to trial. At the same time, however," he bowed in deference to Frank Black who sat just beyond the bar, "public interests demand a fair investigation into this crime. This court stands in recess until tomorrow at ten a.m., at which time defense counsel will support its application for an adjournment with affidavits."

Williams again hammered the gavel. The assembled were surprised by the abrupt and forceful end to the full day in court they had anticipated, and there was much discussion. Shea followed the deputies out.

"How'd it go?" Jack asked when the door squealed closed in the cell.

"He's got a hanging look about him," Shea said, and he went to the window and clasped the grate.

"Why ain't it Houghton or Griffiths?"

"'Cause the governor assigned this here one."

"Where's Murphy in all this?"

"Gone." Shea signed. "George tells me Murphy and the governor are waging a royal blood feud. Murphy wants someone else to run for governor. Himself most likely. The governor wants someone else to head the state party. If I can read it, this judge is here to humiliate Murphy, and my skin is the trophy he's been sent to bring back in his teeth." He sighed again. "Remember when we was camping years back in the Adirondacks?"

"I never went with you guys. I was away."

Shea looked at him and remembered Jack had been in reform school. "Remember I told you about the dogs and the deer?"

"What's that?"

"How the coyotes bring down a deer." He turned toward the window again and spoke slowly. "It's so dark and quiet, Jack, and you're mighty glad for the fire, even as small as it seems, just a wink of light in them vast mountains. First you hear the chase, for nigh on half an hour. Then the barking rises in pitch when they corner it. Merciless barking it is, and though you don't hear the deer, you can feel its fear, you can smell it with the barking echoing in the dark, and the moonlight. Pitiful. Then the barking rises till the deer's brought down, and then, Jack, then there's the silence, and that's worse. Spooks hell out of you as you imagine them feasting on that deer. And your campfire is just one glowing eye in the midst of all that dark." He turned back and looked out the window and heaved a sigh. "They read the indictment, Jack. Weren't a sound in the room. Strange, awful strange after so much commotion."

Jack, as usual, was anxious to dispel the gloom, to put a good face on things.

"So they listen to your motions?"

"Nah, gave Hitt and Norton another day to prepare papers."

"There now. See? Looks like he's at least fair. Fairer than my arraignment last week. I told you, didn't I, how Hitt raised the circular issue, said the circular told them to go to Black's office and get your instructions, and how he called for an investigation."

"You done," Shea nodded.

"And how Black was lurking there like a shadow, impossible to shake. And how both my lawyer and the district attorney asked that Black be removed, but the judge refused?"

"You said so."

"And then how the judge give me hope when he said if any member of the committee approached a juror it was highly improper and the indictment should be dismissed, but then how he wheeled 'round and said there was no proof, no juror testified he'd been approached, and that the circular was just a tract on good citizenship?"

"You done that too."

"Well, looks to me that this judge is fairer giving you the chance to get up your proof."

"But that's what they been doing all along, Jack. Don't you see? It's a game, just for show. They give us a show, then they deny us what we want. Black and company are playing it better, going through all the motions so nothing small trips 'em up, then they'll come out walloping me." Shea squinted. "Now then, Jack, let's get to the meat of the thing. Boland was firing at me. You sure you seen the same?"

"Yeah, Bat. That's the way it was. Why do you keep asking?"

"I ain't got it set in my mind is all."

"Well, Boland was firing at you when Ross got up off of me, and Ross rose up suddenly and caught one in the back of the head."

"Well then, yours is the only version of this thing I'll buy. You saw a deuce more of it than me."

"That was the way of it, Bat, I swear."

"And when they was reading the indictment, Jack, you know three of the counts are for aiding and abetting your escape after you plugged the brother. Looks like we stand or fall together."

"As usual," Jack smiled comfortingly. "You and me, Bat, like it's always been. Right down the line."

Shea nodded and pulled out a cigar.

The next day the courtroom again was filled beyond capacity. Shea's attorneys presented their papers on four separate motions: the governor's order appointing Williams was void, the trial was starting too soon, the court had no jurisdiction and the indictment was tainted.

Hitt, a plump florid man with a high nasal voice, argued that the terms of Oyer and Terminer designated by the Justices of the Appellate Division were the only ones that could sit. There was no provision for the governor to call an extraordinary term at the same time an ordinary term was sitting, and so the court lacked jurisdiction.

Williams interrupted Hitt: "Where is the authority for your proposition that you can have but one Oyer and Terminer in the same county at the same time?"

"In New York City in 1883 the legislature expressly created a second term of the circuit court . . ."

"But that is not a court of record."

"I would concede as much, sir. But the county clerk is charged as clerk of the court, and he cannot serve two masters."

"Yet Mr. Riley is doing an admirable job." Riley nodded and whispered off the record, "At your service, Judge."

"No, Mr. Hitt, I cannot accept your jurisdictional argument. I refuse to dismiss on such ground."

"But . . ."

"Consider this, Mr. Hitt, if I have no power to continue this court, then how can I have power to dismiss? A court has only such power as has been conferred upon it. The most I could do, if I agreed with your view of the law, is to summarily close my court and go away."

"That is precisely my point, sir. The governor had no authority to convene this court in the first place."

"Then the matter shall be addressed on appeal. I have been assigned this case. I have no authority to remove myself from it. Please proceed."

Now John Norton rose: "I move to dismiss the indictment based upon improper and unlawful influence brought to bear upon the grand jurors through public meetings, the grand jury selection process, and by a circular sent to each grand juror."

"And what do you offer in support of your motion?"

"An affidavit of myself and one of the defendant."

Thomas Fagan arose: "I object, your honor. Mr. Shea has been in jail since the shooting. He can have no personal knowledge of any of these events."

The judge peered down at Norton: "Is the defendant's a positive affidavit or one sworn on information and belief?"

Norton was flustered. "A positive affidavit, Judge."

"How could he know about the things he swears to?"

"It is a matter of public notoriety; everybody knows it."

"How could he swear to what took place at the meetings unless he was there?"

"He says he knows it from the public press."

"But that would not be a positive affidavit; that would be upon information and belief."

Norton bowed his head, humbled. "Yes, sir."

The judge continued: "How could he say the circular was placed in the hands of over two hundred jurors? And yet you make him swear to that positively."

"It is a fact, as I have sworn to it as well." Norton then presented his affidavit and a copy of the circular. "Those are the papers upon which we move."

Fagan arose: "The People produce sworn affidavits that Shea has been behind bars since the shooting, and could not have known what he swore to, Judge."

Williams leaned forward. "Upon all the affidavits presented, I fail to see any evidence to convince me there was anything improper."

Norton responded: "But surely our showing is sufficient to set on foot an investigation. The grand jurors should be called, sworn and questioned about their schooling by Black's committee."

"I think I cannot. I think I will have to deny this motion. It is so denied, and the clerk will prepare an order." He nodded to Riley. "Now, gentlemen, what is the plea? The indictment was stated to him yesterday. I suppose he is ready to plead. What do you say to the indictment, Shea?"

Shea stood up, facing the judge.

Norton spoke: "He pleads not guilty."

"Do you plead not guilty?"

"Yes, sir."

"If the court please," Fagan spoke, "I now move the trial of Bartholomew Shea."

A loud grumble rose in the room, and Williams rapped the gavel. "This court will come to order! Mr. Riley, how many passes did you issue for today's proceedings?"

"Three hundred, sir."

"There must be six hundred people in here and another thousand outside, clamoring to get in. There is something going on here that I do not like and will not tolerate. This trial will not become a circus. If there are this many here tomorrow, I will clear the courtroom and proceed behind closed doors."

The scolding quieted the crowd.

"Your honor, we have affidavits now that the trial must be postponed." Norton handed up the papers to the judge, and Williams scrutinized them.

"Is this all?"

"No, your honor. At this moment there is a man in the county jail indicted for murder. He has been there three months. Try him first. Give us time to prepare. Shea's indictment was only handed up last week. Grant us a month's adjournment."

"A month is not required. This is not a mysterious case. This occurrence happened at noon in the presence of a great many people, all of whom live in this city. It will be much more pleasant to have the matter heard now rather than in the heat of August. Your motion is denied. The clerk will prepare an order." Riley again nodded. Williams rapped the gavel. "I will, however, postpone the trial until Monday next, June 4. You will be two or three weeks in obtaining a jury probably, which time will aid you in your preparation. Court stands in recess!"

Again the judge rose abruptly and was out of the courtroom as Riley was calling: "All rise!" Norton and Hitt busied themselves shuffling their papers on the four motions that had just been denied. The deputy, Jem, came to Shea, rolling his eyes, and Shea obediently offered his wrists for the shackles.

26.
THE JURY

The Jury and Court Officers

While the sheriff was summoning a panel of two hundred eighty-six jurors, an appropriations bill was introduced in the state senate and assembly seeking one thousand dollars for Troy attorneys Black and Van Santvoord for services performed in the election abuse cases. The amount was immediately raised by the grateful legislators to four thousand dollars, and the bill went on to the governor for his signature.

In true Yankee fashion, the Gurley brothers of Troy invented a mechanical ballot box and during this session they were seeking state legislative approval for its use statewide. This would mean substantial profit as they outfitted every ward and township in the state. Senator Coughlin sponsored their bill, and he happened by Governor Flower's office to ask that the governor approve the funds for Black and Van Santvoord and sign the bill for the "unstuffable ballot box".

"So, four thousand dollars is the price of Black's civic spirit?" Flower thundered. He instructed his clerk to pull the bill from the cabinet. "Watch this, Mr. Coughlin," and he scrawled "VETOED" across it with thick black ink. "Let these men appear as pure in spirit as they would have us believe," and with that he dismissed the senator.

When news of the veto spread, others disclosed that the Republican Party had retained its own chairman Frank Black with a check for one thousand seven hundred dollars, and that the Committee of Public Safety had paid him the same amount. Other amounts were hinted at from the temperance leagues and even church collections. Black failed to respond to any of these inquiries, yet the purity of his intentions had been impugned.

Meanwhile, out through the rocky hills of Rensselaer County sheriff's deputies rode on horseback. Through sleepy rural village where taverns and general stores were filled with talk of the trial, Poestenkill, Hoosick Falls, Stephentown and Nassau they rode, delivering their summonses for the jury panel. The crops were growing, foals and calves were stretching young limbs, the granges and barn dances calling solitary farm folk together for another summer of socializing and courting. This year important public service summoned many down to the county seat on the river. The corruption of a shiftless class of criminals must be ended, and political power returned to the wholesome, clean-living yeomen.

Into the city wards, too, went sheriff's deputies, to union halls and saloons and grape arbors in the back yards of the Italians, the neighborhoods of European Jews along First Street, the Polish beer garden in South Troy, the iron wards, the wards of collar factories, through the neighboring villages of Lansingburgh and Bath-on-Hudson, jurors were summoned. On a rainy first Monday in June, two hundred and sixty-seven men, short, tall, fat, lean, robust, consumptive, clean-shaven, bearded, bald, old, young, Protestant, Catholic and Jewish farmers, merchants, machinists, carpenters, innkeepers, stovemounters, toolmakers, foremen, painters, scaffold builders, railroad engineers, teachers, bridge-keepers, bartenders, garment makers, roofers, chimneybuilders and a score of the unemployed converged upon the Troy courthouse, directed by Clerk Riley to the proper room, with the intention of doing one of three things: getting on the jury to convict, getting on the jury to acquit, or else ducking the whole clamorous mess with a convenient excuse.

In the presence of judge and defendant, attorneys for either side questioned them. Some were immediately excused because of deafness, to harvest a strawberry crop, because of blindness or the illness of a child. Others were grilled by the four attorneys, Norton and Hitt for the defense, Fagan and Raines for the People:

"If the evidence warrants, would you find the defendant guilty of murder?" George Raines asked. Raines, a Democrat from Rochester, had been brought in to help Fagan with the prosecution.

Jacob Vischer, an old Dutch farmer from the Grafton mountain, bit his whiskered lip: "Yalp."

"And could you send him to the electric chair for a first degree offense?"

"Oh, no, no, no," the farmer slowly shook his head.

"You are opposed to the death penalty?"

"Yes, I am. Christ Jesus spoke, 'Give unto Caesar what belongs to him,' and the state don't own no man's life." This response brought a peal of laughter in the courtroom.

"You may stand down, sir," Raines said.

Charles Hipwell, a Hoosick farmer, when asked the same question, admitted: "Since I was a young man, I've had a holy horror of capital punishment, and now with electrocution . . ."

"Are you afraid of something under your bed?" Raines asked.

"No, sir."

"What do you do in a thunderstorm?"

Again there was laughter.

John Palmer, an illiterate stovemoulder from South Troy, was asked if he could send a man to his death. "Oh, no, sir. I have conshus… conscienc-sus . . . conscientious scruples against that."

"And do you know where your scruples are located?"

"Yes, sir . . . I mean, no, sir."

"Do your scruples hurt when you sit down?"

Palmer paused and thought. "Why, yes, sir," and at the ensuing laughter, "I mean, no, sir."

Hour after hour, day after day, the prospective jurors were examined. The first panel was exhausted in the first week with only seven found acceptable. Another hundred and fifty were called.

During the second week, the Gurley employee who'd invented the unstuffable ballot box, Augustus Bigelman, was called: "Your honor, I do not wish to serve as I am well acquainted with the Ross family."

"Please, sir, allow counsel to question you."

Galen Hitt approached: "Tell me, do you belong to the APA?"

"Yes."

"Will you recite for us the oath your took?"

"I decline to answer."

"Did you take an oath to oppose Catholics?"

"I decline to answer that."

"Challenge for cause," Hitt announced.

"On what grounds?" asked the judge.

"Why, he's an APA. We've already dismissed fifteen jurors because they belong to the APA. Why, I'd rather be kicked to death by a mule than tried by this man."

"He has shown nothing objectionable yet," Williams said. "Please continue."

"Where does your lodge meet?"

Bigelman turned toward the judge. "Must I answer?"

"No," Williams said.

"Well, then, who is president of your lodge?"

"I decline to state."

"Did you take an oath not to employ Catholics?"

"I refuse to state."

Judge Williams intervened: "The juror may step down. If I don't require him to answer your questions, Mr. Hitt, I won't require that he serve."

"Thank you, your honor."

Slowly, tediously the jury selection proceeded. Other members of the APA were found and dismissed for cause; those who objected to the death penalty were likewise dismissed for cause. Soon a new reason for not serving emerged:

Raines was questioning George Miller, a teamster from the tenth ward: "Have you read about the case?"

"Yes, sir."

"Have you formed an opinion?"

"Well, the case seems pretty well settled by the press of this town. Yes, I have an opinion." Williams instructed him to step down.

Another, an Irishman, David Hayes, claimed he had read of the case but had not formed an opinion.

"Did you read of the coroner's inquest?" Raines asked.

"Yes, sir, but I don't know that they weren't making an issue over nothing."

"Nothing?" Raines cried in disbelief. "A man is shot and killed while watching the polls, and you say it's nothing?"

"You says he was kil't," Hayes rejoined, "and the papers say he was kil't, but I don't know that. I don't know nothing 'bout nothing."

"Did you think the coroner was holding an inquest on a live man?"

"I don't know," Hayes replied. "I keep an open mind."

Hitt rose: "It was a pretty lively inquest on a dead man at that." The dwindling venire laughed and Williams called them to order.

Raines hammered away on Hayes for half an hour, but Hayes kept insisting he knew "nothing 'bout nothing." In exasperation, Raines turned to the judge. "I ask he be dismissed for cause."

Hitt was on his feet: "I protest that this man is being challenged just because he is Irish. Messrs. Fagan and Raines have purposely kept Irishmen off this jury."

Judge Williams' expression clouded, and he pointed the gavel at Hitt. "It will not do to talk this kind of stuff to me. I have heard too much of it already. A man of one nationality can kill as well as one of another. The question of nationality does not enter this case. I will keep you down to the real questions."

"But, your honor," Hitt said, "I protest this discrimination."

"Yes, and you have the right to protest against the APA as well."

"But this man has no opinion about the incident, he cannot read, so he has not been poisoned by the press. He can be nothing but an objective juror, and yet he is to be kept off for cause. What is the reason other than he is Irish?"

"You may step down," Williams told Hayes.

When Hiram P. Sherman, a farmer from Cropseyville, was examined, he squinted miserably and admitted to Raines that he had poor eyesight. Yet he insisted he had acute hearing.

"A juror must have all his mental faculties," Hitt insisted. "He must be able to look into a man's face and see if he is lying."

"On the contrary," Raines argued, "a juror need only hear the evidence, not see who is speaking it. Tell me, Mr. Sherman, could you exist on hotel food for some weeks."

"I never et at a hotel in my life."

"You mean you never used dynamite on a Troy hotel steak?"

"Nope."

"Again, I protest, your honor. This juror cannot see."

"That is of no moment," Raines insisted, "some of the smoothest liars make no show, but slink into the witness stand as honest men."

"Mr. Raines, we all know that dynamiters have a peculiar look," Hitt returned. "Since we have been here I have not made a mistake on members of the APA. I could tell them when they sat in the chair, like bloodsuckers to get on the jury."

"Very well," Williams said, "the juror may step down."

The second venire was exhausted during the second week, and a third panel of a hundred and fifty had to be called. Irishmen were reluctant to sit, but members of the APA were all too eager, and those who answered honestly about membership in the secret fraternity were dismissed.

By Thursday of the second week, nine jurors had been chosen out of four hundred examined, and all nine were staunch Protestant farmers from the hill towns who insisted they had nothing to do with the APA. Hitt and Norton had only one preemptory challenge left.

In the long days of selection, the process became a farce, attorneys slinging jokes occasionally to lighten the tone. Thomas Branigan, an iron worker from Lansingburgh, took the stand.

"Could you by your verdict send this prisoner to the electric chair?" asked Raines.

"No, sir. I am opposed to capital punishment."

"This disease of scruples is spreading," remarked Hitt. Most of the Irish had disqualified themselves from jury duty on this ground. "But this is the first case we've found in Lansingburgh." The jurors in the gallery laughed. Thomas Branigan blinked and stared in disbelief.

"Are you sure you didn't just develop a sudden attack for this case?" Raines asked with a smile.

"No, sir," Branigan said definitively, "and I don't think it's a matter to be joked about."

Shea, who had sat impassively for two weeks, raised his eyes and looked keenly at Branigan. He did not know him.

"You're right," Raines said, clearing his throat to hide embarrassment. "But would you entertain these same scruples if your wife or brother were killed in cold blood?"

"Yes, I would, sir." The juror looked at Shea with deep pity.

The judge leaned over his bench. "Don't you think the law has the right to protect society, even by taking the life of a man who committed murder?"

"No, sir. I don't think the law should take away what it cannot give in the first place."

The courtroom was silent. Shea scanned the bench, the witness stand, the jury box, the stenographer's table, the table for the press and the gallery. All eyes were upon him.

"Very well," Williams said, "the juror will step down."

On Friday, June 15, the jury box was filled for the fourteenth time and neither side had any preemptory challenges remaining. Williams instructed Clerk Riley to swear in the jurors and alternates, and then he announced the trial would begin after the noon meal.

Through the pressing crowd and out into the street Shea was led by sheriff's deputies. Many well-wishers called to him, but he passed through the gauntlet without turning his head or acknowledging them.

In the cell, Jack McGough looked up from the barrel lid where he was playing solitaire. "So, things are moving along. How'd it go?"

"Ah!" Shea shrugged.

Jack's father had been in the courtroom, and he entered behind Shea. "Eleven farmers from the hill towns and a Protestant carpenter out of the third ward. Not what I'd call a jury of his peers," Owen McGough said. Jerry Cleary and Owen Judge, held in the jail as material witnesses, came in with Jem to delivering a large pot of ham and boiled greens for their dinner.

"Too bad 'bout them goddamn farmers," Jerry laughed brutishly and took up a tin plate and spoon. "Give us some of that here. They got an imperfect understanding of the system." He doused his greens with vinegar. "They won't listen to the jingle of a few coins."

"What's that, Jerry?" Shea said quietly, but the tone of his voice stopped all conversation in the cell.

"You heard me, Bat. Christ, don't tell me you ain't thought of that? You got to fight fire with goddamn fire. They lie on the stand, we pay off a goddamn juror or two and get it goddamn hung up. Some of the boys figgered . . ."

"You stop figuring, Jerry, do you hear?" Shea's eyes burned with anger, and everyone in the room saw the weeks of tension and rage boiling behind them. "I do what I figure needs to be done, me and my lawyers. I don't want you nor none of the boys screwing this all up."

"Well, don't get so touchy. Jesus. Didn't you pay attention in the inquest? Weren't you goddamn there, Bat? They got the goods on you from what I read in the papers. If you don't do something now, you're going to goddamn swing."

"Fine," Shea said. "Then I'll damned well swing. But I'll swing on my own terms, not yours." Shea tried to check his anger, but suddenly it surged beyond his control. "Goddamn it, Jerry! I can't believe you! All of you! Here we have Frank Black tiptoeing around, committee to committee, making everything look fine, smell right, feel clean and starched, and getting paid for his effort, and look at us! Guns and phony ballots, kickbacks and no-show jobs, and now bribing the goddamned jury! Don't you see? This is what got me here! It don't work! And just because it don't work don't mean you got to do it all the harder! It don't work and it won't work! There ain't none of them you can buy!"

"That was my goddamn point in the first place!" Cleary grumbled.

"We brung down the whole business on us by crossin' a line. We got the flags waving, the speeches from the pulpit, the out-of-town judge, the indictment, all of Troy riding on our backs. Jesus Christ, Jerry, and now you want to bribe the jurors!" Shea flung his plate of ham and greens on the table and pushed out into the hall. He bummed a cigar from Jem, and stalked like a caged beast, up and back, smoking it furiously.

Cleary was glum. His leader had scolded him in front of others, and the gang seemed split beyond repair. "Know what I think, Jack?" he whispered, staring mightily at the floor. "I think Bat's goddamn finished. Not fer what Black and them are doing neither, but fer how his mind is changed." Cleary tapped his temple. "He's gone over to their way of thinking."

"Naw, not so, Jerry. He'll come 'round. Bat's as solid as they come. The pressure's getting to him is all. Trial starts in less than an hour. And it don't take no genius to figger what Black's witnesses'll say, neither."

27.
THE PROSECUTION: WEEK ONE

Hon. George Raines

Word spread that testimony was to begin and by two o'clock the courthouse was filled beyond capacity. Sheriff's deputies checked passes at the high oak doors to the courtroom. The wainscotted halls were solid with people and outside the courthouse steps were packed, the crowd spilling across Second Street onto grounds of the Troy Female Seminary. Shea was grim passing through the crowd. He did not smile, and only waved whenever, "Good luck, Bat!" sailed forth.

At the top of the stairs, his eyes met Mamie Halligan's. In that brief instant he read in her gaze many strong, conflicting emotions. He nodded solemnly, apologetically, then bowed his head. Mamie clasped her hands together and tears welled up in her eyes as deputies hauled him shackled through the crowd.

In the dim hall a photographer's gunpowder flash lit the pressing bodies like a flash of lightning, and undertones of conversation rose in pitch when it shuddered through the crowd that Shea was in the building. Into the packed courtroom the procession swept, and Shea sat with his attorneys, waiting.

After quarter of an hour, Clerk Riley called, "All rise!" and Judge Williams entered. "Bartholomew Shea!" Riley called.

"Here!" Shea answered in a loud, firm voice.

After the roll call of the jury, Thomas Fagan gave his opening address. He was genial, frank and informative delivering his initial remarks, then his tone grew more serious:

"Troy is a city of sixty thousand with a uniformed police force of nearly a hundred men. And yet, gentlemen, with one of these policemen on the grounds, within the sight of school houses, within the hearing of church bells, Robert Ross was shot down in cold blood.

"In the Old World, kings are sacred and an assault on the sovereign is punished by death. Here in America our only sovereign is the ballot and Robert Ross died for that sovereign. The bullet that killed Ross struck at the vitals of our American institutions. It struck at the sacred state itself."

Fagan then left the rail of the jury box and walked across to where Shea sat with Hitt and Norton. He pointed Shea out to them. "Gentlemen of the jury, here and now I enter my protest in the name of Holy Mother Church, against this man seeking to cover with her purple robes the blood of Robert Ross that is upon his hands. And as a Democrat, I protest him wrapping himself in the cloak of that party. Bartholomew Shea may have been a Catholic, and he may have been a Democrat, but both affiliations are incidental. Above all else he is a soldier of fortune, a pirate who demands blood money from the side on which he fights.

"Bartholomew Shea is put on trial here for the purpose of preventing crime and maintaining the safety of our state. Your verdict will endanger his life, but remember you owe a duty to the public as well. At the close of proof, the evidence will demonstrate beyond a reasonable doubt that Bat Shea murdered Robert Ross, and I will at that time ask you to return a verdict of guilty."

Shea's counsel, Galen Hitt, puffed and sweat through his brief opening remarks, urging the jury to keep an open mind, indicating there would be a reasonable doubt at the close of proof. Fagan then called his first witness.

Dr. Sidney Frank Rogers had been summoned to examine Ross's body at the Dugan house immediately after the shooting. He afterward performed the autopsy.

"Robert Ross was a perfectly healthy man," the doctor testified "very fine physique, six foot three. I have performed a great many autopsies, and this was one of the finest specimens of humanity I ever saw.

"I took the usual method of opening the cranial cavity, making an incision from one ear to the other, taking up the scalp and turning the front portion over the face, and the back portion in the same way to expose the entire skull from the eyebrows back. We sawed around the skull in a straight line and removed the skull cap and had the contents of the cranium at our disposal.

"The upper brain was in a perfect normal condition. We took off slices half an inch in thickness, and as we got down a little, made the slices thinner to find any fragments of bullet. We found no trace of a bullet or a wound in the upper brain, and then we went searching in the lower brain. The left lobe of the lower brain had no injury, but the right lobe contained a large hole penetrating clear through it.

"Taking it away in threads with our fingers, and along the track of the wound, we found pieces of bone and bullet, four pieces of bullet."

Raines held up a small box with initials on it. "Are these the fragments of bullet you found at that time?" He opened the box.

"Yes, sir."

Raines offered the fragments of bullet into evidence. Rogers testified that the wound extended four inches past the skull into the brain on an upward course, lacerating the right lower lobe, rendering Ross immediately unconscious. The bullet fragments weighed seventy-eight and one-half grains.

Dr. Rogers also testified Robert Ross had a bandaged ankle. He had sprained it recently, and the prosecution was using this to establish why Ross dropped into a sitting position as he reached the top of the ditch. On cross-examination, Galen Hitt elicited that the doctor could not tell whether the gun was four feet or forty feet from Ross's head, and given the path of the wound, the gun must have been below the skull.

Hitt walked over to where Frank Black sat just outside the railing. "In preparing for this trial, doctor, have you had occasion to visit the office of Frank Black?"

"No, sir, I did not."

"No further questions."

Fagan stood: "The People call Ernest Perry, poll inspector."

"Objection, your honor," Hitt was up. "Evidence of the election is irrelevant to this case." The gallery murmured. "This is a case of murder, not voting fraud, and such testimony would be unduly prejudicial."

"Overruled."

"Exception."

"Exception noted."

Perry testified that the third district polling booths were set up at 18 Orr Street, in the house of William Rabbit. "'Bout noon some men come in to vote. As one of them was voting in the name of William

Armstrong, why, the curtain opens from a booth, and out steps this other gentleman who says he is William Armstrong. Well, Eugene Brush says to me, 'I challenge that vote,' and from the doorway, Jerry Cleary says to us, 'Swear it in. There may be two William Armstrongs here.' Then there was some discussion about addresses, then other votes is challenged on the part of William J. Colby and Charles Craver. It is clear to me the fellow that's voting is not Charles Craver. And during that challenge then the trouble broke out."

Raines offered into evidence the voting books. Hitt objected.

"Gentlemen," Williams said, "it's nearly supper time. Before I hear this objection, let us adjourn and resume Monday morning."

"All rise!" The crowd stood, talking loudly.

Later that night, Hitt, Norton, Shea and McGough conferred in the cell. To watch for inaccuracies and to make suggestions as to proof, it was agreed that Jack would attend the trial each day. Arrangements were made with the sheriff to bring him along and sit him in the front row of the gallery.

"The critical problem I see," Hitt said, "is that this judge will let in all the evidence bearing on the voting and the election. Legally it has nothing to do with the shooting. There is a grave danger the jury may convict, not on any evidence of the shooting, but because you were forcing the vote at that time."

"Well, what can we do about it?"

"Nothing now. Each time I disagree with his ruling, I note the objection and I except to the ruling to preserve the issue for appeal."

"Appeal?"

"Yes. We can appeal to the Court of Appeals if you are convicted. They will then review all of what happened during the trial and decide whether the errors are grave enough to award you a new trial."

"And then we'd have to do this all over again?"

"I'm afraid so."

Shea sighed heavily. "Oh, brother!"

"I know there seems to be no end to this," Norton was apologetic.

"There'll be an end," Shea said.

* * *

Nellie Mae Patton paid no attention to the jury selection or the trial; she paid no attention to the newspapers or the sermons or the cries for vengeance; she paid little attention to anything. In her grief she found herself outside the usual cycles of day and night. She slept lightly and intermittently, dozing on the windowseat while looking out upon the flowers and birds that gaily mocked her sorrow, then starting awake in the dead of night to gaze for hours out of the window upon the moonlit garden, imagining her Rob in his coffin under the cold earth.

Saturday night after testimony began, Nellie Mae Patton awoke late in the night. She lay in bed judging by the angle of moonlight how high the moon was up. The house was quiet, but as she listened more closely, she heard voices, men's voices. The clock on her mantel read one-thirty, and the moon was bright, nearly full. Who were those men talking? Why were they here? Curiosity got the better of her, and she rose. Out the window there were carriages parked in the drive, their horses asleep.

The hallway was dark but for the blue moonlight through the high windows. As she passed the Thomas Cole landscape, Nellie heard the voices again. She pushed aside the painting, took out the wooden plug and peered down into the ballroom.

Below an odd ritual was underway bathed in candlelight. Men in black hoods holding candles were lined across the front of the ballroom. Up an aisle through the chairs proceeded a line of bareheaded men. To one side a white goat was tethered, and occasionally it bleated and neighed. A tall man in a black hood was intoning a ritualistic litany as the initiates advanced to receive their hoods, like a bizarre academic procession. The tall man bent low to place a hood on each of the candidates for admission, and shook hands in warm congratulations, calling each man "Friend."

"No!" she whispered. Then she cried out, "No!" and in her nightgown she rushed down the back stairs, through the kitchen, the butler's pantry, and the swinging doors into the ballroom. Heads turned and there were mutterings, then loud protests. "No!" she cried. "Stop this!" The bareheaded men hid their faces. Only then did Nellie feel self-conscious in her nightgown, her long black hair spilling over her breasts, down her back, her bare feet upon the parquet.

"You men!" she cried. "What are you doing in my house?"

Then someone was grasping her by the forearms. She clenched her fists and resisted. She heard his voice, it was Father, but through the eye-slits in the black hood his eyes looked evil. A tall man, like a wizard in a pointed hood, also bent toward her, and she saw the candlelight reflected in his rimless spectacles. His steel blue eyes chilled her.

"Daughter! Daughter!" Josiah struggled with her and two of the men joined him, lifting her, kicking and protesting, off the floor.

"You men! You and your games! This is what killed my Rob! This is what killed my husband! You and your childish games! You killed my husband! You killed him! You *killed* him! You *men*!"

"Daughter!" Josiah thundered, "Leave this room immediately!" And Nellie was carried kicking and screaming though the swinging doors, into the butler's pantry, then into the kitchen while Fitch and Melody were roused to watch her until a sleeping draught took effect.

* * *

Monday morning, the trial resumed to heightened anticipation. Ernest Perry again took the stand and Judge Williams received the voting books into evidence over Hitt's strong objection. Perry testified again about the entry of "the disreputable looking characters," and their bold attempts to vote on the names of Armstrong, Colby and Craver.

"When the firing commenced outside," he stated, "I saw Captain Murphy standing in the hallway. One of the legal voters, Ahearn, ran around the room two or three times screaming. I saw three men running north on Orr Street, one of them was Shea."

"And did Mr. Shea carry anything in his hand at that time?"

"No, sir."

Perry then described how the ballot box was set on a large dry goods crate, and how the voting procedure worked.

"The ballot clerks sat in the front room between the windows there, and the poll clerks stood at this table back here in the second room," he indicated on a diagram.

"Where were the booths?"

"The booths were on this side in the front room, about seven or eight of them."

"So that a voter, when he came in, would enter this front door, turn to the right in the front room, come up to the register, give his name, you would examine the register to see that his name was there when it was called out, he would turn to the ballot clerks and receive his ballots?"

"He generally stopped by the ballot clerk and gave his name."

"Had to give his name to get his ballots?"

"Yes, sir."

"Then pass to one of the booths?"

"Yes, sir."

"Out of the booth, then, and back to the register?"

"Yes, sir."

"Deposit his ballot and go out again?"

"Yes, sir; the same way he come in."

"How many men were in this little hall when you saw the five men come in?"

"There might have been eight or ten."

"Who were they?"

"I don't know who they were, only Shea and Cleary."

"Did you see any difficulty in the hall?"

"No, sir; not until the trouble we had about the duplicate voters."

"No loud talking?"

"Not till I challenged the vote."

"Who did you challenge?"

"The men giving the names of Ahearn, Armstrong, Colby and, Craver."

"You challenged each of them?"

"Yes; and each of them swore in their vote."

"And after the chairman administered the oath, two men voted on the same name?"

"Yes."

"No further questions."

On cross-examination, Perry testified he worked as a machinist at the Ross Valve factory and that Robert Ross had turned a number of Indian clubs about twenty inches long and three inches thick on a lathe at the shop. Perry said he was given a club by the Rosses, and that he carried it to the polls election day.

"Are you, sir, a member of the APA?"

"Yes."

"And how long have you been so?"

"Three years."

"Were you aware a senate committee came up from Albany last year to inquire into voting fraud in Troy?"

"Yes, sir. I was subpoenaed by Officer Butcher."

"And did you testify?"

"Yes, sir."

"Did you go to Black's office that day?"

"Why, yes, yes, I did, sir."

"Did you see Black?"

"Yes, sir."

"And William Ross?"

"Yes, sir."

"And who else?"

"A man named Hayner."

"And did you recognize anyone at the senate hearing?"

"Only the Troy men, that is, Mr. Black," he nodded at the tall, lean form sitting just behind the bar, "Duncan Kaye, William Ross and

Ellis Hayner."

"When was the last time you attended an APA meeting?"

Perry swallowed hard. "You mean before the killing?"

"Sure."

"Two days before election."

"And was the election discussed?"

"Primarily the violence at the caucus the month before, and how to prevent it this time."

"And where was this meeting held?"

Perry fidgeted on the stand. It had been held in the gracious Patton home out Oakwood Avenue, but his brother worked in the Patton store, and it would not do to pull the family into this. "I can't tell you."

"Was it in the city of Troy?"

"No, sir."

"It was in Lansingburgh, wasn't it?"

"Yes, sir." Perry looked down into his folded hands.

"No further questions."

William Davenport of the Earl & Wilson Collar Shop had served as a Republican poll watcher, but testified he did not know Shea.

"I challenged a repeater voting on the name of William J. Colby just before the ruckus began," he swore. "Things got mixed up then and I didn't see. After there was such shouting in the polls, Officer Murphy heaved Cleary then Hayner out the door. I think Shea punched Hayner right in the face. I recognized Hayner; Shea I am not acquainted with personally; he was only pointed out to me once, and I never saw him again until that day right there in that swath that was cut through the crowd."

"What did you observe then?"

"It was just as the riot was going by the window; then they all rushed around the post and began shooting."

"Did you at the time see who had the revolver or who shot?"

"No, sir."

Davenport told how Boland was ahead of Robert Ross all the while.

"Where was Robert Ross?"

"Sitting on the ground. He had this foot drawn up under him like that, and that foot out straight and his hands on the ground, his head bent forward."

"Did you notice whether there was anyone near Robert Ross?"

"No, sir. I didn't notice anyone there."

"Did you notice where Shea was after he struck Hayner?"

"I didn't see him again that day."

"John McGough?"

"Didn't notice him."

On cross-examination Davenport admitted belonging to the APA, but had never met Robert Ross in an APA lodge. He had visited Black's office twice during the coroner's inquest and was subpoenaed to appear before the senate committee last year.

"About how many shots did you hear fired?"

"Must have been about eighteen."

"Over how long a period of time?"

"Four minutes, probably."

"How many different people did you see with revolvers in their hands?"

"I couldn't say about that."

"Did you see anyone with a gun that day?" Hitt asked.

"Yes, sir."

"And who carried it?"

"John Boland." This caused a great stir in the crowd.

"Is that the only gun you saw?"

Alarmed, Davenport looked over to Frank Black, but Black sat impassively.

"Yes, sir."

"Tell us what you observed of Mr. Boland."

"Uh, he was wearing a green overcoat, and he passed me going westward with a gun in one hand and a club in the other."

"Did you see Boland fire his gun?"

"Yes, sir. I saw smoke from the muzzle."

"Did you see Shea near Ross?"

"No, sir."

"And was your view in any way obstructed?"

"No, sir. My view was unobstructed. I would have seen Shea if he'd been there."

Hitt knew when to stop. "No further questions."

Fagan and Raines conferred about redirect, but Fagan rose, "No questions."

Edward Philip, a stairbuilder, then confirmed that the row began with a repeater voting on Armstrong's name. "When Armstrong emerged from the booth and challenged him, the repeater started to laugh."

The jurors looked to each other, and muttering filled the gallery.

"Jerry Cleary said there could be two of them, and the repeater swore in his vote." Philip testified he did not observe the shooting, but he saw that John Ross was the first to Robert's side. John Ross pointed, screaming, "The blood of my brother is on my hand. My God!" and ten or twelve men chased after John McGough.

On cross-examination, Philip agreed with Hitt that no one was within ten or twelve feet of Robert when John Ross approached.

"Can you tell us about the evening of that day, sir?"

"Well, Dunlop was declared elected, and the outrage at the murder was amplified by Dunlop's victory."

"Did you ever have occasion to visit Frank Black's office?"

"Yes, sir."

"And were there any others present?"

"Yes, sir."

"And who were they?"

"Other witnesses to appear at the coroner's inquest."

"And did Mr. Black rehearse you well?"

"He listened intently."

"No further questions."

After this witness, Williams adjourned, completing the first full day of testimony.

On Tuesday, Reeves Smith, a civil engineer, testified as to distances, referring to a map the prosecutor had prepared: Dunlop's Saloon was 710 feet from the polls, ran 62.4 feet along Sixth Avenue and 32.3 feet along Douw. McGough had traveled 1.75 miles up to his aunt's house at 45 Christie Street. The depression across the lane from the polls was over four feet deep, and had an uneven bottom over five feet deep.

Charles Piper, photographer for James H. Lloyd, testified that he had taken a photograph of the polling place, and the photograph was entered into evidence.

Samuel Taylor, a poll watcher for Mayor Whelan's party, saw Shea, McGough and Cleary talking near the Pearl's home about seven-thirty. Shea returned with five strangers at ten. Shea, he said, wore a wide, twenty-five cent green necktie. On cross-examination he insisted, "I don't belong to no APA." He worked in the shops and earned two dollars seventy-five cents a day. The Shea family lived next to the Quandt Brewery Bottling Plant.

William Armstrong was then called. He had served as alderman of the second ward years before, and he knew the game, he did. He remembered election day, he had gone to the polls where, even while he was in the booth, "a low-sized repeater" had tried to vote on his name. When he challenged the man, the riot erupted. He heard seven or eight shots: "They fired very quick; not over a second; a very short space of time, it was, to be sure."

The continual buzzing in the courtroom rose in pitch when Ellis Hayner was called. It was Hayner who insisted on accompanying Shea and the repeaters into the polls, thus precipitating the riot. Hayner was a stovemounter by trade, and he testified: "I was a Whelan poll watcher. The first I know of was when Bartholomew Shea told me I had got to get out as I was trying to get in; I made the remark, if he would go out with his crowd, I would and if he stayed in I certainly should go in."

"Go on."

"And with that he got me by the throat, struck at my breast and punched me. He kept pushing out the door and off the stoop. Then Cleary started pushing. They told me I could not go in. I told them if they went in, I would too. Then Cleary said, 'I won't talk to no son of a bitch who'll take a poor man's job.' And I answered them I didn't want any trouble because it was election day."

"With that Cleary struck you?"

"Yes, sir."

"Where did he hit you?"

"It was on the head, around here; with that Shea turned around and struck me twice on this side of the face."

"And did you strike anybody?"

"No, sir. I had no chance to do so."

"Were you arrested that day?"

"Yes, sir," he scanned the gallery with pride, "I must say I was."

"Any what was the charge?"

"Carrying a concealed weapon."

"Were you armed that day?"

"No, sir."

"What about a wrench, a stovemounter's wrench?"

"Why, that's the tool of my trade."

"Now, Mr. Hayner, did you notice what Shea was wearing?"

"A derby hat and a green necktie."

"And McGough?"

"McGough had a cap on."

Fagan turned the witness over to Hitt, and Hitt rose and paused dramatically. "Tell us, Mr. Hayner," he then looked behind him to where Frank Black sat in the front row, "have you ever been to Mr. Black's office."

"Yes, sir."

"How often?"

"Two or three times."

"And who was there with you besides Mr. Black?"

Hayner looked at Fagan and Raines to save him, but they did not object. "Why, there was Duncan Kaye, and Bissell and Lee."

"And did you participate in Black's school for witnesses?"

"It weren't no school. He merely wanted to hear what we had to say."

"And did he have you recite your story in the presence of those other men?"

"In the presence of two or three."

"And what did you have to say there?"

"The truth. Same as here."

Hitt then turned to election day. "When there was this talk about taking a poor man's job, Mr. Hayner, what was that about?"

"Why, I'm a non-union man. Always have been. Unions are a blot on the face of the earth."

"And what did you reply when Mr. Cleary said that?"

"Only that I'd take it, I wanted no trouble from him."

"And did Shea strike you?"

"Yes, sir. He struck me on the left eye."

"Did you tell anyone you could free Shea because you knew that Shea did not shoot Ross?"

"I don't know who did the shooting. I saw no shooting."

William Willard, superintendent of police, next told of going to Dunlop's Saloon immediately after the shooting with Chief Detective Markham, Addison Colvin and Officer Butcher. "There was much confusion," he said. "It was in a back room, a kitchen. There were seven or eight people there."

"And did you question the defendant?" Raines asked.

"I asked Shea, 'Where is your revolver?' and he answered, 'I didn't have any, nor did I do any of the shooting.'"

Addison Colvin, New York State Treasurer and a former newspaperman, had come upriver from Albany on the day of Troy's charter elections: "I had read a great deal in the papers about forcing the vote in Troy elections, and I came over to see the thug-work."

"What specifically had you heard, sir?"

"How a man named Boland had his eye blackened and his face disfigured at a Republican primary a month before. I heard there was to be a pitched battle in the thirteenth ward."

"And when you arrived in Troy, you came to the thirteenth?"

"Yes, sir. I took an electric streetcar to Douw Street. As I alighted this man told me if I went down there, I would see the way repeating was worked by the Democrats in Troy."

By that time Ross's corpse had been removed from the site. Colvin accompanied Superintendent Willard to Dunlop's Saloon:

"I heard one of the officers ask Shea about a revolver, and he said he had none; hadn't had any that day and hadn't done any shooting; there were some remarks made then by a young man that Boland was the man that shot Ross; Markham said Boland was the man they wanted, and they all seemed to agree he was, and after a little conversation we went away."

On cross-examination, Hitt asked sarcastically: "Did you expect to see horns on all the Democrats up here?"

"No," Colvin said testily, "I have once in a while seen a Democrat before I came here."

Dr. Phelan, the jail doctor, testified Shea told him he had no weapon with him but his fist.

Osborne Lansing was called. He worked making patterns for collars and cuffs and was a Mason in John Ross's lodge. He had gone over to the polls when the mill whistles were blowing for noon. The crowd was pressed up to the windows of the polls. There was a sudden rush from inside, then three men came out and there was a general scattering. He heard Cleary threaten Hayner: "If you were any kind of man, I would break your jaw." This caused a brief fistfight.

Lansing saw Jack McGough fire at William Ross, "Bill fell, then another started after McGough. That was Robert Ross. McGough ran and Rob chased him, knocking up the gun that McGough pointed at him. Ross tackled McGough down in the ditch with burrs and cinders, then Shea circled back within two feet of where they lay wrassling. He put his gun down within two feet of Ross's head and shot. Then Robert Ross never raised his hand to strike this man under him again; I should judge the man was killed. 'You cur,' I said to him, 'to shoot a man like that.'"

"Objection!" Hitt arose.

"Sustained."

"Did you see Robert Ross strike Jack McGough?"

"Yes, sir. But he had no club like many of these testified. He had only a bare fist."

On cross-examination, Hitt asked if Lansing belonged to the APA.

"I must say with great pleasure I do. What's more, I hope someday to see you a member."

"For how long have you belonged?"

"Two years last February."

"And for what purpose did you join?"

"It made me proud to associate with men that I supposed were men."

"And is it the objective of the APA to keep Catholics down?"

"No, sir."

"You do not ride on a goat and recite an oath to oppress all Catholics?"

"No, sir."

"You do not agree to keep Catholics out of jobs?"

"No, sir." Lansing looked for a cue from Frank Black, and then he asked: "Now, what do you mean by Catholics?"

"Roman Catholics."

"Oh," Lansing said, looking at the floor. "I thought you meant Holy Catholics. Episcopalians. Not Roman Catholics."

Hitt turned to the jury to see their expressions, but the wall of weathered faces from the farm towns was no more sympathetic than Osborne Lansing. At that juncture, Williams adjourned for the day.

Lansing confirmed on cross-examination, when the trial resumed on Wednesday, that Ross tackled McGough, and that McGough was under Ross at the time of the shooting. Hitt called a boy up and Lansing demonstrated how Ross's head was turned when shot. Lansing then indicated he recognized Shea by his large green necktie.

"Wasn't that necktie business hatched up at the coroner's inquest?"

"I only know what I saw."

"Wasn't it a green overcoat?"

"No, sir. A green tie."

Harriet Titus was then called. She had gone to the polls to look after her husband. She stated she heard men talking in a gangway near Reedy's barn:

"All of them looked like men?"

"Some of them looked rather young," she said. "Might have been eighteen or twenty years old."

"Did you know the names of any of them?"

"Not at that time."

"What did you hear?"

"One of them said, 'We're going to slug someone.' And another one said, 'You slug them and kill them if you can and twenty-five dollars is yours.' Then another said, 'What in hell do you take us for over there in that crowd?' And the other one, the older one, said, 'I don't ask you to do it now; wait your chance,' and the other one said, 'Yes, hell, come on, I will go.'"

She described the older man as rather tall, with a black overcoat, soft hat and a muffler around his neck.

"Then one said, 'How do I know I will get the money?' And the man who stood against the barn said, 'The money is here for you.'"

"Where did they go?"

"Over toward Douw Street."

The conspiracy Harriet Titus described made a strong case for premeditated murder. With that groundwork in place, Fagan and Raines now brought out their star witnesses, the Ross brothers.

The three surviving brothers were folk heroes in the city. They too had turned out heroically to protect the honest ballot. Indeed, William Ross had barely escaped death himself, and it was their loss of a brother that people understood most poignantly.

"The People call Adam Ross," Raines announced Thursday morning. There was great expectation as Adam walked toward the witness stand. Adam had a quiet, forceful presence and penetrating brown eyes. Slowly he peered about the courtroom and then his gaze rested upon the jury. The jurors straightened up in their seats to hear him.

Adam described the gang's appearance and reappearance at the polls and how Shea drew blood when he punched William. Adam told how the gang returned at noon, Shea, Cleary and Hayner entering the polls, then their expulsion. He described the incident without passion, but his deadpan style imparted a sense of great tragedy.

"Robert was in a tackle with a man. My brother William started toward him. Robert was backing the man away from him, holding the hand up and forcing the man from him. I saw McGough passing, and as someone touched him on the arm, I saw the gleam of his gun."

"And who took hold of his arm?"

"I learned later it was Quigley who turned McGough about. McGough then wheeled on my brother William, levelled his gun at William and discharged it twice."

"Was William facing him or back to him?"

"Back to him."

"Now, with respect to Robert, was the pistol in the man's hand discharged or not?"

"The man's revolver was discharged almost simultaneously with McGough's. Robert threw aside the man he had been in a tackle with, and started after McGough, disappearing into the declivity and the weeds. Then I saw them start up and out of the gully. On this higher ground, nearly level with Orr Street, I saw a man which I recognized as Shea, and he had a revolver in his hand. He raised his gun or his revolver and fired twice."

"Where was Robert at the time of those two shots?"

"On the high ground."

"How far from Robert was Shea at the time of the shots?"

"Eight or ten feet."

"Is that the nearest you can state from memory?"

"Yes, sir."

"Did you observe in what direction the shots were fired?"

"Yes sir. At my brother and the man he was pursuing."

"What then?"

"My brother fell and Shea went right up behind him, lowered his gun and fired right into the back of his head. As he passed by him he fired again, right at his face."

"Can you imitate Shea's motion?"

"I don't know." Adam Ross arose from the witness chair. "When he fired the first two shots, he fired holding his hand out straight; when he came up to Robert, he lowered the revolver down so that my brother was sitting in a sitting position, and he lowered it down so it was right down towards his head, and he fired. As he passed him, he turned and fired right back like that."

Adam then identified Robert's hat, clothing, the papers and pocketbook that Robert had carried with him, and testified that the hole appearing in the papers matched the hole through Robert's outer coat.

"Now what did you see after Shea shot your brother?"

"Just then there was a revolver flash in my face, and when I turned, the revolver was right against this side of my head."

"What did you do?"

"I threw the hand up, and the revolver went off again over my head. I seized the man and forced him from me and put my hand inside my coat and drew out a stick and struck him."

"A cocobolo stick?"

"Yes. Then he fell. I went to Robert because I had seen him shot."

"And can you describe what Shea wore?"

"He wore a short sack coat. I noticed all of the party had short coats on. Shea wore a derby hat and a green necktie, a broad tie, four-in-hand knot, the tie inside his vest."

"During this incident, did you see Alderman Dunlop?"

"I saw Dunlop less than ten minutes before the shooting."

Hitt arose: "I object, your honor. Seeing Mr. Dunlop ten minutes prior to the shooting is irrelevant and immaterial."

Williams considered. "What is this being asked for, Mr. Raines?"

"We propose to show that Dunlop was engaged in speaking to a number of persons."

"The law is very careful," Judge Williams cautioned, "to prevent any attack on a man's character prior to the transaction. A man should not be tried on evidence of any past conduct. These transactions were far apart, and I am not going to allow them in, subject of course to their admission at a later stage of the trial."

"Your witness," Raines said.

Hitt elicited from Adam Ross that a dozen cocobolo clubs had been turned on a lathe at Ross Valve and that fifteen shots were fired.

"Who was the man Robert was first in a tackle with?"

"I don't know."

"Was it Shea?"

"I don't know."

"When Robert was chasing McGough, did you see McGough fall and your brother fall on top of him?"

"No, sir."

"When your brother went down, how did he fall?"

"I seen him go down."

"Did he stub his toe and fall over flat?"

"No. He went down in a sitting position."

"And remained in that position?"

"Yes."

"Which way did his head tip as he sat upon the ground?"

"To the left. It was inclined to the left."

"Mr. Ross, do you belong to the APA?"

"I have been published as one."

"Did any of your brothers?"

"I don't know."

"Did you notice the color of any other person's necktie that day?"

"I can't say that I did."

As Adam left the stand there was a thoughtful murmuring in the gallery. His testimony had been most persuasive and sincere.

William Quigley, a friend of the Ross family, testified next. He was a watcher for the Prohibition party, and on a trip to a bakery for ginger snaps he had seen the gang crossing North Fourth Street. He distinctly saw that Shea had a gun, and heard Shea state, "I can do him with this." Immediately following McGough's shooting of William Ross, Quigley went to him.

"Were you looking at Robert when you attended to William?"

"I did not see Robert until after he was shot."

Raines held up a revolver. "Do you recognize this, sir?"

"Yes. It is a revolver."

"And where have you seen it before?"

"Just after the shooting, a boy called my attention to it. Napoleon Jentice, he saw the revolver, a rule and two hats lying in the ditch."

"And did you retrieve the revolver?"

"Yes, I did, and I gave it to Coroner Collins when I met him in front of his store."

Raines asked that the pistol be marked, then turned the witness over to Hitt. Quigley testified he was standing on the street in front of Dunlop's Saloon immediately after the shooting when Superintendent Willard's wagon pulled up.

"I went over and demanded the arrest of Bat Shea and John McGough."

"On what grounds?"

"I saw weapons in their hands, and I saw McGough using his weapon."

"Are you a member of the APA, sir?"

"I am."

"And did you take a pledge to oppress Catholics whenever and wherever you could?"

"Objection!" Fagan rose. "Your honor, I strenuously object to the defense trying to clothe itself in the mantle of the Catholic Church. The witness should not be required to divulge the contents of any secret oath."

"Sustained."

Robert P. Dodds, an instrument maker with the firm of W. & L.E. Gurley, testified that he turned at the critical moment and happened to see Robert Ross slumped over, a running form pass behind him and a shot fired.

"And can you identify who fired that shot into Mr. Ross as he was slumped upon the ground?"

"I identify him as Bat Shea."

On cross-examination, Dodds indicated he was a member of the APA, but he declined to answer about the oath he took.

"Now, something bothers me, sir." Hitt leaned back and took a deep breath. "You saw Shea shoot Ross, yet you pursued McGough. Isn't that right?"

"Yes."

"And you saw Shea go north after the shooting?"

"Yes."

"And no one pursued him?"

"No."

"McGough is the only man they followed?"

"Yes."

"And Boland was in the lead?"

"Yes. Boland asked a woman that was nearby which way McGough had gone."

"Is it not so that Boland shot Ross?"

"No, I guess not."

"Now, about this tie business, you saw Shea wearing a green necktie?"

"Yes. It was quite stylish and highfalutin."

"And Boland had a green overcoat on?"

"I guess so."

"How long had you known Shea before that day?"

"Never knew Shea before that day."

"How many feet were you away from where Robert Ross was when he was shot?"

"I couldn't say exactly. Somewheres in the neighborhood of twenty-five or thirty feet."

"Isn't it closer to fifty feet?"

"No. I can't say it was."

"How many people between you and Robert?"

"Wasn't any."

"How high was the muzzle of the gun at the moment of discharge?"

"About on a line with the top of his head."

"And what color necktie did the man who shot Ross have on?"

"Green."

John Collins, the coroner, testified that he had received the pistol the boy found in the ditch and three chambers had been discharged.

Friday morning Eugene Brazee, a locomotive fireman, took the stand: "John McGough was the only man I saw with a revolver." Brazee swore that Shea wore a green necktie. He told how George Dunlop had come to the polls and talked with ex-Captain McGraw of the Third Precinct. On cross-examination he admitted he'd been to Frank Black's office, but he did not see the shooting: "They were running after somebody. I saw the crowd running, and I supposed somebody had gone that way, somebody they were after."

John J. Lewis, a seller of household goods, told how he had heard the noon mill whistles blow, and shortly afterward, fifteen to twenty shots. He watched as Robert Ross clambered up the side of the ditch.

"When Robert Ross was shot in the back of the head, what position was he in?"

"I think he was sitting up a little bit; seemed to me as if he fell or something was the matter with him; I never saw a fellow go down so."

Judge Williams asked: "Did you see Ross go down before any shots were fired, any of those two?"

"Yes, I saw him when he stumbled, I thought, or his legs caught some way or the other. He was leaning over."

"And was there any change of position with the shot?"

"Yes. He went right over back with his hands up, and he went down, kind of sidewise. That was the last shot; I says, 'My God, they have killed him.'"

"Objection."

"Strike that out."

On cross-examination, Lewis admitted he had not been called at the coroner's inquest. Hitt moved closer to the railing: "Didn't you say back then, 'Yes, I was there but I didn't pay any attention to it; I don't know anything about how it happened.' Will you swear, sir, you didn't say that?"

Lewis became indignant. "I will not."

"You didn't know who Shea was at that time, did you?"

"Someone later told me who he was."

"Could you differentiate him from McGough?"

"I did not see McGough."

"When you saw Shea return, did you see any gun in his hand?"

"No sir, but I saw the flash." He sat back, scowled. "I saw a gun in Shea's hand as he left the scene."

"So his was not the revolver found in the ditch?"

"Apparently not."

"And what was he wearing?"

"I have no idea."

The prosecution then called Thomas A. Lee who swore he did not know McGough or Shea. He saw a man double back toward Robert Ross as Ross and McGough grappled in the ditch. Three shots were fired in the gully at Robert Ross's head, then both Ross and McGough arose, and McGough ran west.

On cross-examination, Hitt probed the identification issue:

"You don't know who this man was that fired the three shots?"

"No, sir; only just as I described him."

"Look at Shea; you know him now; you know he is Shea?"

"Yes."

"Will you say that man fired those three shots?"

"I say he was dressed and shaped just like the man that drawed the revolver."

"Will you swear that was positively the man who shot the three shots?"

"I won't swear as to the man who fired the shots." Lee looked imploringly about the courtroom. "I can't swear until I see and I know him. I can't be certain it was Shea."

This brought a general murmur from the gallery, and Lee was told to stand down.

Augustus Paul, a hotelkeeper from Melrose, was called. He lived adjacent to a gangway through which Shea, McGough and Cleary had passed on their way to the polls with five strangers. He heard one say: "To hell with them. There is enough of us. We'll do them." They climbed over a gate that had been nailed shut and proceeded on.

"Tell these twelve men," said Hitt on cross-examination, indicating the jury, "when you concocted that story."

"I didn't concoct the story."

"Who did?"

"No one that I know of."

"Did anybody ever rake it out of your mind?"

"No, sir."

Paul admitted to Hitt that he had not testified at the coroner's inquest, and indeed had not remembered the conversation until subpoenaed to testify at the trial. He swore that Neil Collins, the coroner's brother, met with him in Melrose to discuss the case, and that he told Collins he knew nothing about the election day business.

"Yes, that is good," Hitt said, advancing, encouraging him, "give us a good lot of that."

"Objection."

Hitt continued: "You never told him there was an alleyway down there?"

"Not that I can think of."

"You told them nothing about this conversation?"

"No, sir."

Paul then indicated he did not testify at the coroner's inquest because he was one of the jurors. Hitt hammered him as to bias. Paul insisted that serving on the coroner's jury had no bearing on his testimony. "And why were you not called after the inquest to tell this to the grand jury?"

Paul squinted and looked toward Frank Black. Black folded his arms, drew himself up, and pressed his thin lips together. "But I was."

"You were?" Hitt thundered. "You were a witness before the grand jury?"

Paul nodded. "Yes, sir."

"But your name does not appear on the list provided me! Your honor, I must object! The prosecution did not disclose this witness to us, and it has substantially prejudiced our case."

"Overruled. Proceed."

"No further questions."

When John Ross took the stand Saturday morning, a respectful hush fell upon the gallery. He had been first to kneel at the martyr's side.

"Are you a brother of Robert Ross, the deceased?"

"I am."

"Were you at the polls in the third election district of the thirteenth ward on election day last?"

"I was."

"What time did you arrive to the polls?"

"Shortly after six o'clock."

"When did you first see the defendant Bartholomew Shea in the neighborhood of the polling place?"

"Between eight and nine."

"Was he alone or in the company of others?"

"He was with John McGough and Jerry Cleary."

Ross testified as to the approaches of the gang, the altercation at ten, and then the riot:

"There were some words in the hallway shortly after Hayner went in. I recognized Cleary's voice. I believe Cleary asked the officer to put Hayner out."

"How did Hayner come out of the doorway?"

"Endeavoring to stay in, and they were endeavoring to put him out."

"Which way did he come out?"

"Backwards. He did not fall. Shea came out and threatened Hayner: 'I can do you with my fist.' Cleary then asked a friend for a chew of tobacco, and he crossed three or four steps very rapidly and hit Hayner in the face. Cleary then spat his wad of tobacco at Hayner's feet and stated he would not talk to any son of a bitch who took a poor man's job."

"And what happened then?"

"Then Shea struck Hayner and Hayner drew a wrench. 'I got something better than that,' Shea said, and he pulled a revolver. At the same moment McGough, who stood to the left of Shea, drew a revolver and his arm was up above his shoulder, he either bunked into someone or someone detained him. Someone also grabbed Shea just then."

John Ross described the general flight across Orr Street. "There were some shots fired, one or two, and as Robert came to the edge of the ditch, I saw him throw his hand in that position as though warding a blow or knocking something from in front of him, and then he disappeared," Ross snapped his fingers, "like that."

"What did you see next?"

"I set out to intercept him, and the next thing I saw, Robert was coming out of a declivity and just ahead of him was a person, an object moving between myself and Robert. There was the discharge of a revolver and my brother sank."

"And where was this person who fired the shot?"

"Six to ten feet from my brother."

"Yes?"

"The object still continued in direct line with my brother, where my brother had fallen, and the next shot was placed within a few inches."

"By this same person."

"By the same object."

"At what part of your brother was the revolver pointed?"

"Back part of his head."

"What shot was that directed at your brother?"

"The second."

"As this person, this object turned, did you get a look at his face?"

"Yes, it was Bartholomew Shea." Ross pointed at the defense table, and Shea's eyes narrowed, his scowl deepened.

"What became of Shea?"

"I don't know. I turned around and went back to my brother. I endeavored to stop the flow of blood."

"What did you do?"

"Placed my right hand over the wound, my left hand under his chin, and raised his head up. My brother Adam came up about that instant, pushed my hand away, and I said 'Bat Shea — '"

"Objection!"

"Sustained."

"You made some cry?"

"Yes."

"Did you observe what Shea was wearing?"

"A low crown derby, a sack coat and a long green necktie." John Ross then testified he knew Shea for fifteen or seventeen years. He indicated Robert was in the act of rising when Shea shot him.

On cross-examination, Ross gave self-defense as a motive for carrying a club to the polls and swore that he was not a member of the APA. Hitt could shake little of his testimony.

Then William Bissell, a machine adjuster, took the stand.

"You saw McGough and Robert in the gully; what movement took place?"

"They seemed to be struggling there."

"Did you see McGough and Robert separate?"

"Yes, sir. When I saw McGough, he got from under Robert Ross and seemed to be moving west."

"Where was Robert Ross when McGough went out from under him?"

"I think he was a little distance below the roadway. I lost sight of him then; the next I saw him he sat there shot."

"Did you see any weapons in anybody's hands?"

"Mr. McGough's."

"What did you see?"

"Revolver."

"What was he doing with it?"

"I didn't see him doing anything with it; not down there."

"And what of Shea? Did you see him?"

"Yes. He was east of Ross, in front of him."

"And where was he going?"

"He was turning away."

"And he was in front of Ross?"

"Yes, sir."

"And what position was Ross in?"

"He was sitting, tailor fashion, and I saw his head hanging down, facing southwest, and blood running down; he appeared to me as though he were dead."

"What was the next you saw of McGough?"

"I saw him going west."

"And you followed McGough?"

"I followed McGough."

To Hitt's cross-examination Bissell stated that he did not see Robert Ross try to get up. He saw only one revolver that day in Jack McGough's hand.

"And, Mr. Bissell, have you been to Mr. Black's office?"

"Yes, sir."

"Were there other witnesses there at that time?"

"Yes."

"How many?"

"Ten or twelve, I would guess."

"Did anyone make suggestions while you were telling your story?"

"Yes."

"Were there any suggestions or any attempts made in any manner by Black to influence the statement or change the statement any person made?"

"No, sir."

"Did you learn who Black was appearing for?"

"He was going to assist Mr. Fagan; that is all I knew about it."

It was noontime on a buoyant blue Saturday. Outside, trees filled like sails with the summery wind. Birds were calling, flowers were in bloom and the river was clogged with canal boats. As Judge Pardon Williams adjourned court for the week, a crowd of dark-suited men poured down the white granite steps of the courthouse. Through the crowd came a line of men then, deputies first, then Shea and McGough in straw hats. McGough looked jaunty and pleased; Shea looked glum.

Up Ferry Street among the horses and wagons and wheelbarrows they walked, crowds gawking at them from the storefronts and saloon windows, the malthouse of the Excelsior Brewery smoking and steaming across from the jail. When they were in the dim, dusty cell once more, Shea lit a cigar.

"No one'll be by today, Jack. They'll be up to the ballgame."

"Yep."

"George'll go a keg for 'em, and they'll be betting and cheering. Delaney's brother's a pitcher of considerable skill, and I wanted to watch him come along this year."

"Yep."

Shea stood a long while at the grate, watching his cigar smoke escape upon the wind. The one-thirty express from Albany thundered up the line past the South Troy market, under Ferry Street, behind the jail, its wheels rattling their teeth. The whistle blew long and shrill, then two short blasts as the brakeman applied the brakes and eased it into Union Station.

"The case is getting strong 'gainst me, ain't it, Jack?"

"Damned perjurers! All of 'em!" McGough kicked his feet off the bed and hopped to the floor.

"This last witness, Bissell, why he never told that I went 'round back of Ross. He told the truth. I was in front of Ross, but when I seen him off of you, and with Boland firing at me, I spun away and got out of there myself. It don't add up to me. Everyone says Ross slumped down soon as he was out of the ditch, Jack. It's clear to me he was shot then. This nonsense about his ankle! They're making it up to pin the deed on me."

"You're right, Bat, you're goddamn right! I seen Boland chugging up behind me, his gun a-blazing. Then he'll get up there and tell everyone he was shooting blanks. Sure."

"But with the testimony from the inquest in all the papers, and now witness after witness saying how I went 'round in back of him. It's clear to me the circle's narrowing."

McGough slapped him on the back. "You just wait and see, Bat. We ain't put on our case yet."

Shea sighed. “You know, Jack, I think back to last summer and the ballgames in Rensselaer Park. That was nice. A barrel of beer and four bits on the home team. Mamie even liked to go. Mamie.” He shook his head. “I saw her there today.”

“Some of the boys’ll come visiting tonight, you’ll see.”

Shea turned to the window and his eyes were red, “You know, Jack, thinkin’ back, before the election, I considered what I could gain. That’s what filled my mind before election, what I could gain, what we all could gain by puttin’ George in. I just never gave a thought about what I could lose.” He sighed heavily. “Nor do I think I’m seeing it all yet.”

“Ah, forget it, Bat. You know you’re innocent and I know you’re innocent.”

“Do you, Jack? Do you?”

“’Course I do, Bat. I never doubted your innocence for a second. Don’t worry ’bout what there is to lose, ’cause there ain’t nothing to lose. The boys’ll be by tonight and we’ll have a time. And they’ll tell us all about the ballgame. Just wait. They’ll bring a growler in tonight and we can put on a glow. Won’t be long, Bat. Won’t be long till we’re out of here together.”

28.
THE LORD'S DAY

St. Joseph's Seminary

Blue laws prohibited selling liquor on Sunday, but if you paid the cop on the beat to avert his eyes, you could keep the doors open all week long. And if you were the duly elected alderman from the ward, why you didn't even have to pay. The force and the boss would get their consideration some other way. Being open Sundays was useful because the boys needed a place to come and nurse their hangovers.

In the summer, there were ballgames and the team and the cheering section could get primed before the game, then return and relive the game in lively description all evening. In winter there were sleighing parties down the hills and skating parties on the river. Whatever the season, Dunlop's Saloon was the place to while away the sabbath, away from the shrieks of the kids and the nagging of the wife.

In the past two months, Dunlop's Saloon had been active and cheerful despite its role in the infamous murder. Sightseers frequented it, curious from newspaper accounts to see the scene of the crime, the neighborhood and even to meet characters in the drama: McClure, Delaney, O'Keefe, Judge, Burke and Alderman Dunlop himself. Sunday afternoon crowds flocked aboard streetcars from South Troy, downtown, Albia,

Green Island, Cohoes, Waterford and Albany to pace the streets and gravel lanes, and to hoist an Excelsior Pale Ale in Dunlop's.

But once the trial began, public attention shifted from the crime scene to the courthouse, and the day-to-day battering of Shea, McGough, Dunlop, the police force and the Murphy machine from the witness stand brought a resentful silence down upon the boys whose boots knew the feel of a brass rail. Patronage fell off then, and periodically a snarl or flare-up set the barroom on edge.

George Dunlop, always ebullient, always the politician, now suffered wide mood swings from high indignation at Frank Black and his committee to the depths of despair that Bat's fate was sealed. With a few shots of whiskey in his veins, Dunlop would expound about the "Blackhearted Protestants railroading my poor Bat to the electric chair."

Dunlop wanted to believe in Shea's innocence, and so he accepted Jack's account that Boland's errant bullet had done the fatal work. But no amount of soothing by his erstwhile friends and colleagues, no amount of nagging by his wife could shake George Dunlop out of his despond, and his guilt that it was at his behest the murder occurred. He was quickly becoming his own best customer. He had won the election, but lost much more, and he knew he would never put this crisis behind him. Those around him knew it too, but they still referred to him, hardly concealing their irony, as "Alderman" or "Your Grace."

Half a block from the saloon was St. Patrick's Rectory and there Father John Swift followed the trial each day in the newspapers. Evidence was amassing steadily with the slow, crushing weight of a glacier. By that second Sunday the People's case against Shea looked conclusive to him. Yet Father Swift believed he knew what happened. While clubbing Jack McGough, Robert Ross heard Shea coming. He climbed off McGough, scrambled up the ditch, and as he reached the lip of the ditch to confront Shea, he immediately collapsed into a sitting position. Ross had been shot at that instant. All the evidence about a sprained ankle was beside the point. Ross was shot before Shea got to him, if Shea got to him at all.

The penitent had come again the day before to confession, and as he recited his office Sunday morning, Father Swift heard the whispered words in the confessional: "Father, I know who shot the Ross boy . . . but I cannot come forward."

And his response: "But you must!"

The groan then. "I cannot, Father. My God, I cannot speak. You know why." Father Swift knew why, and the burden weighed heavily upon his conscience. As he sat considering this Sunday afternoon, the irony was not lost on him — the silence of the confessional was being used not to save a guilty party from punishment, as was the usual case, but to prevent saving an innocent man. He placed his face in his hands and rubbed his forehead and temples.

"I know, I know, I know the privilege is to work both ways, all ways, every way and always," he murmured to the crucifix on the wall. "I know I cannot divulge. But is justice, is our imperfect human justice, to be thwarted by Your holy rules? And if so, to what end? Will You allow an innocent to be convicted and executed?"

And as he gazed upon the crucifix for an answer, Father Swift nodded. "I see. I see. But as hard as it must be for that boy, so scared and bewildered, it is no easier for me to witness."

Father Swift placed all faith in Providence, yet here the divine purpose was being deliberately hidden from his eyes. That saddened him. Human justice, as he perceived it, a game of tricks and legal fine points, could not be trusted. Only three hearts in this city of sixty thousand knew the truth. One was the murderer himself, one the penitent, and he was the third. Father Swift doubted Shea knew.

"Yet I must and I shall bow to Thy plan, Lord," he whispered. "Thy will and not mine be done." And he sighed heavily.

29.

THE PROSECUTION: WEEK TWO

Harriet Titus

Monday morning a sense of expectation reigned in the court-house. The prosecution called William Ross who had been shot in the back of the head. William Ross admitted he did not know Shea on the day of the murder, but that Shea had been pointed out to him afterward.

"I saw Robert in a tackle with a man. Robert had a club, and I did not see it fall from his hand."

He told how he himself wrestled with McGough, and how he was then shot in the back of the head, behind the ear. Yet he did not lose consciousness. He watched as Robert chased McGough into the ditch of cans and rocks and briars, then how Robert began to climb up the side of the ditch.

"Commence from the time you got up," the judge instructed.

"I got a glimpse of Robert off to my right; he was falling; and I saw a shot just at the same time."

"Where was your brother Robert when you saw him fall?"

"He was northwest of where I was; about somewheres in the neighborhood of twenty-five to thirty feet, more or less. I saw his hand and saw him fall. I saw a man, as soon as he fell, a man rushed up right behind him, shot right into the back of his head, passed him and turned and shot again, and then passed out of my sight; I got a good view of that man that turned."

The judge leaned over: "Did this man fire the first or the second shot?"

"The third."

"Did the same man fire all three shots?"

"I thought so."

"Objection!"

"The same man fired the last two shots; I saw the first shot, saw the man with the revolver come close to my brother and fire."

"You can't say for certain," the judge asked, "that the first shot was fired by the same man?"

"No."

The gallery registered this. Shea leaned forward and folded his hands intently. Raines resumed the questioning.

"What do you know upon the subject as to whether or not the man who fired the first shot fired the second and third shots?"

"The man who fired the second shot came right from the direction from where they fired the first shot."

"At what part of your brother were the three shots directed?"

"The first one was just a flash and my brother dropped."

"You couldn't see the direction from which it was fired?"

"No. The second shot I saw the man rush right up behind my brother, put the revolver close to his head, fire and pass him."

"What part of his head?"

"Back of his head."

"Who was the man who fired those shots at your brother Robert?"

Judge Williams clarified: "The last two?"

"The man pointed out to me as Bat Shea."

"You see Shea here now?"

"Yes." He pointed to Shea at the defense table. "My brother says as he was going away, 'That is Bat Shea, the man with the green tie.'"

On cross-examination Hitt sought clarification:

"With regard to the first shot, you saw the flash of a pistol and instantly Robert fell?"

"I saw them both together."

"Are you able to tell us which took precedence as to time, the falling of Robert or the flash of the pistol?"

"I can't tell you."

"They were so near together that you were unable to state which was first?"

"They were so near together that I thought my brother was shot."

"The impression then made upon your mind was that the flash was from a pistol that carried the ball that shot your brother?"

"It might have been just at that moment, but I began to reason right off because of the way he fell. I didn't think he was hurt then."

"Didn't you just say that your impression was as you saw the flash, saw Robert fall, that he had then been shot?"

"My other answer covers that. I reasoned it away."

"Was there anybody between you and your brother when he fell?"

"Nobody that I saw."

"Was there anybody between you and the man who fired the first shot, when that shot was fired?"

"I couldn't tell you nothing about that."

"Do you remember anybody being between you?"

"I don't remember."

"Tell us how your brother went down."

"He sank straight down; I saw that go, I saw the flash, I saw my brother fall."

"You say you saw a man pass by?"

"After the first shot."

"Yes, sir."

"And shoot him?"

"Yes."

"Had you been looking for any particular necktie?"

"No."

"You looked over and your brother said he had on a green neck-tie?"

"Yes."

"How many others wore green neckties?"

"No one of that crowd except Shea had a green necktie."

"You can't tell what color necktie the man had on who fired the first shot?"

"No, sir."

"Did you see your brother stretching out for the man?"

"Yes, sir; he seemed to be reaching for a man ahead of him, and just as the shot was fired, he dropped."

"At the coroner's inquest, were you able to say whether Shea is the man who shot your brother?"

"Yes, sir."

Hitt produced a volume of the transcript. "Didn't you ask him to stand and put his hat on?"

"Yes, I did."

"And didn't you state, 'I would rather not swear to anybody except the man that wore the long green necktie; I only saw his face for a short time before the shooting.'"

"Yes, that is what I said."

"I ask you now if you will swear to the jury positively," Hitt motioned Shea to stand, "if that is the man?"

"I will swear positively."

"Then why couldn't you do so before the coroner?"

"I will tell you why; I hadn't seen the face, the men were mixed; that is, Cleary and Shea were the only two that were mixed; if you would stand them side by side, or if I could have seen the face, I could have identified the man."

"Now, didn't you ask Shea at the coroner's inquest to put on his hat, and you still couldn't identify him?"

"I didn't see Shea until he was ordered to stand up, and then I insisted that he put his hat on; I was sure of the man, but I said, 'I don't care to swear positively to the man; he is one of the two, Cleary or Shea;' McGough I had seen before; I knew him from the caucus."

Judge Williams then leaned over: "Can you give us any idea of the length of time between the first and second shot?"

"I can't."

"Was it a very brief period or a little longer?"

"It was a brief period. I saw the shot and the man rushed right up from the same direction; didn't seem to be any interval between seeing the first shot and the man firing the other two in rapid succession."

"Did you see your brother raise his head up after the first shot, or was it continually drooping?"

"I couldn't say as to that."

A Republican poll watcher named George Congdon then testified he had been at the first district polls in the morning and saw Shea voting a repeater on the name of John P. Sayles where he had voted the same repeater on the name of Ezra Bouton earlier. Congdon left the first district to go to the third around noon.

"I saw the approach of Cleary, Shea, McGough, Jack Ryan, Stanley O'Keefe and another man named Keefe." He characterized the gang of repeaters as a football team.

"I then saw Robert Ross in pursuit of a man out of the gully apparently reaching for him; I turned around to see where the police were; and when I turned back, Shea was going around the corner of the fence and Robert Ross was sitting down."

"Who was Boland pursuing after Robert Ross was down?"

"McGough. He seemed trying to hit him or catch him."

"What did you have with you?"

"A revolver."

On cross-examination Congdon admitted that when he reached Robert Ross, Shea was gone off. "I followed in the tracks of McGough."

After the dinner break, there was a stir in the crowd when the prosecution called John H. Boland. Boland was a heavy man, a youthful forty-two, and was self-employed as a wholesale tobacconist. He had been born in Ireland and was an Irish Catholic, yet he was Republican in his politics and a friend to the Ross family.

"Yes, I knew Robert Ross," he said, adjusting himself in the seat for the ordeal. "He was a fellow travelling man who sold valves for his father's firm." Boland testified he bought a revolver the night before election. Raines then turned to the scene at the polls and asked Boland to describe the gang's approach.

"They were very hard looking characters, not very good looking. They looked like a lot of canalers, and they paused in the vacant lot by a pile of flagstones. At the first encounter, Shea hauled off and smashed William Ross in the mouth. They left for a time, and then returned. There was one rather good looking fellow at the front. He braced up and waltzed into the polling place. Cleary and Shea followed him. McGough stood back there on the stoop watching."

Boland told about the beginning of the riot: "I saw the glitter of a revolver in McGough's hands. He put it up over his head; I understood him to say, 'Stand back there,' and by that time the crowd began to scatter, and about that instant there was a shot fired. The next man that came in my range of vision was William Ross going rapidly across Orr Street with his hand down in his coat. I saw a shot and it was McGough who had fired; the next I saw was Robert Ross running at McGough who turned and faced him and ran backward and began firing; the next thing they disappeared into this declivity; they both came scrambling up the other side, McGough ahead, and Robert Ross immediately behind.

"Both McGough and Ross were on their hands and knees, both scrambling to get right in position; Robert had got into a sitting position when Shea run up, right up close to him and shot."

"How far was Shea's pistol from Ross's head when he shot?"

"Twenty inches."

"Then did you encounter Shea?"

"I struck him over the left side with a stick, after the last shot he fired."

"And then you encountered McGough?"

"Yes. I pulled my pistol then, when I was past Robert Ross."

"You pulled your blank cartridges and fired?"

"Yes, just as hot and fast as I could."

"What did McGough do?"

"He fired back at me, then he started and ran."

"What did you do then?"

"I started in pursuit of him."

"Now, Mr. Boland, how long have you known Shea?"

"Since the caucus, February 3rd."

"On the day of the shooting, did you notice anything peculiar about his attire?"

"Yes, sir. He wore a green necktie."

"Did you hear any outcry after Shea shot Ross?"

"Yes sir. John Ross."

"Where was he?"

"Holding his brother's head."

On cross-examination Boland swore he purchased eleven blank cartridges the night before election and had no live rounds with him election day. He testified that after Ross clubbed McGough, he arose to confront Shea.

"Did McGough immediately pick himself up and move on?"

"No. In the meantime, Robert was shot." He positioned McGough off to the side and Shea in front of Ross. "But I can't place it precisely as it was." He told how he and McGough squared off, how McGough fired at him and he fired back.

"But McGough hadn't done anything, had he?"

"I thought he had done some tall shooting."

He then testified how he had gone to John Collins's store. He admitted he presented his gun to Collins after it was reloaded with blanks, and that he stated, "Look, the gun hasn't been fired."

"Have you been to Mr. Black's office?" Hitt turned around and pointed to the attorney.

"Quite a number of times."

"And did Mr. Black visit you in the Troy jail?"

"Yes."

"Now isn't it true that you were in Granville on May 21?"

"Yes."

"And that you stated to a group of men, 'I am satisfied Shea ought not be held, and I can acquit him'?"

Boland's eyes narrowed defiantly. "No, sir."

"Did you see Shea when you were in jail?"

"Yes."

"Did you speak to him?"

"Yes. He confronted me. He said, 'Boland, how do you like your medicine.' I said, 'I can take my medicine, young man. What happened to you?' He was wearing a bandage around his head. 'Don't you know,' he asks me. 'You are the man that shot me.'"

"And was that true?"

"No, sir. I only had blanks in the revolver that day."

Hitt adjusted his great bulk and looked skeptically toward the jury.

"Why did you load your new revolver with blanks?"

"I didn't care to injury anybody. I wouldn't kill a man nohow."

"Objection, your honor."

"Sustained."

Ira P. Humphrey, clerk at Bonesteel's Hardware, corroborated that Boland bought a revolver the night before election. On cross-examination he revealed that Boland did not ask for blank cartridges.

The prosecution then called Junius Mickle, a boy of thirteen. Mickle had come upon the scene shortly after the shooting and discovered the revolver, two hats and a ruler in the ditch. Mickle testified that there was no one under Robert Ross when he was shot, and that Bat Shea threw his revolver in the weeds. On cross-examination he stated that Shea had on a green necktie and a black coat.

As Williams adjourned for the day, the crowd was buzzing thoughtfully. Many thought the tide was turning, that William Ross's uncertainty, and Boland's absurd claim of having blanks had weakened the People's case. Yet there was no way to gauge the impact of the testimony on the twelve minds behind the twelve weathered faces of the jurors.

Outside, the streets were swarming with animated newsboys and onlookers. Frank Black leaned momentarily against a column off to the side, arms folded, watching the prisoners and deputies parade down Second Street. The evening was cool and pigeons cooed above in the stone eaves of the courthouse. In the dark of the school grounds across the street fireflies blinked. Today's road had been rocky, but progress of the trial was satisfactory. Yes, there had been some damage, but his strategy was being vindicated. When Black considered what might have been said, Boland had held up well under cross-examination.

Back at the jail, McGough was jubilant. "Bat, you're going to beat it! I know you are! Didn't I tell you the truth would come out? Hell, his own brother! His own brother testified Ross went down while he was reaching out to you, not while you were behind him! He wouldn't say you fired the first shot! His own goddamned brother!"

"Jesus, Jack, I could go for a beer."

"George'll be in!"

"Aye, it was a good day, a good day all 'round."

George and Gene McClure came in soon with a kid carrying three growlers of beer.

"This calls for a celebration!" George announced. "It did my heart good seeing them blackhearted Protestants telling the truth for a change."

"Here! Here!" Jack cried. He took a mug and held it high. "To Bat Shea! The most loyal son of a bitch I ever met! May he prosper!"

"At this point, Jack, I'd settle for giving the slip to the hospitality of the Rensselaer County sheriff."

Jack slung his arm around Bat Shea. "Did you see the look on Boland's face? Blanks. Yeah, he was shooting blanks! Just ask his goddamn wife!"

There was a round of laughter and more beer and more cheer. Outside the church bells rang and a boat whistle blew from the river.

Dunlop and the boys left about eleven, and as they bunked down for the night, Bat lay on the cot, his hands behind his head: "Goddamn, Jack, I ain't felt this good in some time. Maybe. Maybe the tide is turning after all." And they both lay awake clutching onto the straw to keep themselves afloat.

* * *

That very night, Mamie Halligan also lay awake hundreds of miles away. Ostracism at the collar factory had made life unbearable, so Mamie gave notice and quit. Her brother Tom had a use for her talents.

"You've got a fiery quality, Mamie. More often than not I think my passion, more'n the words I say, is what persuades 'em. Come with me to Johnstown 'n Pittsburgh. Talk to the women about the sweatshops and the child labor. 'Tis pitiful the lives they lead. Help me, Mamie, whilst Bat's on trial. You can do nothing here."

As a prelude to the trip, Mamie had attended the Iron Moulders Union meeting in South Troy and she remained until the ale was served. Tom, a teetotaler, escorted her from the building to the streetcar. She had been deeply affected.

"You've got a natural gift, Tom. You're a leader of men. Your eloquence draws 'em out of theirselves and unites them into a common purpose."

"Until the beer arrives. There'll be some good-natured brawls tonight." The Lansingburgh car stopped and they boarded and sat. "You can do the same with the women, Mamie. They need a voice, one who might focus their rage and sense of injustice to a purpose, who can organize and oppose the inhuman treatment, the poverty, the hunger and privation . . ." and with a lilt he continued his speech for the benefit of those aboard who were eavesdropping.

In the following week, Mamie went with her brother into a foreign world, a world of union halls and ethnic clubs, Polish, German, Irish, Italian, French Canadian, a world where the good spirits and warmth of the people could not distract you from their threadbare clothes and careworn faces and the hollow eyes of the children. They knew poverty, humiliation and despair. They had survived lockouts and strikes. They had protested the iron-fisted demands of increased productivity. The prettier woman knew the crude feel of a supervisor's hand, the degradation of his demands, and then the shame and rejection and demotion when he found a younger, prettier girl. While the men brayed protests and hoisted tankards of ale to soothe their indignation, to bury their resentment, the woman bore it with quiet stoicism. The children, though, understood little of their plight. They had no champion.

Pittsburgh had replaced Troy a generation before as the iron and steel capital of the nation. Located among the coal fields, the city had burst its boundaries as a greedy railroad industry demanded of Pittsburgh's foundries and rolling mills vast quantities of rails and spikes and engines and machinery to get the sprawling nation up and rolling. Coal mines, machine shops, forges and foundries sprang up. And at Johnstown, with the largest machine shop in the world, eight thousand men and boys employed, countless locomotives moving cars about the yards, all was bustle. Like Mamie's hometown, these Pennsylvania cities were coated with a gritty coal film, and the worker families were pale and thin.

Tom was at home in this world, a kind word here, a handclasp there, keeping their spirits up, drawing out the slim strands of their hope and braiding it into a strong cable to pull with a common purpose in the great tug o' war between management and labor.

Late at night, exhausted, he lay down upon the cot or straw tick or pile of coats reserved for him and he slept as if he were dead. Mamie lay awake beside him, thinking about her beloved Bartholomew, his misguided pride, the disgrace he had, rightly or wrongly, brought down upon himself, his family, his neighborhood, his race, his church. Voting fraud was wrong. Carrying a pistol was wrong. Getting drunk was wrong. Bat Shea was guilty of all three. But he did not murder Ross, Mamie knew with the same intuition that produced her premonitions.

Tom was as angry as Bat at the way of the world, and saw the necessity of strikes and occasional violence directed at property. But his view was tempered with respect for law and order. Change the laws, he told the people in the dingy union halls, in the yards of slag after a shift change, in the saloons and ethnic clubs, force the capitalists to reform by law, and you and your children will benefit. Violence only drew retribution and any benefit was short-lived.

Mamie asked him one day what caused the split with Bat. "Two things, Mamie," he replied. "George Dunlop and Jack McGough. Before, he'd listen to me and keep out of trouble. We were blood brothers, you know? Since we were kids. Then George come along with his fool scheme to get on the board of aldermen, and Jack's right there alongside, spinning his pistol 'round his finger, a trick he learnt out West. I warned Bat those fellows were trouble, and he told me what I could do with my 'union stiffs,' as he calls them.

"Now, we hear George got dismissed from the force for letting them boys steal out of the railyard, and that should tell you something about George. Jack, why, I've known Jack his whole life long, and he can't be trusted. So long as Bat's with them, Mamie, why I got nothing to say to him. Now Bat's a solid enough fellow, but he's always had that chip of wood on his shoulder asking the world to knock it off. He hated his old man; he hated the foundry; and he wanted nothing to do with the laboring man. We had words, as I say. I don't believe you got to use criminal measures to change things, and he does. That's the difference. Sure you gotta use force occasionally, and God himself knows what a lot in life these millowners carve out for all of us. You saw my skull cracked back in February. But fraud and thievery? Nah. It's always the path to nowhere, and so we parted company, thank you very much."

And as she lay there, anxious to be on tomorrow's train back to

Troy, anxious to learn of the trial, a prayer went out to her beloved, that God, in the midst of this jarring uneasy world of iron and soot, capital and labor, this tangle of crossed purposes, betrayal and murder, that her God and her Savior would bless Bat Shea and deliver him from the hands of his persecutors, even as she as she prayed for God to deliver the laborers from the hellish foundries and sweatshops. And she prayed for herself, too, very quickly and very humbly, that she might still find, in the midst of so much drudgery and despair, the salvation of human love, and of children.

* * *

When the trial resumed Tuesday morning, Fagan and Raines produced a series of witnesses to sketch in details. A boy, Napoleon Jentis, testified he came upon the scene as they were removing Ross's body and he saw two hats fifteen feet from the gully.

Nicholas Lougham, a boy of thirteen, saw a revolver in Shea's hand and he saw two or three men come up out of the gully. He swore that John Ross told him Shea was the murderer, and when asked to identify Shea in court, he insisted twice: "I ain't positive. Looks like him. Looks like the man who shot Mr. Ross."

Henry Richardson testified he escorted the state treasurer to Douw Street. Over Hitt's strong objection, he told how he had seen Shea emerge from McClure's Saloon a number of times that morning running people across the street to vote them illegally in the first district.

John Crutchley, corroborated this. The first district polls, he stated, were directly opposite McClure's livery stable, and as soon as the polls opened, Shea and a gang came over from the saloon with slips of paper in their pockets. The policeman, Officer Patrick Cahill, silenced the protests of legal voters with: "I'll break your skulls if you don't keep still."

Judge Williams interrupted: "Is Officer Cahill still on the Troy Police Force?"

"Yes, Judge, I believe he is."

Williams shook his head with disgust, and the judicial disfavor was not lost on the jury.

A series of voters in the first and second district was called and over continual defense objections, testified about the forcing of votes for the remainder of the day.

Wednesday morning Frank Wheeler, a coal dealer, described Shea immediately after the shooting as being groggy, that he had to be kept up walking by Mike Delaney and Stanley O'Keefe, and that he had a revolver in his right hand at the time.

John Kilcullen, a boy of fifteen, heard someone say after the shooting, "Let me take it. I will load it again."

Elias Falle witnessed the shooting. "I remained near the polls, near the front of the building."

"You heard the shooting to the west of you?"

"Yes, sir. Hayner was getting up from the ditch to the side of the polls where they'd thrown him. He was bruised pretty bad. 'Did you see my hat, Mr. Falle?' he asked, so's I picked it up and gave it to him. The shooting was going on to the west, right in front, and I saw Mr. William Ross at the edge of the gully, and there was blood coming down from his collar. At the same time my eyes seemed to be placed in the direction of about northwest of that, and I seen there were two men, both had their backs toward me; one was in a sitting position, but the other, I should say about four or five feet to the nor'west of him; I saw the man in front standing up to turn around sharp and shoot at the man that was down, and just at that time I saw Boland go for the man, the assassin."

"How far was the man who fired at Robert Ross from him?"

"About five feet."

On cross-examination, Hitt asked: "The man that was sitting down, from the moment you saw him did you ever see him stir hand, foot or head?"

"I could not say."

"How far ahead was the man in front of him?"

"Four or five feet."

"And he turned around and fired at the man sitting?"

"Yes, sir."

"So it brought them face to face, didn't it?"

"Yes, sir."

"No doubt about it?"

"No, sir."

"You don't recollect of hearing a shot fired after the man in front of Robert Ross turned and fired at his breast, as you think?"

"I didn't hear no other shot."

Frederick Miller, a sewing machine adjuster for Miller, Hall & Hartwell, testified:

"I saw them have their revolvers in their hands; I saw two of them go through the crowd; this is about all I noticed at that time, but an instant after that somewhere near that position I heard one shot; it might have been just west of the post, and very shortly after that I heard several other shots in rapid succession."

"Let's pause there. You saw Robert go over the bank?"

"Yes. I saw Robert Ross stumble or pitch forward."

"Was there a man under him at that time?"

"I did not notice, but he was striking something. He was down on his hands and knees, striking like this." He demonstrated with his arm. "I turned away, and as I looked again at him — this shot came just before, a single shot; then I saw a man point a revolver at him and fire."

"Where was the man standing?"

"On the edge of the gully, just on the edge of the road."

"And where was he in reference to Ross, ahead or behind?"

"Ahead of him, to the north."

"And where was his revolver pointed?"

"At Robert Ross's head."

"At which side, front or back?"

"At the north side; the right hand side, toward the back. Robert Ross appeared then to straighten up, and the man passed by him and turned about and fired again."

"At what?"

"At his head. Then Robert Ross straightened a little more and staggered sidewise and settled down into the road."

"And what became of the man who fired those two shots you saw fired?"

"Disappeared from my view."

"Can you identify him?"

"No, sir, I cannot."

"Was it Mr. Boland?"

"No, sir, it was not."

"Was it this man?" Raines indicated Shea.

"I cannot tell."

Duncan Kaye told of the illegal voting, the visits of the gang, and the beginning of the riot.

"After they came pushing and shoving out of the polls, Cleary seen me and he came over and he says, 'Ah,' and he stuck out his hand to me to shake with him, and I shook hands with him at that time; and James M. Adams stood at my left; Cleary turned around and said, 'Give us a chew of tobacco, Jim;' Adams took his package out of his pocket and handed it to Cleary, and Cleary took a chew, and then he circled out into the crowd, and the next thing I saw Shea haul off and hit Hayner on the mouth, first with his right hand and then with his left, and having dove in the blows, he wheeled south of the polling place; then Shea jumped back and pulled a revolver, and then it kind of turned into a row."

"That is a scattering?"

"Yes, sir. I started in a little westerly direction and I got about five or ten feet from the polling place and the glare of a revolver in a man's hand attracted my attention. I recognized the man's form as Bartholomew Shea; he was in that position and he shot a revolver at a man on the ground. 'My God,' I cried out loud, 'they have killed Boland.'"

"Objection!"

"Sustained."

When Raines turned the witness over for cross-examination, Hitt rose: "You have stated you helped in the investigation. Did you help secure witnesses to go to Mr. Black's office?"

"Yes, sir."

"Did Mr. Black tell you who to get?"

"No, sir, it was Mr. Collins. He told me to get all the evidence I could get."

"Mr. Collins is quite a prominent Republican here?"

"He is a prominent businessman here in the city."

"I am not asking you about his business."

"Yes, sir, he has been Republican Police Commissioner."

"How many witnesses did you take to Black's office in all?"

"Didn't take any there."

"How many did you tell to go there?"

"I told all that I knew."

"How many?"

"Oh, there must have been ten or fifteen, maybe more."

"Now, did you know Shea prior to election day?"

"Yes, sir."

"How long?"

"About fifteen years. We were boys together around the ward and we went to the same school."

"What did he have on his head when he shot Ross."

"I'm not positive, but I think he was bareheaded."

"What kind of coat?"

"Black sack coat."

"How did you know it was Shea?"

"By his form."

"His form. You mean his height and weight?"

"Yes, sir."

"Is that the best you can do about it?"

"And the color of his hair."

"Did you see his face?"

"I saw the side of it; kind of a glimpse; that is all."

"Are you willing to swear positively it was Shea?"

"Yes, sir; I am pretty sure it was him."

"Now when you were getting witnesses, who did you give their names to?"

"Mr. Fagan and Mr. Collins."

"Before the inquest?"

"Yes."

"What did Mr. Collins have to do with this matter before the coroner's inquest met?"

"They had Mr. Collins' best friend locked up on a charge I knew he was innocent of."

"That is Mr. Boland?"

"Yes, sir."

"You and Boland always go to Collins for your political cues?"

"I never got any political cue from Collins."

"You were working in the interest of Collins to get his best friend out of jail, to get all the evidence you could in favor of Boland, and all you could against Shea?"

"Only the truth."

Hitt closed in, leaning over the rail of the witness stand.

"And you didn't care what happened if you only got Boland out?"

"I wanted the truth to come out."

"But you wanted Boland out?"

"I wouldn't want an innocent man to suffer."

Hitt turned dramatically to the jury. "Neither do we, Mr. Kaye. Neither do we."

"Objection!"

"Sustained."

Edward Cipperly, a furniture wagon driver, told how he saw Jack

McGough on a run fire two shots at Ross who was chasing him. As Jack fired, Robert Ross knocked his hand upward.

"Was McGough backing up?"

"No, sir; he was running and then he turned around and shot."

"At whom?"

"At Robert Ross, and after he fired the second time, they went over the embankment and down the gully. It seems to me they were on kind of a side hill."

"Then what?"

"Then McGough got up quick, both about five or six feet west of Ross, and he fired a third shot."

"What became of Ross?"

"After McGough's third shot, I started to run across the road."

"What came between you and them at that time?"

"I don't know; I kept an eye on McGough."

"Did you see anything of what happened to Robert Ross?"

"No, sir, I did not."

"That last shot of McGough was the last you saw in connection with Robert Ross?"

"The last of the shooting."

"Did you hear some shots?"

"Yes, sir."

"But your attention was not on Robert Ross?"

"No, sir; it was on McGough."

"And where did McGough go?"

"Went along the fence, up along in that vacant lot."

"How far did you follow him?"

"Over on the west side of North Fourth Street, and he went into a yard."

On cross-examination, Cipperly testified McGough did not shoot his pistol after he shot a third time at Ross. Cipperly did not see any green necktie and did not know whether Shea ever fired his revolver.

With so many witnesses, the People's case had become repetitive. The jurors, interested and spellbound at the outset, now yawned and fidgeted in their chairs. The evidence had been conclusive and remarkably harmonized. A newspaper reporter from the *Albany Argus* testified, and then the People called Harmon C. Simmons, a teamster.

"I saw Robert Ross grab for somebody and they fell, and the man he grabbed for went under, then he got up and got away from Robert, and at that time there was some man ran in front of me and pulled a pistol down and shot at Robert Ross's head," Simmons said. "I saw the discharge of the pistol and the smoke and the dust from the ground, and he turned and went to the right of him again, and he had his back toward me all the while. I could not identify him."

"Robert Ross was sitting when the man fired?"

"Yes, sir. He appeared to lay with his right hand on the ground, one leg backing the other under him, his head a little southwest towards North Fourth Street."

"Did you notice just how McGough got away from Robert?"

"I did not exactly, only I saw him get away and run towards the west."

"And when was that with reference to the time this man stepped up and fired?"

"It was about a second or so before the shot."

"Was that as much time as there was between McGough's escape and the shot?"

"Yes, sir."

"What was Robert doing at the time, the moment the shot was fired apparently?"

"Apparently trying to get off of the ground and trying to get up."

"And the shot came from where?"

"From in behind the back of the head."

"Will you point the location of the revolver again?"

"He came in from this way or that way, I could not say which; he curved around after coming in just in that shape and pulled the revolver and pointed it at his head. I didn't see his face."

On cross-examination, Simmons testified he knew McGough but he did not know Shea at the time.

Thursday morning, the People called James Adams who testified he could not tell the difference between Shea and McGough. "At the polling place the repeaters all clung together on the stoop and lockstepped into the polls. When Officer Murphy thrust them out, Cleary came over to me and asked for a chew. Then Hayner pulled his wrench, Shea drew a revolver and said, 'If you draw that, I have got something better.'

"At the first shot, they all commenced running westward, Shea first, then McGough, then Robert Ross in pursuit. When Ross tackled McGough, Shea doubled back to help McGough, and shot at Ross at least twice from in front."

Adams disputed Simmons and stated he did not see Simmons anywhere nearby.

The People's case was winding down. Fagan and Raines were drawing out the questioning and concentrating on small details. All the major ones had been covered. They called a Ross cousin, William Ross 2d who had also been at the polls.

"The instant Robert went down there was a man advanced from the east, northeast of him, and pointed a pistol right at his head, and fired instantly. It seemed he no more than fell than this man was right there and pointed a pistol at his head."

"You say Robert didn't seem to have more than fallen or sunk down upon the ground when this man was there?"

"Yes, sir."

"Who was this man?"

"Shea."

"At the time that first shot was fired by Shea into the back of the head of Robert, where was McGough?"

"I couldn't tell you."

"Do you know whether he was down upon the ground or not?"

"I couldn't tell you. But after Ross was down I saw the man running away, McGough."

"Did you see anybody around Robert?"

"Yes. His brother Adam had his arm around his neck, and Loeble was tying a knot in a handkerchief around Robert's head; his brother John was to the southwest of Robert with his hands upraised calling for American citizens."

"How many times did you see Shea that morning?"

"I saw him when he hit Will in the face."

"And can you describe his clothing?"

"He wore a black suit, a derby and a green necktie."

The final witness on the People's case was Eugene M. Partridge. He recited the now-familiar litany of events and described Robert clambering up the side of the embankment.

"Did you see McGough when Robert Ross fell?"

"No. There was no one with him."

"And what was Robert doing?"

"His hands were outstretched. He was reaching for something when he went down. It looked to me as though . . ." Partridge stopped, looked down at the floor.

"Yes?"

"His hands were held up. He whirled around to the west and he went down."

"Was anyone near him at that time?"

"No, sir. No man was near him." Partridge then cleared his throat.

"Was Shea behind him?"

"I saw Shea behind him after he fell."

"And how many shots did Shea fire?"

"Two."

"And when Shea shot the first shot did you see McGough?"

"No, sir."

"Thank you, Mr. Partridge."

When Hitt finished cross-examination, Fagan and Raines conferred, then Fagan announced: "Your honor, at this time the People rest."

There was a communal sigh of relief. Frank Black narrowed his eyes and nodded at Williams, his arms folded.

Williams spoke: "I assume the defense has motions at this time, which I will hear out of the presence of the jury."

"All rise!" called Riley.

The gallery stood and the jurors were escorted out of the courtroom.

"Your honor," Hitt spoke, "at this time the defense asks that all charges against Mr. Shea be dismissed due to the People's failure to prove their case."

There was a wave of laughter through the gallery. It was like a splash of cold water upon the tension that had built for the past two weeks. "Order! Order!" Williams rapped down the gavel. "Motion denied."

Hitt renewed motions aimed at jurisdiction and improper influence with the grand jury and such motions were likewise denied. "Is the defendant ready to proceed?" Williams asked.

"Your honor, could we adjourn for the day? I should like to discuss certain matters with my client."

"No, Mr. Hitt. It is only two o'clock. Proceed. Clerk, please bring the jurors in."

When the jurors were again seated, Hitt arose:

"The defense calls Dr. Herbert DeFreest."

The jurors' interest seemed renewed, but this time with skepticism, not curiosity.

30.
THE DEFENSE

Galen R. Hitt

Because Bat Shea had no burden of proof and was presumed innocent until his guilt was proven beyond a reasonable doubt, he was required to advance no theory of the case, to do nothing in his own behalf. The question swirled through the city whether or not he would testify. So far, Shea had asserted no affirmative defense, no alibi, no insanity, no justification. Beyond bald denial, his only line of defense was mistaken identity, and he looked nothing like the portly John Boland.

The prosecution's showing was strong. The emotional pitch of the crowd each day suggested that Shea was doomed. Yet he sat bolt upright at the defense table day after day, chin forward, his sneer occasionally souring from contempt to disgust. He knew he was innocent and he believed he could prove it and at the close of the People's case he brightened up. Now was his chance. First, two doctors testified that both Shea and McGough had been shot, thus establishing there was a general riot with injuries on both sides. Hitt next called Ellen McLaughlin, a plump woman in a print dress who lived on the pathway between the polls and Dunlop's Saloon.

"My husband was home from work that day. His leg had been scalded at Manning's Paper Mill. We were at the dinner table and we heard the shooting and we ran to the front windows and when we got to the front windows we saw people rush by the side of the house; we got to the side of the house and got out on the landing of the back stairs, and I seen about four or five revolvers; and after the shooting my husband went downstairs and I went down after him, and I seen a man standing at the picket fence with his arm on the fence, or his hand, and his ear was cut and he was bleeding on the back of the head; and he stayed there for a few moments, then he walked away around the O'Brien house."

"Who was the man?"

"I think it was Mr. Boland, there," she pointed at Bat Shea.

"Do you mean Mr. Shea?"

"Him, right there, the one that was identified to me as Mr. Boland."

"Let the record reflect the witness has indicated the defendant, Bartholomew Shea."

Hitt then called her husband Peter who told the jury he was eating soup when he heard three volleys of shots, and he hobbled down the stairs behind his wife. He saw John Boland firing at Stanley O'Keefe, then two or three in the crowd of vigilantes hollered, "Lynch him!" and eight or ten of them set off at a dead run in the other direction. "'Lynch him,' they hollered, and they chased McGough." McLaughlin looked over at Shea, "'Lynch him,' they hollered."

After the first four defense witnesses, Williams recessed. Back through the streets Shea and McGough walked together. Shea swaggered for he believed he could raise a reasonable doubt in the jurors' minds, and he sneered at the crowds in the street who called, "Good luck, Bat."

At the jail later that night, Mike Delaney and Jerry Cleary brought in a half barrel of beer and a box of cigars. The mood was cheerful. "See, ain't I told you all along?" Jack said from the upper bunk after lights out, "The truth is going to come out, Bat, mark my words. You're going to be a free man."

"Maybe so. Maybe so."

Next morning, a bright, hot, muggy Friday, crowds of Irish gathered along Second Street and pressed between the Doric columns of the courthouse portico. Shea nodded to the chorus of well-wishers. He drew up when he saw Mamie Halligan in the throng. Their eyes met. Hers were filled with sorrow, searching in his for a signal of how it would end.

Shea nodded, winked to show his spirits were lifted, and bowed his head to proceed into the dim courthouse. Mamie and Maggie Riley, Jack's girl, went in together.

Hitt called Billy Riley, a brakeman on the Fitchburg railroad, and brother of McGough's girlfriend.

"I saw McGough running in a northwesterly direction, followed by Robert Ross; Robert Ross was being followed by John Boland. I saw Boland fire a shot; I saw Ross fall; Boland fired either two or three shots after that; in the meantime there was a crowd west, north and southwest of them firing shots, too. Ross never rose after he was shot that time."

On cross-examination, Raines brought out that Riley had met Shea in Chicago, and that Riley had served time for wife-beating. Methodically, then, Raines took his account of the fray apart point by point, drawing him out by leading questions into making contradictory statements.

"Why do you keep changing your statement?" Raines asked.

"I am not changing my statement."

"Did you see anyone with a pistol that day?"

"Yes, sir."

"And who was that?"

"Jack McGough."

"And when was that?"

"I guess Robert Ross was down when I saw Jack McGough with the pistol."

"When was that?" Raines repeated.

"Just after Robert Ross fell."

"No further questions."

Hitt announced then, "The defense calls John J. McGough." Jack nudged Shea as he passed and the gallery registered its excitement. "Here we go," he whispered, and a nervous smile flickered across his face. McGough was trembling as he sat in the witness stand.

Jack testified how Cleary, Hayner and Shea entered the polls, then were thrust out by Officer Murphy. "Hayner then bumped against Cleary and Cleary says, 'You scab. Do you see what you're doing? Walking all over my feet.' Hayner says, 'You son of a bitch, don't you call me no scab.' At that point Cleary hit him. Hayner then goes over to Robert Ross and John Boland and Duncan Kaye, and they whisper together for half a minute; turning directly around, he walks toward Shea, making the remark, 'By Christ, I will go in there or I will hurt somebody.' I answer him with the remarks, 'Hayner, you got no more right in there than I have;' he says, 'I ain't going back,' and getting this wrench that he drew from his pocket, he had the large end in his hand, and he struck at me, and I threw up my left arm and warded off the blow; he struck me with the small end of the wrench; Shea called, 'Look out, Jack,' trying to catch the wrench, and Hayner struck him, split him down the left side of the ear; Shea clinched Hayner, and they went off to the south; Quigley drew a club then and began striking Shea, making the remarks, 'Club him, boys, damn him, club him.' And I went in to try and throw up his arm, and that man shoved a gun under my nose."

"Which man?"

"William Ross. Quigley threw up his arm; 'My God, William,' and the gun goes off. I went down and got my revolver and I covered Ross, making the remark, 'Put that up, Ross, and don't you hit him no more, Quigley.' Shea and Hayner were still on the ground."

"Where was Shea when he got up?" Hitt gave Jack a pointer, and he indicated on the map.

"Shea started almost to run north, then he turned to run west. I cut across this way, coming along quickly; I heard a bullet whiz by my head; I heard the discharge of a revolver, and turning I saw that man, William Ross there, turning; I was running and there was a flash, and I was turned around like that, and I went down on my left side, right about on the edge of this ravine. I was hit here in the hip.

"As I fell, there were three shots in rapid succession; the first I could see the flash of it, and into my vision came Robert Ross, and then seven to nine feet behind him, there was John Boland; he discharged a pistol three times; the first shot he fired, this man Robert Ross didn't go down, no sitting position, but he went forward just like if you stand that pencil up and let it drop; at the second or third shot, I heard Shea, who was west of me, cry out, 'I am shot!'

"Throwing my eyes around, I saw Shea on the ground; my line of vision went back again, and by the time I was back, William Ross and his brother Adam Ross and this man Quigley were on me. William Ross gave me a kick in the chest here. These three men forced me into the gully with their cocobolos, and I drew my pistol again and fired two shots as quick as I could. Adam Ross knocked me senseless with his club and I relaxed my hold upon the pistol.

"Shea, who was north of me, came back. I regained my footing again, came up out of the gully and started to run westward, and I heard the remark made, 'There he goes,' and instantly two or three of them starts to pursue me, and there were three shots they fired at me. I run through the gangway as quick as possible, got over into the house; I staggered into the house, washed myself and changed my clothes. I told my father —"

"No."

"I washed myself, came out and went over the back fence directly in front of St. Patrick's Church. I went down Sixth Avenue to Middleburgh Street, up Middleburgh Street to the Fitchburg tracks and down those tracks to a block below the depot. I then took the streetcar up Congress Street to my aunt's house on Ida Hill, 45 Christie Street."

"See if you can pick out your revolver."

"That is mine."

"The one they picked out of the ravine?"

"Yes, with three bullets discharged."

"And where did you get this revolver?"

"I bought it in Albuquerque two years back."

On cross-examination George Raines elicited from McGough that he saw Shea in Chicago in 1892 for an hour; that he and Shea owned a horse together for a month this past winter. Raines explored the theft of tobacco and liquor from the railyard, but Jack dodged the questions by swearing they never had the horse out at night.

"What is your employment?"

"Iron molder."

"When did you last work at it?"

"In June, 1893."

"How long did you work?"

"Three weeks."

"Why did you not work longer?"

"I have been sick. With malaria on several occasions."

Raines then brought up the so-called "revolver caucus," and over Hitt's objection, Judge Williams ruled evidence about the caucus was competent on the issue of McGough's credibility.

"Inform me whether in that caucus you drew a pistol?"

"When my life was in danger, I did draw a revolver."

"Where were you at the time?"

"On the ground."

"Did you strike anybody in that room?"

"I did. John Boland."

"How hard did you hit him?"

"Just as hard as I could."

"Where were you then?"

"By the window."

"The voting window?"

"Yes."

"Have you written to Steve Burke?"

"No, sir."

"You did not write Steve Burke and ask him to swear as to the gun Shea had at the shooting?"

"I did not."

"Did you write any letters for Bartholomew Shea?"

"Yes, sir."

"More than one?"

"Yes, sir."

"Addressed to whom?"

Jack looked over at Mamie. "To a young lady."

Raines picked up McGough's revolver. "Three shots were fired?"

"Two," Jack said.

"There are three empty chambers. When had you fired it before election day?"

"Maybe a month before."

"When did you last load it?"

"In February."

"Do you recollect shooting the third shot off?"

"I do. I was in Dunlop's Saloon."

"Firing at what?"

"At a mark."

"Where?"

"In Dunlop's Saloon."

"And you never fired it again until election day?"

"Election day."

"And you had five cartridges?"

"Four."

"I thought you reloaded it after firing it in Dunlop's Saloon."

"I didn't have enough to reload it; there was one empty chamber there."

"You reloaded it March 6th?"

"No. I left it with four full cartridges and one discharged."

"You fired only two shots?"

"Yes."

"When did you shoot William Ross?"

"I don't think I shot William Ross."

"Did you tell Dr. Phelan you shot the man that shot you?"

"I told him nothing of the kind."

"Will you swear you didn't shoot at William Ross at all?"

"I won't swear anything of the kind; I shot at either of these three men in the ravine."

"Were you on your knees when you fired?"

"On one knee."

"Do you know Margaret Riley?" Jack looked into the gallery and nodded.

"Exactly."

"On the day of the shooting did you tell Margaret Riley you shot William Ross?"

"I told her nothing of the kind."

"Didn't you tell Dr. Phalen you shot the man that shot you?"

"No, sir; I said I shot at the man that shot me, and if I did it, I did it in self-defense."

"Now you have testified you saw Shea fall."

"Yes. I saw a flash and he was on the ground. He went down after I was shot."

"Was this while Robert Ross was on top of you?"

"No. Robert Ross was never on top of me."

"Oh?"

This caused a rumbling in the gallery. Raines turned dramatically and approached the witness stand.

"Robert Ross never tackled you?"

"That was Adam Ross."

"Robert Ross never clubbed you?"

"Nothing occurred between me and Robert Ross all day."

The jurors shook their heads at McGough's brazen lie. Raines paused for effect.

"Finally, McGough, what were you wearing that day?"

"I had on a dark suit, a derby hat and a square cut short coat." He glanced this way and that.

Raines leaned toward him. "What color was your tie?"

"Green," McGough said. "I had on a green necktie."

The judge rapped his gavel to quiet the loud discussion.

Stanley O'Keefe was called and he testified: "I saw Shea over on the west side of Orr Street, in that roadway alongside of the gully. Behind him, I should say fifteen or twenty feet, was John Boland; I saw Boland raise his arm and he fired, and just as Boland fired, Ross fell; and just as he fell, I started over toward the Dugan house on the west side of Orr

Street. I was walking along there and Shea came by me and says, 'I am shot'; I got hold of his arm, left arm, and ran around the corner with him over toward North Fourth Street, and there we met Delaney. On the way back to the saloon, we met Alderman Dunlop who shoved Mike Delaney along the street telling him to go get a doctor."

O'Keefe painted a scene of chaos at Dunlop's Saloon, Superintendent Willard and Chief Markham entering when the doctor reached Dunlop's. "They was all shouting in there that Bat was hit, and someone should get a doctor, yet these men began questioning him."

On cross-examination, Fagan sought to impeach O'Keefe's credibility by showing the jury he had been convicted of stealing a ride on a train and he had spent time in Albany County Jail. When asked if he had worked since the election, O'Keefe replied: "Where are you going to get a job from the 6th of March on after people ruined your character here?"

Judge Williams then adjourned until Saturday morning.

31.
SOLILOQUY

She Walked Out Through The Countryside

Nellie Mae Patton now noted the days passing. The warm sun and the green tapestry of meadows and gardens through her French doors beckoned her thoughts into a silent, benign, natural realm where there were no human voices to interrupt.

A doctor had been called after her intrusion into the APA meeting, and she had been sedated for a week. She now refused to speak to her father whose APA she blamed in large part for Robert's death. On Friday evening she walked out through the countryside, a lone young woman dressed in black, a black veil obscuring her face, passing dairy farms and ponds and mill streams, her pace hesitant, tentative, a shadow through the landscape. She passed into the pine forests where the great trunks and the carpet of pine needles and the lofty fragrant canopy were as still and majestic as a cathedral.

Her religion had been stern Calvinism. She had believed in predestination, that some were born to eternal life, others to damnation, and that regeneration came only through God's influence on the human heart. Before, she believed God foreordained everything, yet now she was not so sure. The coincidence, the futility of Robert's death, those low-life saloon thugs, the ignoble gunshot in a ditch of trash and briars, how could this horror be predestined for someone of Robert's stature? And even while her faith in the harsh creed of Calvinism was shaken, the gulf between life and death seemed no longer so broad nor so deep. She sensed Rob near her day and night. She chided herself for her romanticism, but as birds called and the cattle lowed in the pastures and a church bell tolled, Nellie sensed that only the sheerest of veils separated her from him:

"Oh, Rob, tonight was to be our wedding night! I remember looking forward with such concern that everything would be perfect, the decorations, the menu, the ceremony. It was to be the wedding of the year in Troy! You so handsome in your tails, and my gown, O! Rob! my beautiful white gown!" She held up her black skirt. "And look at me, tonight. Since your departure I've been dreading this night coming and going, but now that it is here, it is like any other, like they all shall be until . . . Whatever am I to do with that beautiful dress? Packed up in a trunk now, never to be worn. Much like the rest of me, never to be of any use to anyone."

She heard the jingle of a harness, and so she stepped off the road as a team and a large wagon came around the bend. A fat man with gray whiskers drove the team and within a hundred feet he pulled up, stood and relieved himself over the side. Nellie hid behind a tree trunk, averting her eyes. The crudities of life were never far off. Then the teamster cracked the whip, "Giddy-ap!" and the horses plodded and the wagon creaked, and he passed her, whistling tunelessly.

"See, my darling?" She looked up into the pine where the golden sunlight lingered. "I am always interrupted. Not even here in the forest can I have an hour alone to speak with you." She hung her head. "I am afraid, Rob, that I took you for granted when you were here among us. I was so proud, so certain of my world and my place in it. My beautiful life was predestined, and I was worthy of it, I thought. Now, now it is in tatters and I never knew how much I loved you until you were gone." She sighed. "But that is life, I suppose, life . . . interruption, shock, coincidence, the unexpected." She shivered and shook off a sob.

"Oh, Rob, if you hear me . . . and I believe you do, I can never love another. I have foresworn a husband and family, yes, but I must not allow the emptiness to prevail. I must use my life to do good, to improve this poor sad world. That is what you want, isn't it?"

She stood and walked on, thinking, then she spoke again in a murmur: "Susan Anthony was here again last week, and she made so very much sense. I am travelling out to Seneca Falls next month. I wish to work with her. I haven't yet told Father, and he will raise a hue and cry, but I shall go nevertheless. Father and I must have a parting of the ways very soon.

"I know you can see and hear them downtown howling for blood. An eye for an eye. A tooth for a tooth. A life for a life. As if one of their miserable lives could ever be worth yours!" Nellie slumped down on a great stone and stroked her slender fingers through the moss, and she clenched her other hand near her womb. "I constantly imagine the children that will never be born. I can hear their laughter and their songs. That's what hurts so very much, Rob, so very deeply. I think of the places we shall never see together as we'd planned. And each night, in my bed, I feel how empty and alone it will be, for me, forever. And you in the cold ground. And tonight . . . was to be . . ." Tears stung her eyes, and streamed down her face. "But if I can join these women, Rob, if I can humanize politics, won't that be something? Won't that carry on what you gave your life for? And won't that remove some of the sting? Won't it . . . won't it, Rob?"

32.
THE ACCUSED

Bartholomew Shea — "I've got one chum ... McGough, I guess."

Saturday morning rumors flew through the city that Shea would testify. By eight o'clock the steps of the courthouse were solid with a dark crowd waiting for the doors to open. Again the line of prisoners and guards came down Ferry Street, then up Second. Shea, in a light summer suit, passed through the dark crowd into the packed, noisy corridors of the courthouse.

Mike Delaney took the stand first and testified he saw Boland shoot Robert Ross. On cross-examination, Delaney answered:

"We started with a drink in McClure's saloon at six. It was still dark. Across the street the people were lining up to vote. We went over, and as I took a place in line, Officer Paddy Cahill was there, and he told me to get back and stop crowding or he'd break my head."

At the third district Delaney saw no revolver with McGough, O'Keefe or Shea.

"As they ran, they were all facing west; Shea was first, Ross second and Boland third."

"Were they on a straight east and west line?"

"After they got straightened out, Ross come up there, cut off that corner of the gully."

"When Boland fired the shot what occurred?"

"Robert Ross sank down."

"What did Boland do then?"

"He fired another one in the same direction."

"How many did Boland fire in all?"

"Two that I saw."

"What did you do?"

"I turned away. O'Keefe and Shea overtook me."

"What was O'Keefe doing?"

"Looked to me as if he was helping Shea along."

"What did you do?"

"I took hold of the right side. I saw Dunlop come running, and he shoved me away and said, 'Go for a doctor.'"

"No further questions."

So far the defense had established that Shea and McGough were shot during a general riot, and that two men saw Boland shoot Ross. In the face of the prosecution's showing, the defense was pitiful. During a short recess, the crowd noted the defense's implausibility. And yet there was hope and keen expectation when Galen Hitt stood after the recess: "The defense now calls the defendant, Bartholomew Shea."

Whereas Jack had been jumpy, Shea was calm and steady. He listened to the questions, paused, then answered, occasionally narrowing his eyes. He testified he was twenty-three and lived at 865 River Street with his parents, his two younger sisters and younger brother. He then gave his narrative of the events:

"Cleary called Hayner a scab; he says, 'Don't you call me no scab, you son of a bitch,' and at that time Cleary hit him, and he goes over and has a whispered conversation south of the polling place with John Ross, William Ross, and Boland and Duncan Kaye, to the best of my opinion; I don't know the whole of the men; but at that time he came back and says, 'By Christ, I will go in there,' and at that McGough says, 'You haven't any more right in there than I have,' and Hayner pulled a wrench then and made a crack at McGough, and McGough threw up his left arm and at that time I hollered, 'Look out, Jack,' and Hayner hit me in the ear and I clinched him and went to the south with him; I hit him a couple of times, if I am not mistaken, and after that we went both on the ground and a crowd got around us and Quigley commenced hollering, 'Club him, boys, club him,' and Quigley hit me over the shoulder with a club.

"At that moment I heard McGough say, 'Don't you club him,' or

'Don't you hit him;' at that time I ran away from Quigley, and there stood William Ross with a gun down the side of his leg like that." Shea demonstrated.

"You mean a revolver?"

"Yes, sir, a revolver; and I ran."

"Where were you then?"

"Down by this post, and I ran about thirty feet north, I think, to the best of my recollection, and then started in a direct line west; there were three shots fired immediately after that; came just one, two, three, just like that, and a third one of those shots hit me; I went down, and after I regained my feet, I got up and staggered over against the fence; I stood there for a few minutes and I saw John H. Boland with a gun in his hand, and he fired and shot at me; at that moment I fired three shots at him; he was directly back of the man that laid on the ground in this roadway; then I put the gun in my pocket and went by this O'Brien house, around the corner of this O'Brien house, and I met O'Keefe and he took hold of me by the arm; I met Delaney on the way over to Dunlop's and he caught hold of my other arm, and they sent for a doctor and he sewed up my head and I went upstairs and went to bed."

"Did you fire any shot at Robert Ross when he sat or lay upon the ground?"

"No, sir."

Hitt then introduced Shea's revolver.

"You had this revolver with you that day?"

"Yes, sir."

"Did you have any other revolver with you that day?"

"No, sir."

"Did you fire any other revolver that day?"

"No, sir."

"Did you tell the police chief you had no revolver that day?"

"Yes, sir."

"How long did you stay in Dunlop's?"

"Oh, until four o'clock. Then I dressed myself and got up from bed, and they fetched the carriage there and I went and voted."

"Then where did you go?"

"Police headquarters."

"Who was with you?"

"Dunlop and McClure and his coachman."

"And have you been a prisoner in the jail ever since?"

"Yes, sir."

"No further questions."

Raines began cross-examination by asking Shea about his gun.

Shea testified he bought the gun for two dollars the previous October from John Dugan in O'Donnell's Saloon on River Street.

"Did you take your gun along with you on election day?"

"Yes."

"Did you expect to be mixed up in a fight?"

"In that ward?" Shea surveyed the crowd and his lip curled in a sneer. "Sure."

"Did you have your gun with you at the February 3rd caucus?"

"Objection!" Hitt called. "Incompetent and immaterial."

"Overruled."

"Yes."

"And where did you take it from?"

"From a dresser in my house."

"You expected difficulty in the caucus?"

"I had no hand in it at all."

"Did you take any part in the proceeding of the caucus?"

"Your honor!" Hitt said with exasperation. "This was a full month before election day!"

"Overruled."

"Yes."

"And at what point?"

"At the point McGough was getting punched and kicked around."

"What did you do?"

"I went around to the back and could not get in."

"How did you try to get in?"

"I didn't try very hard; I got in."

"How did you get in?"

"In through the window."

"Who broke in?"

"Me."

"And what did you do then?"

"McGough handed me the box."

"Did you hit anyone with a revolver?"

"No."

"Who did you level it at?"

"No one."

"Anyone else break in at that time?"

"No."

"You got the ballot box at the caucus?"

"Yes."

"And went through the window with the ballot box all alone?"

"Yes."

"What did you take the ballot box for?"

"Safekeeping."

"How far did you take it from the caucus?"

"Two blocks, to Rapp's meat market."

"And of course I will ask the question, how many more ballots were there in the box when you returned it to McGough than when you took it from the caucus."

"I don't know; I didn't count them."

Bat Shea then testified as to election day. "I went to McClure's Saloon and had a drink, then I went to the first district. At eight I went to Dunlop's Saloon and had breakfast with Dunlop and his wife." He proceeded to the second district, then back to the first, then on to the third.

"There was a group of them there at the third, waiting for us. We went over. Owney Judge struck this man named Kearns. William Ross run up, I thought to hit Judge, so as he did, I hit him."

"Ross hadn't hit anybody?"

"No."

"Where did you hit him?"

"In the mouth."

"Why were you responsible for what became of Judge?"

"He is a friend of mine."

"And did you expect he would have struck you?"

"They would have done it if they got a show, all right."

"Did anyone strike you?"

"They didn't get near enough to me. I wouldn't allow them."

"Where did you go then?"

"I went over to Dunlop's and had a drink."

"With your party?"

"I ain't got any party."

"How long did you stay in Dunlop's?"

"Just long enough to take a drink."

"How many times during the day did you stop at Dunlop's?"

"I stopped there every time I was dry and got a drink." Shea peered into the gallery and Mamie Halligan was looking on sorrowfully. Premonitions. Shea told how he went back toward the third district about noon with three fellows, how McGough came over afterward through the lot, and how he, Cleary and Judge went through the crowd and started into the hallway of the polls.

"How many persons could fit in that small hallway?"

"You might get six on a pinch. But only three like Murphy. McGough, he waited on the stoop." When things went sour inside, Shea told how Officer Murphy cleared them out and then how Cleary pushed Hayner.

"He told him, 'You scab, what are you doing walking all over my feet?' And Hayner replied, 'You son of a bitch, don't call me any scab.' Then he went over to talk with the Rosses and came back howling: 'By Christ, I will go in there.' So McGough tells him, 'You haven't any more right in there than I have, and you won't go in.' At that time I told him, 'You been looking for trouble all day, and you will get some, and you had better shut up.'"

"And was that a bluff remark?"

Shea slowly scanned the gallery and the jury box and he narrowed his eyes looking at Raines. "A bluff?"

"Were you bluffing?"

"I never tried to bluff anybody. Anything I say, I say pretty near what I mean."

"Were you backing up Cleary?"

"I think Cleary could hold his own with Hayner."

"And did you strike anybody?"

"I didn't get a show to do much; they all punched me all right. Hayner hit me with the wrench. Quigley, he struck me two or three times on the shoulders and back. When I tried to get away, they shot me in the head. I went down, then I pulled myself up against the fence."

"You went down, you arose and went up to the fence and stood there?"

"I went to the fence, yes, sir."

"Then what did you do?"

"I raised my revolver then."

"And where did you go?"

"I fired from the fence."

"Right up against the O'Brien fence?"

"Yes, sir."

"Where did you fire?"

"I fired then at Boland.

"Where did Boland stand when you fired at him?"

"He stood directly in back of the man that laid in that roadway."

"Did Boland fire any shot at you?"

"Fired once."

"Where was he then?"

"Directly back of the man in the roadway."

"Didn't you tell a Dr. Phelan that Boland shot Ross?"

"I told Dr. Phelan exactly the way McGough told me. I did not see Robert Ross shot."

"Did you see McGough fire any shots?"

"No, sir."

"Did you see McGough running away?"

"After the polls, I didn't see McGough till jail."

"And you don't know that Boland fired any shot that reached Robert Ross?"

"How could I tell about it?"

"You did not see him shot?"

"I did not see Robert Ross shot, no."

"Did you see McGough at any time while you were firing those three shots?"

"Didn't see him at all; no, sir."

"Did you see him running across the lot?"

"I did not."

"Did you suppose McGough was anywheres close to Robert Ross or Boland at the time you fired the three shots?"

"I didn't suppose anything."

"What were you running away from?"

"From the clubs; what did you want me to do?"

"Shea, did you ever run away before, with a revolver in your pocket, from anybody?"

"I never had any occasion to run away."

"What did you do with your revolver?"

"I gave it to Steve Burke in Dunlop's."

"And is Steve Burke one of your gang?"

"I got no gang."

"Well, is he one of your chums?"

"I don't know whether they are any chums of mine. I have got one chum. I have got no more chums."

"And who is that?"

Shea looked to the first row of the gallery. "McGough, I guess."

Shea then denied that he'd told McGough he'd given his pistol to Steve Burke.

"And did you not tell McGough to write a letter to Steve Burke to substitute another pistol for the one you had?"

"That never happened."

"Didn't McGough write a letter for you from the jail."

"Yes."

"And was that to Steve Burke?"

"No."

"Who was it to?"

Shea looked for a long moment at Mamie. "To a young lady."

"How well did you know Steve Burke?"

"We travelled together out West. Chicago, Pittsburgh, Alleghany, Sioux City, Leeds, Independence, Dubuque and Freeport. We also went hop picking together near Utica one summer."

Raines then steered the questions back to the murder scene. "While you stood by the post, did you hear McGough?"

"I heard him, yes, but I didn't see him."

"Isn't it a little remarkable that you didn't pay some attention to the whereabouts of McGough when you started away?"

"My attention was to those people clubbing me."

"That is not standing by your chum, McGough; didn't you think of him?"

"How did I know where he went? Wouldn't I be foolish to stop and let them club me?"

"You heard testimony that you came back and fired three shots?"

"Yes."

"And that you stood by Robert Ross and fired them?"

"Yes."

"Have you any recollection of doing anything of the kind?"

"I am pretty sure I fired three shots."

"Have you a distinct recollection as to where you stood?"

"Near that fence."

"Your head clear enough to remember that distinctly?"

"Yes."

"Now, then, isn't it remarkable all the time you stood there that you did not look for McGough; can you account for it, knowing Bartholomew Shea as well as you do, you not thinking to look for John McGough?"

"I did not to the best of my recollection."

"You think you were weak when you went up against the fence?"

"I know I felt weak with four or five cracks across the back and shoulders."

"You started to run while over there?"

"I did the best I could."

"You did not think when you were going around there you had shot anybody, did you?"

Shea looked at the jury. "I couldn't say as I thought I did."

Raines moved in closer:

"Now, you are not answering the question. You weren't sure whether you shot a man or not?"

"No, I wasn't sure; to the best of my opinion I didn't shoot him, though, the man I was firing at."

"You thought at the time you didn't hit him?"

"Yes, sir."

"Why didn't you go over and look at this man that was down?"

"What did I want to go over for?"

"There wasn't anybody meddling with you."

"But they would. I had all I could do to take care of myself."

"Did you know who it was down?"

"I did not."

"There was no one attacking you at this time?"

"No. I walked right away."

Raines looked up at the judge. "No further questions, your honor."

Judge Williams looked over the crowded courtroom. "I will recess until Monday, July 2nd at nine-thirty. The witness, the defendant may stand down."

All stood as the jury returned to their sequestration, and when Williams left the courtroom, speculation and comments swirled. As deputies escorted Shea through the pressing crowd, a path parted in the throng, as if they were backing away from a condemned man. Shea threw out his chest and glared defiantly at all the people who fell silent as he walked through.

Outside, the sweltering afternoon hit them and crowds pressed up the courthouse steps. Reporters urged questions at Shea, but he ignored them. Horses stood in the shade of the elms, and the lawn was green and thick on the female seminary campus. Shea took a long drink of the fresh air, and walked proudly to Ferry Street. Men were loafing in the doorways of saloons, and draught horses pulled heavy wagons over the railroad bridge and up the steep incline of Mount Ida to Marshall's mill complex on the Poestenkill.

Like a blot against the sky, the stained brick bulk of the Kennedy & Murphy Brewery poured smoke from its tall stacks, and high atop the hill rose the gracious Tudor mansion of the Warrens.

Shea again breathed deeply. The sunlight felt good and the bustle of the street was comforting after his testimony, yet all too soon they entered the shadows of the jail and the narrow dusty hallways and cell.

Shea went to the window. "The jury had a hanging look about it today, Jack," he said gloomily.

"Aye." McGough was visibly depressed with the day in court. He tried to seem hopeful. "But don't you think if the gunsmith shows the bullet didn't come from your gun, that'll give them the reasonable doubt they need to acquit?"

"They come up with this letter you supposedly wrote to Burkey, but they never produce it. Boland says you wrote a letter for me to Burkey telling him to claim I give him a gun other than the one I give him. That took some pluck out of our case."

"But there weren't no such letter."

"I know that. You were writing to Mamie."

"So Boland's lying. So Boland's covering up for himself. So Boland done it."

"Yeah, Jack. But Boland ain't testifying no more. And Fagan and Raines is laying this doubt before the jury as to what pistol I was packing." He looked around and his lip curled down. "You had a thirty-two rim-fire, Jack."

"So did Boland."

"No. His was a center-fire. They all chased you, Jack. It come out."

"Don't say that, Bat." McGough shook his head. "Don't even think that. Do you think for one instant I'd let you stand patsy for me? You yourself said we was chums. That's just what they want, to split us apart. Don't you turn on your only friend in the world, Bat. Look, they got me for assault first. I didn't even shoot that son of a bitch brother of his. Boland's the one what shot Ross."

"But you said it was Adam Ross when everyone else said it was Robert that tackled you."

"Yeah," Jack nodded his head seriously, ". . . and I commenced to shoot when I rose up. But I didn't plug Ross."

"And that goddamn green tie they all talk about. You had it on. You notice that Raines never asked me what color tie I wore?"

"Yeah." Jack was thoughtful. "I think the witnesses were all confused with Boland's green coat. Never mind. The gunsmith will be the key, Bat. Wait and see. He'll come in with the proof that it weren't your gun, and there'll be some shocked sons of bitches."

Shea shook his head slowly, unconvinced.

33.
COMINGS AND GOINGS

City of Troy Steamboat

Frank Black stood at the railing of the steamboat "City of Troy," gazing thoughtfully across the Hudson at the towers of West Point. Too young for the Civil War, as a boy he had been fascinated by military affairs. The pageantry, the line of command, the dedication to a cause made life simple and orderly, and Black longed for a more military approach to civil authority. That was the prime benefit of the APA. It provided structure, and rank and file members to do the bidding of the leaders.

Frank Black felt himself rising to the surface in the riptide of politics. Indeed, he was directing its flow. The state Republican chairman had called him down to Manhattan for a conference with money people. They had talked. The uproar in Troy, the chairman confided, was causing irreparable damage to Murphy in his own party. Frank Black was being recognized as a reformer, emulated statewide as the citizens of New York mobilized to throw out their political bosses. The clean, pure lines of morality and good citizenship were triumphing over the ignorance and drunkenness and cynicism of bosses.

The chairman urged him to think about a run for Congress, lifting and donning the mantle of political office himself. Frank Black had a saying, though, that expressed a cherished belief: "When you hold public office, you're the public's dog." Surely he had ambitions, and he knew that despite his pinchpenny law office, he had considerable executive talent. He told the chairman he would think about it, talk it over with his family. Washington, a Republican member of the House of Representatives, while the junior senator from New York was Edward J. Murphy. Now there was a thought.

Frank Black watched the river narrow. From the broad expanse at Tappan Zee, it had narrowed by half. At Troy navigation stopped altogether. Yes, at Troy the river was narrow and choked, like the politics. River navigation ended at the dam in the thirteenth ward where the canals began. Frank Black had recently set sail upon the broad currents of state politics, and now a seat in Congress was possible. He enjoyed the wider view. Returning to Troy, to all the unpleasant business of the trial, narrowed his vision, and the closer the boat got, the more irritable he felt. Would that this horrid trial were over, and he might raise his eyes up from petty bank and commercial litigation to matters of public import on the national level. The trial upriver, like the dam in the thirteenth ward where river navigation ceased, was the single obstacle to his clear sailing. And if a fresh new wind were blowing, he might even succeed Murphy in the senate seat. The chairman, though, had inserted one condition to his run: the death sentence in Shea's trial. That seemed odd to Black.

"Why an execution?"

"People need to believe the system works and they will believe only if Shea gets the chair."

As he pondered it in the steady throb of the steam engine and the splash of the sidewheel, Black recalled a public execution in Limington, Maine. It was bloody murder, a husband murdered his wife and his wife's lover with an axe. The community was torn as to whether the hanging was justified. Despite the extreme emotional disturbance defense, malice aforethought was proved because the farmer lay in wait all evening in a hedgerow until the lovers were well beyond flirtation. The jury convicted on the top count, and the judge sentenced death by hanging.

The festive atmosphere of the hanging shocked young Frank Black, the sad look of the criminal, hands bound before him, prodded forward by deputies to the steps of the gallows. His eyes! The sorrow, the fear, the horror twitching in his face! The climb up the gallows steps, the sack cloth hood, then the noose, his muscles trembling in anticipation, the nerves jumping as the noose was tightened, then the lever sprung and the sharp intake of breath in the crowd as the boots danced in the empty air, the body twitched for a full minute, and then the spasms lessened.

They let him hang there for half an hour before cutting him down. This memory, long buried, had arisen by the phrase, "the system works." The system works, all right. The Shea trial was proceeding remarkably well.

"All that is left," Black told the chairman, "are the summations and the jury charge. While it is never intelligent to second-guess a jury, a conviction is very likely. Shea is facing a freight train of evidence against him."

The chairman nodded with satisfaction, and Black felt assured that conviction for premeditated murder would be found.

And yet, one thought nagged at him here in the open air: what if Shea was innocent? Black shook his head. No, impossible. John Ross and Osborne Lansing had told him immediately following the murder that it was Shea, the man in the green tie, who had shot Robert Ross. Others had confirmed this. Shea circled back to rescue his friend McGough from the bludgeoning, and then executed Robert Ross as Ross stumbled out of the ditch. But the angle of the wound troubled Black. Robert Ross's initial fall troubled him. The testimony of that couple on Thursday, the McLaughlins, the woman testifying that Shea stood alone by the fence, then her husband testifying that two or three in the crowd hollered "Lynch him!" and ran off after Jack McGough, he was troubled reading that in the newspaper.

Could John Ross and Osborne Lansing have mistaken McGough for Shea? And what if Boland had indeed killed Ross with a stray bullet? That story about blanks was perjury. Not even Boland was fool enough to pull a gun only to fire blanks. And yet Black had tried enough cases to know not everything fit into neat explanations.

The sun on the river was as bright and gleaming as his future in politics down where the river broadened. West Point was behind him and the river narrowed between rocky shores. He told himself that he must adhere to the principles of right and honor, and not listen to voices of doubt. Then an insidious, cynical voice whispered, someone killed Ross, and Shea was as good a defendant as any. No, he told himself, Shea was certainly the guilty party. It had been proven. Shea would pay for the life he had extinguished. A life for a life. Justice.

Meanwhile, along another river farther south, the Potomac, the capitol dome and the Washington monument and the executive mansion are startling and white amidst the brick Victorian mansions, the bustle and greenery of Washington, DC. Down from hardscrabble New England, up from the subjugated South, in from lively and robust Chicago, the desolate badlands of the Dakotas, the high peaks of Colorado, clear across from Nevada and California on the clattering transcontinental railroad, men come to deliberate and barter power and prestige, then to return with grants and laws and preferments to benefit the folks back home.

New York has produced a good share of presidents, Martin Van Buren, Millard Fillmore, Chester A. Arthur, Grover Cleveland. Indeed, Cleveland's course through the New York governor's office is what Ed Murphy has been eyeing since Roswell Flower's disloyalty. Despite "that business" in cramped little Troy, Murphy believes he can pull the necessary votes from Tammany Hall if a primary becomes necessary to knock Flower out of Albany, and retire him back to Watertown. Murphy is fond of the image that he was born to "soar with the eagles," and his wheelings and dealings on Capitol Hill are legendary.

It took only a few whispers in the cloakroom and the rumored briefcases of cash to glide the Wilson Tariff Bill through the Fifty-third Congress. This bill levied a tariff on detachable collars imported from Britain, thus giving the American product a competitive edge in the marketplace. The manufacturers in Troy, who produced nine of every ten detachable collars in the United States, were overjoyed. Their market, income and investments were secure, and they had the skill and beneficence of Senator Edward J. Murphy, Jr., to thank. Some were now cautioning the upstart Frank Black to refrain from referring to the senator in his remarks.

Yet Senator Murphy has not emerged unscathed from the stormy four months following the murder. Identified in the fledgling national press as an urban political boss, Murphy's reputation has been irreparably battered. The Populist swell toward clean government and its reforms — the secret "Australian" ballot, initiative, referendum and recall — coupled with the Panic of 1893, have cast the urban political boss as an enemy of the people. Yet Murphy denies he's in trouble. He is caught up in heady power plays of Congress. He refuses to cede any of his power, and is now lining up supporters in Tammany for his bid for governor.

In late June, "Racehorse" Cullen, one of the bowler-hatted army of New York City Hall layabouts, was dispatched to Washington from Tammany Hall with a delegation of two to invite Murphy to his own testimonial dinner. "Race" was a veteran in machine politics. He cut his teeth on the public pap under Boss Tweed and had survived the scorching winds of reform that blew a generation before. Down through New Jersey and Pennsylvania, Race regaled the club car with jokes and jigs and song and merriment, hoping to stave off the hour of his unpleasant duty.

Danny O'Marra and Tick Riordan helped him off the train and took a hotel room so Race might sleep off the effects of the journey. Next morning, a foul, muggy, sweltering day with a stench of horse manure and sewage clogging the streets, Race arose with bloodshot eyes and a mottled face. After a shave and hot towel, the boys led him over to Murphy's office on Capitol Hill. The clerk made a fuss that they had no appointment.

"He'll see us," Race insisted, "just tell him it's Racehorse Cullen he's got cooling his heels out here." Race cleared his throat and located the spitoon. With any luck, Murphy'd take them out to noon dinner and he could ease the jangle in his nerves with a touch of the Irish.

"Of course! Of course I have time to see my old friend Race," Murphy's booming voice came from within the office, and the double doors burst open and the boss stood beaming in the doorway. "How're the ponies treating you, Race?"

"Them and the women keep me broke as a beggar, Boss. Me 'n the boys was admiring your spread here."

Murphy came toward them with uplifted arms, and they embraced all four. After pleasantries, the senator invited them to dine at the Jefferson Club, his posh private club in the shadow of the capitol dome. The dining room was a high, chandeliered affair with frescoes and dainty plaster work and French doors that opened onto a lawn with a vista of masts and steamboat stacks at the Navy yard. Leaden clouds hung over the salt marshes. With whiskeys all around and plates of oysters, the men settled in for a seven course dinner.

Tick Riordan said little in response to Murphy, while Danny brought him up to date on the New York City gossip. They were cutting through chops of veal when Murphy broached the subject:

"Now, it's damned good to see you boys. Reminds me of what a group of arsekissers, incompetents and rejects I have 'round me down here in Dixie. None that can hold the candle to our northern boys. But I suspect it's more than a greeting you've brought."

"Aye, 'tis useless to be coy with you, Senator!" Racehorse cut into his third chop and talked with his mouth open. His face carried the scars of many brawls. "Seems the sachems at Tammany want to honor you."

"Is that so?" Murphy smiled at the news. Since the regrettable business in Troy, he had spent too much time in the capital, and he missed his family and his sycophants at home. Murphy chuckled. If the state chairman cannot place himself on the ballot, then what good is being state chairman? Besides, as governor he would be just across the river from

Troy, and a closer watch would insure fewer things went amiss. "I'll go over the guest list with you. We can't forget a soul. This nomination has to be carefully orchestrated."

Race nearly choked and he raised his napkin to his mouth. Tick was twitching at twice his usual speed, and Danny O'Marra stared at the cutlery. Race gagged and poured a tumbler of water down his throat: "Uh, the dinner's t'honor you, of course, Boss. A lavish collation at the hall with all the dignitaries we can't keep away who want to shake your hand and wish you well."

Murphy smiled ear to ear. It proved a maxim he held dear in politics: stay close to the people for they have the power. Flower was out and Murphy was in. "When is the dinner?"

"Why, July 14, Boss."

"Bastille Day?"

"Aye. They sent us down to inform you and take back whatever direction you wish, menu, music, the guest list you mentioned."

Murphy scowled. "But the convention's the week before. I will be a candidate by then."

"A candidate?" Race looked at Danny, then at Tick who was twitching wildly. "A candidate, Boss?"

"The candidate for governor. Ain't that what the dinner is for?"

"Why, no, sir."

"Well, then, why in blazes have you come down here? There's to be a dinner, is there not?"

"Yes."

"Well, what the hell do I need a dinner for if I'm already on the ballot?" Murphy's neck was reddening and his jowls quivered. "You're not bothering me about a goddamn fundraiser, are you, Race?" His fist was clenched on the linen and a few from nearby tables were looking over.

"No, Boss, I ain't." Race took a long swallow of whiskey.

"It's yer retirement," Tick sputtered.

"My what?" Murphy glared at the three of them.

"The kid here's spoken it. The cat's out of the bag," Racehorse eased back in his chair, and leveled his eyes at Murphy. "Your retirement as state chairman. We figgered the week after another successful convention you could announce your retirement nice and graceful."

Murphy's eyes narrowed and he leaned across the table pointing at Race Cullen. "Listen, you double-dealing son of a bitch. You see these hands? You go back to the boys who sent you here and you tell them that Ed Murphy will give up his grip on the Democratic party only after he's snapped their worthless spines."

"Well, that ain't the way they see it, Ed." Race picked his teeth with his fingernail. Deliberately he'd dropped the "boss" appellation. With his fists on the table, he squared off for the confrontation. This was when Race was best, when he felt alive. "They say you've lost your base upstate with the disgrace of that there trial, and the downstate boys ain't been happy with your voting record for sometime. Governor Flower's looking for someone with more modern, more progressive ideas to join him on the ticket."

"Progressive! Flower? I'll bet!"

"Now, you can go out with a fanfare and good cheer, or you can go out with spite and ill will." He opened his arms in a gesture of conciliation. "Your choice. But don't mistake it, Ed. Either way, you're going out."

Murphy wadded his napkin and threw it on his plate. "Have a pleasant trip north." He was up and away before they could respond, yet as he navigated his bulk through the tables and the approving eyes of those seated about, he felt light-headed. Stripped of his state chairmanship, it would be one term in the senate, and then he'd be dumped on the political dungheap. Race was right. Except for what he could salvage in Troy, the upstate base was gone, and the downstaters were striving for the appearance of Populist reform that was sweeping the land. He could protest and argue, but he had no leverage. He took his top hat from the coatcheck, slipped the kid a silver dollar and he was on the street. Murphy felt dizzy and weak, and he returned to his rooms rather than the office.

34.
THE CONVICTION

Rensselaer County Courthouse

When the trial resumed Monday, the atmosphere was less expectant. McGough had testified, Shea had testified, the defense was, in large measure, in and had not sufficiently rebutted Black's twenty-one eye witnesses. Hitt and Norton now sought to prove that Shea was carrying a thirty-two calibre center-fire and therefore, due to the size of the fatal bullet, he could not have shot Ross. Yet as they called their firearms expert, to the stand, Raines stood:

"Your honor, there is no need for this witness's testimony. The People at this time will concede that the revolver Shea produced here is not the revolver which made the mortal wound on Robert Ross."

The crowd murmured. The stipulation threw the defense into disarray.

"What are they saying?" Shea asked Norton.

"That this is not your gun."

"Which one's supposed to be mine then?"

"The one found in the ditch."

"But that's Jack's."

Norton shrugged. "We must convince the jury."

"Mr. Norton?" the judge spoke.

"I call George Gemmill."

Gemmill, a well-known gunsmith took the stand.

"I show you a revolver, the one found in the ditch, and ask that you examine it and describe to us the calibre."

"Thirty-two calibre, rim-fire."

"What make?"

"American Bulldog pattern; double acting, that is, self-cocking."

"What bullet does that accept?"

"Thirty-two short."

"How much lead in one of those bullets?"

"Eighty grains."

"And in the thirty-two longs?"

"Ninety grains."

"I show you another revolver, Mr. Boland's revolver."

"That takes a thirty-two calibre center-fire cartridge, Waltby and Henley make."

"What is the quantity of lead?"

"Eighty-eight grains."

"And what is the difference between the center-fire and the rim-fire?"

"The only difference is in the head of the shell, the method of igniting the charge; one has a primer in the center of the shell, while the other has a percussion lead in the rim."

"Can you tell a ball that came from a center or rim-fire cartridge after it had been exploded?"

"Yes. The rim-fire has three grooves and the center-fire has one large groove. Grooves are around the bullet, put there to hold the lubricator."

"Can you tell us whether this bullet is a center-fire or a rim-fire?" He held out the box that contained the fatal bullet. Gemmill opened the box, examined the fragments.

"No, sir. It must be more intact."

There was much grumbling at this. This witness, the gallery whispered, served no purpose at all. At least not until Raines began his cross-examination:

"There are different weights of bullets for the same calibre revolver?"

"Yes, sir."

"Is that the same with center-fires?"

"Yes, sir."

"When a bullet passes through a substance with no apparent change of shape, the friction along the side will remove some small portion of the weight?"

"A small portion."

"A grain and a half in an eighty grain bullet wouldn't be too much?"

"No. That is liable to come from friction going through the barrel."

"If you had broken bullet pieces weighing seventy-eight and one half grains, that indicates an eighty grain bullet, ordinarily?"

"Yes, sir."

"So it was impossible for this center-fire," he held up Boland's revolver, "which you just testified fires an eighty-eight grain bullet, to have produced the ball that killed Robert Ross?"

"Objection."

"Sustained."

There was much discussion of this testimony. "Order! Order!" Williams rapped his gavel. The stir came because Shea's own witness had suggested that Boland's revolver did not fire the fatal shot. Shea scowled at Norton. Hitt was wiping sweat from his forehead. Their expert witness had immeasurably hurt the defense.

The next witness, Clinton Herrick, was a doctor who performed gunshot experiments on corpses. He was offered to show the difficulty Shea would have in inflicting the mortal wound from above.

"Can you put that skull in any position," Hitt asked, "where a revolver held eighteen inches away from the back of the skull and at least six inches higher than the point of entrance of that wound, with the revolver pointed downward, can you put the head of a living person in such a position?"

"I don't think you can."

"Can you put the skull at right angles?"

"No."

"Why not?" Judge Williams asked.

"It would be a most unnatural position," Herrick showed with his hand. "If the man were lying flat on his face, the other would have to fire from about there; if he was sitting, he would have to fire about there."

"Supposing the person were shot standing up?"

"Not with a revolver pointed downward."

"With a revolver held on about the level?"

"Would depend on the height of the man he was shooting at."

"Assuming the man is six feet three inches tall and the man

shooting him is five feet nine inches, and he holds the revolver about on a line with the lower portion of his breast bone?"

"Everything would depend on the positions of the two men."

When Raines cross-examined, he drew attention to the angle of the wound, and the judge then posed a question:

"Start at the end of the wound and draw a line which would reach the point he suggests to a person standing twelve feet behind."

"Yes."

"Given the angle of the wound, the farther back you go, the lower the person would have to descend with the revolver?"

"Yes, sir."

Raines picked up the questioning. "And at twelve feet the revolver would have to be two feet underground to produce such an angle?"

"If your assumptions are correct, it might."

"Given the angle of the wound, isn't it true that the further back you go the greater the difficulty of keeping the revolver above ground?"

"Yes, sir."

"To produce that wound from twelve feet behind Robert Ross, the gun would have to be underground?"

"Objection!"

"Overruled."

"Yes, sir."

There was much discussion now in the courtroom. Produced to show Shea did not shoot Ross, the last two witnesses had successfully disproved Shea's only theory, that Boland shot Ross. The defense called two additional witnesses, then rested. The People then called a few of their initial witnesses back to the stand on rebuttal. One was John Boland:

"Do I understand you to say after Robert Ross had been shot you ran by Shea and had an encounter with McGough?"

"Yes."

"You left him and went back to Robert Ross?"

"Yes."

"There you made up your mind Robert Ross was dead?"

"Yes."

"You got up and immediately started in your pursuit of McGough?"

"The second time."

"Why did you go to McGough and not for Shea?"

"Shea was out of sight and McGough wasn't."

"You had seen one man shooting?"

"Yes."

"You hadn't seen McGough shoot him at all?"

"No."

"The People have no further witnesses," Raines announced.

"Very well," Judge Williams stated, "testimony is closed."

Since the close of the prosecutor's case, Black had been absent from the courtroom. Yet the net he'd woven was closing and the few struggles the defense put up seemed to have been absorbed with no damage. The prey was ensnared, and now it was merely a matter of summations, jury charge and deliberations to complete the task.

Out of the presence of the jury and with the gallery emptying, Hitt and Norton renewed their motions to dismiss. The motions were denied, and the charge conference held.

"We shall be most of the day hearing summations, gentlemen, and I should like to give the case to the jury by this time tomorrow."

"And what of the holiday, sir?"

"We shall see, Mr. Hitt," the judge remarked. "I do not think deliberations will be long in this case."

All over the city preparations went forward for Troy's Independence Day parade. The many associations and unions from the mills and factories and foundries had constructed floats and drilled their members. The six lodges of Masons, the International Order of Odd Fellows, the Iron Moulders Union, the Knights of Pythias, the Orangemen, the Ancient Order of United Workmen, the Order of United American Mechanics, the Elks, the Druids, the Independent Order of Good Templars, the Master Plumbers Steam and Gas Fitters Association, The Women's Christian Temperance Union, the Ancient Order of Hibernians, The St. Vincent de Paul Society, the League Shirt and Waist Co., the Bakers Union, the Master Painters and Decorators Association, the Troy Collar and Shirt Manufacturers Association, the Troy Yacht Club, cadets from LaSalle Institute, boys from the Troy Catholic Male Orphan Asylum and small children in white frocks from the Mary Warren Free Institute would join Doring's band and the various military companies in Troy's Fourth of July parade. And while the costumes were brushed and the ribbons tied and the florists' wagons busy with deliveries and musical instruments checked, melodies practiced, Shea looked down on it all from behind the grillwork of his cell.

Steve Burke and Mike Delaney stopped by with a growler of beer, but so silent and stoic was Shea they stayed only half an hour. Up in the north end of town, George Dunlop was drunk and on a crying jag at his bar. He went to bed just after supper.

A delegation of citizens visited the law office of Frank Black in the Hall building and asked him to march in the Fourth of July parade at the head of the delegation of Orangemen. There could be no public show of force for the APA, and this was the best they could do to show their appreciation for his effort.

"Gentlemen," Black told them, "in guiding the prosecution of the notorious repeater and murderer Bat Shea, I have sought no preferment. I have merely done my duty as a citizen. I seek no honor, and therefore I must decline."

When this was told and retold in the salons of Washington Park, the board rooms of banks, the offices of the mill executives, Black's stature rose higher than it would have if he had accepted and marched.

The next day, Tuesday, July 3, was scowling and overcast with a yellow sky. The courtroom was stifling. Galen Hitt was first to deliver Shea's summation, trying to cast the People's proof in a doubtful light. He hammered at the ulterior motives in the prosecution and he sweat and repeatedly mopped his brow:

"This prosecution was conceived in politics, reared in politics and matured in politics, and it reaches from a small ward election to the chief executive of this Empire State. The charges against Shea are political charges primarily and criminal charges secondarily. Such an uproar was made by certain citizens calling themselves defenders of the common weal, and by the press, that this young man's conviction was a foregone conclusion. They hadn't the courtesy to submit it first to a court or to you, the jury."

Hitt walked to the reserved seat from which Frank Black had watched the trial, held empty now in case Black returned, and his voice rose with passion: "I say to you, gentlemen of the jury, that Frank Black and company, all their committees and meetings and lofty rhetoric are nothing more than self-appointed executioners!"

The gallery registered shock at Hitt's characterization. Hitt's face was red and his voice quavered with emotion.

"Let us look at the facts, gentlemen of the jury, the bare facts. The Ross brothers, Lansing, Lee, Dodds, Quigley and Hayner, why were they at the polls? Why were they armed with pistols and wrenches and clubs? Gentlemen, they were looking for a fight. They got Zweifel up to preach incendiarism and they held a meeting in one of the largest churches in this city where the squeaky orator of the Empire State tells of the booming of cannon, the bursting of shell with the old flag rolling above him and the congregation."

The gallery erupted with laughter at this hyperbole. Judge Williams rapped his gavel and cautioned the spectators that he would clear the courtroom at the next outburst.

Hitt continued down through the evidence: "And then we have Boland. He takes us for idiots wanting us to believe he bought blank cartridges. After the shooting he runs up on the Fitchburg tracks and reloads, then he surrenders the gun to the coroner. 'Look,' he says, 'I was shooting blanks.' And he reloads! Why? He then visits his APA friends and gets a closed carriage to carry him to a sympathetic judge to set bail. Bail! Bail for what? I ask you. He had been charged with no crime.

"Next we view the coroner's inquest, sprung directly from that gravedigging meeting at Fifth Avenue Presbyterian Church, sprung directly from Frank Black's school for witnesses. Gentlemen of the jury, these citizens, under the claim of justice, then intervened in the picking of the grand jury.

"Then there is the fable of Mrs. Titus. Twenty-five pieces of silver given to execute Ross. You heard that she is related to John Boland whom her words helped free. And that dreamer, Augustus Paul, who hears voices in the wind. I say you could not hang a woodchuck on such evidence!

"All of these stories were weaved into a net, gentlemen, a net to trap this defendant." Hitt walked to the defense table and placed his hands upon Shea's shoulders. "Do you believe that if this man is bound down in the electric chair with leather straps and killed by that horrible current, do you believe that all the repeating and corruption ever done will be atoned for?" His voice rose, and he pointed to Black's empty chair. "That's what they believe! That is what they stated at their church meeting as the old flag was sailing aloft again!

"When Shea and McGough fled across the ravine, gentlemen, they were escaping. At that point the Ross party was the aggressor. Like mad dogs they chased these fleeing men with pistols and clubs and wrenches. And they call themselves keepers of the pure ballot! Shea has identified his revolver and it is in evidence. It is a thirty-two calibre center-fire. Robert Ross was shot with a thirty-two calibre rim-fire. Gentlemen," he went to the clerk's table and picked up Shea's gun, "here is the reasonable doubt, and under the law Shea is entitled to that doubt. No matter who has clamored, the newspapers, the ministry, the APA, I ask for acquittal because these proofs fail to show beyond a reasonable doubt that he is guilty."

Hitt bowed his head. He was sweating profusely. "From

between you and the defendant I now slip. I ask you simply to use the golden rule and do by him as you'd have others do by you. Take the evidence and under the God that made you, decide the guilt or innocence of this man."

He held an open palm towards Shea, and Shea looked up, his jaw set, his eye scrutinizing each one of the jurors, then he looked down at his folded hands. Silence filled the courtroom.

George Raines stood and walked to the jury box. "Gentlemen of the jury, tomorrow is the anniversary of the signing of the Declaration of Independence. Today Robert Ross sleeps peacefully near the home of his birth. He has died upholding the rights of free men.

"I will not call your attention to his family's terrible grief, or to the scene of the murder when young Ross's life blood was spilled upon the ground. I will call your attention rather to the two parties before the bar today. One party," he swept his arm about the courtroom, the judge, the clerk, the officers of the court, "consists of the people of the state of New York, that is, organized society. The other," he jabbed his finger at the defendant's table, "is Bartholomew Shea!" The stir that arose in the gallery was quickly silenced with a look from Williams.

"What are we today, gentlemen? Part of a system in the evolution of civilization nineteen centuries long. We have evolved the most perfect system of justice there ever existed. And yet counsel for the defense would claim that the thought and effort of all these centuries are part of a mighty conspiracy against one miserable young man. In their defense they have impugned the testimony of twenty-one people who swore they saw a man fire a bullet into the back of the head of a sitting Robert Ross, and sixteen or seventeen who actually identified that man as Bartholomew Shea. They have painted Mr. Fagan as an opportunist. They have argued this court has no jurisdiction, that this jury of good men should not be sitting. What then?" he paused dramatically. "Is Bat Shea's revolver to be the arbiter of our disputes?"

Raines shook his head sadly. "But what are they really doing? They have no case, and they are invoking prejudice to induce disagreement among you. Divine Providence gave us so much evidence in this case that Bat Shea should have enlisted it as a co-conspirator. Bat Shea should have arranged for a suspension of the laws of nature while this murder took place. In the name of American institutions, these sacred institutions our fathers gave us, you must see that there is no cowardice in your decision. You too are now called to hold up the banner that Robert Ross so bravely raised. This is the meaning of the coming Fourth of July."

Raines went over the evidence then point by point. He did not perspire, but was cool and rational in his approach. For three hours he weighed and shaded the evidence the People had introduced, and then he concluded:

"Jurymen, this overwhelming evidence warrants me in saying that a verdict of guilty of murder in the first degree is demanded at your hands. While Bartholomew Shea may have no particle of malice toward any man, he is, rather, the enemy of the ballot box. He rises above the classes of criminals that infest our cities. He represents the rule of crime."

Raines folded his arms and looked each juror in the eye. "I say, let the laws be administered. See that there is no surrender of that which is due to justice. Stand, as Robert Ross stood, against this tide of lawlessness, and let justice be done!"

Church bells were chiming nine when Judge Williams began his jury charge. Outside the courthouse, a soft velvet darkness had replaced the muggy day, fireflies winking in the shrubbery across the street, and in the gaslight horses pawed and a crowd waited in anticipation for the conclusion of the trial. Tomorrow was a holiday, and it would not do to run the trial over. Within the courtroom, in the glow of gaslamps, Judge Williams instructed the jurors on the law, the meaning of "reasonable doubt," and he gave a caution that Shea had not been accused of repeating and so if they found he did not shoot Ross, they must acquit.

As the jurors retired to deliberate, the doors to the courthouse flew open and the crowd rushed into the street. After the initial surge, Shea and McGough appeared, jostled by sheriff's deputies. Down the courthouse steps they were carried in a tide of humanity, into the dark, sweltering night where boys were exploding firecrackers, then into the glow of gaslamps, up Ferry Street to the jail.

As Jem removed the handcuffs in the cell, he said, "I wished they'da called me to testify, Mr. Shea. I'da told them about your being a perfect gentleman and all. Best of luck to you, Mr. Shea, and I hope the jury sets you free this very night."

"Thank you, Jem." He waited till the kid left the cell.

"Ain't very likely that'll happen, eh, Jack?"

"You can never tell about juries," McGough said, but his customary optimism had dampened.

"Goddamn kangaroo court!" Shea lashed out with his boot at the spitoon.

"And Black was nowhere to be seen tonight," Jack observed.

"His work's over and he can rest upon it now, seeing where it'll raise him to. A game for whores, Jack, goddamned no-good pickpocketing whores." He lit a cigar with a sulphur match and then rested back, blowing out the smoke. "You know, I never really trusted them, Dunlop, Molloy, Murphy himself. What do they owe such as us? Huh? You and me, why we're just what they scrape off their shoe. Least that's what they think. You, Jack, you're the only one I ever trusted not to put your interest above mine."

"And me you, Bat."

Shea gave a laugh. "Funny now that it's all played out. I see how small my hope was, how foolish, and what I risked for it. Alls I wanted was a seat at the table; I was tired of living on the crumbs and scrapings, and Murphy there, he'll be carving the roast for years."

"I don't see how they can find premeditation, Bat," Jack said.

"And the other day you was saying they'd find Boland's bullet was the one, and before that it was the riot. You keep finding these things, Jack, but they ain't in there." Shea shook his head. "Thanks for trying to cheer me up, but we both know it's coming and there ain't no use to pin false hopes on illusions. Them bigots and hypocrites have had their way. They took the trial and twisted it, just like we was trying to twist the election, and they got what they wanted just like we did, getting George in. Elections, courts of law, they can be twisted, Jack, 'cause they're run by men, and it's only a fool who thinks they're ever pure or truthful. It weren't the strong who won here, but the sly. That Black's a sight darker than anyone I ever encountered before. I'd sooner have a man shove a revolver in my face than to slip a knife in my back like he done."

"I still don't see how they can find premeditation."

"Christ, Jack! Will you stop? We was there. We had guns. We wanted to vote the repeaters. Ross got in the way. Ross died. We're to blame." He spat. "That's how they'll see it, open and shut."

They sat together smoking for a time.

At half-past eleven, Jem was at the door: "The jury's come back, Mr. Shea, and there's a vast crowd about the courthouse. Judge'll be down from the hotel in fifteen minutes for the reading of the verdict, so's I better get you over there."

"How about me?" Jack asked.

"Yeah, you're to come too."

Out through the midnight streets the two were led in handcuffs, under the shadow of the Excelsior Brewery as firecrackers sounded like gunfire in the alleys and yards. "Good luck, Shea," people called along the street. The streetcars had stopped running and horses were stabled for the night. The streets were empty.

As they rounded the corner, a vast crowd filled the street and the square in front of Troy Female Seminary. The mansions and hotels and tenements for blocks about had been emptied. Seeing the prisoners, a great shout went up. Into the crowd Jem and Wilbur plunged, pulling Shea and McGough in their wake: "Step aside, gents. Please."

From every side hands lashed out to touch Shea and McGough, to wish Shea well, and inside, the halls of the courthouse were packed tightly with the curious. Into the courtroom the party finally came, and at the bar stood Shea's mother, brother Tim and his sisters Julia and Frances.

"Hi, Ma. Timbo, Julie, Frannie, how are ya?"

Tears streamed down Frannie's cheeks. Everyone was pale and tired. George Dunlop bustled in, his eyes heavy with drink.

"The old man couldn't make it?"

"No, Barry," Mary Shea apologized. "He's afflicted tonight."

"Too many porters like as not," Shea muttered. "Mamie?"

"Off again with Tom on union business. She's never around no more."

Shea registered this, nodded to George and he sat between Julia and Frannie to wait. For quarter of an hour they waited, and the crowd grew restless. Suddenly, the girls jumped at a knock on wood and Clerk Riley's call: "All rise! The extraordinary term of Oyer and Terminer is now in session, Honorable Pardon C. Williams presiding!" The crowd reacted in the gaslight.

"Order!" Williams commanded. "Bring in the jury."

The door to the deliberation room opened and into the courtroom shuffled the twelve men. They were a motley group, whiskers and haircuts from horse shears, ill fitting clothes, and they sat and glared over at Shea.

"Foreman, has the jury reached a verdict?"

An intake of breath was heard in the courtroom.

"Yes, your honor." The foreman handed Riley a piece of paper and he handed it up to the judge. The judge read it and looked up at Shea. "So say you all?"

"Yes, your honor."

Williams handed back the paper. "Let the defendant rise."

Shea stood, each hand held by a sister, and he faced the jury.

"Please read the verdict, foreman."

The foreman took back the paper, looked at Shea, then his eyes went down to read: "We find the defendant, Bartholomew Shea, guilty of murder in the first degree."

The courtroom exploded. The pent up emotion of three weeks

erupted from six hundred breasts and throats.

"Order! Order!" cried Williams, rapping his gavel, but the storm was unleashed and it raged through the gallery and the balcony, and rolled in waves of joy and anger, disbelief and rage out into the dark street. In its midst, Shea stood still, a grim look on his face. Both his sisters fell crying upon him. Mary Shea lay back in her chair as if she had fainted. "Order!" thundered Williams. "Order in this court!" For a full five minutes the storm raged, and when it subsided, Williams instructed Riley to poll the jurors, and as he was doing so, church bells rang midnight. It was now the Fourth of July.

"The jury is discharged. The prisoner is to be returned to the jail and incarcerated alone. The court fixes sentencing for Thursday, July 5 at ten o'clock. This court stands adjourned," and Williams was back immediately through the velvet curtains. Mary Shea fell upon her son, wailing. George Dunlop was behind her, and he shook Bat's hand.

"There'll be an appeal, Bat, if I have to sell the goddamn saloon!"

Shea said nothing. The worst had happened. He set his jaw and slowly scanned the courtroom, observing all the hysteria, dejection and elation. There was nothing else they could take from him. He was a dead man, and Mamie was not even there to witness it.

35.

INDEPENDENCE DAY

Fourth of July Parade, Franklin Square

Deputies kept Shea and McGough in the courtroom until the crowd dispersed. Jem then took Jack roughly by the arm, "It's time."

"Guess I won't be seeing you no more," Jack said. "In the cell, I mean."

"Nope."

Jack sighed deeply and looked up at the bench. "Might not see you again at all, ever, eh, Bat?"

"Prob'bly not."

"So long," McGough's eyes were red and his lip quivered. "We sure had some high old times, didn't we?" He bit his lip and fought for control. "Sorry 'bout what happened, Bat. I'm real sorry. You don't know how sorry I am."

"Yeah." Shea formed a large fist and gently raised it to McGough's cheekbone. "It weren't your fault, Jack. You're a good man." Their eyes locked. "Take care, Jack."

McGough dissolved into tears, and Jem led Jack away, hunched over, sobbing, "I'm sorry, Bat." Shea watched him go. He was ashen white, but strangely calm with the verdict.

Upon opening the courtroom door to leave with McGough, Jem had to haul McGough forward, shouting, "Back! Please, stand back!" The crowd surged forward, heaving and calling out to him.

The other deputy, Wilbur, allowed Shea's family to sit with him after Jack was gone. Despite his fatigue and shock, Bat tried to keep everyone's spirits up. Mary Shea cried uncontrollably saying over and over, "My boy! My Barry!" Shea shrugged at his sisters. They smiled through their tears at him, and Tim hung back, looking at the floor, unsure what this bar sinister on the family honor would signify. He admired his older brother, despised the Protestants and the APA, and knew that he'd inherited a heavy burden of shame. In his rebellious adolescence he considered that more violence might very well be the answer.

"All right, Shea," Wilbur said, and he caught him under the arm.

"My little boy! They're going to take my little boy!"

"Bye, Ma!"

"Oh, my God! Is there no justice?" She shook her fist at the judge's bench.

"So long, Frannie. You be good, Tim. Get a hold of Tom Halligan. Get in with him and stay away from George."

"Let's go, Shea."

Wilbur led him to the door and when it opened a great cry went up. Yet, rather than press to touch him, as they had an hour before, the crowd shrank away from the condemned man. Shea held his head high and sneered at the reporters who came crowding up, asking him questions. Outside the night was dark and hot, heavy with humidity. Uptown the saloons and brothels were open and the cards and roulette were shifting money about, and the trains were pulling in and out of Union Station. In South Troy sparks flew and the foundries lit the sky orange. Along the river bank canal boats and steamships were berthed and the river flowed dark and tranquil. The square across from the courthouse was cool and dark, moths kept flying into the globes of the gas lamps.

As he left the courthouse, the crowd surged down the street, following Shea at a distance. Up Ferry Street a gang of Italian kids letting off fireworks glowered at the procession. Then into the jail they moved. Wilbur brought Shea down to the basement. "In here," he said gruffly, and he pulled open a heavy metal door that squealed on rusted hinges. The room was damp and foul, and when Wilbur peered in, the lamp revealed a narrow room, four by ten, seven feet high, a dusty cot, a bucket and a wooden chair. "I'll bring you some water and a candle."

Shea entered the cell, beat dust from the bed with his hand, then sat with his head in his hands. So this is it, he thought in the dark, this is how it's going to end.

All night long the saloons were open, the trial the only topic of discussion. From the recesses of people's hearts Shea's conviction brought doubt and anger and resentment that till now had been checked by the possibility of acquittal. Bat Shea was a condemned man, Jack McGough would be convicted surely. Black's committee had done its work. The Murphy machine was discredited. A change in power was in the air.

"One of ours went down!" Jerry Cleary muttered in Dunlop's, his face sagging with drink. "One of ours went down! We gotta bring one of theirs down 'cause one of ours went down!"

George Dunlop was chastened with grief, and he sat behind his bar letting Timmy Shea tend to the customers. He talked low in a group with Mike Delaney, Owen Judge, Gene McClure and Stanley O'Keefe. They talked about the good times with Bat, the smoldering anger of him, the size and effect of his fists, his honor and loyalty as a friend, and now his strength in standing up to a murder conviction.

"The don't make them better'n Bat," Gene observed.

"My boy Bat!" lamented George. "His life's worth more'n Frank Black's and his whole goddamn committee!" And he spat and missed the spitoon.

"One of ours went down," Cleary added. "We gotta bring one of theirs down."

At three-twelve that morning a train clattered into Union Station. Its brakes gasped and as soon as it halted, before the conductor could place the steps, a young girl flounced to the platform, her face hopeful.

"How goes the Shea trial?" she asked of a sleepy porter.

"Why, ma'am, it's over!"

She turned, her eyes lit with excitement and anticipation. "Tom! Oh, Tom! The trial's over! It's over." Her brother then hopped to the platform.

"What's the verdict?" Tom Halligan asked.

"Why, sir, Shea was convicted. Murder in the first degree." The porter looked from one to the other of them. They were rumpled from the journey. "Oh, my God!" Mamie said, her hands to her cheeks.

"Bear up, Mamie."

"Oh, oh, oh! Oh, my God!"

Birds were chirping when he awoke, and gray light filtered

through a grate near the ceiling. Bat Shea arose, stood on the chair and tried to see out. His eyes were at street level with Fifth Avenue. There were explosions, caps and firecrackers heralding the Fourth of July, and he heard young boys crying in delight as they chased each other through the honeycomb of streets and alleys.

Scenes of his conviction in the high courtroom then revisited him, and he sat on the bed pondering it for a long while. Although his mind and his emotions were in confusion, and the deep agony made him lightheaded, there were moments of calm, too, when he nodded and accepted that knowing the worst was better than fearing it.

Suddenly, a loud explosion shook the walls of the jail. He jumped up and tried to climb on a chair to peer out the grate. Boys nearby had discharged a toy cannon and a dog was complaining loudly. The day was overcast and warm, a day for mosquitoes, a day to help George sweep up, sprinkle fresh sawdust on the floor of the saloon, then have that first delicious glass of beer, and maybe a shot of Irish alongside, followed by a plate of steak, eggs and homefries. Then later it'd be a ballgame over to Rensselaer Park with a half keg tapped and a few bucks wagered, and then a picnic thrown by George up to Sunnyside in the evening, and fireworks in the dark. A happy Fourth, ducking the parade and the windy speeches he loathed.

Wilbur brought his breakfast, corn porridge and black coffee. Wilbur took out a flask and poured a healthy shot of brandy into the coffee. "This here's from Alderman Dunlop who instructed me to take good care of you, Shea."

"Then leave the bottle."

"Can't do that, sir. You might break it, and . . ." he shrugged. "But I'll be back later."

The parade stepped out from South Troy. In the shadow of the Burden water wheel, wagons of flowers and floats filled the streets, crowds of uniformed police and firemen formed ranks and files. When the soldiers, Doring's Military Band and Orchestra, the 125th New York Regiment and the Tibbits Cadets were all arrayed, the new mayor, Francis J. Molloy, blew a whistle as grand marshall. He had been placed there by Murphy to show he could unify the city in its time of crisis. Molloy called the first division to order, and they stepped out.

First came the officials for the reviewing stand. Next came the bakers and the carpenters, the Orangemen, the Poestenkill Band, the butchers and letter carriers, the plumbers, steam and gas fitters association, the cigarmakers, the iron moulders, the tailors, the temperance league ladies in their white frocks and dresses, the Troy City Band, the pipes and drums of the Ancient Order of Hibernians, followed by the Emerald Club. On and on they marched, the Ancient Order of United Working Men, the Troy High School band, the girls from League Shirt and Waist Company in their blue pinstripe frocks, firemen from Esek Bussey, a company of blond children in *lederhosen* from Germania Hall.

They marched up Fourth Street. The crowds on the sidewalk were wild with joy and occasionally there was heard a young prankster's explosion. From the flats and rooming houses people came to stand at the curb, and others looked down from windows, their elbows on the sill. Everywhere hung flags, and red, white and blue bunting, bunting from the sooty cornices of buildings, bunting on the floats, bunting across the street, clean bunting over the coal grime of the streets, everywhere the beloved stars and stripes as the parade marched through the Polish and Irish and Italian neighborhoods up Fourth Street into the center of town. And as the whole city in martial array passed to the rousing brass and the snare drums, within the jail in a basement cage sat Bat Shea with his head down in his hands.

At Federal Street, the parade turned toward the river. With the drum majors high-stepping, it turned south through Franklin Square and on towards city hall.

As the first division of the parade marched down Third Street, a large coach drawn by four white horses pulled up, and out stepped Senator Edward Murphy in a top hat. There was polite applause as he ascended the reviewing stand with youthful vigor. "Hi ya, boys!" he called with a mirthful gleam in his blue eyes. "How we doing today?"

"Fine, Senator!"

And he worked the crowd, shaking every hand, kissing all the ladies on the cheek. When sallow Frank Molloy and other dignitaries reached the stand from the front of the parade, Murphy was a one-man reception line. In theatrical tones, he told the tale of when he was mayor and he quelled an uprising of South Troy millhands by wearing an orange top hat and marching at the head of the Orangemen's parade. He was brave, he was brassy, he was confrontational, he was the boss. "What is Troy, eh? That's me! Ha, ha, ha." And the boys nodded and laughed and passed the flask, but did not say openly what they knew in secret — Murphy wasn't marching this year because he feared the criticism of Protestants after Black's success, and he also feared catcalls and rotten fruit from the Irish for selling out Bat Shea. "Hiya, there, Georgie!" the senator smiled upon Dunlop. "Feeling all right? You look a little drained." And he leaned over and whispered, "You've got to stay out of those fifty-cent houses! Those girls'll clap you right up," and George managed a smile, and muttered as he turned away, "You should know."

The night brought fireworks. In mimicry of the siege of an old world city-state, rockets shot into the sky in fiery arcs, exploding in profusion of metallic light and sparkle. But this is no old world city-state, no walled town on a cliff. This is an accessible city on a major artery of commerce, and it is a time of enlightenment, 1894, in America where representative government and law have evolved to their highest apex since men first settled disputes with a club. Electricity is propelling streetcars, carrying messages, lighting streets and public buildings, and even some of the wealthier homes. Through American technology, the thinkers of the age report, mankind is emerging from the Dark Ages of superstition and strife. This is America! In the rockets' red glare the faces of children are lit, their hope and awe at the fireworks, for through technology there will be freedom so long as Frank Black is vigilant and American political institutions are kept pure.

The following morning the courthouse was mobbed. Hitt asked for a week to prepare postverdict motions, and Williams adjourned sentencing until July 10. Down the steps came Shea in a light summer suit, and as he looked over the crowd with his customary sneer, he spied Mamie Halligan. A weak smile fluttered to her lip and she nodded. Though he could not talk with her, it was reassuring to know she was in town.

The weekend passed quietly and on Tuesday, Shea again was escorted through the thronged streets to the courthouse. Summer was fully upon the land, locusts whining in the trees and a mild breeze from the west across the river. Wagons of the earliest vegetables, tomatoes and corn and potatoes, were displayed in the open air market two blocks to the south and horses were frisky in the street. As Wilbur and Jem led Shea from the jail, he was blinking and seemed disoriented. The light and the width of the sky, the fragrance of the wind astonished Shea as he left the confines of his basement cell. Much had changed since his conviction.

Before the proceedings began, Norton and Hitt took Shea into the jurors' room for a conference.

"We're making a motion for a new trial, Shea," Hitt said. "John and I obtained affidavits that prove Lemuel Durfee, one of the jurors, had a bet that you would be found guilty."

"He weren't alone." Shea showed a healthy suspicion at the news.

"But he was a juror," Norton said. "He gave odds. He bet ten dollars of cigars to a man named Clarence Akin and a man named Andrew Finnegan that you would go to the electric chair."

"So what? Black's been railroading me there, making the same wager, and no one's seemed to mind."

"But this is a juror! He had a vested interest in the outcome."

"Will the judge give us a show?"

"He should."

Shea shook his head. "Not here and not now. I'm not saying don't try, but I doubt it'll amount to much."

In the courtroom Bat Shea sat with his family and with Mamie Halligan. Thomas Fagan moved that the court fix the time for the execution. Norton interrupted to make his motion and put his affidavits before the court. Then Fagan surprised them by producing answering affidavits.

"Mr. Fagan," Judge Williams said, "where did you learn of this bet? You seem to have known of it before today."

Fagan adjusted his spectacles. "Your honor, I knew the defense would be grasping at straws even after the verdict. Mr. Durfee came to me and informed me he had been approached with this bet at the place named, but that he declined the wager because he was sitting on the jury. He was afraid of prejudicing the case."

"Why, his refusal to bet on that ground alone shows he was predisposed to find a guilty verdict, Judge," Norton argued.

Judge Williams spoke: "Mr. Norton, I see nothing in your affidavits but hearsay."

"These affidavits are from the men who made the bet with Durfee, Judge. It wasn't hearsay. They swore positively. We ask for a hearing. Put the men who swore these affidavits under oath and subject them to cross examination."

"But Durfee's affidavit states he made no bet, and so it's his word against the others'."

"Even more of a reason to grant a hearing."

The judge persisted: "If you had an affidavit from Durfee, Mr. Norton, that might be sufficient for a new trial, but this is not enough. Motion denied."

"Thank you, Judge," Fagan said.

"Will the prisoner rise?" Clerk Riley's voice rang through the courtroom.

Shea dropped his sister Frannie's hand, but held Mamie's as he stood, then he squeezed and dropped Mamie's and folded his arms across his chest.

"Do you have anything to say before I pass sentence?" Williams asked.

"Yes, your honor." Shea spoke in a loud, clear voice. "Before

God and man I am innocent of this crime."

"Is that all?"

"That is all."

"Mr. Shea," Williams said, "in a calm and orderly way this verdict has been arrived at and I do not see given the evidence how a different one could have been rendered. Your sentence is mandated by the conviction and I only have to fix the time. You will suffer the punishment of death by electrocution at Clinton State Prison in Dannemora during the week of August 21, 1894."

Shea stood impassively, a sneer curling his mouth downward. His sister Frannie cried out.

"I will not add to the burden that rests upon you," Williams continued. "I will say instead some kind word. I am sorry you are in this position. It is sad so young and intelligent a man as you are should have committed such a crime. I sympathize with your parents and loved ones and pray that God may have mercy upon your soul." Down came the gavel.

"Court is adjourned!" called Clerk Riley, and a general uproar filled the courtroom. Mrs. Shea was weeping and Frannie clasped onto his wrist. Mamie embraced him a last time.

"Oh, Bat! Bat!" she placed a desperate kiss upon his lips. "I am so sorry! So very, very sorry!"

"Now, stand back there, ma'am," Wilbur said. Wilbur and Jem escorted Mamie behind the railing. She was weeping and reaching out for him. "They can't do this!" she implored.

They had the shackles on Shea again, and were muscling him through the crowd. "Make way! Make way!" There was a covered carriage waiting by the curb outside, and it spirited him directly back to the jail.

Shea was confined to his basement cell with no visitors. For days he sat upon his bunk, hands folded, considering his fate. He was surprised one morning when Wilbur opened the door and Father Swift entered.

"Hello, Father. What brings you by?"

The priest waited till Wilbur had departed. "I came to see if I might offer you spiritual comfort."

Shea hung his head. "I was never too keen on church and the sacraments and so forth."

"Well, now is your time to make peace."

"I s'pose that's so." Shea eyed him keenly. "But if you come to hear me confess to the killing, like I told the judge, I didn't do it."

Father Swift frowned. Shea suspected the curiosity behind his visit. "Even so, Bartholomew, would you like to make a confession?"

Shea looked down at the floor. He coughed. "This cell is terrible damp," he explained the cough. He wanted to be left alone. He looked at the priest. "Nah, I don't think so, Father. Not just now. There really ain't much to tell. I think I'd rather wait and do it all at once. But thank you, Father, thanks for coming by."

Father Swift closed his eyes and murmured something. "Very well, Bartholomew." Then he stood, blessed Shea and called for the guard.

Next morning, two deputies escorted Bat Shea out of the jail into a carriage and drove directly to Union Station. The conductor was calling "All aboard!" as they hustled him onto the waiting train. The movement was sudden and unannounced because the authorities feared there might be an escape attempt by the North Troy Irish.

Shea took a seat between the deputies charged with delivering him to Dannemora. They removed one handcuff and locked it around the railing of the seat. The train whistle blew, then the train jerked, the couplings caught with a metallic clang, and with great labor it picked up steam. Through the streets dark with summer's grit, across the broad river on the Green Island Bridge, and along the river's west bank the train gathered speed. Shea looked across the river to the east. He saw his home momentarily, and up the street, Mamie's and Tom's. On the brow of the hill was the Ross Valve Company, and the Ross home. There was St. Patrick's Church, and on the hill, Sunnyside. Below Sunnyside, against the foot of the hill, was the polling place. Shea turned from the window and looked straight ahead, at the handcuffs and the armed guards escorting him up from the river valley into the mountains.

36. AMBITION

Jack McGough

McGough's trial for assaulting William Ross with intent to kill began the day Shea was sentenced. It lasted three weeks. During summation, Thomas Fagan addressed the jury:

"Look at this man, McGough. He is a parasite, gentlemen. He is one of the thugs that breed in the night in the slums of Troy. They fasten bad officers on our community. They put in our offices men who must have pay, who tap the public treasury, who haunt the low groggeries, the gambling hells, the dives and disorderly houses. All this crime and corruption needs protection from decent law and order, and when all this is protected, it becomes part of the official system.

"Recall, gentlemen, that infamous Tweed Ring where indictments were pigeon-holed, where injunctions flew with the speed of wings, the whim of birds. Here! Here is that same cancerous ring. It is only an accident that William Ross is not lying next to his brother in the Oakwood Cemetery on the hill. This man, this McGough, shot William Ross with an intent to commit murder, and the full measure of the law must be visited upon him."

The jury returned a verdict of guilty of assault with intent to kill. Three days later, at his sentencing, Jack accepted Judge Williams' invitation to speak:

"Yes, Judge, I do have something to say. I ask you to consider what I have suffered. The Rosses weren't the only ones who suffered. I was deeply wounded in the right side and for twenty-four hours my life hung in the balance. That is all I have to say, your honor."

McGough sat, and Judge Williams scowled down at him. "I am sorry for you, first and foremost, John, sorry that you kept such bad company at an early age. Because of your prior burglary, I must give you a longer sentence. I feel especially sorry for your father," Judge Williams said, and nodded toward Owen McGough. "Here is a man who served his country in the bloody war of rebellion and to all appearances is an honest and hard-working man. Cases of this sort are always hardest upon friends and relatives."

McGough was jumpy, and the mention of his father angered him. Owen McGough sat next to him, and sought to hold him down as Jack raised his hand: "Judge, excuse me, but may I say something else?"

"You may, John."

Jack stood and threw his arms to the sides: "Is this a court of law? Or is it a lynching court? What I want to know is who are these men who come in here and sit in the witness chair and calmly tell what they saw that day? Nobody saw nothing that day. It was a riot. There were bodies flying every which way. There were clubs everywhere and pistols firing. The man who wasn't looking after his own skin was a fool. And still these liars, these damned perjurers sit up there and say they saw this and that, all using the same expressions. By just using the same lies cooked up by Mr. Black and Mr. Fagan, and telling enough of them, they have convinced the jury that their lies are the truth."

Reporters scribbled upon their pads and the crowd buzzed at McGough's tirade. Jack continued: "Now Mr. Shea stood here with his arms folded three weeks ago and told you of his innocence. He was too proud to tell you what he thought of you. This serious and grave procedure! I know a railroad job when I see it!

"Now, maybe I am wrong and maybe I am as bad as they have painted me. Maybe Shea and McGough were the cause of all the trouble that day. I am convicted and I must now go to prison, yet regardless of any other thing that happened that day, I am innocent."

Jack went over to the table of reporters: "Look at the facts, will you? You say it was only by chance that William Ross wasn't killed. It is only by chance that I wasn't killed, or Shea who was shot in the head. Are the lives of the Rosses worth more than the lives of Shea and McGough?"

Slowly, evenly Jack looked into the eyes of the reporters daring them to answer his question honestly.

"Raines and Fagan say that Shea shot me. If he did, he did not shoot Robert Ross. The bullet that shot me came from a different gun than the one that shot Ross. And yet why isn't anyone on trial for shooting me? Why?" he implored.

McGough turned back. "Look at these two men. Raines and Fagan, and Black, too, who is behind this railroad job. They are blinded by their ambitions. They want to make names for themselves rather than reach the truth and arrive at justice. They sent Shea to the chair and now they are locking me up for the best part of my life, and this court will pack up and go home and everyone will say the trouble is over."

Jack turned toward the gallery and he pointed his finger into the crowd and his voice rose. "You hear me! All of you! The trouble ain't over, not by a long shot. The trouble is inside of you! You, not me and surely not Bat Shea. The trouble comes from the spite and the vileness that you accuse me of. The trouble is in the ambition of Black and Fagan and Raines who have seized upon this incident to make careers for themselves at my expense. There is the evil that you must seek out and rid yourselves of, the evil in your hearts. Ambition!" He turned to the bench. "That is all I have to say, Judge."

Williams nodded gravely. "I have patiently waited to hear something not raised in the trial, and I have waited in vain. Considering your past life, I cannot extend leniency to you. You show no tendency toward reformation, but stick to the story you've been telling all along. It is rare to see a criminal with so much intelligence and so much vim. Now you are to be shut up in prison where you will have a chance to ponder your past life. If your talents had been otherwise applied, you would not be here today.

"I hereby sentence you, John McGough, to nineteen years and six months in Clinton State Prison at Dannemora. If you show by good behavior you have reformed, you may apply for parole in seven and a half years." Williams rapped the gavel and stood. "This court stands adjourned."

For the final time, the crowd surged forward and reporters fired off questions. McGough's family hugged him, his father looking ashen and tired, his sisters weeping. The Extraordinary Term of the Court of Oyer and Terminer was now adjourned, and Pardon C. Williams, packed his portmanteau and left Troy for Watertown by the evening train.

With two successful convictions, one with a death sentence, Frank Black met again with state Republican leaders. He was perceived as a champion of the people and he accepted the nomination to run for Congress. All summer he campaigned through the district on a reform platform. Citywide, the Murphy machine had been discredited. The Gurley brothers, the Frears, Josiah Patton, the Burden family, the merchants and manufacturers all flocked back to political life to reclaim what they believed had been stolen from them by Irish immigrants. In November, Republicans swept Democrats out of office throughout the county, the Board of Supervisors was placed into Republican hands and Frank Black was elected to Congress. In January, Black went off to Washington and served in the House of Representatives, his arch enemy Edward Murphy still in the Senate.

With Black gone and with the Shea trial over, the heat and light of reform abated in Troy. The righteous went about their daily pursuits, satisfied their sacred public institutions had been redeemed. Troy fell back into its industrial and commercial rhythms. Yet beneath, fires of unrest and resentment smoldered. The Irish believed they had been cheated and oppressed, but their response was muted because most of them believed Shea guilty. All awaited with expectation and with dread the execution that would irrevocably end the ugly and unfortunate affair.

BOOK THREE

THE EXECUTION

37.
DANNEMORA

Prisoners In Lockstep.

North along the river, Green Island, Cohoes, Waterford then overland to Saratoga and Glens Falls, then into the deep forests, over streams on trestle bridges and out again upon stark terrain, mountains of stumps and slashings left by logging companies, Shea gazed out the window of the train. He had seen much open country riding the rails in boxcars out West. He'd seen more dramatic open country through the high peaks of the Rockies, the painted deserts and down the Sierra Nevada to the Coast, but he'd never seen open country for the last time.

"Mind if we have some air?" he asked. His deep cough was bothering him and the car was dusty.

"The clean air up here'll tucker you plumb out. Healthy air, Shea. They bring consumption patients up from all over the state, air's so good and pure. Hell, even cures some of 'em." The guard exhibited the forced good humor used with the condemned. He opened the window. "Ah, now smell that will you!" He drew in a lungful. "Healthy clean air." He sat back and looked out the window. "Look at that view, Shea! No sight on earth prettier'n a sunset in the mountains. If I live to be a hundred . . ."

"Ain't much chance of that," Shea said.

The guard looked insulted momentarily. Then the other guard stifled a laugh, reached into his pocket and pulled out a flask. "Here, have a snort, Shea. You're all right."

"Thanks." Shea took the flask and drank the smooth whiskey that warmed him down his throat and charged into his empty stomach. So this was what it was like. Evening sunset in a train with two portly guards in derbies, handcuffed to the railing, enjoying a nip as the train rattled over frost heaves in the railroad bed. The whistle blew, echoing back as the sun set in orange fire, and blue shades deepened into violet and deep gray, and coal smoke came through the window when you took a curve.

They reached Plattsburgh at ten. The narrow gauge Chateaugay railroad ran the seventeen miles through the mountains to Dannemora, but the next train wasn't until morning. Shea stood on the platform staring out over the lamplights of Plattsburgh, and up into the sky at the rising moon. It was pleasant on the platform, as if you could just step aboard the next train and go somewhere else, anywhere in the country, anywhere in the world. Freedom. He inhaled the dark fragrant wind. It was chilly, but quiet and lovely with the pine. So this is what it is like, he thought.

The guard returned from a livery stable with a hired carriage and horse.

"Which way to the prison?" he asked the stationmaster.

"Just foller the road in the moonlight there. What nag you got? Jim? Why, he knows the way, been there and back enough. Foller the ribbon in the moonlight and when you see the great wall, he, he, why, there you are!"

As they drove, the forest was dark and deep. The road was chalky, pale blue in the wash of moonlight. They heard owls and coyotes, and the moon hung overhead, a silver ball against the diamond stars. The dark quiet forest and the dips and turns of the mountain road lengthened the night. It was dreamlike and pleasant.

"Long seventeen miles," one deputy observed.

"Shea ain't complaining," the other said.

With his hands shackled before him, slumped on the seat, a coat over his shoulders, Shea was docile enough, enjoying the drive.

"Ah, shut up, Mason," the first guard said. "Let him enjoy his last hour of freedom."

So this is what it is like, Shea thought, this is what the moon looks like, this is how the forest sounds and smells, this is how it feels on the last night, the last hours of freedom. And they drove on in silence past dripping cliffs and swaying pine trees, the moon large and luminous, appearing suddenly around bends of the chalky road.

It was after three in the morning when they saw the wall. Shea's jaw clenched. It was a high massive stone wall, white in the moonlight and atop the thirty-foot wall were guard towers, like the watchtowers of a fortress. A lamp was burning at the guardhouse. The deputies presented Shea's commitment order at the gate, and through the thick stone walls, as if into a castle, the buggy rolled. The heavy iron door clanged behind. In the admissions building an old turnkey brought Shea into a high barren stone room.

"Now, lad, you've got special accommodations with us here. The condemned cell they call it. Take them clothes off and put this here on." He measured a heavy striped woolen suit against Shea. "This one'll do, and these." He gave him a pair of boots. Shea stripped naked. He was thin, his ribs showed as he shivered and coughed. They let him stand naked a moment. Then he pulled on a pair of cotton drawers and the scratchy striped prison suit. After a barber shaved his head, a phrenologist carefully measured his skull with metal implements, and then two guards led him across the yard to the condemned cell. As the heavy iron gate clanged shut, the sun was rising, cold and stark upon the trampled mud of the prison yard.

There were no windows near his cell, just an electric lamp down the hall that burned night and day. He inspected the cell, six feet wide, ten feet long, eight feet high. The bunk with a cornhusk tick was welcome, and he lay down, pulled the wool blanket up about him and tried to sleep. So this is where you wait to die, Dannemora.

Named after an iron mining district of Sweden, Dannemora had been founded fifty years before to use prison labor in mining and smelting iron. At first a log palisade separated prison huts from the village. For thirty years the iron ore was rich enough for mining, and far enough away from civilization that it did not compete with foundries and labor unions in the cities. But because of lower and lower grades of ore and frequent escapes, mining ceased by 1877. A decade later the great stone wall sealed off the inmates from the rest of the world. The purpose of incarceration, too, had changed.

Clinton Prison was not a place of industry and rehabilitation that Shea came to, but a place of penitence, a "penitentiary" as prisons were characterized. Silence was the rule. Inmates were not allowed to speak to each other and only with permission to speak to the guards. Their heads were shaved to avoid lice. They bathed twice a month. They wore striped woolen suits night and day. They ate in silence, sitting on wooden stools and spooned from tin bowls the corn gruel and molasses and, infrequently, meat stew. They walked everywhere in a "lockstep," a sort of jog with hands on the shoulders of the man in front, legs interlocked. The guards gave orders in a series of taps from a wooden baton. Infractions brought confinement in the "dark cell" or whippings, the prisoner tied face down, spread-eagled on the floor, and whipped with a cat o' nine tails. It was a cruel, tedious, hopeless life with only Father Belanger, the Catholic priest from the village, to uplift spirits on Sunday. And yet the hardships the prisoners suffered were luxuries compared with inmates of the condemned cell, for the condemned had no expectation of release.

Days in the condemned cell were long and empty. Because of his appeal to the Court of Appeals, Shea's execution had been stayed. Bobby Griffith who brought his food and water was afraid at first, then shy. After two weeks he spoke to Bat Shea and told him about "That crazy I-talian," executed the previous year, a vegetable vendor in Brooklyn who murdered his partner for stealing. "He'd have these dreams, y'see? And he'd be wrassling with the partner, cursing in I-talian so's I couldn't unnerstand." And Bobby narrowed his eyes like a necromancer. "And that feller'd be fightin' back, and I'd slide the grate like this," he demonstrated the metallic squeal, "and he'd wake up and the evil that come out of him, out of his eyes!"

Shea was withdrawn and declined Bobby's invitation to talk. In the dark, damp cell he pondered his life, the misguided steps, the trip out West, the arrogance with George and the false security in believing the game was rigged in his favor. He regretted deeply the swaggering, brawling, pistol-brandishing way they forced the vote. While the APA bigots deserved no better, he saw how the violence he had unleashed caused all the heartache and tragedy on both sides. Shea chided himself for his blindness in thinking that churchgoers did not lie, that lawyers and judges and juries could not convict upon false evidence, and that a lynch mob could not be methodical.

Yet as he continually relived the early months of '94 when his gang of desperados got George in, as he revisited the trial again and again, reliving the spite and hate and recrimination with the newspapers blazing away, even as he awaited the result of his appeal, the anger and the bitterness left him. Slowly through the autumn and the numbing cold of winter while he huddled and coughed in his cell, then through the spring, the mountains gushing with meltwater and yellow flowers among the pine, he came to accept what happened. It was his lot in life. He was in large part to blame. What happened happened, what was done was done. Then the autumn came again.

A steam pipe ran along the ceiling giving off its meager heat, and the electric light burned day and night so he hardly knew the time. Once a day for an hour he exercised in the hall where there was a small window. All day and sometimes all night he sat on the edge of his bed, bundled in his blankets against the bitter cold, thinking, remembering, awaiting with small hope the outcome of his appeal. His hacking cough worsened and it reminded him, when the seizures came, of his father. Once a day a guard visited to bring a tray of food and remove the slop bucket, and occasionally the priest came to talk in low tones about repentance.

The year had been a dull blur of memories from his past life, the trips to Saratoga, the horses, the bookies, hanging off the train blissfully drunk on the way back while the conductor passed; the beer parties near the railroad tracks below Oakwood Cemetery; the ballgames over near the river where a homer could hit a tugboat; camping on Center Island in the Hudson with nothing but a bedroll, a skillet and a fishing pole.

Shea observed that the river was behind most of his memories, the broad blue river in summer where Mike Delaney and Steve Burke would steal a rowboat and launch out to fish, trading swigs from a flask; the frozen waste of the river in winter, a channel for the howling north wind to rage down from the mountains into Troy's narrow brick streets; then the grinding ice floes and the flooding each spring where the dark water snarled over the bank and filled the streets and basements, rowboats replacing wagons in the streets; the river, the great buoyant sparkling breast of the river upon which canal boats and steamboats and old river sloops floated on a breezy summer's afternoon; the river lit at night with the flare of the mills and foundries; the river choked with logs and barges of lumber from the north; the river flowing south to New York Harbor and the sea; the river ebbing and flooding with the tide, like a great breathing thing.

And there was Mamie, too. He reserved remembrances of Mamie for the twilight state between sleep and waking, her soft voice and gentle hands, her modesty that had made him so impatient, but drew his admiration. Her hope and faith in him when no other human, including Jack, thought of him as anything but a scoundrel. He remembered how she had come to him that night with premonitions, and he had scoffed. He loved her, but he had denied such a simple, true and innocent emotion in favor of ambition and his cynical servitude to Dunlop and Murphy.

Poetry to Bat Shea was doggerel verse, sentimental Irish ballads and bawdy limericks. He did not equate any noble sentiment with poetry. The sanctified thoughts he had for Mamie and for the river were closer to the fragments of religion he recalled from his schooling. Certainly the muddy Hudson, the canals, the slag heaps, mills and sooty tenements filled on Friday nights with drunken rage and wife-beatings, the bawdy houses and smoky saloons were a far cry from Eden. Yet those times when he was with Mamie, just walking with her, two kids through those noisy streets, reminded him of the story of Adam and Eve, as Sister Bernadette read it in the second grade, the Garden of Eden before the serpent spoke. And the serpent had spoken of ambition, and now the knowledge of good and evil was his.

In reviewing the trial, Shea saw Judge Williams as Flower's hatchetman to appease the bloodthirst of Black and his Committee of Public Safety and to disgrace Murphy. He viewed the trial as a parade of perjurers. The harshness of the verdict seemed out of the old testament, Abraham being called to sacrifice Isaac, Solomon ordering the baby cut in half. Perhaps, as in those two stories, the execution would be forestalled, the appeal would give him a new trial and justice might yet be done.

Shea saw with supreme and chilling irony that Frank Black had done the very thing he and Jack set out to do: advance his political ambition by threatening opponents with death. Black had done it differently and certainly better, but it was the same thing, and his success in obtaining a death sentence had raised him high on a tide of popular approval. In Shea's view, there was no difference that he and Jack carried guns and Black used lawbooks, sermons and editorials. The result was the same. Law and justice were sidestepped to serve political ends. Seeing the game, Shea accepted the result. It was like he used to say about cards — "Don't sit at the table if you ain't prepared to lose."

For fifteen months the regularity dulled Bat Shea with the complacency of the doomed. Then one day the guard was at his cell: "Shea, rouse yerself. You've a visitor."

He walked with the guard down the hall uncertain as to what this could mean. He squinted because the daylight hurt his eyes. As the great iron door opened, and he was shown into an anteroom, he winced. It was John Norton.

"Sit down, Shea," Norton said.

"I thought no one but my family . . ."

"There's an exception for attorneys." Norton stared at Shea and his blue eyes seemed sad. Shea saw the dismay and pity. "I wanted to bring this news myself, and it is at considerable hardship getting up here as you will understand."

Shea nodded, but he knew the news and he hung his head.

"The Court of Appeals denied your appeal. You've been sentenced to die December 23."

Shea looked up. "I ain't surprised, sir. I expected as much."

"Do you want to hear the decision?"

"Nah. I know what it says. It says Robert Ross was a saint, and I was not supposed to be there with the repeaters, and so I'm responsible because he died."

"Pretty near."

Shea began coughing and he doubled up. Norton turned to the guard who stood with folded arms by the door. "Would you get him a glass of water, please?"

"Ain't s'posta leave the priz'ner, sir."

In a few seconds Shea stopped coughing, and he looked up and wiped his eyes. "So, nothing else?"

Norton waved the decision at him. "I'd like to read from it, Shea. I came all the way up here to see you. We raised some compelling points that the court summarily dismissed. And the rhetoric!"

"Go ahead. Sure."

Norton read, but Shea did not listen. Instead he looked up toward the ceiling at a window through which muted October light fell. It occurred to him then he would not see another summer. Ah, so this was what it was like.

"'He is a young man,'" Norton looked up, reading from the decision, and nodded his way, "'being then but about twenty-three years of age and a molder by trade. He and his friend McGough and one or two others with them were very greatly interested in the success of Dunlop, and so far did they carry their interest that during election day they carried on, as leaders and conductors of a number of ruffians, the most open, shameless and reckless system of fraudulent voting, by means of repeating and by false personation of legal voters, that has ever come to our notice.'"

Norton kept reading, and Shea looked about.

"'In the light of such events it is a somewhat difficult task to preserve that judicial temper which ought always to characterize the expression of the views of this court. Such acts as those above described are not alone a gross outrage upon the rights of the citizen, but they lead directly to riot, bloodshed and murder; and if they should become habitual, there would cease to be a government by the people, might would become right, and anarchy and despotism would be the result.'"

"Sounds like Black wrote that," Shea remarked.

"Wait. The court characterizes your testimony with: 'Such manifest and reckless perjury is sickening to read.'"

"The perjury was theirs, Mr. Norton." Shea sat back, folded his arms and regarded Norton. "Hell," he sighed, "What does it matter? I been going over the testimony in my head. Got little else to do. Now, you go back to the testimony. There was one fellow named Harmon Simmons, toward the end of the trial. He swore that he saw a man run in front of him, point a gun at Ross who was on the ground, and then discharge it. He testified he saw the smoke and he saw dust rise from the ground. Don't you see Mr. Norton? Dust from the ground! If that was me, if I shot twice, then I did not shoot Ross. If I got that close and if I shot at Ross at all, the shot he saw raised up dust! It never went into Ross's head, it went into the ground." Norton nodded. Shea continued.

"The next fellow to the stand was named Adams, as I recall, and he swore that just as Ross reached the top of the ditch, his arms flung out and he fell. Why didn't the jury see that? Ross was dead when he went down, his head slumped over."

Norton frowned. "Unfortunately that is an issue of fact, Shea. The jury has determined it already, and it can't be undone. We could only raise issues of law before this court."

"But it don't square."

Norton shrugged. He continued: "The decision refers obliquely to Senator Murphy, too: 'We cannot, and we do not, for one moment believe that there are prominent public or party men of either political party who countenance or who would sustain these modes of conducting an election, otherwise we should despair of the republic.'" Norton then went point by point through the decision, the jurisdictional attack, the evidentiary rulings, the post verdict motion, and when he finished, he looked up: "That's it. Conviction affirmed."

Shea nodded. "Look, Mr. Norton, I admire all that you and Mr. Hitt did for me. I know it weren't easy down in Troy with the bloodhounds out baying for my hide. But you stood up to them and you drew a lot of ridicule for even speaking to me. I appreciate that." Shea held out his hand. "I want you to know, sir, and I want everyone else to know, that I understand now what the game was all about, and how I got caught in it, and how I'm going to pay the price now. It's all right. I understand and it is what I've got to do."

Shea looked into Norton's eye and held his gaze for a full minute. "I want you, sir, when you think of me, sir, in the future, if you ever do think of me at all, sir, to think of someone like yourself who didn't shy away from what needed to be done. I was awful angry before, and I lashed out, but that's all gone. I got no anger towards no one, not even Black. They did what they needed to do. I just got caught in the middle, in the shift of the parties. Now it's time for me to stand up and swallow the bitter cup. And I'll do it, sir. I will, sir, as best I can."

Shea turned away and nodded to the guard who accompanied him back to the condemned cell. Norton took a deep breath of air when he reached the outside. The mountains beyond the prison were aflame with autumn color.

The warden, Walter Thayer, a Troy man put in charge of the prison by Flower at the behest of Boss Murphy, had invited Jack Norton to dinner and to stay the night. As they sat in the elegant dining room of the warden's house, Norton lifted his brandy snifter: "I've defended a lot of young men, Walt, but there's a quality about this Shea. He's smart and he's tough. He has no schooling, no refinement, can't even read or write, yet there is a dignity to him that I have never seen before."

"He's been a model prisoner," Thayer agreed.

"It's a shame, really. A wasted life."

"Let's hope it's not wasted," Thayer said.

"What do you mean by that?"

"Only that others, perhaps, will learn from his example."

38.
CONFESSION

So now it was final. Bat Shea's slender thread of hope, the appeal, was severed and he was condemned to die December 23, 1895. In the days that followed Shea stared at the blank wall of his cell. When the guard entered with his tray and a clean slop bucket, Shea did not notice. The cough worsened. They suspected consumption, but in view of the pending execution, there was little alarm.

Meanwhile, the Troy Republicans prepared for the execution that would vindicate their quest for power. On the state level Murphy punished Flower for ousting him as state chairman. Flower was not renominated for governor, but neither was Murphy chosen. The nomination went to the senior senator from New York, David Hill, who had previously served as governor. Times were changing and reform was needed. Hill lost to the Republican and APA-backed Levi Morton. Murphy's spite had cost him. It was generally discussed he would retire from the senate seat at the end of his term rather than air dirty laundry in another campaign.

Frank Black continued to distinguish himself in Congress, and rumor, that ready servant of political intrigue, touted him as a gubernatorial contender in 1896. Imperious and austere, when he strode upon the deck of the riverboat on his trips to and from Washington, Black cut an impressive figure. The conviction and pending execution had raised him into statewide prominence. His ambition had triumphed.

Even so, as the execution approached, the Irish neighborhoods smoldered with resentment. The saloons, the corner groceries, the barbershops were filled with rebellious talk. Shea was elevated to the status of folk hero. Shea had been framed by the Committee of Public Safety. The testimony was harmonized, much of it perjury, and Shea never fired the fatal bullet. The facts made no sense. Why would Shea circle around behind Ross and twist his arm upward? Yet it was bothersome that Boland would have to be underground to fire the fatal shot. Many prayed for a miracle, and one of these was Father Swift.

The Shea family sought a stay of execution until after Christmas, and Governor Morton granted it by executive order. Shea was now to be executed Tuesday, January 7, 1896. Invitations edged in black were mailed just after Christmas to the press, to members of the Committee of Public Safety and other concerned citizens, inviting them to witness the execution. Friday before the execution, Mary Shea and her daughter Frances prepared to go north to say good-bye. They took a streetcar to the station, and boarding the train, they were surprised to see Father John Swift.

"Where be you going, Father?" Mary sat across the aisle from him.

"Same place you are, Mary," he said.

"And what for now, though to be sure, my boy'll be honored?"

"To hear a confession."

"Ah, he'll like that," she nodded. "He's a changed lad since all this took place, Father. Sad to say, but it's straightened him out, and he's embracing the Good Lord and the blessed sacraments."

The train jolted forward, and they settled into seats as it pulled out of Union Station. The train chugged and clanged and creaked over the Green Island Bridge, picking up speed. The priest was reticent. He had his breviary out and was murmuring prayers, so Mary and Frances talked in low, respectful voices not to disturb him. The car was drafty, the day cold and grim and overcast. It was comforting on such a journey to see Father Swift.

Yet the priest was not reading. He was considering questions of life and death, guilt and innocence, human justice, divine justice, betrayal, treachery, fate, coincidence and precisely where his mission of mercy lay today. Recently appointed vicar general of the vast Albany Diocese, his spiritual calling had now been joined to daunting secular tasks, financial management, disciplinary procedures, the curricula of schools. He had little time for reading or contemplation. Yet the administrative work showed him that action, not simple thought or prayer, got results in the secular world. The prayer book lay open in his lap:

"What man of you, having a hundred sheep, if he lose one of them, doth not leave the ninety and nine in the wilderness, and go after that which is lost, until he find it?" *Luke XV:4*

This was the genesis of his unpleasant task today. He was prepared if need be to break the secrecy of the confessional in order to save a life and he was unsure in the eternal scheme of things which was the greater wrong. Yet when he looked at Mary Shea, of solid peasant stock, and Frances, already a spinster at twenty-three, he sensed it was the right thing to do.

A heavy blizzard was blowing when they reached Plattsburgh next morning, and the Chateaugay railroad was unable to get through. Father Swift hired a horse and cutter for himself and the Sheas and they set out merrily enough. The woods were deep and silently filling with snow, and trees were frosted into fantastic shapes. The horse made good time and they reached Dannemora by three. Mary was overawed by the height of the wall, and could not take her eyes off of it, saying, "So he's in there, Frannie. Your brother's in there." Frances had frostbite on her right foot, and so Mary left her at the hotel and she and the priest crossed the road together.

"Now, I'd prefer, Father, if you'd wait till I had my say with the boy. It'd be a kindness if you would, for I have something very special to tell him from his mates, and from a young lady, too, who's been nothing but kind and above board with him."

"Of course, Mary."

Warden Thayer was happy to see Father Swift. He consoled Mary Shea, telling her how courageous her son had been through the past year and a half. "Still, I'm afraid you'll find him much changed." After Mary left with a guard for the condemned cell, Thayer started to excuse himself: "You can wait here . . ."

"Actually, Warden, I didn't come to see Shea."

"No?"

"I came to see John McGough."

"McGough?"

"He's here on the assault charge."

"Yes." Thayer scowled. "Can I ask what it concerns? Usually we allow only family and attorneys to visit the inmates. Father Belanger administers to our inmates' spiritual needs."

"I'm afraid I cannot say, Warden."

Thayer looked concerned. "Well, I'll make an exception. He'll be in the conference room in thirty minutes."

Mary Shea was relieved Frannie was back at the hotel, and that the priest stayed behind. The wind raged in the prison yard, blowing the snow horizontally and the guard pulled her against it until they reached the squat grim building of gray stone.

The air was stale and chilly and musty inside. She waited in a low whitewashed room, and in half an hour she was shown down a narrow hallway, through a heavy door of bars into the small cell. Her son looked haggard and thin and he grimaced with embarrassment when he saw her.

"Ain't much, is it, Ma?" He reached out for her, kissed her and led her to the pallet that hung from the wall by chains. "How've you been, Ma? You look all right. How's the old man, and Timmy?" They caught up on news from Troy. Occasionally Shea coughed, and when he coughed, he doubled up and his frame shook. Mrs. Shea fidgeted with the strings of her purse, and glanced nervously towards the door.

Finally she said:

"I come up here to ask you a favor, Barry."

"What is it, Ma?"

"It ain't very Christian of me, I'm afraid," her eyes narrowed, "but I want you t'do something for me, and for your family and for anyone in Troy who has an ounce of pride left."

"I'm afraid I can't do much for them up here."

"Ah, but you can." She took a white packet from her purse. "I brung you this from Boylan's Pharmacy. It's strychnine. P'ison. I want you to take it 'tween now and the execution and save whatever sense of pride we got. Now, Father Swift's here to take your confession." She frowned, unsure whether absolution for sins could be given prospectively. Shea looked at his mother for a long moment. In the year and a half in the dark at Dannemora, circles had formed about his eyes, and the pale blue lustre of his eyes seemed unearthly. There was a hint of moisture in them now as he stared at his mother who had come all this way to end the life she had created.

"Can't do that, Ma."

"But you must, Barry! You don't know what they're saying about you at home, about us. How they call you a dog and a coward. You ain't a coward, Barry! You never was that."

"No, I never was that."

"Here. Don't do it today, but next week, just before the electrocution. I can't bear the publicity, the newspapers reporting how you walk to the chair, the priest, the hood, the 'lectricity," she buried her face in her hands and sobbed. "Oh, you'll never know what I've suffered!"

Tears were in his eyes now, and he put his arm around her woolen coat and held her to him. "I'm sorry, Ma. I wanted to make you proud of me. I wanted to be somebody, to wear elegant clothes and have people doing what I told 'em. Look at these rags. Look at 'em. I wanted to drive in a carriage with a team of stallions, and be pulled on the railroads in private cars. I can't move beyond these walls! That's why I threw in with George. I never saw this to be the end of it all. But this is it, Ma. These are the cards they dealt me, and there ain't no bluffing my way out."

"But you'd cheat them at their own game! They don't deserve to take your life. You never killed that boy!"

"No, I didn't. But I ain't going to kill myself now neither. It ain't right, Ma."

She fell upon him now, sobbing wildly. "Oh, it's a harsh life, Barry. Your father ain't been no joy t'live with, particularly when he's had his drink, and now Tim's heading down the same path as you."

"What's that?"

"George give him a job at the saloon! Tim learnt how to roll cigars, he had a good job, but George stole him away. George thinks it's a favor he's doing. And we protested, your father and me, but he's there, and he's growed and we can't say nothing about it."

This saddened Shea. "You got to bear up, Ma. You got to meet it at least. Maybe you can't overcome it, but at least you gotta meet it face on. Tell Tim to stay away from George. Tell him I said so." He pulled her away from him and looked at her. "Now there ain't no use feeling anger or hate, Ma. Others is just doing what they think'll help themselves. Just do what you can to cope with it. Here, put this away so's the guard don't see it. I'll be fine. I'm at peace. I won't shy from the chair. That's only the last thing they can do to me, and then I'll be out of their grasp forever."

"Oh, Barry! Oh, my God! Take the p'ison, Barry. If you won't do it for yourself, do it for the poor mother what bore you into this harsh world, and who reared you up. Them strappin' you down and sending jolts of 'lectricity through you . . ."

"No, Ma. Put it away."

"Please!"

"C'mon, Ma. Sit you down."

He led her to the pallet again and talked in a consoling voice. "Remember the old days, Ma?"

She brightened to this. "I remember when your father would be out on a bender, and I'd sit you in my lap, and we'd look down upon the wagons passing on River Street; and in summer, in the back yard, watching the boats up and down the river . . ."

"That's it, Ma. Let's talk about folks in the neighborhood. How's the Widow Polk? Let's remember about those we've known. How's the mad pair of Rafferty twins? How's Tag Foley?"

Jack McGough shambled into the room in striped woolens, turning a cap in his hands. A sly smile flickered at his lips. "Hey, Father. Bet I know why you're way up here."

"Please sit down, John." He pointed to a chair.

"How's everyone back home? My old man? You seen him? And Maggie Riley? She writes me, but they open the letters and black out a lot of what she says. And George, he going to run again? Nearly two years since all this started. His term must be just about up. Hell of a thing, pardon the expression, Father, and pardon me running on like this. They don't let us talk, and it just kinda builds up, if you know what I mean."

"John, there is a very serious matter I'd like to discuss with you. Now you needn't say a word, yet I must speak with you about this, and it must be done now."

McGough shifted in his chair. "Sure, Father, I know what it is. I do. And I'm glad you came. But I was going to take care of it. On my own. I was."

Father Swift chose his words carefully. He could not breach the sanctity of the confessional. He could not tell McGough what his father confessed. The knowledge of Jack's guilt weighed heavily on Owen McGough, and he wanted the priest's permission to keep the truth from the authorities. Let the boy make the decision, had been Owen McGough's argument, and Father Swift explained it was the father's duty as a Christian to see truth and justice were served. While Father Swift had refused to give absolution until either of the McGoughs came forward, beyond the note to Fagan, he decided to do nothing until the appeal was adverse, and Bat Shea's fate sealed.

"John, do you know more about the murder of young Robert Ross than you stated at Shea's trial?"

Jack's smile got more sly, and his eyes hardened. "Got a smoke, Father?"

The priest took a cigarette from a box on the warden's desk.

"Thayer's own brand, eh." Slowly, to buy time, McGough sniffed it, tapped it on the back of his left hand, lit the cigarette, drew in the smoke, then exhaled. "Yeah, I know more, Father. I know who shot Ross, and nobody else does. But you must've figgered it out to be way up here." Father Swift nodded. "Now, Black never bothered to figger out the truth, and the lawyers never did much with the bullet nor with the angle of the shot nor with which gun was used." He gave a laugh. "And all that rubbish about the green tie! Hell, I was the one with the green tie on, and half them black Protestant bastards, 'xcuse me, Father, testified that's who shot Ross. Even so, nobody picked up on it. Not even Bat." He shook his head. "Poor old Bat! But now I been here a year and a half. It's a hard life, Father, and I've had a lot of time to think. I was meaning to come clean. I was. Today, in fact."

"Why didn't you tell someone before?"

"Confess back then?" He shook his head. "Nah. You saw what they did to Bat? You saw how he took it? I ain't that strong, Father. I couldn't've stood it. I wanted to tell him while we was together in the cell all that time. Maybe he suspected. He asked me once or twice in a rage, but I lied to him. Yeah, Father. I lied to my own best friend."

"You could have saved him."

"Yeah. But I ain't crazy. I figgered the truth would come out eventually. Ain't that what's supposed to happen? Ain't that what you fellows teach? The truth always comes out? And I told myself it would, 'least regarding Bat's innocence, and then their blood lust would be tempered somewhat and they could've tried me on a lesser charge, say, manslaughter 'stead of murder one. And all that rabble-rousing with Black and his people would be over and done, like a storm blown out to sea, and I'd get what they saw fit to give me, but it wouldn't be the chair, and Bat'd be free as a bird. And there he was with me, Father, in the jail cell all that time. If I confessed, I would have been in it all alone."

"But what about Shea? Didn't you ever think of him?"

McGough paused for a long moment. "That there's the toughest part, Father. When the trial started, I wanted to tell him in the strongest way. But you know how it is. Once you start down a hill, it's hard to turn and go back up. You just keep going down and it gets easier all the time."

The priest rose and went to the window. The snow had not abated and the wind blew it furiously into drifts against the high granite wall. The gun turrets peered down along the wall. "So, what are you going to do now?"

"As I say, I was meaning to do the right thing. I ain't told no one, not George, not Gene, not Owen. . ."

"Your father?"

Jack laughed. "No, Owen Judge. Come to think of it, I mentioned it to the old man that very day when I came dancing in with the slug in my hip. Whew! He was awful upset. He told me he'd clout me worse'n ever if I breathed a word about it. 'Course that's before they picked Bat out to crucify. That's when all fingers were still pointing at Boland."

"Well now, you say you are going to tell the warden?"

"Yes, Father. And maybe . . . maybe you'd hear my confession now."

Father Swift removed the purple stole from a small leather case. "Please kneel."

"Sure, Father." McGough stabbed out his cigarette and knelt on the rug. "I think I remember how this goes." He made the sign of the cross. "Bless me, Father, for I have sinned . . ." and Father Swift sat, closed his eyes, kissed his purple stole and put it around his neck.

39.

A RESPITE

Governor Levi P. Morton

Amid the smoke and sparks and clanging of the smithy late Saturday afternoon, Jack McGough broke silence to a guard: "Hey, I gotta speak to the warden!" The din drowned out the guard's response. Jack shouted: "It's important. About Shea." The guard nodded, pointed him back to the anvil and forge and left the shed. Half an hour later the guard came for him and they walked in silence across the snowy yard.

"Is there any hope for poor Shea?" Jack asked when ushered into the warden's office.

"No there isn't, John."

McGough turned his cap about in his hands. "I got . . . sir . . . I got something to tell you and everyone else regarding the Ross murder."

"Sit down, John."

The warden heard Jack out, then called for his secretary, Gleason, who spilled a pot of ink across the desk when McGough admitted killing Robert Ross.

"You understand, John," the warden was concerned, almost fatherly, "that even if Shea is executed, you still forfeit parole by this admission?"

"Sure," Jack nodded, his smile twitching nervously around one of the warden's cigarettes. "It don't matter now, Warden. It's the truth. Should have come out long ago."

Jack then gave a detailed statement. Thayer dispatched a note to the telegraph room with Gleason. Gleason returned a minute later: "Can't get through, sir. The lines are down with the storm."

"Well, then, Gleason, you had better get into Plattsburgh and catch the Montreal sleeper to Albany. I want a letter in the governor's hand tomorrow. Shea's execution is scheduled for Monday and we haven't much time."

Gleason then took a letter from McGough:

January 4, 1896

To his Excellency Hon. Levi P. Morton:

I, the undersigned, do hereby acknowledge in the presence of a witness that it was I, in a moment of anger and excitement, and not Bartholomew Shea, that killed the deceased Robert Ross.

Knowing full well the serious consequences of my unfortunate act and also that it would be wrong for me to let an innocent man die for a crime he did not commit, I affix my signature,

John McGough.

"And I want you to wait there, Gleason," Thayer's eyes were intense, his voice insistent, "wait until the governor gives you a response. And not a word of this to anyone." He turned to McGough. "We must isolate you from the rest of the population."

"Figgered that," Jack said with a shrug. He crushed out the cigarette and followed a guard to solitary confinement to await the governor's decision.

Mary Shea sat in the coach of the Montreal sleeper with Frannie. Father Swift was across the aisle and Gleason who'd overtaken them in Plattsburgh, sat in the back of the car. All of them swayed to the rhythm of the wheels, each tight-lipped, possessing a secret, the bereaved mother her packet of poison, the priest his burden of the confessional, his doubt McGough would step forward, and the secretary McGough's letter. Occasionally they regarded each other in the swaying coach, surmising, but small talk and silence were observed until the conductor made up the beds in the sleeping compartments. Mary Shea and Frannie shared a berth and retired early. Gleason retired an hour later.

Far into the night Father Swift gazed out the window as the train whistle blared and echoed through the Adirondack wastes, and its lamp scoured a path in the dark blizzard for the smoking, clattering hulk of steel.

Gleason caught Governor Levi Morton on the street Sunday morning as church bells were tolling. After reading the letter, the governor questioned the secretary as to the validity of the statement, then he summoned Galen Hitt to his home by telegram. Hitt reached the governor's house early in the afternoon.

"Two questions, Mr. Hitt," the governor asked when Gleason had relayed McGough's statement to him. "First, is it possible? Second, is it plausible?"

Hitt was deeply affected by the news. He paced before the window, his hands clasped behind his back. "Not only is it both, sir, this statement explains all the facts that did not fit into Mr. Fagan's case."

"You recall, Mr. Hitt, I was in Europe during this trial. Would you be so kind?"

"Well, this statement explains the lack of powder burns on Ross, it explains the angle of the wound, and most importantly, it explains why the men chased McGough from the scene and let Shea walk away unmolested. There was much testimony at trial that a man in a green tie shot Ross. McGough testified he was wearing a green tie that day. Above all, it explains the weapon. McGough's gun was found in the ditch and the fatal bullet was the proper calibre and weight to have come from it. As Mr. Norton suspected, as we have both suspected, someone early on made a mistaken identification, and Black and his group fastened on Shea as the culprit, harmonizing testimony to secure a conviction."

Morton raised his eyebrows. "That is a strong allegation against a fellow member of the bar and a member of Congress."

"He wasn't in Congress when he did it, sir. That's what got him there." Hitt paced before the French windows. The snow was deep and the sky above the unfinished Capitol across the square was streaked yellow and gray. "They picked Shea out when it looked like one of theirs, Boland, was to blame . . ."

"What, Mr. Hitt?"

"Uh, as I say, there's no use speculating, sir. Here we have a man's admission, a man who was armed, who had an opportunity and a motive. Most importantly it explains why Ross was on the ground when

Shea approached. He was on the ground, not because of any ankle problem, but because he was dead."

"So, what should be done, sir?"

"Why, Shea is entitled to a new trial, of course."

"Not so quickly, Mr. Hitt. I can stay the execution, but a court must determine if a new trial is warranted."

"Of course, sir. I will then make an immediate motion for a new trial on the ground of newly discovered evidence."

Later that afternoon, Morton issued a stay of execution and dispatched Gleason with it back to Dannemora. The governor referred Hitt to special term in rural Schoharie County to make his motion.

News of McGough's confession hit the Troy papers Sunday afternoon. Newsboys flew through the snowy streets as horsedrawn sleighs headed for vespers at the downtown churches: "Extra! Extra! Shea's execution stayed! McGough confesses!"

Home from Washington for the holiday season and due to return the next day, Frank Black heard the racket as he dined with Lewis Gurley at the Mansion House. He sent a waiter for a newspaper. He carefully read the headline and the first paragraphs of the news story with his thin lips pressed white.

"I'm afraid my return to Washington must be postponed," he told Gurley, struggling for composure. There was anger in his manner, but something else, too — fear. He showed Gurley the paper.

"Oh, my!"

"We will convene the executive committee tonight. Justice must not be balked. These are desperate men and they will lie to the last possible moment to cheat the hangman!"

"Yes, Frank, they will lie. But to put their own neck in the noose?"

Black glared at Gurley. "This is a deliberate attempt by these scoundrels to usurp justice, and they will not succeed!"

Well into the night gas lamps and electric lights blazed in the houses of Second and First Streets, in the gracious mansions of Washington Park, and in the gothic homes high upon the bluffs as the merchants and manufacturers discussed the case. Plans were laid for rallies in the Protestant churches to decry what surely was a desperate attempt to thwart justice by a crafty gang of Irish.

And the candles and gas and oil lamps burned in the tenements on Scotch Hill, through St. Joseph's parish in South Troy and throughout St. Francis' parish on Ida Hill, St. Paul's, St. Peter's near the Hoosick

Road, and St. Patrick's in North Troy. The conviction of Bat Shea, till now so final and irrevocable, was a colossal sham! McGough pulled the trigger, not Shea! All the rumors were true! People then remembered it was Black who had first publicly named Bat Shea. It was Black who had doggedly pursued him, interviewing witnesses, selecting and advising grand jurors, appearing at the trial. Now Congressman Black's integrity hung in the balance.

In North Troy, Dunlop's Saloon was in a spirit of hilarity. There was a makeshift band with fiddler, squeezebox and tin whistle. Timmy Shea, the newest bartender and bouncer, was a celebrity, and George was dancing with glee. "He's coming home," he cried out again and again, "my boy Bat who stood with me through thick and thin, he's coming home! I can feel it! I can smell it! Another round, boys! Stuff your money! Drinks on the house! It'll be like old times!"

Far in the snowbound mountains, Warden Thayer received the stay of execution Monday morning with the governor's seal. Thayer immediately ordered Electrician Davis, who was even then in the death chamber testing "Old Sparky," to board up the room. With Gleason, two of the governor's counsel had come north to gauge the veracity of McGough's statement by taking an affidavit. Norton and Hitt had journeyed up too, but were not allowed to see McGough.

Jack came into the interview blinking and stretching from two days and two nights in solitary. They pointed him to a chair. A stenographer copied down the questions and answers.

"When did you decide to make this statement?"

"Saturday morning."

"That was the first time?"

"Yeah." McGough laughed nervously.

"Did anyone influence you to make this statement?"

"No."

"It was of your own volition?"

"Certainly."

"What was your object?"

"I did not want to see an innocent man die for a crime he did not commit."

"You considered yourself a friend of Shea at the time of his trial?"

"Yes, sir. Certainly." Jack's lip twitched, and a nervous smile flickered on his lip.

"Do you still consider yourself a friend of his?" They were trying to evaluate bias.

"That all depends."

"Upon what?"

"Upon what Mr. Shea has to say of the matter."

"Are you willing to make a sworn statement that you killed Robert Ross?"

"Isn't that what we're all doing here?"

"Do you expect to be put on trial for your life."

Jack snickered at the idiocy of the question and he shook his head. "Yes. Certainly."

"Is this something to laugh about?"

"No, sir," he shook his head, "but I wouldn't have made the confession if I didn't know what was coming."

Prodded by their questions, Jack discussed the murder in detail.

The stenographer scribbled for over an hour:

" . . . In the course of the melee, previously to the firing of the fatal shot, deponent had been himself shot in the back and had fallen into the ravine. Said Robert Ross either jumped or fell on top of deponent. Said Ross then and there struck deponent several blows with a club, and then suddenly arose from deponent and started out of the ravine, up the bank onto the path in pursuit of Bartholomew Shea, the defendant.

"Deponent raised himself to a kneeling position, kneeling upon his right knee, and as the feet of said Ross, being at that instant about three feet higher than deponent's head, and said Ross being headed in a northwesterly direction, with his face turned partly toward the east, deponent discharged his pistol at said Ross, and said Ross immediately sank to the ground and did not move again.

"Deponent further says that at that time there were three shots fired to the right of deponent by one John Boland, said Boland being on level ground, that almost immediately, deponent being still in the ravine, he came in conflict with William Quigley and Adam Ross who struck deponent with clubs. Deponent was knocked senseless by one of such blows and relaxed his hold upon his said revolver.

"Deponent recovered in a very few seconds, arose and ran as best he could and after going a little distance, John Boland and a number of persons, in all about twenty, pursued deponent up North Fourth Street to the residence of deponent's father; that deponent went into his father's house, and took off his clothes, which were covered with ashes, dirt and briars from said ravine, had his wounds dressed, put on other clothing, and departed for the residence of his aunt, where deponent remained until he was arrested.

"Deponent further says that the foregoing is a correct and truthful narrative of the manner in which Robert Ross met his death, and that said confession was made by deponent voluntarily without solicitation from anyone. Deponent only regrets that he did not tell the truth upon the defendant's trial."

Jack was then sworn, and he affirmed the statement and signed it in the presence of the notary. After Jack had been returned to solitary confinement, the warden asked the governor's men about the likelihood of a respite.

"There has been no formal announcement yet," one replied, "but the governor indicated this matter would go back to the courts unless McGough was clearly lying."

"He certainly was nonchalant," the other observed.

"Yes, but his story holds together," the first counsel noted. "I have been following this matter, and it explains all the questions raised at trial, everything except how so many witnesses saw Shea fire his pistol at Ross."

"Yes," the warden mused. "And that needs no explanation."

Hitt and Norton were informed of the contents of the statement, but were allowed no interview with McGough. When the group had departed by sleigh to Plattsburgh, the warden bundled himself in his bear coat and crossed the prison yard to the small squat building where Shea sat, ignorant of all that had happened.

"The warden's here," the guard growled, "stand up!"

"The warden?" Shea blinked as if awakening. "Is it time?"

The metal door squealed open and Thayer entered: "Sit down, Shea, sit down." Thayer sat on the wooden chair and Shea sat on the bunk. "There's been a development in your case."

"What's that?" Shea seemed mildly interested. His eyes were luminous in the dark, and he was quiet and composed and reserved.

Thayer paused, uncertain of his phrasing. "Best just to tell it straight out. John McGough has confessed to the murder of Robert Ross. Your execution has been stayed pending an investigation."

"What?" Shea looked at the warden as if he were peering through a thick murk, his eyes narrow, his face skeptical. He had aged considerably in two years, and had acquired many mannerisms of an old man. "Jack?"

"Yes. The governor sent two men up today and they took a sworn statement from him. Hitt and Norton were here too. I must say, Shea, McGough's statement sounds plausible."

"But why didn't he say so sooner?" Doubt registered. "Nah.

He's trying to take the fall for me."

"I don't think so, Shea. I heard him give the statement. There was no hesitation."

Shea hung his head a moment, then he looked up. "You got a chew, Warden?"

"I can give you a cigar."

Shea stuck the cigar in his mouth and lit it. It had been a year and a half since he had a smoke due to the cough. The first few puffs of the fragrant smoke sent him coughing and hacking and wheezing backward, but he shook off the fit of coughing, spit into the bucket, and looked with watering eyes at the warden. "So, what does this mean?"

"They'll decide now if you get a new trial. If you do, I would think Jack's statement conclusive as to your innocence. I'm no attorney, mind you."

Shea stood up and paced in the cell. "But, Warden, Jack wouldn't have done me like this. He never would. He ain't that sort. Jack! He was like a brother to me. The things we went through together! Aw, no, Warden, he's just trying to take the fall for me. That's the Jack I know, trying to help out a friend. All that time I shared a cell with him in Troy, he woulda said something, let something slip, maybe in his sleep."

Thayer shook his head. It was pitiful to watch, the thin convict with a shaved head, eyes luminous, cheeks sunken, hunched over from a year and a half sitting on this bunk, trying to convince himself his best friend had not betrayed him even to the door of the death chamber.

"Jack and me was tight, Warden. I stubbed my toe, he said ouch. Jack and me was a team. We knew the score. We had the same thoughts about the same people, and we knew where we wanted to be, and where we woulda been if this here didn't befall us."

"Well, I'll leave you to that. Your case is going to special term in Schoharie County very shortly, and the judge there will rule whether or not you get a new trial." The warden stood. Shea still refused to believe what he heard and was shaking his head. "I just want to say, Shea, that I wish you the best of luck. I have never seen the like of this case. Your story is a unique one, and you've been a model prisoner. I hope the new trial comes through for your sake, and for your family."

"Thanks, Warden. Thank you for coming personally to tell me, too." He offered his hand in a warm handshake.

When the warden and the guard left, Shea pensively finished the cigar, then sat with his head in his hands. The news overwhelmed him. So long accused and reviled and insulted, he had met it all with brave defiance. Till now he had borne the insults and raillery without a flinch, his anger and spite directed at Black and his committee. With not a whimper of rebuke he suffered the machine selling him out, Murphy cutting him loose. So it surprised him, now, when sobs welled up as he felt the impact of Jack's keen betrayal.

Bat Shea rose from the bed and began to pace, punching his fist into his palm. "Now, only now, you step up and tell them what you done. Now, after I spend a year and a half in this hole thinking with every thought directed at the moment I will die. Maybe this'll save me, maybe not. But you shoulda never done it to me, Jack. You shoulda never put me in this position." He shook off another bout of sobbing. "I never woulda done it to you! And that there's the hardest part to swallow."

He fought back the tears. Why should he weep now? After everything he suffered, now there was hope. Yet while he could take the lies and the double-dealing from enemies, it was a different thing altogether when it came from Jack.

"Jack! You son of a bitch!" he growled through clenched teeth. "You sold me out! You son of a bitch! Jack! Down the goddamned river! It weren't the Rosses! It weren't Black! It weren't the APA! It weren't Murphy! It weren't the judge nor the jury! It was you all along, Jack! You!" He grit his teeth and clenched his fists and he pressed back the sobs and he cursed. "Nobody ever sold me out so bad! You son of a bitch! To let them take my life away from me without a protest, without a word just to save your miserable arse. And you was my best friend! I, I loved you, Jack, and look, look what you done to me." He waved his hands at the cell. "Look at me! Look!"

Then sobs seized him and he buried his face in his hands. "I stood it all. The APA, the lawyers, the judge, the jury. But it was you, Jack. You was the enemy. And I was too stupid to see! I could handle it, Jack, before I knew it was you who done this to me," and he coughed uncontrollably. "O, my God," he whispered as the tears came hot and cleansing, and his frame heaved with sobs, "O, my God! There ain't one man to trust. No one! And I never saw how alone I was! How alone we all are!" Again he grabbed the bars of his cell, and he growled like a caged beast.

40.
SPECIAL TERM

"No, my dear sisters, we must never, ever, ever, rest ..."

Monday evening doors to the Protestant churches flew open in Troy, and orations thundered from the pulpits that justice must not be balked, the trial had found guilt beyond a reasonable doubt, and no lying thug from Shea's gang must now be allowed to save him. The Committee of Public Safety passed resolutions memorializing the governor as to why the sentence must not be commuted, nor a pardon or new trial granted. Congressman Black was desperate. If a new trial freed Shea, his status as a reformer would sour to that of a political opportunist willing to use a lynching to advance his career.

Ascending the pulpit, Black denounced the confession and again invoked the moral superiority of the committee:

"This is the same situation that confronted us during the fifteen years previous to the shooting," he said. "If there had been an objection, it would be met by a bullet. Two years ago you said 'Stop,' and the gun went off. Two years ago we entered upon a contest that involved a life. If we surrender now, after conquering, we lose all."

"No!" the congregation cried and the organist struck up "Onward Christian Soldiers."

Tuesday afternoon Congressman Black met with editorial boards, and editorials followed the next day in the Republican papers to bolster up sagging public confidence in the verdict.

From its convention in Rochester that week, the National APA movement announced it controlled three and a half million voters. Rensselaer County chapters boasted four thousand, three hundred members. This year, 1896, would be the year the APA elected a president and the APA boasted its anonymous legions would be the deciding factor in all elections "from the President to the pound master."

With Jack's confession, the Irish were emboldened. At last a sensible explanation had surfaced, something the vigilantes ignored and had foreclosed in petitioning the governor for a special court and a special prosecutor and calling for biased grand jurors. Gangs of toughs prowled the streets and hurled rocks through windows of members of the Committee of Public Safety. No other topic was discussed in the stove foundries, the shirt and collar mills, the bakeries, the groceries, the saloons. Weary Shea seemed more sprightly, and Mary was beside herself with joy. She dared not think what she herself might have accomplished if she'd convinced her "Barry" to swallow the poison.

Curiously few of the Irish rebuked Jack McGough. In part it was due to his reputation as a rogue. No one expected any different of him than to duck blame even if it was his best friend who was to be executed. Part of it was due to his manliness in stepping forward even at this eleventh hour, but much of it was due to a suspicion that he might indeed be lying to save Bat Shea, shouldering the guilt that might belong indeed to John Boland or even to Shea.

Father Swift passed through his parish that dark, snowy Wednesday night, lightened by his secret as to how his intervention may have resurrected a hope for justice.

Boss Murphy was silent as to the confession. Cleansed and rehabilitated by his manipulations in Washington on behalf of the millowners, the able politician had put the whole issue behind him and did not want to revisit it. Indeed, the *Troy Times*, a Republican paper, ran a column denying it had ever accused Murphy of voting fraud. His reputation had been tarnished, he had been dropped as chairman of the Democratic State Committee, and he had forfeited the governor's chair, but at least he retained his senate seat. One local politician, though, Alderman George Dunlop, bawled for justice from behind his bar, and some of the union mobilizers, led by Tom Halligan, raised a cry for justice at meetings.

Galen Hitt told the press he had every confidence a new trial would be granted and that justice would be done. Thomas Fagan took the news with a sinking heart. Raines had received most of the credit for the conviction, and so he had not prospered politically. Fagan had harbored strong misgivings about Black's involvement from the first day, and the meddling and secrecy of the committee had caused him much grief before and during the trial. Yet he dutifully put his case in and he obtained a conviction. Now to have the verdict impugned! He saw the entire matter as a sham. Yet what could he do? He had a duty to see that justice was done, but if he slackened in his pursuit of Shea, the people would remove him, howl for his skin, and his legal and political career would be destroyed. No, he had a duty to oppose the motion for a new trial, not out of fear like Black, but to uphold the integrity of the verdict. Shea had his day in court, and if McGough lied, then everyone must live with the consequences. And yet, when George Raines asked if he could help present the People's case in opposition to the motion, Fagan acceded to his wish.

Out through the snowy landscape to the village of Schoharie, Hitt and Norton, Raines and Fagan went together on the train two weeks later to argue the motion for a new trial. Schoharie slept under a blanket of snow, and the halls of its ancient courthouse echoed with the eloquence of Shea's attorneys, and with the logic of Thomas Fagan and George Raines. For two full days oral arguments persisted, Hitt, red-faced, perspiring in the frigid room, imploring the court to allow a new and impartial jury to pass upon the credibility of McGough's confession at a new trial, Raines arguing that the matter had been decided, McGough's confession changed nothing, and the execution should proceed.

Judge Rufus Mayham reserved decision, and while Troy boiled like a cauldron with Frank Black at the ladle, stirring up public opinion and occasionally tasting how sweet, how bitter, how explosive it was, the attorneys boarded the train and rode back to the Hudson Valley together.

The intervening week was tense in the Shea household, so Tim ducked out whenever he could to Dunlop's Saloon where the mood was celebratory. It was certain, the hangers-on averred to a man, that Shea would be back. One of the girls from upstairs promised she'd give him a whole week free of charge if he made bail, and she confessed to her sisters in the trade that there would be something exciting with a man who just escaped the electric chair.

George Dunlop tested his latest version of the election and the trial on his saloon patrons, and it was a good one. The boys he chose were good boys. Shea took the punishment, the brunt of the trial, and now Jack was "fessing up," taking the blame for the deed. No one could bring young Ross back. Maybe Jack would get manslaughter and be out in twenty, which was his sentence on the assault anyway. In any event, these boys had the character to withstand the resistance and beat it back. In light of the festive spirit, few wanted to inform George that they knew his view was fiction, particularly since he was pouring so many free mugs of Excelsior Porter and Excelsior Pale Ale to make them believers.

On the intervening weekend a large convocation of women gathered in Albany on its way to a national convention in Washington, DC, women from around the state led by Susan B. Anthony. They came to address the opening of the 1896 legislative session about reforms they were seeking both statewide and nationally: woman's suffrage, temperance and a prohibition amendment, a ten hour workday, the outlawing of child labor, and a mandatory minimum wage.

Nellie Mae Patton was a featured speaker Sunday afternoon as the women prepared to visit the offices of their legislators the next day. Nellie gave an articulate speech about the evils of mixing whiskey, gunsmoke and politics. Her voice was filled with emotion, as she referred to the deadly mixture of these "forces." She was restrained in deploring the tactics of men. Even though she merely mentioned in passing her own terrible loss, the assembled women were aware of her personal tragedy. They listened intently, empathized with her pain, applauded enthusiastically.

In the audience sat Mamie Halligan, feeling mighty uneasy. She had attended to advocate labor reform, particularly outlawing child labor, but hearing Nellie's allusion to the Ross murder, and with the recent revelations about Jack, her tears began to flow. It was a sorry affair on all sides. Nellie Mae Patton was so elegant, her features so perfect, the strong chin, the upturned nose, the high cheekbones, the violet, passionate eyes. Her delivery was aristocratic, her emotions lofty, filled with strong but tender passion. Mamie felt coarse and common.

"And so, my dear sisters," Nellie's eyes flashed enthusiastically, "we must never, ever, ever rest until our voices are heard, nay, until we become leaders ourselves at the highest pinnacles of government. It is our women's sense that must temper ambition with caring for others, restrain the monopolies and trusts from crushing the lives of the workers and the public alike, reform the electoral process so that the secret ballot and temperance, particularly on election day, may insure an accurate and just election." Applause resounded.

"We must never rest, my dear sisters, until we demonstrate that we are every bit as capable as men, and in many ways worthier of holding public office." Loud applause. "No, my dear sisters, we must never, ever, ever rest until we fashion for our children, our daughters, but more importantly for our sons," loud and sustained applause, "a more merciful and rational world where might does not make right, and people need not live in fear, but can fulfill the Creator's plans in peace and harmony." Nellie Mae Patton bowed quickly and was off the stage, ignoring the thunderous applause and the standing ovation.

Mamie Halligan was overwhelmed. Never had she been so affected by an orator, indeed, never had she heard a woman speak so. She felt great shame to be associated in any way with the murder of Nellie's betrothed. Such a noble heart deserved a strong, proud husband, just like everyone said Robert Ross had been, and children, beautiful, intelligent children. Had Bartholomew prevented that? In not heeding her premonitions, in leading his gang to the polls, had he indirectly caused the death? In a great confusion Mamie left the auditorium and retired to a far corner of the lobby to be out of the way, to clear her mind, to think. As she stood near the heavy maroon and tasseled curtains, the backstage door opened and she found herself, to her horror, face to face with Nellie Mae Patton. She froze.

"Hello," Nellie said pleasantly.

"Hello."

"It's deathly cold backstage and I'm trying to get warm." Nellie Mae rubbed her hands together, and seemed shy after the speech. She looked at Mamie. "Aren't you from Troy?"

Mamie's eyes opened completely in shock, while Nellie's eyes narrowed and she nodded. "You are, aren't you?"

"Yes, ma'am."

"Why, I recognize you. You were pointed out to me once. Aren't you the sweetheart of that fellow Bat Shea?"

Mamie gasped and stared up and down the hall. Her throat was suddenly dry, and she felt lightheaded and weak. Tears threatened to flow. She wanted to hide behind the curtains. She wanted to run down the hall. The shame, the rebuke. But she looked into Nellie's eyes and saw kindness. "Why, yes, ma'am, uh, that's right, I was, I mean, I am."

"You must be overjoyed at the respite and the possibility for a new trial." Not a hint of rancor. Mamie was suspicious of her kindness. She narrowed her eyes.

"Why, yes, ma'am, yes, I am." She nodded, pressing her lips tightly together.

"Perhaps you'll be spared, Miss — ."

"Halligan, ma'am, Mamie Halligan."

"Perhaps you'll be given another chance, Mamie Halligan. Perhaps." And she gently touched Mamie's face. "I've heard about your brother. Tom, isn't it? And his work with the unions. Remarkable man. And yourself, I've heard about your speaking out on behalf of the spindle girls and the children." She nodded at Mamie. "It's so important we save the children from the mills, and you are doing noble work." She smiled, and her beneficent smile lifted Mamie's heart. "Isn't it curious, Mamie Halligan, how we turn to public causes when love is gone from our lives?"

Mamie winced. "You don't despise me?"

"You had nothing to do with the murder, did you?"

"Why, no. I, I tried to stop Bat from going that day. I told him I felt something awful would happen, and it did. It did." Mamie felt tears welling up, and her breath came in short fits.

"Well, why should I be angry with you? I was angry, terribly angry for a long while. But anger passes. You will see if there is no new trial. You must get over it, the great gulf of emptiness. That must be filled, Mamie Halligan, replaced by, well, by this. This caring. You know. You wouldn't be here today if you didn't."

The lobby was filling with women from the auditorium, and many flocked to Nellie, but held off seeing she was engaged in a private conversation.

Overcome with emotion, Mamie fell upon her in an embrace. "Oh, thank you, ma'am! Thank you ever so much." Other women then pressed forward to speak with Nellie.

"There. There. Things may work out for you with the new trial. Best of luck, Mamie Halligan!" And a look of ineffable sadness passed over her features, and she turned to speak with the crowd of admirers.

41.

THE DECISION

Bartholomew Shea

Shea received the news a week later with a clenched jaw and a lowered brow. "I expected as much," he said. "Someone made the call. Maybe Black himself." He nodded and scowled. "The APA got to the judge. That is, if he ain't one himself."

"I have read the decision, Shea," Warden Thayer was sitting in the cell. The warden had taken a great liking to this young man who seemed day by day to be coughing out his life. "I'm no attorney, but I will tell you that it strikes me as rather far-fetched."

"But it don't matter now, does it?" Shea had his arms folded and he held one of the warden's cigars.

"But it bothers me, Shea. You see, there's four things you must show to get a new trial, and the judge himself admits you show three of them: first, there must be new evidence; second, it could not have been discovered with due diligence; and third, it's likely the evidence would change the verdict. But there's that fourth thing he says you miss: the new evidence can't be cumulative."

Shea had lapsed into a stony silence, trying to let the finality of the decision register and the shock pass.

"What's that?"

"Cumulative? It can't be the same as evidence that you produced at the trial."

"So Jack confessed. He didn't confess at the trial. Where's the problem?" Shea's eyes narrowed. He bit into the cigar, and spit out the end.

"Ah, but here's where Judge Mayham goes far afield. He says that when McGough testified at your trial 'Boland shot Ross,' he was not legally saying 'Boland shot Ross.' He was saying, 'Shea did not shoot Ross.' Now, by virtue of his confession, he is not saying, 'McGough shot Ross,' he's once more saying, 'Shea did not shoot Ross.' Legally speaking, the trial testimony and the confession say the same thing: 'Shea did not shoot Ross,' and so Jack's confession is cumulative."

Shea spit out the cigar. "What?"

"The judge also says McGough's confession is not absolute, it still leaves room to find that Boland shot Ross."

"So Jack's confession's no good? Even though he's putting his own miserable arse in the chair? Just because both times he's said I was innocent in two different ways?"

"That's what the decision says."

"Ah, it's nothing more than the railroad job they give me from day one. This one's as bad as Black, as bad as Williams, as bad as any of them. What have they got to fear on a new trial if their proof's so good?"

"I agree, Shea. The judge does state he is not being bulldozed by Black and the committee. He has a whole paragraph in there about the howling of these men."

"One thing to say it, another for it to be true. If he opened this trial again, they'd come after him with a rope. He would see what it's been like for me for near on two years, the son of a bitch." Shea spat into the slop bucket. He caught himself before the bitterness took over. "Ah, the game's been played, Warden. Everybody did what they could. It's over. I'd like to write some letters."

"You need paper?"

"Yeah."

"I'll send in some paper."

"Yeah, and someone to write it out for me."

"I'll send my secretary over tonight."

"Thanks."

When the warden left, Shea paced back and forth in the cell for quarter of an hour. "So this is what finally sends me to the chair, a judge with the flick of his wrist, swatting me dead like a fly," he murmured.

"Jack got me into this bind, and there's no way out now. Because Jack twice swore I was innocent, they won't give me a show. Jack must feel like hell. And he should for what he done. But it don't matter. He's like the rest of them, and I ain't." Shea spread his arms out in the cell. "So this here is what it's like! Goddamnit! This here is what it's like staring death in the face." And he sneered and nodded and hung his head. "And I never knew how alone I was before."

That night Shea lay upon his pallet, his arms folded behind his head. What should you remember? he asked himself. You only got a few days left, and there's so much to remember, and it's important to remember in these few days 'cause if you don't remember, then it'll be gone.

So you remember the sunlight on your skin when you swam in the lake, camping back then, and the deep pine forests and the taste of fish cooked on a fire of oak chips, and you folded your hands behind your head and thought, looking into the sky, of the great things you would do, the esteem you'd win, but for now it was all right to breathe the mountain air and await the day of opportunity;

And you remember the first girl and how the older guys in the pool hall built it up to be such a big deal, and you were surprised that she was willing, and the appearance of it, and the quick furtiveness in the alley, like dogs, like horses, her skirts up, then it's over and she's looking slyly like she owned you, and it weren't such a big thing, though it felt all right, but it sure weren't worth working day in and day out in the mill for, which was the mistake all the fellows were making, and if you had made the same mistake and now had a couple of plump little babies, and a steady job and some chums to attend the ballgame with, and then some ale in the saloon of a Saturday night, you'd never know this disgrace nor this pain, nor this dizzying revelation about life, and about the death that is coming just around the corner, so quick you can feel it like a dark and silent fog;

And you remember the first step into politics, the feeling of the organization, greater than the sum of its parts, the camaraderie, the ability to get things done with a whisper in the right ear, the great feeds where the party faithful turned out for clams and roast ox and fried chicken and countless kegs of Kennedy & Murphy Pale Ale, and the baseball and horseshoe toss; and then the fear you could instill in the opposition by marching a group of repeaters to the polls, the cops looking the other way as you shoved your men in quick to stuff the box, and you were out again, clean, sailing on to the next saloon to juice up the repeaters for the next polling place, and the high glee of taking what they held away from you, what was rightfully yours because you had the courage to seize it, laughing in the face of them who ridiculed and denied you;

And you remember the fights, oh, all the fights, one by one, Timmy Kerwin and Jack Sheehan and Willy Burke and Joe Carey and Dave Delaney, the fights in the schoolyard where you split their noses, cracked their skulls, got them on the ground and twisted their arms till they screamed for mercy, and the nuns came running; and fights later at the mill to take your place in the hierarchy, and the men around holding greenbacks as you stripped down to longjohns and braces and walloped the factory tough. How about Big Kevin Muldoon the day you whacked him with the two-by-four whilst he was taking bows for whipping you? The surprise on his face was worth the thumping that followed. And later, on the lam in the Midwest, then out to the mining camps, the simple country boys from Arkansas and Indiana who didn't know much about alley fighting, the eye-gouging and ballbashing and headbutting, taking rank advantage of them in the railyards to advance your reputation and line your pocket. And Silver City, and San Francisco. Good rough and tumble times!

But the lure of the big fight at home was always drawing you back, the fight for a place, for dignity and recognition in Troy; pulling you back even across the continent, and then falling in with George and Jack to wage the proper war against the blackhearted Protestants who you underestimated because they knew how to wage a war of their own, the proof of which is you sitting in a cage awaiting death; and you remember "the Line" in the fog, the red lamps of the whorehouses, and the skinny black fellow on the piano with his big eyes rolling, and the redheads and the blondes and the brunettes with the breasts and thighs and buttocks all trussed up, the girls high on opium and cocaine and belladonna and nightshade, and the rank perfume to cover up the other stench and Jack the soothsayer, dreamer of dreams, the seven fat kine and then the seven lean, he called them, the troupe with flesh enough for a battalion, and then the consumptive ones with bony ribcages and hips, all earnest elbows and knees;

And you remember the love of a girl, of Mamie Halligan, how simpering and useless it seemed back then because it advanced nothing, was apart from the stuff with George's girls, how it slowed you down and siphoned off the necessary meanness with its sweet delusion; but you remember that in the light of her eyes you saw yourself as someone worthy and capable, as someone who fit in and could do anything, and could settle down and raise up some proper children, not like you were raised, cuffed and clouted by anyone with a fist or boot, but happy children who had clothing and good food and hope, who wouldn't leave school to brawl and ramble around looking for scraps; but the timing was off, you couldn't think anything about love nor marrying nor a family until after election and you were in city hall with a clean white collar, silk tie and a proper job;

And you remember the river, for there was always the river, how you swam over to Cohoes, diving beneath the mossy bottoms of canal boats, the river swollen in the spring with ice and treetrunks, flooding its banks, filling the streets, the river bristling and calm in the summer, the river, dark and swift and silent as you walked down from the house at night, the river clogged with steamboats, alive with men shouting and the whistles and bells, the river dead and frozen all winter whilst you sat indoors warming your hands by the stove; the river rising and pulling with the tide, with the seasons, a great living thing, the living, breathing river;

And you remember the first pistol, the cold steel and how it fit and balanced in your hand, and how confident you felt with it in your side pocket, and the target practice on Kennedy & Murphy bottles, and seeing at the end of the barrel all the opposition against you, and how with a squeeze of the trigger, all your problems would simply fall away. And what was it that Jack used to say? "Ain't a problem on earth what can't be solved with a revolver." Yet, other problems immediately rose to take the place of the ones you slew.

And you feel the remorse again, the sorrow for Robert Ross and his girl and his family. Even though you never condoned the APA and their tactics, and Ross was in thick with them, but still he didn't deserve to die. It had bothered you deeply all along that murder was the end result of the repeating, and it bothered you, too, for you knew you were capable of it even though it weren't you who pulled the trigger. Death was a horrible thing, because it could never be undone. And soon you would know.

And then you slowly work around to remembering Jack, clever Jack, sneaky Jack, Jack be nimble and Jack be quick, and there were signs of the betrayal in all the remembrances; how he screamed out at the caucus, and you busted through the shop window to save him; how he screamed in the ditch and you doubled back to rescue him; your best friend who betrayed you, the friend you showed so many things to, who you trusted and confided in, who you protected, and then who lied to save his own skin even when he saw yours in peril; and now the misery he must feel at the ruin he made of everything. You remember him, the joking, happy fellow who cured a hangover with raw eggs and gin, then directed everyone's attention to the next song, the next girl, the next bar, all the while keeping up the momentum out of his sheer joy for life, the antics and the absurdity of the saloons and whorehouses till the beast within, as he called it, grew shy and sleepy.

And in the midst of his remembering, Shea slept at last, and he dreamed he was flying up through mists and dark thunderstorms, flying effortlessly upward and he was naked, and he felt the cold clouds on his skin, and then the clouds opened above and it was a warm, golden blue. The light that bathed him was warm and liquid, the sweetest bright light of blue and gold that quivered in a harmony that was splendid and new, and as he flew upward, the light grew brighter and brighter, and he was flooded with a radiant warmth and sense of well-being. He flew toward the source of the light where he sensed a vast and intelligent sympathy emanated with the warmth and faint harmonious music.

The entanglements of earth, his sins, his vices, the plots and intrigues had fallen off like his clothing, needless complications in this warm and naked bliss. The cacophony of voices striving to be heard was behind him, and there was faint music here that swelled all about him, like the harmony of a great choir as he drew near the source of the light, as he closed his eyes against its brightness and suddenly, squeezing his eyes closed, he was awake.

It was dark and cold in the cell. The corn husk tick was lumpy and the wool blanket scratched. He had been dreaming, yet it seemed more real, far more real than this cold, dark, damp cell, and this waiting to die. He coughed, and the phlegm came and he spit and huddled into the blanket and sat up. When he sat up, the coughing wasn't so bad, and he stared, wrapped in his blanket, at the stone wall of his cell.

42.
FINAL DAYS

Union Station

An invitation arrived at St. Patrick's Rectory in an envelope edged in black.

> Dannemora, New York
> February 7, 1896
>
> Dear Sir:
>
> In compliance with the laws of the State of New York relating to the infliction of the death penalty, you are respectfully invited to be present at this prison as a witness, without compensation, at the execution of Bartholomew Shea to take place Tuesday, February 11, 1896. Your immediate acceptance or declination is requested.
>
> Respectfully,
>
> Walter N. Thayer
> Agent and Warden
>
> This invitation is not transferable.

Father John Swift closed his eyes, crossed himself, and breathed deeply, steadying himself against the door jamb. He had heard the newsboys yesterday announce the decision, and he had prayed far into the night. His plan had been completely undone. An innocent man was going to die in the electric chair. He fetched the small leather pouch containing his stole and chrism for Extreme Unction, and seeing his hand tremble as he packed his grip for the journey north, he murmured to the crucifix: "Thy will and not mine be done."

There was a shout in the street. Father Swift stood for a moment in the rectory's dining room. Everything in the room, the silver flatware and candelabra, the Waterford crystal, everything gleamed in the wintry light. Everything seemed suddenly to quiver. He blinked and steadied himself. The gray light grew brighter. His suitcase open on the dining room table, the houseplants in the window reaching toward the feeble winter sun, the humble black clothing of his vocation, the white linen, the worn carpet, the ticking clock that seemed so loud just now, tick-tock, tick-tock, each object in the room seemed irradiated by an ethereal light. Clutching the invitation, Father Swift knelt.

From the street came the calling of children. Children. Innocent children who would grow into adolescence and adulthood on these streets, blessed with not seeing so deeply into matters of fate and providence and truth and justice, matters of betrayal, perjury and the harsh aggression of seizing political power. They would marry, they would beget more children in these tenements to run through these streets, they would die and be buried up on the hill in the cemeteries, and a new generation would inherit this place, raise up its buildings, its children, make its mistakes, deify its heroes, scorn its villains, and then another, and another, and another in an endless succession. But would they heed the lessons of this great misfortune?

The suffusion of light grew brighter as if the sun were peering from behind dark clouds. Father Swift wondered if his senses were deceiving him, then he wondered if he were dying. And as he knelt and crossed himself, he suddenly knew what this was, and it sent a cold chill through him. It was a realization that Shea's death had been preordained, fated. His meddling in destiny had served no one. His meddling had only reinforced for him that destiny could not be averted. His meddling in the course of events only showed him his own vanity, for his actions as a self-appointed agent of justice were the measure of his sinful pride. The clarity in the room astonished him. He saw objects as he had never seen them, as if each possessed its own soul, and then another depth to the matter was revealed to him — without his meddling, the full force of the wrong would have been known to no one but himself. Both Jack's guilt and Bat's innocence would have died with Shea. "Perhaps I have been of some service, after all," he murmured to the crucifix, bowing his head, breathing deeply.

And the silence was maddening! The clarity! This was it! This was all there was! Life replete with its doubts and jagged edges and injustices, and what was there beyond all this, outside the loud ticking of the clock, beyond this life? The calling of the children from the street? What was there? Shea would soon know. The electrocution was a mere spark in the long night, and Shea would soon be set loose on a journey that theologians had sought to observe for millennia, so simple, so fundamental, life and death, like Ross, dispatched with a spark, and in the scheme of things, Shea's absence would be as if a salt cellar were missing from this dining room table. And yet, the magnitude to Shea! "How alone we all are," murmured Father Swift to the crucifix, and he folded his hands to pray, dropping the black-edged invitation on the carpet.

The next afternoon, Father Swift boarded the train at Union Station along with Mary and Frances Shea, and Michael Davis, the electrician who would throw the switch. Davis sat by himself. Mary Shea and Frances, too, sat silently apart from the others. It was Sunday afternoon. They'd arrive at Dannemora Monday, and Shea would die Tuesday. The train whistle blew loud and long, then with a jolt and a clang the train moved slowly through the brick maze and over the bridge to Green Island.

As they passed through Saratoga, dinner was served in the club car. Mary Shea gazed out the window and barely touched the fare. She had spoken with the newspapers and her statement appeared today: "I have always believed my son to be innocent. They have hounded him and roasted him and after he is dead I suppose they will be satisfied. The only friend I have now is God." She sat in a daze, looking out the window. There were card games later, and when the conductor turned down the beds, the train clattered and clanged at full speed, bodies steaming in the darkness, someone coughing down the car, all restless, hurtling through the frozen landscape on their deadly mission.

Up in the engine, Timothy "Cork" Corcoran rested in the engineer's chair. The red glare from the furnace lit his features devilishly. He gazed out over the back of the great boiler. Nothing to encounter up here north of Glens Falls, a deer once in a while, and he's seen bears, but there was time to think tonight. He had a layover Monday in Montreal, so he'd be bringing the casket of the dead man home. "Just freight to me," he said when the fireman told him, but now that he starts thinking, with the passengers asleep, it was more than that.

He'd heard of Shea's innocence for a year and a half, and now he'd won the dubious honor of bringing the body home. His old fireman, Sparky, still on the belt line, was related to Shea in some distant way by marriage. Cork considered what it must be like to die, and so rattling through the pine forest, the red glare of the firebox in his eyes, he suddenly reached for the whistle pull and the whistle roared defiantly into the night. The noise of the whistle made him feel less alone.

"Whatcha do that for?" the fireman chided him, huddled on the floor in his bearskin robe. "Enough to wake the dead!"

"Aw, go back to sleep, Lester."

Mary and Frances Shea were ushered into the condemned cell at noon Monday. They'd arrived before the crowd of witnesses to spend a few hours with Bat on his last day. Mary tried to put a good face on things, but Frannie sat upon the floor, laying her head in her brother's lap. As he stroked her hair, she wept quietly.

Shea seemed thin and sick and sallow and distracted to his mother, as if he was not hearing her, following her thoughts or remembering her memories. He seemed to be listening to other voices. And yet, he seemed strong and noble too, calm and forgiving and dispassionate.

Father Belanger, the prison chaplain, spent an hour in the cell, leading them in the rosary. Just before supper, Father Swift entered to hear Shea's last confession, and all the others filed respectfully out.

"Well, Bartholomew, I am here for your last confession. I am sure I needn't tell you to cleanse yourself of all your sins."

"I will, Father."

"Proceed."

"Bless me, Father, for I have sinned," Shea made the sign of the cross. "I confessed a month back to Father Belanger so there ain't much now." He closed his eyes and he groaned. "I found it terrible hard to forgive Jack for what he done, Father."

"Have you forgiven him now?"

"Yeah, I have. You know, Father, looking back, he always was that way. That's his nature to duck the blame. Yeah. I forgive old Jack. So, that is all, Father. I am sorry for all my sins."

There was a long silence.

"Anything about the murder, Bartholomew, or about the trial?"

"Nah." He shook his head, then he looked askance at the priest.

"I forgive all those who plotted to get me to this point."

"That is good. Your forgiveness."

"Yeah, you see, Father, I think this here is the way it is supposed to work out. Even though I tried to make it different, this is the way it happened, and I got to take it. I don't know what it's supposed to mean, to me or anybody else. I guess it'll mean whatever folks want it to."

The priest took a deep breath. He wanted to stop Shea, get him back to the confessing, safer ground.

"I can't read nor write, Father, and I don't know much about a lot of things, but I seen a lot of treachery and betrayal. And you know, it hurts when your best friend does what mine gone and done. I was all right up till Jack spilled it. Then I just sat down on this bed here and cried like when I was a little kid and the old man'd have at me. And I ain't been right since. That, Father, what Jack done, that showed me how alone we all really are, and so there's nothing left to do but face this last thing and move on." Father Swift swallowed hard. In his simple words, Shea was articulating the priest's emotions.

"And your last confession, Bartholomew?"

"What? The murder?" He shook his head slowly. "I been saying it all along, Father, and it's the truth as only God can know, I never killed that man. I had rage in my heart for what he was doing to Jack, but when I seen him he just rose up from the ditch and sat down heavy. Now I might have potted him one in the chest, and likely as not mine was the ball stopped by his pocketbook. I might have squeezed off another if I ran toward him as they say, but I never killed him, and Jack did, and that's all there is to it. But I ain't bitter, Father. This is the way it worked out, and this is what I gotta do, face it."

The priest had his eyes closed for tears were coming.

"Let me ask you, Father, would you recite me something, I wanted to hear it again before I . . . before tomorrow. I been trying to remember it, how it goes in English. Would you recite that part of the mass when you hold up the host?"

"Hoc est enim corpus meum?"

"Yeah, but so's I can understand it."

The priest closed his eyes. "On the night He was betrayed, He took the bread and broke it and gave it to His disciples saying, 'Take this, all of you, and eat it. For this is My body which will be given up for you.' And in a like manner when the supper was done, He took the cup filled with wine and He gave thanks and giving the cup to His disciples said, 'Take this all of you and drink from it, for this is the cup of My blood, the blood of the new and eternal covenant that will be shed for you and for all so that sins may be forgiven. Do this in memory of Me.'"

"And that was before they come for Him, for Jesus Christ? He saw His own death coming, right?"

"Yes." Tears spilled down the priest's face.

"Now, I sure ain't no holy man, nor no teacher, Father, like the human side of Jesus. In fact I've been a pretty rotten individual all around. My death'll be forgot completely this time next year. But ain't their conduct just the same, the crowd's. And that Barabbas? The other one they wanted sprung. Who's that? Boland? But the crowd needs someone to kill, and it's me this time, whether I'm guilty or no don't matter. Whether it's a holy man like Jesus or just some saloon bouncer like me, it don't matter. When the crowd gets its rage up, they gotta kill at all costs. Black knew this, and with his committee howling, it's the same as the mob that called, 'Crucify him! Crucify him!' Why, Father? Why does the same thing happen over and over? Why do they need to kill? What does it do for them? Why can't they let me live? Just, just live? I just want to live, Father. Why does Frank Black need me dead? I got no anger for the man. Don't know as I've ever met him. Why must they crush out my life? What do they gain by it? And Judas, he flung away the silver and hanged himself. Maybe that's like Jack there. Won't it ever end, Father? The hate, and the betrayers and the executions? I been thinking this out, Father, and it seems so needless." He paused, hung his head. "But after tomorrow, I guess, it won't be none of my concern."

"Is there anything else to confess?"

"That's about it." Shea clenched his fists. "But I just want you to know that if my death could bring Ross back, Father, I'd give it in an instant. Give him back to his family and his girl. But I ain't got that power. I can only die and hope to be forgotten, and hope everyone else forgives and forgets too."

"Very well then, Bartholomew. Let me administer the last rites to you now in preparation for tomorrow. Please lie down."

And Father Swift opened the small gold jar of chrism as Shea lay down and folded his arms and the priest murmured the ancient rite in Latin.

43.
THE EXECUTION

"Old Sparky"

A cold wind's howling out of the north. The canals are frozen, the river icebound. Like battlements of a medieval city, brick mills and warehouses line the frozen river, taking the brunt of the wind. Whistles blow at dawn, and men in dark clothing come spilling out of the tenements over the snow toward the mills. A vile yellow smoke rises from the foundries and steel mills, and the snow is stained by coal soot from chimneys. Now and again the winter sun appears like a white communion host behind dark clouds passing. As gray light seeps under the eastern rim of clouds and snow begins to fall, sixty thousand souls in this city go about their daily business with thoughts upon one soul far in the north.

Galen Hitt was at the capitol last night petitioning the governor for a commutation of sentence to a life term. Hitt was shown through the panel door to the governor's inner chamber, but when Morton reviewed his papers and heard him out, he declined to intervene. A bill had been introduced in the state legislature to amend the law allowing an appeal from Mayham's decision, yet members of the Committee of Public Safety called legislators personally, and it failed in both houses. All avenues have been exhausted. Shea is doomed. This morning, two letters appeared in the *Troy Press*:

Dannemora, New York

To the Editor of the Troy Press:

As I am about to leave this world, I think it is my duty to express my feelings in regard to my trial and conviction. To my attorneys, Mr. Norton and Mr. Hitt, I wish to say I am very thankful to them for their earnest and untiring efforts in my behalf. I wish to say also that I do not think I had a fair trial and that people used extraordinary means to bring about my conviction through the Committee of Public Safety.

And as to some of the witnesses that testified against me. That one Lansing's testimony in regard to the way I shot Robert Ross was false. And also as to Mrs. Titus who swore she saw six men standing near a barn with a man, who they claimed to be a politician, who was urging us to go ahead and earn money. That was also false as nothing of the kind ever took place.

As to shooting Robert Ross, as sworn to by witnesses against me, the evidence was false. I am innocent of the crime I am to die for. I never went to the polls on the sixth day of March, 1894 with any feeling against Robert Ross or any of his friends and no one feels worse about his death and the sorrow of his family and the gloom it has cast over them and my own family than myself. I wish to thank my friends one and all, for what they have done in my behalf, and all who have aided me in my trial. I wish to thank Warden Thayer, Deputy Warden McKenna and the officers who have had charge of me since my confinement at Dannemora.

I forgive all who wronged me, and I hope to be forgiven, and bid you all a last farewell.

BARTHOLOMEW SHEA

There was another letter to Tom Halligan, who as a boy had tattooed Shea's initials on his leg in a pledge of blood-brotherhood:

Mr. Thomas Halligan
899 River Street
Troy, Rensselaer County, New York

Friend Thomas:

I now take the pleasure to write you these few lines before I leave this world forever, as it is the last letter I will ever write to you or anyone else. I wish you would kindly cheer up my mother and father and sisters and my brother and give him a little advice for me about whom he travels with and his habits and not to go around drinking, and not to go with bad company.

My health is good at the present time, and my courage stays by me, and I hope and pray to God it will till it is all over. Remember me to all my friends and to all your own friends and especially to your sister and to the Kanes. Having no more to say, I will close with a good-bye and farewell forever. From your true friend,

BAT SHEA

P.S. Yours, forever and ever.
Bat.

In the worst blizzard of the decade witnesses travelled up from the river valley into the mountains for the execution: city and county officials, two members of the Committee of Public Safety who were instructed to report details of the execution directly to Black; and members of the press, reporters from the Troy, Albany and New York City newspapers. None of the witnesses has ever seen an execution, though some of the reporters have researched and carried stories about the debate over the electric chair — is it indeed a more humane way of execution than hanging? A woman reporter, Kate McGuirk of the *New York Morning Journal*, came north to watch and report the execution. Yet by wire Superintendent of Prisons Lathrop forbade her attendance. The death chamber was no place for a woman.

The blizzard was raging and the wind in the telegraph wires sent forth a dismal wail. Snow drifts were neck-high. In the shadow of the prison wall, the witnesses huddled for breakfast, discussing mundane topics, awaiting the execution with a mixture of curiosity, righteousness, horror and disgust.

Thayer issued a lockdown order. Since inmates became restless and sometimes violent each time the state extracted this last full measure of punishment, since sentiment about Shea's execution was running high and the warden feared inmates would cut the electric wires, and since

Thayer was under investigation by the state senate for his leniency and could not afford an "incident," the prisoners were to be locked in their cells until after the execution. The uniformed men in the guard towers, the keepers with their great rings of keys, the silent, sullen men themselves are so advised, and they sit upon their bunks, hands folded, heads bowed, waiting for the electric lights in the cellblocks to dim when the switch is thrown.

Mary Shea had been allowed to spend the night in her son's cell on a cot. She recalled the long night of labor just twenty-five years before when her Barry was born. Bat Shea lay upon his pallet, gazing into thin air, hovering between sleep and waking, praying in vain for the splendid dream of blue and golden light. From time to time Shea turned his head and when he saw his mother gazing at him, he spoke:

"Mornin', Ma." She was sobbing. "Ah, Ma," he pulled himself off the pallet and knelt by her cot. "I'm awful sorry about all this."

"I been telling everyone you're innocent, Barry. No one believed me till Jack spoke up. Now they believe, but," she burst into tears, "there's nothing we can do."

"No, and that's the truth of it. So you got to bear up, Ma. Don't let them see you like this, weeping. We'll get through it, ain't that what you always taught us when the old man was locked out of the foundry? Or on strike? We'll get through it, and we always did. Now come on, we'll get the guard to help you on your way. You don't want to be around here when they do me up."

She rose up, looking haggard and suddenly much older than he remembered. He called the guard. "Good-bye, Ma. Let's not make this long and sorrowful. You say good-bye to everyone for me. Tell 'em I love 'em all, and that I don't harbor no blame for anyone but myself for what happened. They gotta put all this behind them now, and try to forget. Same with you. Try to forget all this, and think of the happier times. All right? Now bear up there, Ma. Father Swift and the warden'll be coming for me soon."

She was weeping as she embraced him one last time. "Oh, Barry! My boy!"

"There you go, Ma," and he gave her over to the guard. "See she gets to the hotel with my sister, and onto the train for Plattsburgh, will you?"

"It's blowing awful hard out there, mum," the guard said, offering her a bearskin coat. "Better put this here on."

As the door creaked shut, Bat Shea took a deep breath. He wanted to do so much, to say so much, to call the secretary in and write more letters to people. He also wanted to pray, but that time would come. It was a giddy, unnerving feeling that filled him. He was at a crossroad, and one way there was horror and fear and on the other was relief and joy that the entire lamentable business would soon be over. He closed his eyes, clenched his fists and tried to compose himself. He concentrated with effort — there would be the chair and then, what? The pretty dream of sun and clouds and music? Or darkness? Or nothing? There were foot-steps in the hall, and the door creaked open.

"Barber's here, Shea," the guard said gruffly. In came a swarthy Italian barber who was in the mountains because he applied his razor to geld his wife's lover. He had a tin basin, shaving soap, a razor and tow-els.

"*Buon giorno, Señor Shea*," he said cheerfully. "We'll clean-a you up a bit, eh?" As he began his work, the fragrant soap brought back memories. So this is what it is like on the day you die, Shea thought as the humming barber expertly shaved his chin, his upper lip, his cheeks and jaw, then lathered the top of his skull and shaved off a circle for the electrode. He did the same on Shea's right leg, talking all the while. "God bless you, *Señor Shea*," the barber said, leaving the cell.

Next was breakfast. Instead of the usual corn porridge, the war-den sent in ham and eggs, toast, fried potatoes and coffee. The breakfast came on a large tray with two cigars. Yet Shea had no appetite when it came, and he just nibbled at it and sipped the coffee, and sat back with a cigar.

Again the door creaked open and Father Swift entered. They talked, and went through the ritual of another confession. It seemed anti-climactic. Then they were joined by Father Belanger. Shea lit the second of the cigars, waiting with the two priests for the call. Next came a guard with the dark suit he had worn through the trial. Shea exchanged his striped woolens for the street clothes, and when he had buttoned on the high collar and tied the striped tie, he felt more dignified, more himself.

Meanwhile in the death chamber, twenty-seven chairs had been arranged in a semicircle about "Old Sparky," the heavy oaken chair with electrodes snaking about it. The blizzard raged outside the grim stone building and on the way from the hotel just across the street the witness-es and reporters had to stop to catch their breath three times. They filed in, stamping and blowing into their hands, astonished at the sparse utility of the stone room, the wooden chair and the deadly electric wires. They hung their coats and hats upon pegs. It was dark and chilly in the death chamber.

Over the armrests of the chair lay a bank of incandescent lamps, and Electrician Davis was rearranging the wires he had arranged and rearranged a dozen times. The warden then entered alone to greet them.

"Gentlemen, let me now explain that you are to remain seated at all times. There have been situations at executions in the past where the first jolt of electricity did not kill the individual. This electric chair was most recently tested upon a cow, so we are certain it works."

Again there were nervous murmurs and a smirk from the reporters. "Dr. Ransom is in attendance and he will take care of everything. You are to do nothing but watch. Understood?" They nodded their heads in unison. "Mr. Davis will now give a demonstration as though the man were in the chair."

"The electric current passes through these wires and enters the head here," Davis spoke as he attached the top electrode to one end of a bank of lamps, "and then it passes through the body and exits through the leg here," he attached the other electrode, then stepped into a booth and threw a switch. There was a low hum and the lamps lit brightly. Davis emerged.

"The electric current travels much faster than the nerve signals to the brain, and so Mr. Shea will be dead before he feels any pain whatsoever." Davis stepped back into the booth and cut the power. A few showed interest in the scientific explanation, as if it sanitized the event.

Davis unhooked the lamps and lay the electric cords aside in readiness. The witnesses sat in nervous expectation as the warden left by the door leading to the corridor and the condemned cell.

It was nine forty-five when the warden entered Shea's cell. He looked somber and careworn. "Morning, Shea."

"Warden Thayer," Shea held up the stub of the cigar, "thank you for this." The warden nodded. "Did Ma and Frannie get off all right?"

"The Chateaugay tracks are impassable so I had my driver hitch up the sleigh to run them down to Plattsburgh."

"So long as they're away and gone. Thanks for allowing her to spend the night here. It meant a lot to her." He took a long pull on the cigar. "If possible, I'd like to ask you one more favor."

"Yes?"

"Let me walk into the room all alone. I've made my peace. I don't need no guards leading me to the chair. There won't be any incident."

"Very well, Shea. It's time."

The priests were murmuring prayers as Shea rose to go.

A metal clang startled the witnesses, and the door opened. First came the warden, next two priests murmuring prayers from prayer books in their hands, then Shea walked in, head held high, followed by four guards. Shea passed down the aisle between the spectators, looking easily at the electric chair. The priests went to either side of the chair, murmuring prayers for the dying, and Shea approached the chair, turned and sat down. He looked at each witness and then at the ceiling of the room.

Immediately Davis and the guards buckled the leather straps about his arms, legs and body. Shea helped with the strap across his waist. He tipped his head back, swallowed, closed his eyes, then brought his chin down level and opened his eyes. Slowly he looked along the semicircle of witnesses, pausing at each pair of eyes.

Davis anointed Shea's tonsure with a sponge of saline solution to aid conductivity. While he did so, Shea stared each of the witnesses in the eye, sizing them up, his pale blue eyes boring into them, his jaw set, inquiring, searching, challenging each to witness, and to understand, and to report accurately what they were about to see. His face was impassive, his hands resting easily upon the armrests. He seemed more of a spectator to the scene than its victim. Then he closed his eyes. He sat easily. There was not a tremor of a muscle.

Davis was behind him then, and he suddenly pulled the black hood down over Shea's face. The hood had a hole in the center for the wire and the electrode. Davis quickly circled in front, knelt on one knee and sliced the leg of Shea's trousers, found the shaved circle on his calf, dabbed it with saltwater and strapped the electrode there. Then he stood aside and looked at the warden. Thayer nodded as the priests intoned: "Into your hands I commend my spirit . . ." Then Davis stepped into his booth and closed the door.

Immediately there was a high pitched whirring and Shea's body flew out against the straps, bulging and straining against the thick leather restraints. A sharp intake of breath was heard among the witnesses as the priests continued to pray, and the smell of burning flesh, the smell of meat cooking, stole through the room, and one of the witnesses leaned forward and vomited on the floor. In fascinated horror the witnesses watched as a deep red burn stole down Shea's neck and beneath his collar as the heavy oak chair creaked under the strain and his arm and chest and thigh muscles bunched and pushed against the straps. Now the smell of excrement joined the smell of meat cooking, and others gagged and groaned. The whirring stopped suddenly, and Shea's body went limp, a slim line of blood flowing from under the hood, from where he bit his lip.

The attending doctor stepped forward and felt for a pulse. "He is dead," Dr. Ransom announced to the sighing relief of the witnesses who looked about for the door. "However, to be sure, I recommend another treatment."

The warden rapped at the door to the booth, told Davis, and again the whirring sounded, again Shea's body flew out against the straps and a spark and a tongue of flame appeared at the hole in the hood, lighting the dim room in a halo of smoke and fire as hair burned.

"For God's sake!" a witness cried.

Davis cut the power, and the body was limp, deep purple in color, the hooded head falling forward. A guard opened a door at the rear of the room, and the witnesses rose slowly, some fascinated, others disgusted, and quickly they were led back to the hotel through the chill, white, cleansing blizzard.

Immediately the straps were removed and Shea's body carried into the adjoining pathology room for the autopsy. Left upon a stone slab to cool, the steaming corpse was still one hundred twelve degrees a quarter of an hour later by rectal thermometer. Three doctors in lab coats then stripped the body, swollen and deep purple in color from the scalp to the toes. Expertly they probed and prodded with their steel implements, a scribe recording the data in a notebook. There were seminal and fecal discharges and under the microscope the spermatozoa were dead. On the right calf there was a round blistered burn, at the right knee was a tatoo, "T.H." The doctors opened the thorax cavity. The left lung was filled with miliary tubercles.

"Note an advance of tubercular consumption," Dr. Ransom said. "This boy couldn't have survived another trial. He would have been dead within a year."

The heart and liver were normal, the kidneys small, and the stomach filled with a watery liquid. They did not dissect the brain. After turning over various organs of Bartholomew Shea, Jr., in the light, making their observations, they put them back within the corpse and sewed up the incision. The cadaver was signed over to Troy undertaker Connie Burns for embalming, and he proceeded with his work to make the corpse presentable and to transport it home.

Immediately after the execution, Father Swift hurried from the prison and struggled through the drifts to the train station. There he learned the Chateaugay tracks were impassable. He hired a sleigh to take him to Plattsburgh. He wanted to catch the morning train from Montreal and avoid the crowd of reporters.

Faced with a restless prison population still locked down, the warden telegraphed the Delaware & Hudson to send a special train to Dannemora for the body and for the reporters and witnesses. By noon the corpse was ready for transport in its coffin of quartered oak lined with satin. The D & H engine, a huge snowplow affixed, came smoking and steaming through the storm.

Waiting in the hotel across the street, reporters heard that Thayer would allow them to speak briefly with McGough before he was returned to general population from solitary confinement. They scrambled back across the street in the blizzard to the warden's home and after a time Jack came in, nervously glancing about, grinning sheepishly.

"Do you know Shea is dead?" one of the newsmen asked.

"Yes."

"Do you still insist that you are the real murderer of Robert Ross?"

"Yes, sir. I killed Ross and Shea didn't and they had no business putting him to death."

"Do you believe other witnesses were mistaken?"

"Well," Jack said, "if Shea hadn't been arrested, and if it hadn't been decided to make him the victim, every one of those fellows would have sworn that I shot Ross."

"Do you realize you have forfeited parole by your confession?"

"They killed an innocent man." Jack was offended by the tone of the question. "What do I care about parole?"

"Do you understand you cannot be convicted of the crime now that Shea's been electrocuted?"

"I'm perfectly willing to stand any punishment now."

McGough was then shackled with leg irons and led by a guard to his old cell in East Prison Hall.

The train arrived before one and Connie Burns supervised the transfer of the coffin to the baggage car as reporters watched. Everyone boarded, and the train backed its way down seventeen miles of track to Plattsburgh.

Mary and Frances Shea had caught the morning train to Troy and they were well on their way, but Father Swift arrived too late. As the reporters entered the Plattsburgh station, cheered now that they were away from the grim gray fortress of Dannemora, an Albany newsman spied the priest and cornered him. Father Swift's eyes were red, and though he was reading his breviary, it was obvious he'd been weeping.

"Father, you gave Shea the last rites?"

"Yes."

"You heard his last confession?"

"Yes."

"And you believe that he was innocent?"

Tears welled up in the priest's eyes, and he looked with a mixture of anger and disdain at the reporter: "I cannot violate the secrecy of the confessional. But," he said hoarsely, "as has come out, that boy was no murderer. He never pulled the fatal trigger."

At this Father Swift turned away, holding his handkerchief to his face and murmuring to no one in particular, "Thy will and not mine be done."

44.
THE FUNERAL

Victorian Hearse

Since the recent decision that Shea must die, Mamie Halligan remained home, scarcely eating, sleeping fitfully. She could not visit Bat in prison as only family and clergy were permitted. She remained in a haze of inactivity and despond, stunned by the finality of the decision.

Yet on the morning of the execution, she awoke at six, dressed and walked five blocks through the blizzard to St. Patrick's Church. No one was about except an old lamplighter extinguishing the gas lamps.

"Morning, ma'am."

"Morning." The word stuck in her throat and the lamplighter's dog looked quizzically.

"Come along, Buster. Ain't polite to stare," and after she passed he whispered to the dog, "Looks like she's got a heap of sorrow in her heart, poor thing."

Alone in the dim quiet of the church, Mamie lit a votive lamp and awaited until the hour specified in the order of execution, her imagination conjuring horrible scenes as her beloved was strapped into the chair, electrodes fastened and the deadly current sent through him like a lightning bolt. Just before ten, tears streaming down her face, she looked up imploringly at the crucified Christ, knowing now the sorrow of Mary at the cross.

Shortly after ten she arose, made the sign of the cross and turned toward home. Still it was snowing and the gentle snowfall eased the dark angles of tenements and factories and saloons. The funeral would be Friday. Now would begin a three day ordeal until Bartholomew Shea was in the cold earth. It occurred to her she could easily join him. There was always the river. Many leapt from the Green Island Bridge to end it, and the ice would crush her now. Yet the image of Nellie Mae Patton, staunch, heroic, triumphant, prevailed and she thought also about her darling Bat Shea, the courage with which he faced his accusers, the perjury, the specially convened court, the newspapers shouting for his blood and now the electric chair. No, she must live through it.

The day in Troy was quiet and uneventful. The newsboard outside the papers carried blurbs about the execution and the funeral train, relayed down by telegraph. At twilight in Dunlop's Saloon, George Dunlop was stinko. The regulars rested in attitudes of dejection and drunkenness all about, and a large polished brass spitoon stood on top of the bar. Lil, one of the upstairs girls sat at the bar, which was never permitted. She had a cheroot in her teeth and, all elbows and knees, was cursing with the energy and expertise of a canaler. When the door opened, Alderman Dunlop looked up and gave Lightning Kilcullen a sidelong glance:

"Let's see a couple of greenbacks float in here, Lightning!" he ordered.

"Fer what?"

"As if you didn't know!" Dunlop snarled. "T'give to poor Tim here who lost his big brother today." He slung his arm around the thin kid brother with the pronounced adams apple. Their eyes were red. "And a finer big brother this sorry goddamn world ain't never seen. Loyal. Tough. No one ever broke Bat Shea. Not that goddamn APA Frank Black, nor the goddamn APA judge, nor the goddamn APA jury of goddamn APA farmers, nor the goddamn APA electric chair. So ante up, Lightning, and the drinks are on the house tonight now that my poor boy Bat has been taken from us all." He slapped his billy club on the bar. "And this is one sorry goddamn lot of goddamn mourners, I'll tell you that now. But I swear, I goddamn swear before God and before you my goddamn loyal patrons, if any goddamn newspaper reporter writes a bad word about my boy Bat and his death, I'll use Old Hickory on his worthless goddamn skull." And he rapped the club again on the bar.

Kilcullen dropped two dollars into the spitoon.

"Can't you play me a song, Lil?" George called to the skinny jade. "'Feeney's Lament' or ''Tis a Green Glade Yonder' or 'Night on a Troubled Sea?' C'mon, Lil, you used to play before you lost the cherry."

"Goddamn classy gent, ain't he, boys? Alderman goddamn Dunlop! Ain't he that too, boys? Hah! Not fer long." And Lil sidled up to the piano and began to play while George passed along the bar with a fresh bottle of bonded Irish.

At midnight there was a knock on Mamie Halligan's door that startled her awake. She'd been sleeping in the chair, and her coal fire had gone out. She wrapped the shawl about her tightly in the chilled room. When she opened the door, Emma Delaney and Maggie Riley, Jack's girl, were in their bonnets and cloaks.

"Ain't you coming to meet the train?" Maggie asked.

"We thought you of all people would," Emma chided her.

"What?"

"Get your cloak. The train, the funeral train, Bat's coming home. They're bringing him in in the middle of the night so's there'll be no fuss, but the word is out and everyone's leaving the saloons and their stoves and hearths to go down to Union Station and welcome him back."

"Come with us!"

The streetcars had stopped running, and so the three girls walked the mile to Union Station. To Mamie's surprise, for blocks around the station hundreds of people stood in groups in the streetlamps as the snow fell. The hourly newsboard at the Evening Standard in Franklin Square revealed the funeral train had passed through Glens Falls, and was now racing through the forests toward Troy.

Emma and Maggie put on airs with Mamie along as they pushed through the crowd. "This is the girl he left behind," they said to people, advancing through the crowd.

When they introduced Mamie to the stationmaster, he brought the three young women upstairs to his office that had a pot-bellied stove and a commanding view of the railyard. Mamie looked out upon a bobbing sea of derbies and umbrellas, and for the first time, she understood the great regard that common folks had for Bat Shea. It was no longer her private and solitary grief.

On his way through Plattsburgh, Cork had picked up the execution witnesses and the casket of Bartholomew Shea. Down through the snowy countryside he propelled the train, its headlamp scouring out a hole in the snowstorm, Cork occasionally yanking on the whistle, squinting into the blue dark, imagining the body within the box in the baggage car. It wasn't just cargo, he concluded, not by a long shot, and he had Lester pile on the coal to get the body back as soon as possible.

By his pocket watch they reached the river at two-twelve and Cork eased on the throttle to cross the Hudson. The ice of the river was jagged and broken, and across Federal and Grand Street and Fifth Avenue, the train rolled. Swinging wide around a brick wall, the beacon lamp then fell upon a vast crowd of derbies, bonnets and umbrellas waiting in the snow:

"Who's coming in here tonight, Lester?"

The fireman, his face grimy and sweaty from the work, looked out: "Don't know. President Cleveland?"

"Couldn't be the fellah what was executed today, could it?" They traded astonished looks in the red glow of the firebox.

Mamie Halligan watched the train halt beneath the iron canopy, steam rising, couplings clanging, and the crowd pressing forward. The conductor stepped down and parted the crowd for Father Swift and the Troy witnesses to detrain, and then farther back the baggage car door slid open and a great roar arose in the crowd. All the men on the platform removed their derbies and caps, and three cheers for Bat Shea arose from a thousand throats.

Connie Burns, the undertaker, barked commands at the porters for he feared the crowd might forcibly steal the casket. Gingerly it was handed down. Mamie cried, and Maggie and Emma hugged her as the casket was spirited through the crowd, into the station and then through a loading dock onto the Burns hearse where high stepping black geldings carried it north to the Shea home.

Mrs. Shea was pacing in the dim light of her kitchen lamp wringing her hands. She'd arrived home earlier in the evening, and was now awaiting to see her Barry who would be waked on the dining room table of their second story flat. Tom Halligan sat at her kitchen table over a cup of tea. He had been affected by Bat's final letter, and he had forgiven him, their feud at an end.

Mr. Shea limped in from the parlor on his cane. "There's some sleighs pulled up outside, Mary. I think Connie Burns is come."

The woman's face blanched and she clutched her throat. "Come along, Mrs. Shea," Tom Halligan took her by the arm. "The worst is over now." They went to the parlor and watched below as the men moved in the swirling snow opening the door of the hearse and pulling out the casket. Connie Burns was downstairs at the front door, and Tom went down to answer it. With a groan they carried the coffin up to the small flat and laid it on the dining room table.

"Is he . . . can you open it?" asked Mrs. Shea.

"If you'd like," Burns said comfortingly. He stepped to the coffin, undid a latch and slowly raised the lid.

"Oh, my Barry!" Mary shrieked and she fell upon him, kissing his face. In the coffin in a black morning suit, white shirt, high starched collar and a black lawn tie lay Bat Shea, a look of peace upon his face. After the electric chair, Connie Burns had spent much time and expertise fixing it there. All was silent except for Mary Shea's sobbing.

Weary Shea hobbled into the kitchen and called for Tom to help. They returned with a tray of glasses and a bottle of Irish whiskey. Mr. Shea pulled out the cork, wet his finger with the liquor and touched it to his dead son's lips, then he poured out the glasses and toasted the memory of the man.

Just then there were footfalls on the back stairs, and Tim Shea entered the kitchen. "Ma? Hey, Ma!" he called with excitement, and he came through the door and paused. His excitement vanished as he peered into the coffin.

"Look at him!" Mary Shea commanded. "Look good. This is what comes of hanging about in saloons."

"Ma," Tim said with a slurred voice, "George went and took up a collection." He held up a cloth bag. "There's a hunnerd twenty-six dollars and fifty-two cents . . ."

"What?" her eyes opened wide.

"A hunnerd twenty-six . . ."

"Dunlop is sending me money?" she cried.

"Why, sure, to pay for the funeral."

"No!" she shrieked. "No!" She grabbed the bag and hurled it against the wall where a shower of coins fell and scattered. "Throw it back into the gutter where it come from. Get George Dunlop's filth out of my house!" With a loud crack she slapped her son across the face and pushed him toward the door. "You tell Dunlop to give me back my son!"

"Mary? Mary!" Mr. Shea said. "Leave the boy be. George is only trying to make amends."

"George Dunlop was the cause of it all. There is nothing I want from George Dunlop."

Frannie and Julia began to pick up the coins with Tom Halligan who offered: "I'll take it back, Mrs. Shea. You just sit quiet."

Tim slunk back into the hallway nursing his dignity. Tom gave the bag of money to Connie Burns and instructed him that if there was any left after funeral expenses, he should put it towards a stone.

"Well," Connie Burns announced, "I'll be going now. I think we should all get some sleep. If the crowd at the station was any indication, we'll have a tiring few days ahead." He closed the coffin and left the family in the lamplight to mourn.

River Street outside the Shea home began to fill before sunrise. The saloons along the way served coffee and something stronger to those who came to pay their respects. No one knocked until Frannie Shea opened the door at eight, and a cheer rose from three hundred people. The mourners began to file in, kicking snow from their shoes.

Mary Shea opened the back door for the file of mourners to exit. She lit the fourteen candles around the body, and arranged a receiving line to greet the crowds. After nine, floral arrangements began arriving from shops throughout Troy, and in the afternoon from across the river, Watervliet, Green Island, Cohoes and Waterford, then toward evening from Albany. By nightfall floral shops in the area were sold out. A silver tray near the coffin filled with Mass cards and had to be cleared hourly. All day and into the night the crowds came. Lincoln's Birthday was not a holiday in the mills, but many workers took it anyway. When the collar factories let out at six, the street in front of the Shea home filled so that traffic could not pass.

At the Troy Club that evening a hastily convened meeting of industrialists and merchants was called. This demonstration for the young man could bring civil unrest, riots, sabotage. Accordingly, it was agreed that all the foremen would tell the workers tomorrow that anyone absent from work during the week would be fired.

And still they came, hundreds upon hundreds of people, men and women who paused above the body, whispered a prayer, dabbed a tear with a handkerchief, gave a pleasant word to the family, left a Mass card, then descended the back stairs. Encouraged by the scene at the train station, Mamie Halligan joined the receiving line, and the sympathy and well-wishing bolstered her spirits throughout the day.

At midnight there were still over a hundred people in the street. Connie Burns closed the door, then joined the family to close the coffin lid and share a cup of tea. The great outpouring of sympathy had surprised everyone, and Father Swift agreed to move the funeral forward from Friday to Thursday so that Bat Shea could be buried, the strain upon his family relieved, and any threat to public safety averted. Burns told them to get some sleep, and said he'd return at half-past eight.

The Republican Party held its annual Lincoln's Day dinner that year in Syracuse, and the principal speaker was Congressman Frank Black. Late into the night the party bosses sat over their cigars and brandy discussing a candidate for governor. Levi Morton was planning to run for president. It was the consensus that they need look no farther than their dinner speaker. They sent a deputation to Black in his hotel room.

"Before I agree to accept the nomination," he said, "I shall require committed financial support."

"That will be no problem, Mr. Black. There are many bankers and Wall Street financiers in our ranks."

"I will need to see some numbers, and I should like the night to consider. I shall give you my answer in the morning."

As he closed the door on the men, Frank Black's thin lip turned up in a smile. The drive had been successful. His constant emphasis upon reform, imbuing politics with morality, had elevated him in two years above all his peers who had been playing the game of politics far longer. They did not understand that the rules were changing. It had been his address at the dinner that secured him the nomination:

"Just yesterday, gentlemen, the murderer of Robert Ross was executed in the electric chair at Dannemora as a direct result of our reform. Boss rule and forced voting are coming to an end in our cities. The people will not stand for it, and are visiting just punishment upon these criminals."

He would extract commitments for funds from the state committee tomorrow, and then graciously accept the offer to be nominated in the summer.

Thursday morning dawned ashen and overcast, and a fine snow was falling. All streetcars passing north carried large crowds in dark clothing. The doors to St. Patrick's Church opened at half-past seven and the assembled crowd rushed in, immediately filling the church.

Four blocks away at the Shea home, Gene McClure and Tim Shea collected a score of young men to help load the floral arrangements, and they filled three sleighs with four dozen large sprays, and countless small baskets of flowers along with one grisly arrangement — a floral electric chair with "MARTYR" on a wide ribbon across the back.

The Shea household was a flurry of activity. When Connie Burns arrived, Mary Shea leaned into the coffin and kissed her son. Weary Shea kissed him on the forehead. The girls hugged him, lifting him slightly from the satin pillow. Wax from the candles had dripped upon the threadbare carpet, and slush and mud had been tracked through the house. It was chilly with the door being open. "Goodbye, Bat!" Tim said, and he turned aside with reddened eyes.

At half-past nine, Tom Halligan and the other pallbearers carried the coffin downstairs to the hearse, and the black geldings with plumes upon their heads pulled the hearse on sleigh runners around to St. Patrick's Church.

As the hearse passed Dunlop's Saloon, the boys gave a toast through the window. George had been to the barber to clean up. By now he had "drunk himself sober," an exercise that required a nip now and then from a flask to keep him functional. George Dunlop did not know what to say to anyone. He fully believed that people blamed him, yet he was enough of a politician to deflect criticism to Black and the Committee. The Murphy machine took no position on the funeral. There would be no police escort, and city hall was frowning upon the large crowds, fearing a populist uprising.

Father Swift looked out upon the crowd amassing in the street from his study in the rectory. He held the rewritten sermon in his hands. The bishop had summoned him to Albany after the newspapers reported he thought Shea innocent. The bishop had chastised him. He could not very well exalt Bat Shea, for his life had been short and troubled and violent. Any recognition by the Church could sanction civil unrest. Father Swift rewrote his sermon. But it was heart-wrenching, too, to know what he knew and what this great, dark and silent crowd believed. The bishop was right, perhaps. As pastor, he must steer their attention away from sorrow and thwarted justice onto some spiritual middle ground. It would serve no purpose now to blame. He rolled up the sermon and left the window for the sacristy.

The edict from the millowners was ignored. Labor unions and associations called out their workers to attend the funeral. St. Patrick's Church was filled well beyond capacity, and thousands of people waited in the street outside as gentle snow coated their umbrellas, derbies and bonnets, the flowers in the sleighs, the horses snorting beneath their blankets.

Bearers carried the coffin through the tight crowd, and then wheeled it up the center aisle. With a blast of organ notes the Requiem Mass began. The church was filled with sobbing, and when he turned occasionally, Father Swift was astonished at the number of young women attending. After the gospel, he paused, then he looked down from the pulpit upon the vast crowd:

"The remains of our departed brother are brought into this church not for the purpose of doing him special honor. We did not consider him during his life as representing the sentiment of the church, and in his latter days he was far from being faithful to the rules of the church and the laws of God."

The stern note to this address surprised the congregation. Perhaps recognizing Bat Shea's misdeeds was only a prelude to a celebration of his innocence? Yet Father Swift continued in this vein:

"The Church was established for the salvation of man. It is a Christian church. The relatives of the deceased have a right to bring him into the Church for the benefit of prayers for the repose of the soul when he returns in sincerity and repents of his transgressions, or even crimes. Bartholomew Shea has paid the debt of human justice." There were loud sobs among the pews and many handkerchiefs seen.

"Whether he was innocent or guilty of the death which occurred, I know not. Neither do I believe he knew." The altar was solemn with the black vestments, the four acolytes and the candles. Outside, pressing at the door, thousands of people stood in the falling snow, craning to hear Father Swift. "If he was guilty," the priest continued, "I firmly believe he was not conscious of it. He forgave all for the part they took in the tragedy as he expected to be forgiven, and his last request was that his relatives forgive and try to forget."

Women in the church began to wail in a high-pitched keen. Father Swift paused until they ceased. He wanted the ceremony and the day to be devoid of hysteria and eruptions.

"His life was not one I would advise young Catholics to follow, and all his trouble was due to his failure to remember the instructions of the Catholic Church. It should be a lesson to young men. We Catholics are a law-abiding community." Father Swift paused. "Human justice," the words caught in his throat, "imperfect as it must be because of our human imperfections, has been satisfied." He bowed his head and folded his hands in prayer. "Let us unite and pray that divine justice may be satisfied and that the deceased may find eternal rest."

Father Swift stepped down and resumed the sacrifice of the mass. Weeping was loud in the church. The congregation was murmuring, disturbed with the harshness of the sermon. The girls, hundreds upon hundreds of them, dabbed at their eyes with handkerchiefs.

After the mass, the body was commended to eternal rest and was carried out of the church as *O, Salutaris* rang from the choir loft, and the bell of St. Patrick's began to toll. As the coffin reached the street, a cheer went up, loud and deep and long. The flowers were by now blanketed with snow.

Tom Halligan and the other pallbearers loaded the coffin into the hearse, and the black geldings stepped out, leading the funeral procession down Sixth Avenue, only two blocks from the murder site. The snow was deep, the wind picking up and the walking was bad. It was two miles out to the cemetery, and the great, dark, silent crowd moved like a vast shadow through the streets. There were no military ranks and files, no uniform, no drum. Up Hoosick Street to Tenth Street the dark crowd moved, then up the grade past Robert Ross's firehouse and Presbyterian church, to the fork of Oakwood Avenue, past Ross Valve, past the Ross home, then, half a mile farther, past the gracious mansion of Josiah Patton.

Nellie Mae Patton was home today, and she stood at the French windows watching the dark crowd pass, like a vast shadow in the snow. So fruitless, such a waste! Another young man to lay in the ground over politics. If she were to do anything worthwhile, it would be to clean up the process so that young men no longer had to die.

The spirited geldings turned in at the main gate of St. Peter's Cemetery. The great throng poured in through a side gate and spilled in a dark wave over the snow.

At a turn in the cemetery road, a hole had been hewn from the clay, snow and water collecting at the bottom. Connie Burns pulled the horses up at the hole, and the pallbearers set the coffin on a small bier. Now the young men brought the flowers, shaking off the snow, bright colors against the gray and black and white landscape. They placed the flowers about the coffin. When the vast crowd of five thousand was assembled around the hole twenty and thirty deep, Father Swift offered a final prayer, then sprinkled the coffin with holy water that mingled with beads of melting snow.

Mary Shea stood at the hole, her eyes red with weeping. Timmy Shea looked tipsy. The sisters hugged each other, crying together. Mamie Halligan seemed exhausted from the rigors of the week, standing with Maggie Riley and Emma Delaney. Weary Shea looked spiteful. George Dunlop, who elbowed his way to the front, looked clean and fresh, and he invited everyone back to the saloon for lunch. Soon Connie Burns was urging people away. Yet they stayed to look upon the coffin and down into the hole.

As the snow deepened, gravediggers appeared with ropes, and they lowered the coffin into the earth. It hit the bottom with a slap. Mary Shea turned and buried her face in Tom Halligan's breast. "There now, Mum!" he said. Still Connie Burns urged people to turn about, but still they remained, staring at the box in the hole.

Now Mamie Halligan stepped forward and took a flower as a keepsake. Maggie Riley and Emma Delaney did the same. Then Bat's sisters, Frannie and Julia, and his mother stepped forward and from the colorful sprays of flowers each took a blossom. There was a pause, and then other women moved forward, the collar factory girls, store clerks and bookkeepers and seamstresses and spindle girls, and even girls from the brothels, all advancing slowly with shivering lips, to take away a memento of the slain man.

Soon in slow and steady procession, as the gravediggers began to shovel, young mothers, and nuns, chambermaids and scullery girls all advanced to the great heaps of greenery and color by the side of the hole. Some pressed a blossom to their pale cheek, some held it to their lips, some clasped it to their bosom. And as they passed, they glanced with sorrow down into the hole where the snow was melting upon the box and yellow clay was falling from shovels.

An hour later, the mound of fresh earth was covered by a soft gauze of snow. The great, dark and silent crowd was gone, back down to the city by the river. Snow was still falling here in the city of the dead upon the hill, easing the corners of the gravestones and the wings of stone angels, the piking of the iron fence, effacing all footsteps. Around the fresh grave of the young man lay empty wicker baskets and greenery, but nowhere was there a flower, nowhere a blossom. By women they'd all been taken up and borne away.

THE END

Robert Ross Monument

EPILOGUE

On the day of Shea's funeral, Frank Black informed Republican officials he would accept their offer to nominate him for governor. Levi Morton was running for president. Nominated at the summer convention, Black stood for election in November and won. He served one term as New York governor, but was passed over in 1898 when party leaders, irritated by his haughty and imperious ways, chose Teddy Roosevelt, the popular "Rough Rider" of San Juan Hill. Frank Black maintained his home in Troy and commuted by train each week to a law office he opened in Manhattan.

The American Protective Association attempted to field a candidate for the presidential election of 1896, but when the narrowness and bigotry of its platform became known, it was discredited. The organization lost its impetus, its membership dwindled and it soon faded as a political power.

Boss Edward Murphy, who lost his chairmanship of the state Democratic Party due to the outcry surrounding the Shea case, finished his single term as United States senator, and retired to his brewery.

George Dunlop was not re-elected alderman in Troy. Eli Hancox, the original designee of Robert Ross in 1894, handily won the seat in 1896, shortly after Shea's funeral. George Dunlop died of consumption in January, 1897.

Nellie Mae Patton continued her volunteer work. Mamie Halligan and Tom Halligan persisted in their work improving conditions for the laboring masses. The chronicles do not record whether either woman married.

The Ross brothers prospered in the family business as municipal water and sewer systems were installed across the nation. A shrine to the slain hero was erected in the company's office on Oakwood Avenue.

Jack McGough served fourteen years at Dannemora. Despite Warden Thayer's prediction, McGough did make parole in 1908, and he returned home to Troy and married Maggie Riley. When parole released him in 1914, Jack moved West with Maggie to California.

The women of Troy subscribed sufficient funds to commission an eight-foot bronze statue of Robert Ross, a ballot box in his right hand, the American flag in his left. The statue stands on the rock outcrop of Oakwood Cemetery above North Troy and Lansingburgh, facing eastward from the confluence of the Hudson and Mohawk Rivers. Tom Halligan collected funds among the laboring people and raised a granite monument across the road in St. Peter's Cemetery at the grave of Bartholomew Shea.

After two more decades of protest, women won the right to vote. The temperance leagues for a time closed the saloons. Capital punishment and the electric chair were eventually outlawed in New York. Voting machines and electoral reforms did much to reduce election day violence nationwide, yet politics in the City of Troy and in Rensselaer County remained tempestuous.

The Erie and Champlain Canals were superseded by highways and by the St. Lawrence Seaway. The railroad and steamboats fell into disuse with the coming of automobiles and trucks. Troy's manufacturing concerns closed or moved on as their products — collars and cuffs, parlor stoves, textiles, shirts, iron and steel — became obsolete, or as cheaper labor was found. Today the riverbank is visited only by pleasure craft and the occasional barge. Only dams and the ruins of mills and factories remain in the gorges.

In a century many things have changed: architecture, technology, sanitation, religion, social mores, nutrition, medical care, fashion. Yet many things that caused the trial of Bat Shea remain — tyranny, violence, vigilantism, racial bigotry, political opportunism, unbridled ambition — and these still beget bloodshed, injustice and tragedy. The same battle fought in Troy's wards and courthouse in 1894, for example, has been fought recently in Belfast. As with sunrises and sunsets, each new generation raises hope such tragedies may be averted, and the passing of the old generation allows its sorrows and its mistakes and its tragedies to be buried. But these sorrows and these mistakes and these tragedies should never be buried so deeply that they are ignored and forgotten.

Because of the killing, the trial and the execution, the city ward of streets and alleys and houses and saloons on the east bank of the Hudson at the dam where river navigation ceases and the canals begin, where the spires of St. Patrick's rise and the bells still peal, that ward is known even to this day as "The Bloody Thirteenth."

AUTHOR'S NOTE

This novel portrays events in Troy, New York a century ago. It is a true story, true because these things happened, and true, in a deeper sense, because tragedy often is the fruit of bigotry, injustice and ambition.

My first goal was accuracy. I exhausted all primary sources — newspapers, city directories, the red book, biographies, the letters and public papers of Frank Black, writings about Robert Ross, accounts of the American Protective Association, the reported decisions in *People v Shea* and the 2,500 page trial transcript. I have conveyed the facts as accurately and succinctly as I was able.

My second goal was to reveal the tragic dimension of this American revenge saga. It has been the work of a decade and more to gain the necessary legal and political insights and to observe my fellow mortals so I could charge these facts with emotional energy and strike at deeper themes. While excerpts of an earlier version of this novel appeared in the Troy *Sunday Record* in 1977, the story has been substantially rewritten for its centennial appearance.

Few liberties were taken with fact, but necessary extrapolations from fact were made to breathe life into the characters. Thus, even though the characters are based upon historical figures and bear historical names, they are creations, compilations, inventions. These characters are all fictitious as to what they thought, what they said, what they hoped, what they feared and above all why they acted so. This leap from fact to fiction, from life to art, is essential whenever themes behind the veil of history are explored.

I have tried in this work to hold a simple mirror up to nature. Doubtless it is cracked and defective in places. Yet I have tried in my way to reflect life as it was in this brief time, 1894-96, and this obscure place, Victorian Troy, New York, so that a more universal truth might be glimpsed. If the reader has caught a glimpse of himself or herself in this looking glass as well, then I have accomplished all I set out to do.

Troy, New York
March 6, 1994

JACK CASEY